I0760582

M.G. HERRON

Cover art by Lucas Panda.

Cover design by Vivid Covers.

For Eben, my firstborn son.

THE GUNN FILES

Book 1: **Culture Shock**
Book 2: **Overdose**
Book 3: **Quantum Flare**
Book 4: **Nick of Time**

CHAPTER ONE

HAVE you ever tried scaling a wall while hoisting two duffel bags full of cash?

I hadn't. Not until tonight.

I had *not* come prepared.

Sweating and grumpy, I stood on a cardboard box, which rested on a plastic crate, which was perched atop the lid of a stinking dumpster. I stretched up, steadied myself, and reached out with my right hand.

My metal fingertips dug into the concrete lip of the high wall, scraping out grooves as they caught hold.

The annoying part of my new prosthetic was that I didn't have feeling in my alloy fingers. That, and metal detectors. Airport security had become my nemesis.

But the upside? Sweet Jesus, the upside was something else. Nothing could hurt them, for starters. I once deflected a bullet with my knuckles. My grip was rock solid, powerful enough to make pretzels out of dumbbells—and I had done so on several occasions. It was barely an effort to suspend myself by a single pinky.

That kind of unexpected power carries a certain reassuring weight. Even when I wasn't carrying my sidearm, I would never be without a weapon. As a bounty hunter who earns his living catching bail jumpers of all stripes, from mundane deadbeats to dangerous offworld fugitives, I took comfort in that fact.

Surely, a high wall couldn't keep *me* out.

I shifted my weight, all hundred and ninety pounds plus two gym bags of cash—onto my cyborg hand. My leg wobbled on the crate. I felt strain at my elbow and shoulder. Not painful, mind you, but not comfortable either. As I readjusted my grip, my left hand—a mere flesh-and-bone thing—reached up. The pile of boxes under my feet shifted.

Concrete crumbled beneath my too-powerful fingertips. Rock dust sprayed into my face, and I found myself falling through the air.

My ribcage slammed into the dumpster's edge, knocking the air from my lungs. A duffle bag strap snapped tight across my neck, choking off my airflow.

"Ngh," I managed to say before twisting sideways and bringing one arm up to give my windpipe some relief. This motion earned me another tumble. I landed on my side on the alley floor, my cheek resting in a rancid puddle.

After a moment, my lungs refilled with a gasp, and I was able to breathe again.

"Ow," I said, the picture of eloquence.

A chuckle echoed across the alley, piling insult upon injury.

I scowled into the night as I lumbered up, brushing myself off and panting.

"I know that laugh," I said, wiping one cheek on the sleeve of my denim jacket. "How long you been watching?"

"Long enough," a gravelly voice responded. Samael the Daacro winged gracefully through the air to land on the dumpster's edge. He looked me in the eye, smirked and said, "I'm so glad I waited. That was quite the comedy of errors."

Samael was an offworlder, an extraterrestrial, one of many who lived here in Austin. Recently, events had brought the existence of alien life into mainstream conversation, but most people still mistook Samael for a strange-looking grackle. Or, perched on the edge of a rooftop, a gargoyle. Most didn't know any better.

For better or for worse, I did.

"I live to entertain," I said. Embarrassed, I retrieved the two duffel bags and set them on top of the dumpster. "Now, get lost. I've got business with the Gatekeeper."

"Not in there, you don't," he grated out. The creature's gravelly voice matched his rough skin.

I froze. The Gatekeeper was a local alien *capo*, his monopoly on offworlder transit and trade sanctioned by the Federation. The Gatekeeper also happened to be Samael's boss.

"What are you talking about?" I asked.

"They moved the door."

I groaned and leaned against the alley wall to collect myself.

The Gatekeeper had been a hard body hopper to get ahold of. That was why I was scaling the wall to sneak into the Museum of the Weird's courtyard at 4 AM. The access point to his secret alien nightclub, Harbor, was located beneath our feet.

At least, it *used to be.*

I tugged at a soreness in my neck as the diminutive creature regarded me with two bulging, oversized eyes.

"Are you planning on telling me where the door is now?" I asked. "Or are we gonna stare at each other for the rest of the night?"

"That depends."

I frowned. I just wanted this to be over with. My debt to the Gatekeeper had been hanging over my head like a shameful reminder of my worst impulses. This piece of unfinished business went back years, originally as a business loan to expand Gunn Bounties and then as a way to cover the cost of my mother's funeral (and inadvertently fund my father's binge drinking habit).

I needed to get the Gatekeeper out of my life for good so I could put all that behind me.

"Depends on what?" I asked.

"On whether you've activated your Peacekeeper mods or not."

If he told me there was cause for concern, I'd be a fool not to listen. Samael and I weren't friends, but he was reliable. I'd saved his life once. In exchange, he'd risked the Gatekeeper's wrath to give me key information. It led to a missing offworlder for a client of mine.

At the same time, it pissed me right off. I'd brought enough money to settle my debt to the Gatekeeper, but I'd made zero progress on this other piece of unfinished business.

"Now, why'd you have to go and bring that up?" I asked.

"Because if you *have* activated the augments, my instructions are to keep you as far away from the Gatekeeper as possible."

That gave me pause. It meant I actually posed a threat to the Gatekeeper. "I haven't," I said after a moment. "Honestly, I don't even know how."

And not for lack of trying. Annabelle, Vinny, and I had worked hard to find a way to undo the changes Dyna had made to my body. We'd come up empty-handed.

However it worked, those chemical agents still pumped through my veins like a Trojan horse: dangerous, dormant and likely to kill—myself or others.

"You'll forgive me if I don't take your word for it, bounty hunter." The Daacro produced a small, pen-shaped device from beneath a flap in his wings and scanned me with it. Twin lights at either end throbbed in a strobing pattern as he drew it up and down my body.

When it stopped blinking, Samael stowed the device and stretched his wings. "You're clear," he said. "Follow me."

Looked like I passed the test. I hefted my bags and hurried after him as he flapped away.

WALKING into the Museum of the Weird was like stepping into a time warp.

It looked just like before its destruction. Shrunken heads and dreamcatchers sat beside cursed baby rattles from the 1800s, and a cast of Bigfoot's footprint. A tight maze of walls and shelving wound through glass cabinets and wall-mounted displays, each exhibit packed with evidence of the unexplained.

I stopped. A mummified corpse lay beneath a shelf of humanoid skulls.

Are they human? I wondered. *Or are these remains extraterrestrial in origin?*

I didn't know how they'd replaced every item with such precision, but I suspected I knew where the funding had come from. A sign by the ticket desk thanked an anonymous donor for funding the rebuild.

Samael shuffled by my knees. I ignored my curiosity and followed him deeper into the maze. It was lit only by dim, orange safety lights in the floor and ceiling. He pushed aside a narrow curtain, then laid one claw on a digital scanner.

The smell of ozone filled the air, and a circular hatch swung open from the bare wall.

We stepped through into a tunnel painted with a large skull-and-crossbones symbol in bright orange. Hazard signs in a dozen languages, human and offworlder alike, shouted warnings from the walls.

I adjusted my bags so the shoulder straps crossed my chest. This arrangement was easier, but it forced me to step sideways through a series of five more hatches. Each stank of ozone like a sudden mountain storm. The final threshold dumped us out on the edge of an empty, dust-blown tarmac.

"This isn't Harbor!" I shouted into a strong wind. "Where on Earth did those subspace tunnels take us?"

I glanced back. A narrow guardhouse stood at a corner where two fourteen-foot metal fences met. The fences were topped with heavy-duty barbed wire. Electrical boxes poked up from the ground at fifty-yard intervals as far as the eye could see in either direction.

"Welcome to Hub!" Samael grated, then dipped his head, flapped forward—and vanished.

I froze. These offworlders were always up to something. I expected the unexpected. But his sudden disappearance caught me off guard.

Something large and unseen whipped past me, displacing an enormous volume of air.

"Gatekeeper's patience is running thin these days." Samael's voice came from in front of me. "Let's go."

I glanced back at the guardhouse once more. Having used subspace tunnels before, I knew that this was a one-way trip. I also knew that when it came to offworlders, things were not always as they appeared. I took a deep breath, relaxing my vision and clearing my mind. After a moment, a shimmering vertical barrier became visible in my sight. It stretched up to the sky and in either direction parallel to the fences.

I stepped forward and felt a tingle along my skin as I passed through the secret barrier. Four alien spacecraft were taxiing along a runway. Beyond them, dozens of offworlders ambled within two open aircraft hangars. Loading vehicles and cranes drove between the outbuildings. Another half-dozen alien ships were parked inside.

This was brazen. A whole alien airfield just sitting here in the open? Everything had been hidden behind that reflective photon cloaking shield I just passed through, but what if the authorities paid an unexpected visit? What if some ignorant human visitor stumbled upon it?

Experience with the Gatekeeper told me that visitors wouldn't be likely to survive the experience. And whatever authorities inspected airfields had already been thoroughly bribed to stay away.

As the alien ships came into closer view, I noted that most of them were utilitarian in nature—sleek, oblong bus-looking things. I'd seen these transport ships before. A few ships of a different design sported aggressive angles and imposing silver plate armor. While the transport ships didn't have any visible defenses, weapons barrels were clearly mounted into the wings of the others.

Still airborne, the Daacro flapped toward a heavy-duty, canvas-walled mobile barracks. His flight left me to wobble along with my bags in his wake.

If I ever had to do this again, I'd bring a cart. Or maybe a USB stick with the funds in cryptocurrency.

Live and learn, Gunn. Live and learn.

Upon passing through the tent flaps that served as the front doors, I was assaulted by the sound of a pained moaning.

My hackles shot straight up.

Two security guards, built like pro wrestlers but each bearing three bulldog-like heads, parted at Samael's approach. They let us through without a word.

I'd have preferred to be frisked. Not confiscating the firearm in my waistband meant that the Gatekeeper had already decided I wasn't a threat.

At least not without those augments active.

I chewed on that thought. It was worth investigating in detail—later.

Samael led me to the source of the noise in a central room of the building. Here, the ceiling rose up like a circus tent. A tall human male with a square jaw and glowing blue eyes bent over a whimpering Torlik.

Physiologically, the main difference between you or me and a Torlik was their orange skin and two extra arms. Currently, both pairs of this dude's upper limbs were wrapped around his knees, clutching his legs to his chest and rocking back and forth. Tears tracked down his cheeks, and he shook visibly. He didn't seem to be conscious of the noise he was making. Or if he was, he couldn't help it.

"You have strict instructions to thoroughly inspect every single offworlder who boards that shuttle," the tall man said, "So, tell me again how Tetrad soldiers got past your scanners *carrying weapons*?"

"I don't know! They must have concealed them in a quantum device."

The tall man scoffed. "Unacceptable." He snapped, and two of the security henchdogs strode forward.

Seeing them come toward him, the orange-skinned alien scrabbled backward and fell to his face with his arms covering his head. "P-p-please, you've got to believe me, it was just an oversight!"

"Oh, just an oversight. Oops! Shall I ring the Federation and let them know that we let wanted terrorists onto a silent planet?"

"No! Please. I'll make it up to you."

"I wonder how this news might change the terms of your parole, if the Peacekeepers caught wind of it."

"I can't go back. Please, give me another chance. It won't happen again. I promise."

"I don't believe you," the man said. "Besides, there are few things I despise more than incompetent underlings."

"Please. Please! I'll make it up to you, I swear."

"How? Are you going to track down the terrorists and arrest them, like some kind of Peacekeeper hero?"

"I'll—I'll think of something. Please. I just need a little time."

The tall man's shoulders slumped as the Gatekeeper separated from his host, revealing an ethereal blue creature that any normal person, being of sound mind and honest faith, might mistake for an angel—or a demon.

I knew better. The Gatekeeper was no immortal being, but an alien life form who survived by draining the energy of other living beings. In other words, he was a parasite. He had weaknesses—sonic cannons and telepathic abilities like those possessed by the Peacekeeper, Dyna, could disrupt his ethereal form—but otherwise he was immune to physical damage.

Which is probably why he'd sent Samael to make sure I hadn't activated the Peacekeeper mods lurking in my bloodstream. Vanilla human beings, even those with high-tech cyborg hands and a loaded pistol in his belt, couldn't easily harm the Gatekeeper.

The body hopper dove into the Torlik's mouth, causing the orange alien to gasp in surprise. His eyes rolled into the back of his head before shining with a faint blue light. Using the alien's own lips, the Gatekeeper said, "Time's up."

The Torlik's top two hands clutched his throat. The bottom pair flailed, slapping the floor.

The body hopper once again separated from its host, exiting through the mouth. Only this time, it seemed to experience some kind of resistance. The Gatekeeper's winged form turned. Its claws wrapped around something lodged deep in the Torlik's throat. He tugged once, hard, and tumbled free bearing a turgid slug of a creature in his grasp. Like the Gatekeeper, this new creature's form was translucent. It existed on a plane beyond the physical. A spirit? A soul? I didn't know what to call it, but seeing it sent a shock of cold fear slithering through my gut. I took a long, slow breath to control my nausea.

Unlike the Gatekeeper's rich blue glow, this slug-like creature was a sickly yellow-orange. The Gatekeeper's claws ripped and sliced, tearing the slug to pieces. As they separated, each section disintegrated into smaller and smaller particles until they vanished in the air.

The Torlik's body slumped to the ground and went still.

The henchdogs strode forward. They dragged the body between me and Samael. Its heels bumped the threshold as they passed through the only exit.

The Gatekeeper, meanwhile, had slammed back into the tall man's head. His current ride. Where had he gotten the guy? The body hopper preferred to subsist on beautiful people. I think it gave him some kind of twisted pleasure to devour and then discard them. It made my stomach churn just thinking about it.

Seeing my discomfort, the Gatekeeper's broad mouth opened in a toothy smile. He turned in our direction, as if noticing us for the first time.

"Hello, Mr. Gunn," the Gatekeeper said. "I've been expecting you."

CHAPTER TWO

I FELT VERY EXPOSED.

Here I was—without backup—standing on the Gatekeeper's home turf with more than a hundred thousand in cash hanging from my shoulders, planning to reason with a violent offworld mafioso who just murdered someone in front of me.

That was my choice. Maybe not the wisest decision I'd ever made, but I still had a hard time asking my friends to risk their lives to dig me out of a hole I'd buried myself in.

I straightened my spine and picked up the metaphorical shovel.

"I'm here to settle up." I unslung both duffels from my shoulder and set them on the floor where the Torlik's body had been moments before. "That should cover the balance of my loan plus interest."

At a nod from the Gatekeeper, one of the henchdogs unzipped the bags, revealing the stacks of cash inside.

The tall man regarded me with an unreadable expression. I reminded myself that the Gatekeeper was a businessman first. From his point of view, I was an asset, not the enemy. He had no reason to harm me.

My reminders were a cold comfort under that burning azure glare.

"Where'd you get the money?" he asked.

I gave up my office, sold my house, worked overtime—I even flipped garage sale junk for extra cash, for God's sake. But he didn't need to know any of that. "That's not important," I said.

"Sure it is. Did you borrow it from another lender? No, you wouldn't do that. Too pigheaded." His toothy smile widened. "This wipes you out, doesn't it?"

He was more right than I wanted to admit. I wasn't scraping the bottom of the barrel. I had pawned the barrel to buy the duffel bags, and now I had nothing left.

After this, I wouldn't owe anything to anybody. I'd be a free man. A broke man, sure. But I'd rather be cash-poor and free than rich and enslaved to someone like him.

"I thought so," he said in an amused tone. "What's the rush? Leave half and take the rest home. Use it to invest in growing your business."

A warning siren blared in my mind. *This* was where it got sticky. The Gatekeeper liked lackeys and lapdogs. I'd refused jobs from him in the past, and he'd still managed to use his leverage to trick me into helping him.

"I've already got a partner," I said.

"So I've heard. You possess a skill set uniquely attractive to offworlders. Mr. Ludwig is wise to seize the opportunity."

My blood ran cold. How did he know Alek was my partner? It wasn't a secret, but we hadn't advertised the agreement. One of my new offworlder clients must have noticed and spilled the beans. So much for that NDA I made them all sign.

"How about an investor, then, hmm? In exchange, I'd be happy to serve in an... advisory role."

"Those seats are filled. I've got all the advice I need. I'll be going now." I turned on my heel.

"Wait, Mr. Gunn."

I clenched my jaw and froze. I didn't want to make an enemy out of him if I could avoid it. Anna's voice whispered in my head, counseling patience. Sheila wasn't far behind. Hers was telling me not to be an idiot. "Yeah?"

"A word in private?"

"It's late."

"Or early, depending on how you look at it. Please. It'll only take a moment. No strings attached."

There were always strings with the Gatekeeper, I'd learned. But that was the world I lived in now—straddling two societies, taking offworlder clients while most of the people around me lived in ignorance of the aliens next door.

I followed the Gatekeeper to an office set up like some kind of control room. A wall was filled with widescreen monitors. Holographic displays, which made modern projectors look like relics, scrolled through shipping manifests and other records in an alien script I could not decipher.

The Gatekeeper dismissed a few security people, a couple of Lodians and a Pangozil who had been drinking coffee and scanning the screens.

He gestured to a swivel chair. "Have a seat."

I did. The cushion was still warm. I sat across from this stranger whose head was filled with the Gatekeeper's presence, loathing how he steered a human being around like a vehicle with no regard for their well-being. He wasn't in the habit of murdering his hosts, but after what I'd just seen him do to that poor Torlik, I had no illusions about his view on the sanctity of life.

"Have you been watching the news?" he asked.

I looked up. Half the monitors showed security footage. The rest were on various mainstream media channels. There was only one thing news anchors wanted to talk about these days. A piece of footage panned over a bone-dry lakebed formerly known as Lake Travis. They cut to a journalist walking along its dry, rocky depths. He spoke into a microphone, rehashing the water's sudden disappearance. No doubt all these media companies were making bank off the clicks this story drove.

I grunted. "Who hasn't? Bodies of water don't usually turn into flashbangs you can see from space."

On another channel, the chyron read, "ISS Video Shows Austin Light Phenomenon." The screen showed the familiar curve of Earth, as seen from the International Space Station. It was as beautiful as ever, this shining blue-green marvel. It looked peaceful from space. In slow motion, a flash so big and so dazzling it grew to consume the lower half of North America for more than sixty seconds suddenly erupted from the heart of Texas. The flash spread over the curve of the planet, causing a lens flare that blotted out most of the view, before fading away.

What this video didn't show was how the sudden transformation of water molecules into photons left the lakebed dry as a mummy's tongue.

"Despite the efforts of your Peacekeeper friends—"

"We're not friends," I interjected.

"Regardless, this knowledge is out there now. Your

entire world is aware of the existence of an event that can't be explained by their current technology. On other planets that have become Tetrad bases of operations, this is how we've seen it begin."

"Tanamir's 'Illumination'." I used my fingers to put air quotes around the word.

"Ah, so you do know."

"Guess you aren't omniscient."

He scoffed. "Hardly. I just make it my business to be aware of... certain events, and happen to have the resources to do so."

"Why are we having this conversation, Gatekeeper?"

"Because of how it ends. If Tanamir gets his way, he will put me out of business. Myself and many other offworlders will be forced to take our leave for more..." He glanced up as he searched for the right word. "Suitable economies. I make much more money in times of peace. Offworlders who pay to travel to remote, silent planets like Earth only come if they know it's safe. If they know that, once they arrive, they will have the freedom to live their lives in peace."

"Provided they don't cross you."

"Indeed. And that all ends post-Illumination."

"Why's that?"

"Once a planet becomes aware of the existence of alien life, Federation bylaws will force them to recognize Earth as a sentient world, annexing them into the Federation and installing outposts and embassies. Life on Earth would be forever changed. Your species might get a seat at the table—a small, minor, inconsequential seat, to be sure—but your independence would become an artifact of a past you'll never regain."

Ah, yes, I thought. *Intergalactic politics.*

"That is," the Gatekeeper said, "unless they choose to side with the Tetrad."

I took a deep breath and blew it out.

This information made me see the Peacekeepers in a new light. They were not just protectors who chased down offworld criminals. They were also the enforcers of Earth's ignorance. Without them, humanity would have discovered aliens among them long ago.

"So," I said as I traced his logic, "it's either be annexed by the Federation, or be used as a pawn in Tanamir's games."

"This is no game. If Earth joins the Tetrad's rebellion, it will have declared war on the Federation by proxy. Either way, conflict will come to this planet if Earth is Illuminated."

"What does that mean, Illuminated? No one's been able to give me any specifics."

He waved a hand. "It's a political term. It means we can no longer suppress the existence of offworlders. Suffice to say your world won't take to it any more than the Pangozil did when theirs was inducted." I frowned. I didn't know the reference. I didn't want to waste time asking for details. I made a note to look into that later. "If you believe nothing else I tell you, believe that, Mr. Gunn."

My mind turned to wondering how the people of Earth would come to see the Lake Travis phenomenon. Would they blame Tanamir for causing it, which was what I knew to be true? Or would they point the finger at the Federation for trying to keep them in ignorance?

Would Earth ever side with the Tetrad? I was raised in Texas, where we believed that freedom and independence were inalienable rights for which we'd paid in blood. But not everyone on—or off—this planet saw the world the way I did. That much I'd learned beyond a shred of doubt.

"Needless to say," the Gatekeeper went on, "Earthbound arrivals have dropped by half since the event. Departures are up four hundred percent."

"You still sell tickets for departures at a profit, don't you?"

"Of course. It's eroding my customer base, however, which is terribly irritating. If it continues..." He shrugged. "My business here will no longer be viable."

"Thanks for sharing," I said. "Don't let the door hit your ass on the way out."

"You don't understand. If I leave Earth, it's for one of two reasons: either the Federation is in control, or the Tetrad is. Neither outcome is beneficial to either of us."

I huffed a deep breath. I didn't want to admit it, but he was right.

"Conflict is bad for business, Mr. Gunn. My operation may exploit some intergalactic laws. But I won't join the Tetrad's blood feud."

"Me neither." I closed my eyes and rubbed at my temples. *These damned warring factions and their designs on Earth!* I could barely keep my own house in order. How was one lone bounty hunter supposed to divert the course of an interstellar conflict?

"Now, you see." The Gatekeeper spread his host's fingers as his glowing azure eyes shone brighter. "Our interests are aligned."

I grunted. I hated it, but he was right. The best outcome would be to maintain the status quo. Get rid of Tanamir. Prevent the Illumination. Keep the Federation away to maintain Earth's independence.

Maybe Dyna and I also had more in common than I wanted to admit.

"More immediately, Tanamir is using my ships to send more operatives to Earth. Unfortunately, offworlders here sympathize with the Tetrad's cause. Even I am having trouble keeping them out."

"Not my monkeys, not my circus."

"That may well be. And I respect that. I just want to make sure you understand what's happening."

He pointed at another monitor. In this segment, the chyron read, "From Washington to Cairo: New UFO Footage Emerges."

I grunted. Although national media coverage in the US focused primarily on the disappearance of Lake Travis, in recent weeks, Tanamir's UFOs had begun to make appearances around the world. The difference distinguishing these UFO sightings was that they came with clear photos and videos of flying saucers hovering over national landmarks. The TV screen currently showed a saucer hovering over the pyramids at Giza in full view of a crowd of gawking tourists.

Now I understood what Tanamir was trying to do. Not just give the Federation the finger by violating their non-interference laws on silent planets. He wanted to trigger a larger event that would erase Earth's status as a silent planet.

Annabelle had been following the stories closely. She covered them on her pseudonymous website as the paranormal investigator Marsha Marshall.

"Marsha thinks the Peacekeepers are chasing him, erasing evidence as they go."

"Your blonde friend is an astute observer," he said. "I've been following her coverage. She's right. But Tanamir is clever. He's been able to stay ahead of the Peacekeepers. And once these images are online, it's nearly impossible to erase all signs of them completely."

Something had been bothering me about Anna's theories. "Why hasn't Tanamir shown his face yet? So far, all he's accomplished is to stir up rumors about UFOs and give these media companies free clickbait."

"He's waiting."

"For what?"

"Some advantage," the Gatekeeper said. "Reinforcements? The right moment? I don't know."

"Why don't the UFOs trigger the Illumination?"

"Because he's playing into human preconceptions. These flying saucers are a human invention."

I grunted. That made a certain kind of sense.

"Tanamir used to be one of the Federation's best military strategists. He knows how to walk the lines of the law, and he won't make his next move until all the pieces are in place." The parasite-piloted man stood and opened the door for me. "I doubt we'll be waiting much longer. I'd prefer you keep some of that money, in case you need it for what's to come."

I'd never heard the Gatekeeper sound so... genuine. I almost preferred intimidation and veiled threats.

My phone vibrated in my pocket, causing me to flinch. I silenced it.

"Thanks for the offer, but no thanks. I'm a free man now, and I'd like to keep it that way." I turned to leave, then paused. "But I appreciate you sharing this information."

I fled temptation without waiting for a response.

CHAPTER THREE

I HIKED a couple of miles along a winding gravel road. When I came to a paved street, a cab I'd called with my smartphone met me. I didn't relax until Hub was long gone from the rearview, and Austin's skyline rose in the distance.

Hub turned out to be located east of town near the airport. Brazen, as I'd said, but Federation shielding tech was beyond anything the FAA could detect. And what better place to hide an alien airport than under the nose of another airport? As far as I knew, the Gatekeeper had been operating here since before they decommissioned Bergstrom Air Force Base and turned it into the commercial airline operation it was today.

Counting my hike, it took two hours for me to get back to the city. The driver dropped me at my truck as the sun bathed East Sixth Street in the soft, golden light of dawn.

I'd left my truck in front of my old office. I got out and stood still for a minute, breathing deeply, drinking in the cold breeze and basking in the weightlessness of freedom.

I studied the worn old building where I used to work.

They'd leased my office to an insurance salesman, which was no surprise given the city's growth trajectory. I tried to console myself with the knowledge that rising rents and soaring property taxes would have priced me out in a year or two anyway. As a testament to inflation, a high-class Italian restaurant had opened two blocks away; a new condo building was nearly complete across the street; and I'd even heard rumors about plans for a Whole Foods on the east side.

You know you're falling down the bell curve of gentrification when Whole Foods moves in.

My phone vibrated again. I hadn't wanted to talk where the cab driver could hear, but now that I was alone, I accepted the call and hoped Sheila wouldn't be too mad that I'd been ignoring her. "Hey, Sheila, what's up?"

"I've been calling for an hour."

"Sorry, I was working late. I just got back to town."

"Are you having a hard time keeping up with Annabelle?"

I was grateful she wasn't here to see me blush. "No, nothing like that. I finally went to see the Gatekeeper and bought back my freedom."

"Well, good for you, knucklehead. How's it feel?"

I hadn't told Sheila about my plans in any specific sense. Didn't want her to worry. But she knew I'd been struggling with money problems for years, and that I'd been working to resolve them.

"Light. Freeing." I sighed. "I'm exhausted. And not just from the all-nighter."

"You've been carrying that weight around for a long time, Anderson. I'm happy for you. You know who else would be happy for you? Your mom."

I blinked away tears as my throat constricted. I searched for words and found I had none.

"Gunn? You still there?"

"Yup." I sniffed. "Thanks, Sheila. I'm beat. I need to hit the hay. Did you need something? You don't generally call me at 5:30 in the morning without a good reason."

She sucked air through her teeth. "Don't hate me, but do you think you could postpone the slumber party? I need your help. Meet me at—" a pause as she seemed to check her notes "—3412 South Congress. ASAP." Her brusque tone made the back of my neck tingle.

"What is it?"

"I've got a weird feeling."

Static came over the line as she muffled the microphone. When she came back on, her voice had lowered to a whisper. "Honestly, Gunn, I can't tell if I can trust my instincts here or if I'm going cross-eyed from all the goofy, bass-ackwards cases they've dumped on SIT since they formed the unit. I need a second opinion."

In her new role as head of the APD's Special Incident Team, Sheila had brought me on as a consultant. She was swamped, and I needed the extra work. It was a good arrangement for us both. We cooperated better as colleagues than we ever had as an incompatible couple back in our college days. Even better, some SIT cases were connected to offworlder business, which led me to new jobs for other clients.

Even so, I was beyond tired. "Can it wait?"

"Don't you even want to know what it is first?"

"Fine. What is it?"

"At least a missing persons case. Your specialty."

"Whaddya mean, 'at least?'"

"That's the interesting part. It might also be a homicide."

"Oh. Is that all?"

"That's all I can say until you agree to come."

I weighed my exhaustion against my bank account balance. It didn't take me long to decide. "Alright, I'll be there in ten."

"I'm not made of money," she said. "I've already got three guys doing overtime. Clock starts when you get here."

I PARKED my battered Ford F-150 outside the police barricade at the El Ranchito Motel. There was no yellow ticker tape, but the boys in blue had double-parked two cruisers and an unmarked car around the entrance to the hotel lobby. They gave the stink-eye to any curious pedestrian or nosy resident who drifted too close.

I flashed my consultant badge at two officers flanking the entrance and made to duck between them, only to meet the brick wall of one's barrel-chest as he stepped into me.

I was tall, but this guy was built like an NFL linebacker. "Identification," he rumbled.

"What, consultant badges are no good today, Daniels?"

"That's Officer Daniels to you. I'm required to confirm your identity."

"Ok, Robocop. I know you recognize me. We talked at the HEB crime scene a couple weeks ago." I glanced meaningfully at his partner. "Remember? You complained that crocheting is an expensive hobby. I said it would be cheaper to buy yarn in bulk."

Daniels blushed, evidently displeased that I had remembered this particular detail about him. I wasn't one to judge a man and his hobbies. Whatever got you through the day, you know? But he didn't take kindly to being ribbed about it.

The man's square jaw tightened. "ID, *please*."

I rolled my eyes and dug my wallet from my back pocket. Officer Daniels studied my driver's license, dutifully checking the old mugshot against a face now fuzzy with graying stubble. He nodded to his partner, who stepped forward to frisk me.

"Is this really necessary?" I complained while he patted me down.

The second cop was shorter than Daniels but still taller than me. He had a slight paunch, full jowls, and my father's comb-over. He removed my Kimber from its holster and disarmed it with practiced motions of his big hands. He ejected the magazine and handed it to Officer Daniels.

"Thanks, Officer Gelder. We'll hang onto this for ya, Gunn."

I rolled my eyes. He stepped around me, opened the door of the nearest cruiser and stowed my gun in the glove box.

"Dick move, man. Is this because you have to pull overtime today?"

"I have to be at my kid's birthday party in two hours," Gelder grumbled. "Work quickly."

"Oh yeah, today's Saturday. Where's the party?"

He glared at me for a long minute before scraping out the words, "Dave and Buster's."

"I dig that place. Kids' parties are always better when there's a full bar." He continued to stare at me, his irritation evident. Then he blinked, and when he did, his eyelids came together in a vertical seam—a very inhuman direction.

I rubbed my sleepy eyes. Had I missed something, or was

this cop really an offworlder in disguise? It was hard to peer through cloaking shields in broad daylight, especially if I hadn't slept well. I tried to relax my mind to peer through his, but either he wasn't using one or I was too tired. I decided it wasn't any of my business and gave up trying. Not like he was the first offworlder in hiding I'd seen today.

"I want my gun back," I said.

"Let us know when you're ready to leave."

"So, I'm good to go in, then?"

They glared at me. No more weird vertical eye blinks from Gelder, only the irritable frown of every bored beat cop. I tiptoed between them, exaggerating my motions like a cartoon character. I took an excruciatingly long time opening the door, enjoying the way their faces reddened as they tried to ignore me.

I probably shouldn't have antagonized them, but it was so much fun.

Inside, the motel was ratty and rundown. It had low, popcorn ceilings and water-stained carpets. I followed a trail of cops and "No Entry" signs to a room on the second floor near the fire exit. Someone had propped the door open, and two more uniformed officers stood outside. These ones didn't bother me.

"Gunn, that you?" Sheila called. "Get your ass in here."

I craned my neck and saw Detective Gonzalez holding her nose by the window.

"What is that smell?" I asked, cringing as a musky odor assaulted my nostrils. It was weirdly sweet, with an undertone of citrus.

"Watch your step." She made her way across the room, moving gingerly to avoid dark stains on the floor. It wasn't only the floor that was stained. Blood dripped from the walls, the television screen, the messy bedsheets. Cheap, floral curtains were torn and ragged, as if a tiger had used them to sharpen its claws. A suitcase had literally exploded. The remains of its hard plastic shell were charred and melted. A sliver of plastic ejected with such force that it lodged three inches into the bed's wooden headboard.

"Whaaaaat in the hell happened here?" I asked.

"That's what I've been wondering." She released her nose and sniffed. "It was still wet when we got here."

"Which was when?"

"Couple hours ago."

"So you didn't sleep much, either."

"Nope."

The stains had mostly dried by now. My eyebrows bunched up together as a sense of wrongness came over me. "Wait a minute, where's the body?" I asked.

"Hah!" Gonzalez barked. "Simmons, pay up!"

A man in a tan suit two sizes too big for him stepped out of the bathroom and groaned loudly. He reached into a pocket and palmed Gonzalez a twenty folded up hot dog style. "He just don't look that smart."

"Ouch," I said, touching my cyborg hand to my chest. Detective Simmons glanced down at it, swallowing hard. My hand made him really uncomfortable. I guess I reminded him of things he'd rather forget.

"No body," Detective Gonzalez confirmed.

"So, why do you think it's murder?"

She made wide gestures at the room and rolled her eyes. "With this much blood, how could it not be?"

I shrugged. "Maybe."

"Reports from people sleeping in other rooms up and

down the hall, too. They heard fighting, screams, an explosion. Then silence."

My eyes roamed the room. I stepped forward, studying the cracked LED screen of the TV. It was flecked with fleshy bits of gore.

Distinctly orange-tinted, non-human flesh.

I looked down at where I was standing in a clean oval relatively free of bloodstains. It was located between the foot of the bed and the television.

"Something was lying here when it happened."

"I agree. And see how the bloodstains are heavier there, and there?" she pointed left and right.

"You think the body was lying here as it bled out?"

"It seems likely."

"If that's the case, where'd the body go?"

She shrugged. "Don't know."

"Perp does the deed, panics and leaves without checking the body. When he's gone, the victim comes back to consciousness. Second guy gets up and leaves, too."

Gonzalez was shaking her head before I even finished speaking. "No one was seen leaving this room. Not the murderer, and not the victim."

"Are you sure?" I asked.

"Sure as I can be. We have the footage." She glanced up at Simmons. "Show him."

Simmons pulled up a video on his phone and handed it to me.

Timestamp read 02:30. A bald man in a leather jacket lumbered down the hall. He wasn't staggering drunk, but he was walking like his sneakers were too heavy and he didn't know what to do with his feet. He clutched a biker's helmet in the crook of one elbow and dragged a suitcase behind him—the one that lay charred and melted nearby, I noted. After fumbling with the keycard, the man slipped inside.

Simmons reached over and fast forwarded the footage by tapping on the screen a couple times.

"Wait," I said.

"We don't have time to scrub through hours of nothing. I did that when I got here. This is the important part."

At four o'clock, the camera trembled. Smoke puffed out from under the hotel room door. Moments later, other doors in the hall were thrown wide. An old lady in rollers sprinted out of a neighboring room and banged on the closed door. Someone else stepped out and shouted, "Fire!" with hands cupped around their mouth. Simmons grabbed the video feed manually this time and dragged the cursor forward. More people began to rush back and forth. Eventually, a staffer, maybe the night manager or something, arrived to open the door. She stepped inside for a moment. Then she staggered out and shooed people to the exits.

"That's when the motel phoned us," Gonzalez said. "We'd already received three 911 calls and I was in my car on the way here."

I watched it twice more. "No one came in or out."

"Exactly. So where'd the man go?"

"Maybe the perp entered and exited through the window," Simmons suggested.

Even as he said it, I knew I didn't believe it. The window was dirty but hadn't broken or even cracked. It had been out of the path of the incendiary device.

"It's a picture window," Gonzalez said. "Doesn't open."

"Better question is, who attacked the guy? Or did some

creature just crawl out of his suitcase and try to eat him? I read once that a guy in Wilmington, Delaware was eaten alive by his komodo dragons."

"You think a komodo dragon would fit in that suitcase?"

I shrugged. "I've seen stranger things."

"Okay, it is suspicious," she admitted.

"There's a reasonable explanation," Simmons said. "Always is."

Gonzalez slowly raised her eyebrows.

"What? Occam's blade, right?" Simmons asked.

I shook my head. "Occam's razor, genius. And you're using it wrong."

"Pfah," Simmons said. "What do you know?'

Gonzalez studied me as silence stretched out over the grim scene. I shook my head and then shrugged. "How can I help?"

"You think it's some kind of offworlder thing?" Gonzalez asked.

"Could be," I admitted. "Concealment, manipulating video feeds and unexpected disappearances are basically their MO. Although all the blood and gore does puzzle me. It's not quite the right color, is it?"

"Our forensics guys are analyzing it now." Simmons pocketed his phone. He coughed into his hand, then muttered an excuse and left the room.

"What's up with him?" I asked.

"He hates when we talk about offworlder stuff."

"Is he still in denial about the memory gap?" I asked. A Federation Peacekeeper I knew had wiped Simmons' memories of an alien land-squid climbing Frost Tower. He and several others, including Annabelle, had been involved. Annabelle and I had been able to work through our issues about the event, but I guess old Simmons' mind wasn't so flexible.

"He didn't live through the same nightmare we did." Gonzalez was talking about earlier that same night when the violent, telepathic Pharsei had tried to unalive us. Elekatch had been his name, and his kind were an alien species out of Ridley Scott's worst nightmare. "Still doesn't believe it, not really," the detective went on. "He thinks I'm turning into some kind of crazed conspiracy theorist."

I shook my head. "Even after that Lodian we talked to about the grocery store robbery?"

"Simmons thinks the guy was just into body modification, like the Lizardman."

I grunted. "Well. People can make themselves believe anything if they try hard enough."

"Did you believe it, at first?"

I thought back to my nauseating reaction and all the emotions I'd gone through. Shock, dread, elation, fear. I hadn't wanted to believe... but it had been impossible not to, with two genetically modified offworlders standing in front of me, one with cybernetic implants in her head, the other an albino, feline half-breed. My throat went dry as visions of dormant nanobots in my bloodstream swam through my mind.

"Suppose I would have been able to make more excuses in his situation."

"Gunn, why do you think Dyna hasn't come back to wipe *our* memories?" Sheila asked.

"She still wants us to side with her against whatever mischief Tanamir and his Tetrad cult of Lodian zealots are up to."

Sheila scoffed. “I don’t want two masters. Or two governments.”

“I hear you.” I fell silent, not sure if I should tell her about my conversation with the Gatekeeper earlier. She had enough to worry about.

“What is it?” she asked.

“I don’t know yet. It was something the Gatekeeper said. He told me Tanamir was waiting for something.”

“What does he care? I thought the Gatekeeper was in the import/export business.”

“He’s having trouble keeping the Tetrad’s people out. And apparently offworlders are fleeing Earth. Says it’s hurting his business.”

“Great. Something else to look forward to.”

“So what do you want to do here?” I gestured at the messy room, wrinkling my nose against that awful sour lemon odor.

“Look around, see if you can find any evidence that I missed. Then ask your friends if there’s any kind of offworlder tech that could make a body disappear.”

“It’s not much to go on.”

“We have to work with what we’ve got. Which is damn little in this case.”

“Heh. We seem to get all the SIT jobs.”

“Don’t you start with me. I get enough dog jokes at the station, I don’t need to take crap from you, too.”

“And to think, they formed this team just for you guys,” I said.

“How kind of them,” Simmons replied, deadpan, with only his head visible in the doorway. “Let’s just hope we’re not barking up the wrong tree again.”

“Dammit, Simmons!” Gonzalez yelled. “Make yourself useful and get me a coffee.”

He grunted and wandered off, leaving two old friends to stare at the bloodstained room and wonder what would cause a biker’s body and his helmet to vanish into thin air.

CHAPTER FOUR

"GUNN, you keep asking crazy questions like this and I'm gonna hafta start chargin' ya," said the beak-nosed New Yorker sitting across from me.

I was at Vinny's restaurant, a pizza parlor tucked off Sixth Street in downtown Austin. Normally, the place was packed to the gills with salivating customers while the delicious aroma of brick-oven pizza poured through the open windows.

Today, it was as empty as the hotel room I'd come from. The front door was locked. The windows were covered with newspapers. All the lights were off except for a few.

"Because, Vinny," I said, "there's no one else I trust more when it comes to matters of offworlders."

"Bah," he scoffed. "Why not call Zavis? He's forgotten more about Federation tech than I've ever known."

"I don't need technical details, just a general direction to search in. Besides, Zavis is a recluse, and he gets grouchy when I drop in for a visit."

"Don't *I* seem grouchy to you?"

"Well, yeah, man, usually." I grinned. "But I know you're all warm and fuzzy on the inside."

Vinny heaved a sigh and drummed his fingers on the table as he studied me. The joke was double-pointed. He was a warm-hearted person despite his gruff exterior. But Vinny was also a Pangozil, a race of fur-covered, bipedal marsupials.

Vinny had come to Earth to escape his past, a war-hardened life of combat serving the Federation in its many military conflicts. Unfortunately, his past followed him to Earth despite his best efforts to retire.

"I suppose it's possible for a body to disappear, but it ain't likely. Our tech still follows the laws of physics. Matter don't just vanish. It has to *go* somewhere."

I thought about how much blood was covering the walls of that hotel room. "Is it possible to liquefy a body?"

"Sure. But that's a *lot* of liquid. And what about their clothes and other personal effects?"

"Yeah. I'm not sure. Just tossing ideas around right now."

"It seems more likely that you're missing a piece of the puzzle. Earth cameras don't catch everything."

To emphasize his point, Vinny flicked off his cloaking shield. It revealed a long snout, matted tan fur, and beady, tired eyes set deep into his head. His disguise slid back into place a moment later. Once again, he was a clean-shaven, beak-nosed New Yorker with mousy brown hair.

"Yeah, I suppose," I said. "It's just odd. We canvassed the building. No eyewitnesses saw anyone else go in or out."

Vinny shrugged. "Weirder things have happened."

"Weird is my business these days. OK, how about this? They used a subspace tunnel to escape the room."

"Sure, that's as likely an explanation as any."

I chewed over the possibility, which was the first and most obvious answer. The tunnel system I'd used to get out to Hub belonged to the Gatekeeper. Someone else could have used it—or could have built their own system, like Zavis had out at his lake house. But you have to deliberately place those things. They're expensive and require specialized tools to install. Why would someone put a subspace tunnel entrance in a cheap motel room? That would have required an enormous amount of forethought and preparation.

A knock sounded at the door, causing Vinny to tense. Normally, we'd be able to glance over and see who it was through the glass. Since the windows had been pasted over, all we saw were three shadowy silhouettes.

Vinny reached into the duffel bag at his feet. I grabbed his wrist. "Easy, pal."

He glanced up at me and narrowed his eyes. "What are you up to?"

"Me? Nothin'. Get the door, dude."

Vinny let go of the sawed-off shotgun he had hidden in the bag and shuffled over. He'd barely cracked the door when a chorus of "SURPRISE!!" came surging through.

I grinned as Annabelle, Alek, and Sheila burst in. They showered a disgruntled Vinny with hugs, cheek kisses, and handshakes. Annabelle popped the cork on a bottle of champagne, and we all laughed as the bubbles poured onto the floor.

"What in all the livable worlds is this?" Vinny asked.

"A proper sendoff, silly," Annabelle said. "You didn't think we'd let you go without saying goodbye, did you?"

He spun on me. "You set me up!"

I shrugged and smirked, leaning back in the booth to interlace my hands behind my head.

Vinny grumbled and blushed. Damn, but those reflective photon cloaking shields were good. I was sure that translating Pangozil emotions was no small task. It had fooled me for years before I discovered Vinny's true identity.

Maybe the murderer got that body out of the hotel room using a similar disguise. But if they did... why? What were they trying to hide?

"I don't want you to make a fuss over me," Vinny said.

"Oh, shut up," Sheila said, pressing an overflowing plastic champagne flute into his hand.

"You've made a living serving others, Vinny," Alek said. "Ain't it fittin' that we serve you? I brought barbecue, by the way, just have to grab it from the car."

Alek left and returned a moment later with two heavy plastic bags full of a dozen packages wrapped in butcher paper. We pushed two freestanding tables together. Then, we spread out a buffet of brisket and ribs, biscuits and coleslaw, mac 'n' cheese, and peach cobbler. We chatted as we ate, and I stuffed myself with enough meat to put an elephant into a coma.

Annabelle elbowed me gently. "Hey, sleepyhead."

It felt like I had to bench press my eyelids open. "Hey, yourself." I laid my arm across her shoulders and pulled her close.

"It's done, then?" she asked.

"Sure is. You're looking at a free man."

"Congratulations! What are you going to do with your newfound freedom?"

"Go to work. I'm broke, hun."

Her smile brightened my whole world. “There are worse things to be.”

“No doubt.” I stifled a yawn. “I need to puzzle through this next gig. But I’m afraid my brain won’t work right until I get some sleep.”

Sheila glanced up over a pork rib—picked completely clean, the psycho. “Blood samples are being run against regional and federal criminal databases. Did Vinny give you any ideas?”

“A few,” I said. “Maybe they used a cloaking shield to hide from the camera.”

“Aren’t those for personal use? We would have seen the door open or... or *something*.”

We both glanced at Vinny. “Don’t look at me,” he said. “My short-lived career as a consultant is over. You’re on your own, kids.”

Sheila gave him a fake pout. “You’ll still take my calls, won’t you?”

“There’s no service where I’m going.”

“Where you headed?” Alek glanced up from his cigar cutter. He’d finished eating and was focused on trimming the end off a new stogie.

“The mountains are calling,” Vinny said. “And I must go.”

“OK, John Muir,” I said. “When did you become interested in outback adventuring?”

“When I heard there was a new Pangozil settlement out in Wyoming. I want to check it out, see if I can scare up any news about what happened to the rest of my kin.” A darkness clouded Vinny’s eyes as he thought about the cousin he’d killed. Ezembaster had gone over to Tanamir’s side and come to Earth to incite a rebellion. Annabelle reached over and rubbed Vinny's back.

"Why would they come here?" I asked.

"Not like they were left with much choice, Gunn, after what the Tetrad did to Pango." He took a final swig of his beer. "Better Earth than a Lodian world where they'd be relegated to some filthy ghetto. Regardless, I need to be with my people right now."

"I get it, Vinny. I hope you find what you're looking for."

How did I phrase my next question in a way that wouldn't anger him? Ezembaster had turned on his kind—why not others like him? "These new Pangos. Are they, uh, sympathetic to the cause?"

"I don't know yet, Gunn. I can't get ahold of 'em. They're way, *way* off grid. My guess is they went far enough out that even if the war did come to Earth, they wouldn't get dragged into it. They holed up in the way of my people."

"There's wisdom in that," Sheila said.

"We're really good at hiding when we don't want to be found. Only reason I told all of yous is so you won't be worried about me when I disappear."

I was worried about him, but I kept my mouth shut. Vinny had to do what he thought was right, and who was I to tell him how to live his life?

"You guys," Annabelle said. "Look."

She'd wandered off during our conversation and flicked on the television. A news channel was playing. She pointed the remote and cranked up the volume.

"—anonymous reports linked to Arizona's National Park Service and the National Guard claim a flying saucer saved the life of eleven-year-old Bellamie Taylor. She was visiting the park around eight-thirty this morning when she tripped off a cliff and fell into the Grand Canyon. Multiple *eyewit-*

nesses say that although the child bounced off a rock wall and was in free fall, something caught her about halfway down and raised her back to safety."

"That sounds like science fiction," said the news anchor back at the station.

"Indeed, it does, Jim. As viewers can see in the still image on their screen, it almost looks like the girl was lifted up by some kind of tractor beam."

The image of the reporter faded out, and a still shot of the Grand Canyon replaced it, featuring one of Tanamir's flying saucers—the round, flat design like something straight out of a Roswell conspiracy theory—holding a young girl within a translucent column of lime-green light.

I was happy the girl didn't get hurt. But after my talk with the Gatekeeper this morning, it was overshadowed by a sinking feeling in the pit of my stomach.

What in the world was Tanamir up to?

CHAPTER FIVE

WHILE I WAS CONTEMPLATING my next move at Alek's office, my phone rang.

"Hello?"

"I have another referral for you," Lulamina said. "Any chance you'd be able to come out to the house?"

"Another one?" I asked. "Pretty soon you'll be wanting a commission."

"Neeeeever gonna happen," Alek drawled around the burnt end of his cigar. A different one from earlier. The man smoked more than an old Chevy pickup's exhaust pipe.

"Oh no," Lulamina said, "it's not the money I'm interested in. It's the *story*."

Since reuniting with her husband, I had discovered that my former client was quite the savvy connoisseur: a collector of rare paintings, a breeder of premium Jel'ka eggs, and an expert in offworld antiquities... And what do rare art and racing raptors have in common if not a compelling story? Referring new offworld clients to me had become her obsession.

Not that I minded. They paid well. I'd even been able to use it as an opportunity to raise my rates.

"This connection came through Zavis," Lulamina said. "And to think, my husband didn't see the point of staying in touch with his colleagues. Back in those days, he gave no thought to anything but solving technical problems with his own inventions."

I thought about the jumpy, reclusive engineer, Zavis. He had concealed much from his wife—and me—a couple of months ago. "Is that any different from how he acts now? Seems like he spends all his time holed up in that workshop of his."

"I assure you, sharing a meal with me once every other day is *frequent* for Zavis. He's been practically *sociable* since you returned him to me. So, will you do it?"

My brain had rebooted after a midday catnap, so I had the presence of mind to ask for more details. "Tell me about this friend of yours first."

She proceeded to describe a Torlik academic with more accolades than you could shake a stick at. He'd shown up on their doorstep, unannounced and distraught, begging Lulamina to help him track down a well-known Pangozil.

The Pangozil had one of those long, tongue twister names they fancied. "What'd you say the Pangozil's name was again?" I asked.

"Amberen Geveraux."

"And he's some kind of offworld celebrity?" I asked.

"No, not a celebrity. That word comes with baggage. More like a... clan leader or respected elder. The Pangozil don't have elected politicians or even royalty among themselves, but they're creatures of the pack, and each clan has a council of elders. This man's business was tied up in the galactic entertainment feeds, but he's so much more than that to his people."

"If no one else can find him, what makes you think I can?"

"After the attack on Pango, they evacuated the clan leaders. Their planet was no longer safe to inhabit, something about an arrested singularity. Zavis can tell you more. My point is, our friend believes he came here to Earth."

That stiffened the hairs on the back of my neck. Was this guy hiding out in Wyoming with Vinny's kin? Out of respect for Vinny, I kept that thought to myself. "Did you check with the Gatekeeper? They probably traveled here using his shuttle service."

"Yes, and either they used a pseudonym or a different transportation method. Still, my friend thinks he's Earthside somewhere."

"Earthside. That has a nice ring to it."

Now I could *really* use Vinny's advice in this situation. It was too bad he'd already left town. I'd have to call him before he traveled too far off-grid.

"And how is your Torlik engineer friend involved, exactly?"

"I think you need to ask him that for yourself."

"Okay. Where is he now?"

"In the desert room. The climate there is a lot like his home planet."

I shuddered. That was the room in their Opsilax mansion where Tanamir had held me prisoner and used Peacekeeper tech to repeatedly murder me in a simulated reality.

"I'm a little busy right now... I took another case this morning."

"We'll come to town to meet you, then."

She wasn't going to take no for an answer. I chewed on that for a moment. Lulamina let me take my time.

What bothered me was this: If I took this case, I'd have to deal with two nosy Pinkers, a stubborn Torlik, *and then* locate a missing Pangozil celebrity. Even if Vinny could help —and there was no guarantee of that—how was I supposed to juggle both cases? "Here's the thing, Lula. I'm in the middle of another job with the APD, and that needs to be my priority. I won't make any promises, at least not until I have more detail. Also, I'm supposed to meet Annabelle tonight to help her with something.

"What if we meet around seven at The Poached Pig?"

I sighed. That would be more convenient for me. "I'll meet you, but no promises."

"Great! All I can ask is that you hear him out. We'll see you there at seven."

"All right, Lula. Appreciate you reaching out."

When I hung up the phone, I dialed Vinny straight away. No ringtone answered me. No personalized voicemail greeting either, just a standard "inbox full" message.

"Well, shit," I muttered before heaving a sigh.

"He don't wanna talk, Gunn," Alek said.

"I know, but I really need to pick his brain right now..." I looked up at Alek, who smiled sadly at me. "I miss him already," I admitted.

"Did you tell him that before he left?"

I grimaced. I didn't have many deep connections in my life and, unlike Lulamina, I didn't have a knack for cultivating them. Aside from my new relationship with Annabelle and my partnership with Alek, I was close to no one else. I was estranged from my deadbeat dad. My mom had passed away. I worked with Gonzalez, and we went way back, but she was too busy to chat much outside of assignments.

Vinny was my only other close friend.

A shade of loneliness passed over me. I shivered, and my mind wandered to a dark place. I opened my messaging app and sent Vinny a text.

"Miss you already, pal," I wrote. "Safe travels. Call me if you need anything."

I couldn't bring myself to ask him to verify any of Lulamina's assertions. It would have been selfish of me. Frankly, I wanted to be a better friend than that.

I shook off the cloud, said goodbye to Alek, and went to meet Annabelle.

"AS AN EXPERT IN SUPERNATURAL PHENOMENA, what caused the light seen from space, Ms. Marshall?" asked the interviewer, his nasally voice echoing through the laptop speakers.

Annabelle shifted in her seat and focused on a middle distance. She wasn't one to speak rashly and was prone to biting the inside of her cheeks while she collected her thoughts.

"Ms. Marshall" was also more accustomed to hiding behind the anonymity of her keyboard than giving video interviews, even if it was only to third-rate YouTube channels like this one. She'd taken all the precautions we agreed to, which is why her face was obscured by offworlder cloaking tech, her voice distorted by a microphone filter, and we were sitting on the side of the road in her recon van, streaming from a satellite connection rather than enjoying the comfort of her air-conditioned home office.

"I don't think it was supernatural, for one," she finally said. "Every phenomenon has a scientific explanation, even if we don't know what it is yet."

"No one can agree on the cause, so what's your prevailing theory?"

Annabelle shifted in her seat again. I adjusted the monitor so that her blurred face remained centered in it.

"Here's what I can tell you," she said. "Millions of gallons of water vanished from Lake Travis in an instant. A split second later, a flash of light blinded the cameras of the International Space Station. That sort of thing doesn't happen spontaneously. It's not *super*natural, but it's not natural either."

"What do you think about the theory that a solar flare vaporized the lake?"

She scoffed. "Utter nonsense."

"So what caused it, then?"

"My guess is a chemical reaction of some kind. The lake water rapidly changed states, resulting in a massive emission of photon particles. The water got eaten up like so many fuel cells."

"I read this theory on your website in an article you wrote titled 'Quantum Flare.' I contacted a NASA scientist, and he told me it was impossible to convert water to light."

She smirked. "Implausible, maybe. Not impossible. All I did in that piece was record eyewitness testimony."

"Right. I heard you were having some kind of fan convention nearby. Lucky break."

"You could say that." She smirked at me.

"It still doesn't seem possible for particles of H2O to transform into photons."

"Keep in mind, I didn't say the water *transformed* into light. I said a chemical reaction caused the water to change states, perhaps from a liquid to a gas. The reaction emitted a massive number of photons all at once."

"Wouldn't such a reaction have to emit heat, too? Wouldn't it leave behind some kind of residue? Investigations by multiple parties have turned up nothing of the sort. And local authorities still have their cases wrapped up tighter than a hypochondriac at a brothel. What I can't explain is how it all happened so quickly. One minute it was there. The next minute, poof, gone."

"I spoke to a boater who was by the lake when it happened," said Annabelle. "He didn't report any heat or side effects except for blinding light. It's puzzling, I'll admit, but my explanation is the simplest and most likely."

"So you don't buy the 'leaky dam' theory either, eh?"

"Not for a second."

The interviewer paused as he butted up against Anna's absolute certainty. Which made sense—she didn't need a theory. She'd seen it happen. But we couldn't come out and say such things, knowing Tanamir was still out there in his ships, agitating the offworlder community and, now, doing random acts of kindness to draw the world's attention.

Not without giving away our advantage.

The interviewer took a left turn. "I look forward to hearing more details as your theory develops. Now, while I have you, I want to ask your thoughts about the UFO spotted in the Grand Canyon."

Annabelle frowned. "I'm not quite sure what to make of that. What I can tell you is that it's the clearest footage of unidentified aerial phenomena we've seen in decades—maybe ever."

"Is this some kind of trick? A government hoax? Is this our generation's crop circles?"

"I'm not sure. That girl's testimony was awfully convincing, don't you think?"

"Nah, I don't buy it. Either she was in on the con, or she's some random rube who got tricked like the rest of us. An eleven-year-old wouldn't know an actual ET from a Hollywood prop."

"It's not like they could rig a boom and suspend someone over the Grand Canyon with strings, Bennett."

"Why not, Marsha? It could have been a trick of the light. Or mirrors. Or an augmented reality experiment."

"And what do you make of the other sightings?"

Silence on the other end as Bennett the Believer checked his notes. "Cairo, Rio de Janeiro. Are there others?"

"The US government has documented three times as many UFO sighting reports in the past two months as in the previous two years. I filed the Freedom of Information Act request myself."

"Uh—I—hadn't heard about that."

"That's because I haven't broken the story yet, honey."

At this, ol' Benny boy's eyes shone like two spotlights. "Is that right?" he asked, realizing she was using his channel to tease the information.

"It is. I'll have more details on it soon. Until then, I hope more witnesses come forward to corroborate these sightings. I want to hear their side of the story."

"Still seems like a government hoax to me."

"This is different, Bennett. Something is happening. It's only a matter of time before the truth comes out."

She cut the interview short after that. Bennett took the hint and let her go. Annabelle shut down her equipment as I started the van's engine. I drove us back to town in silence.

"Normally, I don't mind quiet, but this is too much," I said. "What are you thinking?"

"I don't know, Andy. Tanamir's up to something. We have to figure out what."

"My guess is he's agitating. Gaming for sympathy. The first thing revolutionaries do is take over the airwaves, right? The real front line of any war is in the minds of the people."

"That's what I'm worried about. But look at the history of revolutions on Earth. It starts with propaganda, but it always ends in violence—wars, pogroms, uprisings."

"I won't let anyone hurt you."

She reached out and cupped my cheek in her hand. "That's sweet, hun, but you can't protect me from everything."

She glanced down at my cyborg hand and her brow furrowed—ever so slightly, just the barest of squints. "We've got to make a plan."

"You mean if this becomes a combat situation?" I asked.

She nodded.

"We can pick rendezvous points in case of an emergency. Do you have a weapon?"

"My Paw Paw's old revolver is in the lockbox at home."

"Better than nothing. I'll look for something manufactured in this century that's small enough for you to conceal carry. Beyond that, I'll do anything in my power to keep you safe, Anna," I said. "Anything."

"I don't even like being on camera, let alone caught in a gunfight." Her hand drifted up to my bicep and squeezed.

Then her jaw tightened. "But what I'm *really* worried about is what happens afterward."

"What do you mean?"

"Well," she said, "think about it. What does Tanamir want? You told me yourself. He wants Earth to be Illuminated. In more legalistic terms, he wants us to lose our status as a silent planet and bring his conflict to our shores."

"That sounds about right, from what I've heard."

"The question I keep asking myself is, what for? He's not being altruistic. He says he wants to help us, but help us how? God knows I want the truth about offworlders to be made public. But I want it to happen in a way that won't cause people to panic or riot. Or worse."

I chewed this over for a minute. It hurt my brain. As usual, Annabelle was thinking four steps ahead of me. Eventually, I caught up. "He doesn't want us to be part of the Federation either. If I believe what the Gatekeeper said, he's trying to annex us into this Tetrad alliance of his, which sounds equally awful."

"Earth won't want any part of it," Annabelle said. "We can barely agree to keep peace with each other in this country. Human beings and, apparently, most offworlders are incredibly territorial."

"Neither the Federation nor the Tetrad will let us keep our independence without a fight."

"Andy, if we fight back, you *know* we're gonna lose."

"The only other choice is to pick a side." I grimaced. "That's not a choice I want anyone to have to make."

"Right. So we've got to be *smarter* than him," she said. "We've got to get ahead of the curve. Otherwise, what happened to Vinny's homeworld could easily happen to ours."

"Hiroshima but for the whole world."

"And unlike Vinny's people, we can't just get in a spaceship and hop over to some other planet. No one's thinking about our exit plan."

That thought put me in a dark place. Nothing I liked less than being cornered. "So what do we do?"

"I don't know. It frightens me, too, because in a way I want what Tanamir wants. I want people to know the truth about offworlders! I want Earth to be part of the galactic community. We have a lot to give—and even more to learn. But I don't want to do it his way."

"I know that. You've done a great job treading the line."

"I won't be able to do it forever. I agonize over every word I publish or say these days."

"We'll figure something out."

"Yeah?"

"Yeah, of course. We're a team now. We'll figure it out. We're in this together."

She stared into my eyes with those shining baby blues. Must have liked what she found, too, because after a minute she smiled and leaned across the center console for a kiss.

Eventually, we got out and went into the bar. It was a quiet night. I waved to Barry the bartender, then spotted the rainbow-colored hair of Lulamina's human vessel in a booth at the back. She was dressed in a sparkly blue dress that hugged her petite, curvy figure. She sat across from a bald man wearing a leather jacket and wire-rimmed spectacles.

The moment I laid eyes on him, goosebumps broke out along my arms.

CHAPTER SIX

"THIS IS FELIX, the friend I wanted you to meet," Lulamina said.

He put down a spiral-bound book and stood. "Mr. Gunn! Thank you for coming. I've heard so much about you." He held out his hand as he approached.

His jacket was smooth, worn, and full of patches. It looked like he'd bought it from a pawn shop near the Hell's Angels' HQ.

Had I found my missing biker?

What really tipped me off were the dark brown stains on his jeans and shirt. Also, a gash on his jacket had been hastily sewn up with leather thread. Burn marks radiated out from the seam.

It could have been a coincidence, right? Some other offworlder sporting a leather jacket?

Fat chance.

I took the direct route to get confirmation. I reached past his hand and pressed the off button on the device on his belt. It deactivated his reflective photon cloaking shield.

A shocked Torlik stared aghast at me. His single, oversized eyeball darted around the room, as if he'd been caught naked in public.

I suppose he had, in a sense.

The bar was empty enough that no one but the proprietor had noticed the exchange or the alien among them. And Barry was already up on things; more than he let on. One reason I liked meeting clients here was his discretion. I saw the saloon doors swing as he ducked back into the kitchen.

"Who are you?" I demanded, "and how in the world did you get out of that hotel room alive?"

"Uhhh," Felix said, frowning and pressing his lower set of hands to his stomach, as if nervous. Except for the cyclopean eye, his facial features and frame were similar in size and shape to a human being's. His Torlik skin, however, was the color of an orange prison jumpsuit. He finally gathered his senses enough to reactivate the shield so that he appeared, once again, like a pudgy biker with a bad fake tan. "I was hoping to avoid that discussion. Events are moving at such a pace that we don't have—"

"How the flip did you sneak by the cameras?" I interrupted him and stepped closer to the Torlik. I wanted to study his clothes in more detail. Those were definitely bloodstains on the shirt. "No one went in or out after you. Is it some kind of special cloaking tech, like you use to change your appearance? Or a subspace tunnel system? Or some kind of teleportation? That's the last thing I need."

Felix flinched and drew away from me. He looked between me and Lulamina, apparently too shocked to respond. He definitely did not possess the aggressive, come-at-me attitude of a card-carrying motorcycle club member. I'd run some of them down over my years as a bounty hunter. Annabelle laid a hand on my shoulder, an unspoken request to calm down.

"How about we all sit down and talk this over?" Annabelle suggested.

I unclenched my cyborg fist and gave Felix a little space.

The Torlik reseated himself in the booth. He fidgeted with his book, some kind of nerdy engineering text full of diagrams and tiny fonts in an alien language.

"Okay," Annabelle said after we'd made ourselves comfortable in the bench seat across from them. "Who wants to fill me in on what happened?"

Lulamina's mouth was hanging open. She breathed more heavily than usual. "Annabelle, are you surprised that Gunn knows something you don't, or that he figured it out so quickly?"

"I'm not sure yet what he figured out. Obviously, I missed something."

"She's always a little annoyed when I'm not a complete idiot," I said, "Which makes sense because I've been a complete idiot so often. But this one's not her fault. She wasn't at the crime scene and we haven't had a reason to discuss it yet." I scowled at Lulamina. "You could have warned me."

"And deprive myself of this wonderful moment?" Her shoulders lifted in a slight shrug.

"Too many people using me for their amusement today," I muttered, thinking about the fall I'd taken in front of Samael. My ribs still smarted from the experience. I took a breath and refocused my attention. "OK, Felix. Allow me to be blunt. Who attacked you, and how do we find them?"

"Well, I'd like to figure out who killed me, too, but that's hardly the most pressing order of business." He seemed really agitated now.

"Killed you?" I rubbed my eyes and sighed. "Hey Barry, got any coffee?"

"I'll put some on," he hollered from the kitchen.

"I'm sorry, Felix," I said. "We got off on the wrong foot. I'm a little cranky today."

"Imagine how I feel," he muttered.

"I can imagine. I saw the motel room."

He swallowed hard and nodded. I let my eyes relax, focusing a thousand yards away. If I looked at him from the corner of my eye, I could see his lower arms gripping his hands tightly around his stomach. Seeing through cloaking shields by relaxing my mind was one of the skills Dyna, the Federation Peacekeeper, had taught me. I didn't realize until later that her augmentations had given me this ability. Augmentations she'd given me without my permission.

"So, just to confirm," I said, "you said you were killed this morning. Correct?"

He hesitated.

"Listen, man, you're gonna have to be straight with me. Last chance, or I'm calling my detective friend at the APD who's working this case. She's *dying* to speak to you."

He did not find any humor in my comment.

"I can't tell you everything," he said.

"Why not?"

"For security reasons."

"Don't keep anything from me that could put me in danger—or my friends," I added. *I don't have many to spare.* "Otherwise, I can't help you."

"That's reasonable."

"So, please, answer the question."

"Yes, I was murdered."

"By who?"

"I don't know, exactly. I'm fairly certain it was female, judging by her scent, but she caught me by surprise. She blinded me with a flash of light and there was a sharp pain in my stomach where she stabbed me with a blade, or maybe a claw. Gouged out both my eyes and then...." Felix's body trembled as a shiver passed over him. "Horrid memory. I'd prefer not to dwell on it."

"So I have to ask the other obvious question here. How in the world did you survive? That room was painted with your blood."

He hesitated again, this time glancing at Lulamina, who nodded encouragingly. "You can trust him."

Barry set four steaming coffee mugs on the bar. Lulamina got up and went to retrieve them.

Felix looked back at me and rested one hand on his belly. "I had a personal rewinder."

"In your stomach?"

"In my heart. A Torlik's heart is located in our gut."

"I guess that explains all the blood. That first knife wound was a direct hit, wasn't it?" I gestured to his jacket.

"Incapacitated me straight away."

Annabelle tapped rapidly on her phone. She'd been taking notes while we talked. Annabelle took a lot of notes on every offworlder species we encountered. This quirk of anatomy was an interesting detail I knew she'd want to capture.

"OK. Pretend I'm slow for a second."

Annabelle snorted.

I cast a sly smile in her direction. "You hush." I turned back to Felix. "What's a personal rewinder?"

"All I can tell you is that it saved my life."

"Not good enough. How's it work?"

"Can't tell you that."

"What *can* you tell me?"

"It was a device Zavis and I developed together, many years ago."

I knew a bit about the engineer's background. "When you worked together in the Federation's weapons labs?" I asked.

He stared at me blankly. I read that as a tacit confirmation. Zavis was also tight-lipped about the work he did for the Federation.

I didn't really need the details, so I switched my line of questioning. "How'd you get out of the hotel room without being seen?"

The skin bunched up on both sides of his single, oversized eye.

I got up as if to go.

"Wait," he said. "Okay, I'll tell you. The rewinder takes advantage of a quirk of the temporal fabric of reality. It's designed to activate when my heart stops and return me to a recent moment when I was alive and healthy. Due to the intercircumplexity of spacetime, in this particular situation, my body was transported a short distance at the same time."

I blinked, still standing. "Are you telling me you died, and then traveled *back through space and time* to a point when you were still alive?"

"It's not technically time travel. More like time reversion. But that's accurate enough for this conversation, yes."

I fell silent as I wrapped my mind around this information. True to form, Annabelle's mind was far more nimble.

"That explains how you got out," she said. "But how did your assailant escape unnoticed?"

I snapped my fingers and pointed to emphasize her point. "Yeah, that."

"The device she took from me," Felix said. "I need you to help me recover it. It's incredibly valuable and there's only one of them. If it falls into the wrong hands, your world is in real danger… and I'm responsible." He swallowed heavily as an oversized bead of sweat trailed down his face.

"What is it?" I asked. "Another personal rewinder?"

He hesitated again. "If I tell you, you mustn't speak of it to *anyone*."

"Just Anna, here, and my detective friend working the case."

"Not the detective. Only you and this lovely human."

"Aww, thanks, sugar," Annabelle said with an exaggerated Southern twang—the kind that was either very sweet or very dangerous.

It seemed like a conflict of interest, not telling Sheila what he'd shared. I silently promised to disentangle myself as soon as these secrets became inconvenient. In the meantime, I wanted the whole story. "Fine. I'll keep it between us—for now."

He heaved a sigh of relief. "Good. Good."

"I have a theory," I offered, to get him talking again. "It was hidden in that motorcycle helmet, wasn't it?"

He nodded. "It's a piece of time."

"What's that mean?"

"Sorry, translation error. It's a *time*piece."

"That doesn't give me much to go on," I said. "Tell me more. What does it do?"

"It has the ability to speed up or slow down time." His

face grew very serious. “It can temporarily bring a moment from the future—or the past—into the present. In the wrong hands, it’s incredibly dangerous. That’s all I’m willing to share.”

“The Federation keeps it under their strict protection, don’t they?”

“That’s an understatement,” Felix said. “They locked it away, and I didn’t exactly ask permission before I took it.”

I ground my jaw in frustration and breathed through my teeth a few times. “These Feds need better security.” A thought occurred to me. “Do you think maybe it was a Peacekeeper who gutted you like a fish?”

“I doubt it. Not their style.”

I had to agree with that. The Peacekeepers could be dishonest, but they weren’t cold-blooded killers. At least not the ones I knew.

“What about the Tetrad?”

“Possibly. I’ve heard of their presence here. Although that seems unlikely, too, given that I stole the device and no one else knew I was bringing it to Earth.”

“How *did* you get here?”

“I took a shuttle using an assumed identity.”

“One of the Gatekeeper’s ships?”

“That’s right.”

I thought about what the Gatekeeper had told me about Tetrad spies aboard his transports. “Did you happen to take the timepiece out on the shuttle, by chance?”

He fell silent, wiping an upper hand across his brow and squeezing his abdomen tighter with the lower set. “Now that you mention it, the lock on my suitcase did freeze up at one point in the journey. I opened it a couple of times to fix the mechanism. Just a scant crack. The parts didn’t come out. Some passengers may have seen what was inside... not that most would even know what they were looking at."

I leaned forward so my elbows were on my knees. "I need names and descriptions of every person on that shuttle. Especially the females. Annabelle?"

"Ready," she said, thumbs poised over her phone.

We took as many notes as the Torlik's vague memory could conjure up, easily a dozen different species in total. My head spun with descriptions of slime and scales, of fur and fangs, of unhinged jaws and too many eyes and other ways of being that my feeble human brain could barely comprehend.

I also collected a down payment on the job. Lulamina was insistent on pointing out that she hadn't taken a cut. It seemed to be a point of pride for her, so I tried to act graciously. Not my best color, but I said all the right words even if they seemed stiff and awkward on my tongue.

Finally, I drained the rest of my mug's cold coffee and knocked it down on the table in a note of finality.

"Don't go wandering off," I warned Felix.

He shook his head. "I'm not going anywhere without the timepiece. Besides, my personal rewinder was only good for one use. I'm too exposed to be wandering around a silent planet without security, and I'm the only one who can deliver the timepiece to Amberen. If you can track it down, I'll focus on finding him."

"Who's that?" I asked.

He gave me the side-eye and glanced at Lulamina.

"Amberen Geveraux," she said, "The Pango I told you about. The being for whom this timepiece is intended."

"Oh, right," I said, "The Pango celebrity."

He gave me a thin smile. *Cagey Torlik*, I thought.

“I need a place to work from,” Felix said.

“My home is at your disposal, Felix,” Lulamina said. “Zavis will get you set up with the Federation uplink.”

“Thank you, Lulamina. I’m in your debt,” he said. “Mr. Gunn.”

Like two oddball, costumed attendants sneaking away from the masque early, they checked their disguises, then hurried out. Felix’s battered leather jacket clashed with her form-fitting gown like a pair of mismatched socks.

CHAPTER SEVEN

OUTSIDE, a flat ceiling of slate gray clouds threatened rain. A brisk cold front had blown in while we met with Felix and Lulamina. I stopped on the street corner and inhaled cold air and exhaust fumes. Traffic streamed by as a band warmed up in Shangri-La. The slow, insistent kick drum thud of a mic check drifted out of the bar.

One two, one two. Is this thing on?

Annabelle paused beside me and slid her hands into thin black gloves. Winters in Austin are mild, and it was still above freezing, but thirty degrees is cold for two Texans.

We walked toward her minivan, shiny and new-looking. I'd given her a hard time about buying it, but I shut my mouth when I remembered that she had the money to spend while I didn't. If Annabelle wanted to buy a luxury minivan and equip it with a mobile recording studio, who was I to judge? She was a grown-up. She could make her own decisions.

Even if she spent more to buy it than I made in a bad year.

"Want to grab a bite?" I asked. My appetite was growing. I needed something to do while my brain churned on deciding my next move.

"I've got to get back to work. Long night ahead of me. I'm late publishing that UFO article I told Benny about." She shook her phone as if it held a secret gift. "There was another sighting tonight."

"Where?"

"Kyoto."

I let out a low whistle. "The Peacekeepers are slipping up. News is getting out faster than they can suppress it."

"Which is the point, isn't it? The sightings are getting more frequent. Tanamir's working toward something. I can *feel* it. I need to find the pattern."

Passion flared as a glittering intensity in her eyes. But those baby blues were also shadowed, almost haunted. She was tough, Annabelle, but I still worried about her. The hungry little grin she gave me swelled my heart with a fierce pride. I wasn't sure if her smile lines had deepened in the last couple of months, or if we'd both been working too much. She had perfect cheekbones that glowed a rosy red in the cold wind.

"Good luck," I said. "See you tomorrow?"

"I'll be up late, so make sure you let me sleep in this time." She hip-checked me gently.

"No problem."

"You've got your key?"

"I do."

"Do you want a ride?"

"Nah, I'll walk."

"Okay, tough guy."

“I love this weather. It’s bracing.” I gripped the lapels of my jean jacket. “Besides, moving my legs helps me think.”

We embraced and then parted ways. I watched Annabelle climb into her minivan and glide around a corner. Then I turned and walked across the highway into the heart of the city.

Putting some pavement beneath my feet normally got my thoughts moving. One of my favorite places to walk and think was the Shoal Creek trail. Half paved walkway, half dirt path, it spilled out near the tiny, cheap apartment I rented.

I stretched my legs and crossed the city through a bustle of traffic and sparse crowds, thinned out by the cold. As the sun set behind me, the temperature dropped five, even ten degrees, in a matter of minutes. I was lucky to have the fur-lined jean jacket Annabelle bought me. But I hadn’t brought a hat or gloves, so I popped the collar to keep my neck warm and shoved my hands in the pockets.

I found the trail entrance near the central library and dropped down along the creek, sighing as I left the busy world above and entered a nature sanctuary. Well, as much nature as you got in the city.

Here, I could breathe. Away from the crowds, away from my case. Away, even, from my debts.

Then I remembered—I had paid my debt. I may live in a shitty apartment and be worried about the Tetrad’s war and my strange new caseload, but I didn’t owe anybody anything. I was a free man.

It took me a moment to adjust to that fact. I inhaled deeply. This time, instead of exhaust, I smelled brackish water from the creek and roasting meat from a restaurant’s smoker.

The breeze picked up, driving wind into my eyes. I grinned broadly into the cold. I've always felt that cold could show you who you really are. It could expose your weaknesses.

I spread my arms and tilted back my head. The wind whipped around me like a tempest raging over a high mountain crag.

Feeling full of vitality, I got moving again, ducking under a bridge and around the next corner. A shadow flitted across the limestone walkway. I tensed for just a moment before laughter broke the silence of the night. A couple in puffy vests hurried by me on the cold, narrow trail, giggling. They huddled together for warmth.

A mean-looking vagrant limped by, toting a plastic bag and a dirty shovel. I tensed and found myself instinctively shuffling sideways. I forced myself to hold my course and pass shoulder to shoulder with the foul-smelling hobo.

Ahead, I spotted the stone steps that led up out of the creek bed—my exit. As I approached, a woman in joggers and new, neon sneakers pattered down the stairs and ran by me. She left a faint scent of citrus, or maybe lemon balm, in her wake. It wasn't a bad smell, but it was overpowering, like a strong perfume.

Why women wore perfume when they exercised, I'd never understand. I was glad Annabelle didn't wear any.

As I stepped into the cloud the jogger's breath had left behind, my gut knotted up. I turned and caught a flash of her shoulders as she loped around the corner and out of sight.

It might have been a trick of the light, but I could have sworn I caught sight of powerful, muscled legs with a strangely inverted set of knees, like those belonging to a wolf or a deer.

Was my mind playing tricks on me, or was she an offworlder?

I rubbed at my eyes, which were heavy and gritty. That catnap hadn't been enough; not even the coffee had helped. Maybe I could get a full night's rest before picking up the trail of my timepiece thief tomorrow.

A piercing scream interrupted my reverie, stopping me in my tracks. I turned to stare in the direction the jogging woman had gone.

"Help!" cried her frightened voice.

Without pausing to think, I ran.

Once again without backup, I thanked my lucky stars that this time I'd had enough wits about me to go armed. I slipped my Kimber from its holster at my back and gripped the pistol's cool metal grip with my off hand.

I'd been range-training with my left, but it didn't feel natural. There was nothing to be done about it right now. I might need my cyborg hand as a weapon or shield. I couldn't risk bending the gun in a panic.

As I turned around the corner and crossed beneath the bridge, I stepped into a blinding sheet of rain.

I gasped. I was drenched to the core before my foot came down on the other side. A roaring noise filled my ears as a storm washed over me. I squinted through the haze, looking for the woman, but saw no one in the driving rain. A torrent poured down the slanted walls of the creek. Water sloshed into the tops of my boots as I stood in a puddle.

"What in the h—oufff!"

Air huffed from my lungs as something heavy slammed into my ribcage. I bent toward the pain and was lucky to catch sight of a clawed foot coming around to sweep my feet.

I turned into the strike, taking the kick on my shins. Pain radiated into my knees. My attacker pressed the advantage, shoving me backward. Through torrents of stormwater, I caught glimpses of a black motorcycle helmet. Its surface was curved and shiny, cut as if by a laser in precise geometric shapes, like a prop from the movie Blade Runner. Set into the forehead was a medallion with a shape like a tuning fork that reminded me of a Yamaha logo, but wasn't.

The helmet rested on the muscled body of a creature that resembled a human. My ability to see through cloaking shields confirmed my fears. Her jogging outfit flickered away, revealing muscle-bound arms coated with dark, spotted fur. She had wide hips and pants covering muscular legs with inverted knees atop powerful, padded feet the size of a tiger's.

Felix's first description of his attacker echoed in my mind: *A female,* he'd said, *judging by her scent.* My own survival instincts couldn't help but come alive in recognition. I realized, with a jolt, that it was the same citrusy musk from the hotel room. A shiver crawled up my spine, cooling my skin and spiking my adrenaline in the same instant.

I'd never seen a creature like her before, but I'd spent enough time around offworlders to know one thing for certain: she posed a significant danger.

I aimed for center mass and squeezed the trigger. The heavy rainfall muted the deafening crack of the gunshot.

The offworlder vanished. No longer standing in front of me, just completely gone. Shocked, I let my arms drop a few inches.

Oh, no.

The thought struck me at the same time as her powerful foot. Claws sliced through my jacket near my kidneys as her foot snapped away. I staggered into a puddle, slipped to the ground, and my Kimber fell from my grasp. Tilting my face to keep from inhaling water, I groped around for my weapon. I'd located it in a six-inch eddy off the edge of the paved path when a clawed foot came down hard on my ankle. She dragged me out of reach of the gun, then leaned her weight on my ankle, pinning me there.

I cried out in pain as a bone popped. Sure hands searched my waistline, and though I endured the agony, she kept my leg pinned in place with her superior strength. It felt like she weighed over three hundred pounds. Her body must have been incredibly dense.

A female voice muttered in an unrecognizable, yowling language. Then, in English, she snarled, "No cloaking shield? I hadn't expected an Earthling." Her voice came through the helmet muffled. It had a strong accent but enunciated clearly. I could only make out the shadow of her face through the visor. Were those whiskers?

"I'd known the locals were mingling," she went on with that throaty, growling voice, "but this *is* a surprise. Who are you, and why did you meet with the watchmaker?"

"Who?" I said, even as I realized she must mean Lulamina's friend, Felix. I wasn't about to squeal on my new client. I groaned as I realized the money Lulamina had paid me as a deposit was getting soaked inside my jean jacket.

You idiot, I cursed myself. Even in this predicament, my mind wouldn't stop worrying about money. *Damn the feeble human brain!*

When I didn't say anything else, my assailant leaned forward, grinding my ankle into the pavement beneath those callused pads. My fingernails dug into the paving stones as I gritted my teeth against the pain. Her kind must be built tougher than humans. Certainly larger. I snarled and swallowed a second cry so as not to give her the satisfaction.

"Answer the question," she said.

"Make me," I snarled.

I gazed up into the visor of that helmet. Something was going on inside the machine, visible through the geometric cuts around the medallion on the forehead. The tuning fork-looking mechanism was whirring now with a bright, unnatural light. Could I knock it off her head with an uppercut?

"Ah," she said, leaning forward. Her mouth formed a kind of snubby snout inside the helmet. "Watchmaker wants his toy back, doesn't he? That's too bad."

Leaning upward, I swung at her kidneys with my cyborg hand, putting all my strength into the blow. Right as I was about to connect, her form shimmered, blurring, and I twisted as my arm passed through her body. Momentum carried me forward, leaving me a twisted, painful knot.

Her foot had never left my ankle.

"I can think faster than you can move, Earthling," she said. "You're not going to win with those tactics. Or your poor grappling skills."

She headbutted me in the nose with the helmet, sending pain flaring across my face in a wet splash. She pulled my wallet out of my back pocket. Blood ran over my lips and the rain washed it away. Bones in my ankle and foot ground together as she twisted, sending more pain lancing up my leg. I struck at her a few more times, desperately, and hit nothing but air. She extended my elbow in a twisting hold. I screamed as she yanked the joint backward.

"Anderson Gunn," she said, reading from my business card. "Bounty hunter. Is that right? You're not very good at your job."

She wanted something, or she'd have killed me already. I spat blood to clear my mouth. She released my cyborg hand, as if daring me to punch her again. I shook out the arm and waited.

This offworlder was dangerous. I knew of only one place that dangerous offworlders came from.

"Did the Tetrad send you?" I asked.

She shocked me with her answer. "So the general's here after all, is he? Thank you for confirming that. Where can I find him? I have something he's interested in."

My mind raced. She wasn't working with the Tetrad? Was she a free agent? Why had she come to Earth? I didn't want to give anything else away, so I kept my thoughts to myself this time. Instead, I said, "He and I aren't exactly on speaking terms."

"Then what good are you to me?"

The rain increased in intensity, as if ten storms raged at once. She grabbed my neck and, moving faster than the speed of thought, shoved my face into the rising pool of water. I struggled against her superior strength. My lungs burned as she held me down. I opened my eyes underwater. Twisting and looking back, I saw her watching me through that mirrored visor. Her clothes changed from colorful joggers to sleek fur and back as my ability to see through cloaking shields flickered.

I began to swallow water, choking.

Desperate for air, I ignored the pain and yanked my foot back. This time, it slid out of my boot.

My head broke the surface. I gasped for breath, blinking

water out of my eyes and turning to locate my attacker. She wasn't there. A rushing current picked me up and swept me back toward the bridge.

The water's rapids were splashing against the struts of the pedestrian bridge. I reacted on instinct, gulping air and submerging myself to go under it.

I opened my eyes underwater and saw the helmeted creature beneath me, walking on the sidewalk as if the flash flood had no hold on her.

While I scrabbled for the surface, she caught my injured ankle with two clawed paws and held me underwater.

CHAPTER EIGHT

NO! I thought desperately as I kicked and squirmed, swallowing a mouthful of water for my efforts. *Not like this!*

Choking, I thrashed again, this time hard enough to slip her grasp. She was strong but still nothing more than an alien with fancy hardware. I clawed my way to the surface and gasped as my head popped up.

"Gunn!" A bright soprano voice called to me. It was melodic but hoarse, as if she'd been yelling for some time. "Gunn! Can you hear me?"

I flailed my arms and swam in the direction of the voice.

"To me! There, I have you now."

Relief flooded my body as invisible hooks curled under my arms. They hauled me out of the water onto the side of the creek, one bare and one booted heel dragging through the grass. My body convulsed with spasms. I coughed so hard I vomited water.

Stiff hands rubbed my back. When I looked up, it was into the familiar face of a Lodian woman, her expression creased with concern. She had large, intelligent eyes and dark skin. Dozens of red and yellow cybernetic nodes covered her head. She studied me calmly as her hand moved across my wet shoulders.

"Dyna?" I asked. "What are you doing here?"

"Saving your life," she said, somewhat miffed. "What does it look like to you?"

Her head was backlit by a slate-gray sky free of rain. A waxing blue half-moon peeked through wispy fringes of clouds floating near the horizon. Looking down the slope of dirt at the paved path in the creek bed, I shivered. Not because of the sudden cold that I felt, but because it was perfectly dry.

Not so much as a wet spot in sight.

My assailant was nowhere to be found, either. I mentally added this disappearing act to her growing record. Embarrassed, I checked my jacket pocket. I patted it with my uninjured hand and sighed in relief. Miraculously, the bound stack of soaking wet cash was still there where I had put it.

I rolled over and braced myself on my knees as I caught my breath. The presence of that money was reassuring. It represented a thin layer of padding between me and the world. It wasn't much money, to be sure, but it was better than nothing.

My heart continued to thunder in my chest for a long minute. The fight was over, but my body didn't want to admit it. I began to shake from the cold as a gust of frigid wind passed over me.

I could still taste the brackish, unnaturally warm rainwater on my tongue. It gave me a strong sense of *déjà vu*, that uncanny vertigo of the mind. I steadied myself and focused on my breathing until the world leveled out.

"Gunn, are you all right?" Dyna asked in her sing-song

voice. No other Lodian I'd met sounded like she did. It was a side effect of her augments, the cybernetic nodes which gave her extrasensory perception and telekinetic powers.

"I look like a half-drowned cat," I chattered. "Or maybe a man who got half-drowned by some kind of cat. Guess I owe you one."

She studied me intently. "Just doing my duty."

I'd once seen Dyna catch her partner, the Peacekeeper Kilos, as he was flung off the side of the building, using nothing more than the power of her mind. She saved his fur-covered hide, just as she saved mine, but I recalled how he had been hurt a second time. It hadn't been Dyna's fault, but I didn't like the parallels.

I chose my next words with caution.

"Duty, huh?" I responded. "Have you been following me?"

"You live in that building, do you not?"

"So, that's a yes." I narrowed my eyes. "I didn't tell you I'd moved."

"It is my job to know the whereabouts of all... persons of interest."

"I see you're picking up the lingo."

"Your television dramas are strangely compelling," she said excitedly. "I watched a few in transit on my way back to Earth. Once I got used to reading human faces, I began to be able to tolerate them. To answer your question, we were flying in the region when our ship's sensors detected an unauthorized temporal anomaly. It didn't take long to locate its source."

"Temporal anomaly, huh?" Did she know about the timepiece? Or was this just dumb luck?

"You were flickering in and out. It was only once you

heard me that I was able to grab hold of you and pull you back to the present."

"Right," I said, as if that didn't sound like a pulp science fiction novel. "What happened to my attacker?"

Dyna blinked as her eyes went distant. I waited. She refocused on me a second later. "Kilos tells me the suspect disappeared from our sensors."

"Fluffy?" I asked. "He's alive? Is he here?"

"Nearby." Dyna nodded as if she were speaking to someone on the other end of a phone call. "He wishes me to convey that he still dislikes your nicknames."

"In more colorful terms, I'm sure." I grinned. "Did you get a good look at that offworlder when you pulled me out of the water?"

"No. Did you?"

I nodded. "Somewhat. I couldn't see her face through the visor, but..."

Dyna was cocking her head at me. "Visor?"

"She was wearing a helmet."

"Ah. Is that the source of the temporal anomaly?" It seems she didn't know about the timepiece, at least not in specific terms. I clamped my mouth shut, cautious lest I put my foot in it again. This week was turning out to be a series of flubs and fumbles on my part. I was determined to break the cycle.

"More of Tanamir's agents have been coming to Earth," Dyna said when I didn't respond right away. "We're having trouble keeping track of them all."

"That's big of you to admit. I've been keeping tabs on the news. How many stories have you managed to smother before they went mainstream?"

"Twelve. Nothing specifically Tetrad in nature has leaked."

Not yet. I kept the thought to myself.

"Whoever she was, she wasn't Tetrad. But she's definitely looking for Tanamir now. I can tell you that much."

"How do you know?" she asked.

"She told me," I said. "The old general has a reputation."

I watched Dyna's face carefully as my hook landed and took her right in the lip. "Why did you call him that?"

I simply shrugged. "That's what she called him."

Her face crumpled, and Dyna suddenly looked haggard. Her skin was more wan than usual, and she was obviously in need of a good night's sleep. Her hands played over her lined face, searching. "We cannot keep up with Tanamir and his network. We have decommissioned two of their ships. They have seven remaining—an entire squadron."

"Enough to distract and divert you."

"To lay traps and lead us down false trails, wasting our time and precious resources. Yes."

"And every day you spend chasing them, more Tetrad rebels arrive on the Gatekeeper's transport shuttles."

"So you have heard about that." Dyna paced back and forth before me. "News of Tanamir's presence opened a floodgate. The chaos attracts Tetrad revolutionaries and other opportunistic criminal types."

"Like flies to dung. I noticed things have gotten weirder." I thought about all the strange cases Gonzalez had investigated. The jobs Lulamina had funneled in my direction. I'd taken several new clients, many who'd come to Earth to retrieve their loved ones or escape Federation scrutiny for some misunderstanding.

"Perhaps this offworlder who attacked you is one of Tanamir's former soldiers."

"That's not reassuring."

I slowed down and considered my next words carefully. The Peacekeeper may have saved my life tonight, but she'd deceived me often enough that I didn't trust her. I didn't want to work with her if I could avoid it. But as a professional, I also couldn't afford not to make use of every resource at my disposal.

"Can you help me figure out where my attacker's going next?" I asked.

"It might be possible," Dyna said. "I cannot sense her presence like I could the Pharsei, but our starship's systems can detect temporal disruptions. Part of standard Federation scans." She went quiet for a minute. "I have not seen this particular technology in the Tetrad's arsenal yet. Spacetime manipulation is banned in Federation space."

My heart sank. I *had to* recover that helmet before it fell into Tanamir's hands.

"We certainly cannot let the Tetrad have it," Dyna said, anticipating my thoughts. "We will watch for any activity in the region—and elsewhere as we hunt the Tetrad's agents, now that we know it's in play. I will have Kilos run a profile check on your attacker too. Would you be willing to give him a description?"

"Just a minute," I said. I glanced down at my mismatched wet feet and shuddered. "Mind if I grab my missing boot first?" Not to mention my sidearm, I added in silence.

I pushed myself to my feet and hissed when I put weight on my injured ankle. It might be broken or badly sprained. I limped back to the bridge, leaning over and looking down at the path below. No sign of my boot or the Kimber. Drat.

Had they been swept downstream in the deluge? The whole encounter made no sense to me. Why hadn't she just killed me like she had done with Felix? I'd surprised her. I was a pest, not a target.

Or maybe she'd seen Dyna and fled.

I leaned my weight on the bridge's railing and off my injured ankle. It was already swelling to fill the damp leg of my jeans. I dug a chunk of pavement out of my palm and flicked it contemptuously into the creek.

"You need medical attention," Dyna said.

"No kidding."

"We can help."

I made a disgruntled sound in my throat. "Hold that thought. I need a new pair of shoes and some dry clothes first."

I limped over to my apartment building, leaving Dyna standing by the creek. Once inside, I stripped out of the wet clothes, hung them in the bathroom to dry, and took a moment to examine my ankle. Now that the adrenaline was wearing off, I could see it was worse than I thought. Red, swollen and definitely broken.

I looked at it in the mirror and tried to flex my foot. My range of motion was severely limited and spikes of pain radiated into my foot and calf when I moved it.

"Dammit," I said. "I can't believe I'm considering this."

I couldn't think clearly in this state, so I did the only thing I could think of and called Annabelle. She sounded distracted, but she came to attention when I told her what had happened. Lucky for me, she was a fast thinker. I skimmed over the details of the fight and told her about Dyna's offer.

"Are you thinking of going in with the Peacekeepers again?" she asked.

"I can't recover the timepiece in this condition. Imagine what would happen if Tanamir gets it first."

"I don't want to."

I shuddered, remembering how my previous conversations with the old general went, from the innocuous to the horribly violent. "This case isn't one of Lula's casual offworlder reunions. It seems dramatic to say this, but I truly think the fate of Earth is on the line."

We chatted a minute more. I asked several follow-up questions to vet my reasoning. I listened quietly as she dished out advice about staying level-headed and watching out for needles, given the Peacekeepers' fondness for body modification.

"I have to go," she finally said. "One more interview before sleep. Meet for breakfast?"

I agreed. Then I went back to try and make a deal with the Peacekeepers. One I hoped would help keep the timepiece out of Tetrad hands.

CHAPTER NINE

OUTSIDE, I found Dyna in a new disguise. She looked like a middle-aged hippie with medium dark skin and a broad face free of makeup. Her hair was done up in a dozen knots, each dyed red on top. She wore a leather coat and blue jeans which flared out over sturdy low-cut black boots. The Peacekeeper rose to my eye level on two-inch heels.

"Have we met?" I joked. "You look familiar."

She snorted. "I have had much practice at fine-tuning my disguise for Earth. What do you think?"

"Wrong century, but impressive nonetheless." I hesitated before asking, "Can you actually heal my ankle?"

"Affirmative."

I narrowed my eyes. "I'm full up on surprises for the day. No funny business."

She held her hands up in surrender. "I am not in the habit of telling jokes."

"That's not what I mean."

"I find it amusing when you feel frustrated."

"It frustrates me when you hide things from me."

"I have learned much about your language since we last spent time together." She gave me an innocuous smile. "I promise I will not attempt to deceive you."

"And you won't inject me with anything without my permission." It still bothered me, what she'd done. I took a deep breath. "Agreed?"

"Agreed." She inclined her head. "I must inform you. The serum we gave you is not as harmful as you think. Nor is it necessary to inject you with any more."

"We doing this here?" I asked.

"No. The medical facilities are in my ship, and it would be better if you spoke to Kilos away from prying eyes." She scanned the sky warily. Finding nothing there and nobody in the parking lot, the knots on her head flashed a pattern I didn't miss through her cloak.

She lets me see what she wants me to see, I reminded myself. *Remember who made it possible for you to look through these disguises*.

A rush of air poured down as their invisible starship lowered to engulf us. It lifted us skyward, as if we flew on an elevator made of air. My gut somersaulted and my mind flashed back to a ride on the Tower of Terror, which both delighted and haunted my childhood memories in equal measure. We soared up through a hatch, which cycled open just in time to swallow us.

Doors inside the ship opened with a chime. From his place at a control panel, a giant, fur-covered albino rotated to take us in.

"Sasquatch!" I said. "It's good to see you whole again."

The Peacekeepers wore no disguise in this place. I took

in Kilos's giant, muscular form. He looked just as I'd last seen him, although his eyes were more tired than I remembered.

"That's not my name." A soft, warning rumble accompanied his words.

I knew better than to be intimidated. Leaving Dyna's side, I approached and studied his torso where the street sign had impaled him. "Not even a scratch, huh?" His coat was smooth and white. "Impressive, what this medical technology of yours can do."

Kilos considered me for a long moment. Then he sniffed and parted his fur with meaty fingers—each as thick as a piston—so I could see his pale skin. A jagged scar six inches long ran along his ribcage.

"Very impressive." I chucked him on a shoulder the size of a truck fender. Kilos was white and furry on the outside, but he was brave and noble-hearted on the inside. The last time I'd seen the Lodian-Kilgar hybrid, a steel pole had been sticking out of his chest right in that spot. In that moment, he'd urged us to leave him to suffer, mortally wounded and unprotected.

"I never told you how much I appreciated you letting me go after Annabelle while you lay dying. Thank you."

Kilos bowed at the waist. "You are welcome."

I hadn't known, at the time, that Federation tech could restore the Peacekeeper from that kind of a wound. Still, it must have hurt. Choosing to endure pain to save my friend's life was the act of a total stud.

"I am glad to see you alive, Beast," I said.

"Likewise." The Peacekeeper guffawed. "Although, I'm surprised some offworlder thug hasn't eaten you for breakfast. Even with a machine hand, you humans are so fragile and defenseless."

"Believe me, they've tried," I spread my arms wide, wincing as I shifted weight on my bad ankle. "Yet here I am!"

The mutant Peacekeeper's mouth twisted into a wicked smirk. "Must be your charming personality."

"You're one to talk."

The smile on his face faltered, and our banter fell silent as Dyna crossed the room between us. She yanked a panel out of the wall and gestured to a fold-out bench seat.

"We don't have much time," she said. "Allow me to examine you."

I exchanged a glance with Kilos, but he wasn't giving anything away for free. He kept his face empty of expression as he picked up a device labeled with compact alien symbols on its buttons.

I limped over to Dyna, studying the area around the exposed bench. It was packed with all manner of shelving, sealed compartments, and what appeared to be medical implements with sharp edges and pointy bits.

"Our first aid station," Dyna explained. "This is what saved Kilos' life. It stabilized him until we could get back for more intense medical treatment." She nodded at her partner. He was eyeballing two spider-like contraptions which were folded against one wall.

"When was the last time you did a maintenance check?" I asked.

I'd noted the many sparsely filled supply containers, empty or low on items like gel packets, various-sized needles, bandages, and gauze. Many of these items were like what we used here on Earth. Some had been re-filled with local replacements. A few tubes were broken or cracked. Plugs were missing or replaced in mis-matched colors. Tubes that could belong to life support systems and IVs appeared creased and worn.

"We have been on the move quite a lot lately," Dyna said. "There has not been time. But the main tools work fine. This one monitors vitals. This one closes wounds. This one examines and repairs internal damage." She laid her hand on each item in turn as she spoke.

The last box she touched beeped ominously and then clicked open. She unfolded the panel into a long rectangle, and then unfolded a screen from the wall and pointed it at herself.

"Place your injured foot inside, please."

"Oh hell no," I said. "I've seen *Dune*. I'm not putting my foot in that."

"It is safe," she insisted.

Kilos had followed us over. He shoved his hand into the contraption. It had to adjust itself to fit his meaty forearm. Bits of fur stuck out around the band. "Safe, sure," he added. "Still hurts like the void. Are you scared, Earthling?"

He withdrew his arm.

" 'Hurts like the void' is not my definition of a good time, no."

He shrugged. "More pain now, or more pain later. Might as well get it done. Either way, you were going to tell me about this offworlder you saw?" He poised his fingers over his device.

"You taking notes?"

He nodded. I liked the side of Kilos I was now seeing—the detail-oriented investigator. I could work with this.

"Well, I didn't get a good look at her face, like I told

Dyna. She had spotted, grey fur. Knees were inverted, and big heavy paws. She must have weighed twice what I do, although she was about my height. I think I saw whiskers and a snout, but I can't be sure about that. I would recognize her voice if I heard it again. It sounded like a tiger hawking up a furball."

"Can you give me a rough register?" Kilos played a few musical notes and asked me to pick a range. I did. He took notes with one deft hand.

"Well, it's either a Thaym or a Sevrit, although judging from her size and weight, I'm guessing Sevrit."

I glanced at the medical contraption, then unlaced my shoe. I lifted my injured foot and put it inside. The walls condensed around my ankle, adjusting to sense my foot and form to it. They were gentle as they hardened over my ankle and calf, causing no more than the slightest weight of discomfort.

I rolled my shoulders and cleared my throat. "She was incredibly strong, too. Is that normal?"

"Not so unusual. Most Sevrit are genetically augmented in some way, and strength is enhanced in over fifty percent of the population. Anything else notable? Her mode of dress?"

"No. She had some kind of tunic on her torso but her arms were bare and her pants form fitting. Nothing that stood out to me except the lack of shoes and the knife-like claws."

He sighed. "Not much to go on, but I'll look through the Federation database and cross reference it with your description."

"And keep an eye out for signs of her? You can send coordinates to my cell phone."

He hesitated. "Not if you're going to take her on without backup a second time."

I scowled at him. "I'll have backup—ouch!"

A jab of pain stabbed into my leg. I turned to see an oversized, exploded 3D model of my leg, bones and tendons visible, resting in Dyna's hands. She'd picked apart the pieces and was pressing on the ankle bone, which showed a neat fracture in her display.

"Well, that confirms it," I said. "Definitely broken."

"I'm surprised you're not in more pain."

She tapped on the model in a couple different places, causing spooky, crawling sensations to slither in my gut.

"How are you doing that?" It wasn't a hologram or digital twin, but an actual physical twin that seemed to congeal on the fly... an autonomous, organic 3D printing machine, or some such voodoo.

"These models allow us to examine your internal bone structure," Dyna explained. "And give feedback to specific parts of your leg to clearly identify the damage, and map a potential repair."

I looked at the pliable model. "You're not going to try to put that clay stuff into me, are you?"

Dyna shook her head. "No. The nanobots already in your blood are going to do the work for us. We only need to map the procedure."

She tapped, then went back to the machine and made a few selections with the interface. More symbols in the Lodian language the Peacekeepers used. "There. Now, we wait."

"How long?"

"Finish your conversation. It'll take your mind off it."

A weird, tickling, buzzing sensation started up in the

outside bone of my broken ankle. It wasn't painful, exactly, but it made me grind my teeth with the uncomfortable sensation.

"Wait," I said.

Dyna hit a button. The sensation paused.

"This isn't... activating some kind of Peacekeeper augment, is it?"

Dyna stiffened. "I intend to abide by my word, bounty hunter. Have I given you reason to doubt me?"

I squirmed in my seat and remembered what Annabelle had said: Don't lie, even if they have you cornered.

So I gave them a small truth. "No it's... Devices can scan for your Peacekeeper augments. It's bad for business if I'm setting off alarms without my knowledge, you know?"

Dyna frowned. "Those devices are rare. I don't have any record of their presence here on Earth."

"And yet, one of them has been used on me." I shrugged.

She looked at me like I'd shown her something ugly in her own closet. I had a tense moment where I was prepared to yank my leg out of the tube and bolt, but then Dyna said, "No. It does not activate any Peacekeeper augmentations. It takes advantage of the nanobots already in your bloodstream to rebuild your bones, and direct a steroid to the right places to speed the healing of bruised and torn ligaments and muscles."

"Huh," I said. "That sounds awful nice."

"It is, I can assure you. It has saved our lives more times than I can count."

"And here I was thinking these Peacekeeper augments were like some kind of landmine waiting to be triggered."

The two of them exchanged a glance.

"Waiiiit a minute. I know that look. What are you hiding?"

"Nothing," Kilos said.

"What do you mean, nothing? Anytime someone says it's nothing, that means it's really something!"

"It is not important," Dyna said. "You are not in any danger, Gunn. Peacekeeper augments are a highly classified and protected technology."

"Oh sure, like your tech doesn't get stolen all the time. What else can these nanobots do to me?"

"It is classified," she said. "Trust me, you are not in any danger."

I glared at her. "Trust you?"

"Can you please let me heal you so we can get back to work?" she asked.

"No," I said.

"Fine," Dyna said. "Fine! How about this? I will heal your ankle, then I will deactivate the nanobots so that they cannot be used to introduce more augmentations."

"I have to assume that's reversible," I observed dryly.

"Yes, but—"

"I want you to take them out."

"No, you don't," Kilos said. I didn't think the albino could get any paler, but his face actually blanched beneath the thin layer of white fur. "Not only does it hurt like crazy, but it would render your hand unusable—the nanobots are the only reason your body has not tried to reject the cybernetic parts. And, it would mean that should you be injured in the future, we won't be able to treat you."

I hesitated. I actually hesitated! I felt like the worst kind of hypocrite... But then, Annabelle hadn't advised me to *give up* any advantages, had she? That woman was my conscience. If she wanted me to get rid of these nanobots, she would have told me to do so. Instead, she'd been focused on my health and safety, first. Do no harm.

"Okay, I guess I don't want that," I admitted to Kilos. "But I don't want you screwing around inside my body either."

Dyna and Kilos exchanged a glance again.

"What is it now?"

"I agree with the human," Kilos said.

"But—"

"Dyna," the albino warned, clearly irritated with her. "Do it."

"All right, fine. Yes, Gunn, there *is* a protocol to lock down your nanobots. I will give you the code to unlock it, should you wish to do so in the future."

"Great," I said. "Make it happen, lady. You should have done this before you left the first time."

"I am doing it now, okay? By the seven suns, I swear, you Earthlings are among the most stubborn people I have ever met."

"Just me," I said, grinning.

Kilos and I exchanged smiles. Now that she had capitulated, a thrill of elation shot through me.

Dyna punched a button and reactivated the healing device. My leg tingled, and then it itched and burned.

"Keep your leg *inside*," Dyna said, "or it'll break the mapping and we'll have to start over."

"I am," I gritted through my teeth as I dented the bench seat with the cyborg fingertips of my other hand.

All told, it took about fifteen minutes of discomfort. Dyna spent most of the time tapping and muttering commands into a console, like the one Kilos had been using. At the end of it, she asked me to enter a passcode.

"Seriously?" I asked. "No biometrics for the Federation? Just a passcode of my choice?"

She had to translate the symbols on her device for me. I took a photo with my phone. "In case I forget," I explained.

She grunted and stared at my phone, although she didn't object to me taking the photo. The passcode I entered was the old street address of my office plus the zip code all smushed together.

"It is done. Your ankle is healed and your nanobots have been deactivated, save for what's needed to maintain the cybernetic implants in your hand. Only you with this passcode can enter it."

"Much obliged," I said. "It was a pleasure doing business with you."

I felt drained. Zapped. My eyelids drooped. I rubbed at my face.

"Let us stay in touch this time, Gunn," said Dyna. "I am the agent in charge of this mission, and you are too wrapped up in it to step away entirely."

"Not exactly planning on taking a vacation," I said. "And you let me know when that temporal whatsit goes off again. My client has a vested interest in keeping the device out of the Tetrad's hands."

That wasn't exactly the truth, but they hadn't asked how Felix had gotten the device or what he intended to do with it. I wasn't about to tell them.

"Very well," Dyna said, although I could tell she was skeptical. "We will be in touch. It is in *our* mutual interest to foil the Tetrad's plans. I hope that, when the opportunity presents itself, you are prepared to assist me in that endeavor. I did save your life, after all."

"I'll do what I can. Thanks for fixing my ankle." I said. "Kilos."

"Gunn."

I stood up, marveling at the way my ankle moved normally now—free of pain.

I walked back onto the elevator platform. My stomach tumbled as it took me down.

CHAPTER TEN

FIRST THINGS FIRST: I went to my storage unit and stocked up on weapons and ammunition.

I'd lost my Kimber in the creek, but that didn't mean I had to go unarmed. I retrieved a tactical automatic shotgun, two Glock 9mm pistols, a Smith & Wesson handgun with six preloaded .45 magazines, and a semi-automatic rifle.

Only with my arsenal cleaned and arrayed at my bedside did I finally allow myself to collapse on top of my covers.

Sleep took me. A deep, dreamless slumber. Although full function had been restored to my foot, my energy reserves had been depleted by the procedure, as if my body had been fighting a sickness. I woke up with my heart pounding at 6:45 a.m. and reached for a weapon. I lay there for a long time, gritty eyes closed, mouth parched, with one hand resting on the cool, reassuring solidity of the loaded Glock on my chest.

I don't know about you, but nearly drowning has a tendency to pique my anxiety.

I finally got up and stepped into a long, hot shower.

As I dressed for a brisk winter day, I pulled up YouTube on my phone and watched Annabelle's latest interview. It had aired early this morning and I'd slept through it.

"Honestly," Annabelle was saying, "after the congressional hearings on UFOs, the biggest surprise is that other people are acting so shocked about it."

"That flying saucer stopped a Russian tank dead in its tracks!" exclaimed the host—not Barry this time, but a female news anchor with a strong European accent. Czech, or maybe Bulgarian. Whoever she was, her channel had a seven-figure following. "This isn't some blurry photograph of Bigfoot or a cloud shaped like a saucer, Ms. Marshall. The ship's captain intervened in an illegal war, saving dozens of lives and causing a full-on rout of the Russian forces!"

"Please." Anna's face was blurred in the video, but even so I could see her scoff, her face drawn into an expression of pure contempt. "Putin will be back. This is a diversion."

"A diversion from what?"

Annabelle chewed on her lip. "I don't know yet. That's my gut feeling about it."

"Regardless, you have to admit that it has caught the public's attention."

"The footage is compelling," Annabelle admitted.

"Who do you think the pilot is?"

"I'm sure I have no idea," Annabelle said in a tone I recognized as a hedge.

"Here it is again."

The video feed cut to shaky handheld footage of a flying saucer parked in front of a Russian tank. The two vehicles sat still for a long pause. Soldiers shouted useless orders at the Tetrad ship, their faces frightened. Then a pulse of force shot out in a ring, sending the tank flipping backward into the air and scattering dozens of the infantrymen surrounding the alien craft. The soldiers hit the walls of nearby buildings, their bodies crumpling like ragdolls, while the tank crunched onto its top and rocked until it was still.

Another four saucers then descended into Mariupol in the background, settling along the street as the thoroughfare cleared of people. The camera rattled as the videographer repositioned themselves on the run. Rifles fired at the saucers. Bullets bounced off, leaving the hulls of the ships undamaged.

Next, a tank fired at one of the craft. The shell exploded against the hull. When the smoke cleared, the saucer remained standing; a scorch mark was visible where the shell detonated, but otherwise the ship was undamaged.

More nauseating movement of the camera. When the image came back into focus again, it showed a grainy shot of a hatch popping on top of a saucer, viewed from a distance through a narrow window and along the alleyway between two buildings. A man-shaped figure rose from the hatch.

His shoulders were broad and raised, like a cobra's flared hood. To the trained eye, it was unmistakable: he was a Lodian.

To everyone else, it probably looked like he was wearing some kind of shoulder pauldrons.

Indeed, he wore modern armor of some kind. The shoulder ridges were more prominent than usual.

Annabelle had postulated that a Lodian's ridges were something like a fish's gills, connected to their breathing apparatus. Lodian ridges had the ability to extend and contract, which likely increased the amount of oxygen flowing into their bodies, unlike human beings with lungs fully inside their chests. The ridges also expressed emotions, and his flared aggressively in a position that I associated with excitement or anticipation.

With a sinking feeling in my gut, I realized that it must be Tanamir. The camera wasn't positioned at the correct angle to see his face, but the Tetrad leader had a flair for the dramatic. I intuited that he had planted the videographer to ensure this appearance was broadcast internationally.

"I don't know," Annabelle said after they'd cut back to the interview. "But it dispels some of the mystery, don't you think? Just another manned craft, now."

"Several of them."

"Indeed."

"Do you think it's an opposition nation interfering with events in Ukraine? Or is this some kind of private crusade?"

"I wouldn't say that. Here's what we do know: A pilot flies these ships. We know they're well protected, and must have been difficult to manufacture. The design alone is spectacular, completely different from any aircraft in use today."

"How do you think the Russians will take it if this turns out to be a special operation orchestrated by the United States?"

"I'm not here to talk politics, Miss Krupka. Stop trying to pin the tail on the partisan donkey. The only thing I wish to happen is that we all start taking these sightings more seriously. UFOs aren't a fringe experience anymore. They're here. I don't know who's piloting them, but there have been six sightings since the Austin Light Phenomenon."

"Five, isn't it?"

"Not if you count the Beijing cover-up from December 28th," Annabelle said.

"Ah, yes," said Krupka. "But that hasn't been verified."

"Hasn't it?" Annabelle asked. "What I want to know is,

what are they trying to accomplish? They've proven they can fly through international airspace without detection or interference. Departments of Defense all over the world are frantically auditing their active protection systems to try to figure out how the ships are getting through."

"Everywhere these ships appear, they save lives. Children in danger, illegal wars with massive civilian casualties. People are saying they're heroes."

"If you say so," Annabelle said. "When people start doing random acts of kindness, I find myself questioning their motives."

"That's an awfully negative way to view the world, don't you think, Ms. Marshall?"

"When a woman spends her life studying cover-ups and misdirections, she finds it hard to take everything she sees at face value."

"What does it take to convince the infamous Marsha Marshall that a good deed is a good deed no matter who does it?"

"The ends justify the means? Is that what you're suggesting, Ms. Krupka?"

"Grand Canyon. Mariupol. Who knows where they'll go next?"

"Two points is a vector, not a trend line."

They exchanged a few more ripostes, and then Miss Krupka ended the interview. "Thanks for having me," Annabelle said.

"Distinctly my pleasure, Ms. Marshall," Krupka answered. She then refocused on the camera and gave a branded outro about liking and subscribing, blah blah blah.

I closed the video and stood, my back popping. I was on Annabelle's side with this one. I didn't trust Tanamir's motivations at all. Annabelle's skill as a reporter was deft enough to paint that picture without going into detail about the Tetrad or Tanamir himself, which spoke volumes. She had a way of parsing information combined with an earnest delivery that made people feel confident, even if the subject matter was of the strange and outlandish variety.

A quick Google search caused a sinkhole to form in my stomach. It was a top story: The governor of Texas had proclaimed on social media that he'd give a million-dollar reward—out of his own personal funds—to the "Hero of Mariupol," if he came forward to identify himself.

My feed showed between two and three million reactions, piled on by thousands of comments and branching discussions.

The President of the United States had reposted it to all ninety million of his followers before I'd even had my coffee.

Jeepers, that escalated fast. Not even the best Peacekeeper tech could erase it from the public consciousness.

Did this count toward Tanamir's "Illumination"? The Gatekeeper hadn't been specific about what would trigger it. Tanamir was trying to draw someone's attention, but I'd be damned if I could make heads or tails of who or what the consequences would be of violating this obscure alien bylaw.

If the Federation got word of this event... what then? Would they send more Peacekeepers? Would they ask the Gatekeeper for help?

Would they nuke us from orbit?

That's a frightening prospect, I thought as I got in my truck and drove across town, pondering how weird it was, this world I lived in.

Annabelle called as I was pulling into a parking space at

the breakfast spot, which was nothing more than a fenced-in yard with two food trucks and a dozen picnic tables. Simple and unassuming, with good food for the money. It was my kind of place.

"I'm not going to make it," said Annabelle as I put the phone to my ear.

"Oh?" I asked, throwing the vehicle into park. "Why not?"

"You haven't seen the news, have you?"

"I watched your interview with that hot Czech reporter."

"She is hot, isn't she? If I had lips like that, I'd be unstoppable. But no, not that. You're gonna want to see this. Here, hang tight... I sent you the first video."

I opened our secure chat and tapped the link she texted me.

It took me to a publicly hosted video showing two police officers—a dark-skinned woman and a hulking pale man—fighting a protester who was swinging a large sign at the pair. The protester moved with surprising speed, but he was no match for the dark-skinned enforcer, who sent an incredible flying kick into the man's jaw, dropping the protester to the ground with his neck at a cringe-inducing angle. People began to riot when they saw the man dead, and only the hulking pale officer kept the other people from tearing his dark-skinned partner to pieces.

A cohort of police officers closed in around the pair and forced the rest of the group to retreat. The angle of the footage was tight, taken by someone standing among the incensed mob. The signs and colorful tie-dye shirts marked the protesters as a group of UFO die-hards.

"This is all over the internet," Annabelle said. "I think it's in Austin, but there's no geolocation on the footage."

The shaky footage continued, showing flashes of a city street, fairly broad, lined with grass and old oaks. Could have been taken in Austin—perhaps north of the Capitol building, where the protesters had been gathering since the Austin Light Phenomenon event? I couldn't be sure.

"It's them." Even with cloaking shields disguising them as police officers, the two Peacekeepers' identities were unmistakable to me.

"The protesters are calling themselves Truthers," Annabelle said. "See the signs? 'The Truth Will Out'," she quoted. It was painted slapdash on one of the larger stick-mounted poster boards.

The two Peacekeepers conferred for a moment while the cops held the rest of the group back. A beefcake cop in the front row looked familiar to me—*where had I seen him before?* I couldn't place him. Regardless, they'd strung yellow caution tape in a makeshift cordon and though it appeared flimsy and blew in the wind, the protesters shrieked each time they brushed up against it.

Dyna came to a decision, then approached the knot of scared people. They were beginning to panic, shoving each other now. She held her hands aloft as a light from her head blazed to painful, solar-flare brightness—it almost seemed like a camera flash, but I knew better. The lights came from the cybernetic nodes set into her skull.

The camera tumbled to the ground and pointed back at the cops—the Peacekeepers—who swiftly collected the caution tape and moved off-screen to the left.

With their memories wiped clean, the crowd of people blinked in confusion. They looked at each other with slack faces and bleary eyes before turning, one by one, and ambling away in a dozen different directions, as if they'd caught each other sleepwalking and were making their way home to return to bed.

"I suppose it was only a matter of time," I said, "before someone caught them erasing people's memories."

"Agreed. It doesn't look good that they disguised themselves as police."

"Those weren't cops. I guarantee you that."

"Of course not. But now the protesters will be more agitated than ever. It's a big deal when the government shuts down a protest of any kind by using violence against people. Now, it's become an issue of free speech."

"The guy Kilos beat up," I said, "had to have been a Tetrad agent."

"Maybe. But do you think anyone else will come to the same conclusion?"

I grimaced. "Not anyone in the media, except for you."

"Right. And even if I had evidence that they weren't local human cops, I'm only one person. Plus, something else happened at the protest those people were coming from."

I tapped the next link she sent. Its URL was a random string of letters and numbers. Once again, I observed a scene.

This time the footage showed another city street, this one somewhere in the projects. Stark, stone apartment buildings rose on one side. An overpass loomed in the background. Hooptys and battered trucks lined the street in front of a long row of single-story shotgun houses. The projects of some kind.

A storm of protesters marched by, moving down the center of the street. They bore signs proclaiming, "UFOs are real and the government knows it" and "Truth to the People" alongside photos of the Tetrad's saucers—from the tank faceoff in Russia to a glorious shot of a flying saucer hovering over Christ the Redeemer's outstretched arms high above Rio de Janeiro. One man wore a broad tinfoil hat. Most of the protesters had medical masks or black cotton masks stretched across their faces—likely to protect their identities, rather than to prevent the spread of sickness. A half-dozen black hoodies bore the words, "You can't murder free speech" printed in red.

"Scrub forward to 32 minutes," Annabelle said.

I did. The person holding the camera had stepped into the stream of marchers, moving down a wide thoroughfare as drivers yelled at them, heading toward the domed peak of the Texas State Capitol building in the distance.

"This took place before the other video? It's lighter outside."

Annabelle snorted. "Probably. These marches are taking place in cities all over the world, Andy, but they're the largest in Austin. The Austin Light Phenomenon has attracted a lot of interest."

"I'll bet the Tetrad helped them organize. What's special about this video?"

"Just watch."

As the protesters got closer, I could see that several police cars were parked in front of the Capitol's gates, which were closed and locked. There was an altercation as the protesters attempted to push through. One or two guys jumped onto the hoods of the cop cars and threw themselves on the fences. Officers hauled them down and shoved them back into the crowds with riot shields.

"Little aggressive for a UFO protest, don't you think?"

Annabelle remained silent. She must have known what I'd see next. As I watched, one of Tanamir's round ships glided down the street and startled the police officers enough to cause them all to draw their weapons and point them at the sky.

A pair of mounted officers—Lord knew why they thought it was a good idea to have horses on duty at a protest, but they did—turned and galloped off around the sides of the Capitol. Sirens began to whine in the distance, and the knot of protesters around the cameraman screamed with an excitement I can only compare to a religious rapture.

“Good grief,” I said. “Who let those nutters out of the asylum?”

“Be nice. Remember, Tanamir is manipulating them. He’s studied our conspiracy theories and is playing into people’s expectations.”

“Well, it’s working. They’re eating it up.”

In an excited fervor, a wild-eyed protester dance-stumbled in front of one of the horses. The officer drew back on the reins, causing the horse to rear and strike out with its front hooves.

A tall Latina woman in a patch-covered jean jacket bowled into the man, sending him staggering out of the path of the horse. As the pair hit the ground, an object bounced out of the man’s pocket—right into the foot of a police officer who had been looking up at the flying saucer, and discharged.

Startled by the gunshot, the cop drew his own weapon on the man and woman tumbling on the ground and began to shout at them to put their hands on their heads.

This time, his weapon fired—once, twice, three times.

Three shots left the female protester bleeding and wounded on the pavement. Dozens more police officers shouted and struggled as they vied for control of the tragic situation.

The video abruptly ended.

"Wait, what happened? Is that it?"

"That's all the footage I can find. Rumors are flying around, though, that the Hero of Mariupol descended in his saucer and intervened, saving the man and the woman's lives, but there's not a single photograph or video."

"Oh, hell," I said darkly. All this had taken place right after I'd parted ways with Dyna and Kilos. "Peacekeepers got to the footage."

"That's what I was thinking, too," Annabelle said.

"The survivor claims she was healed. She's giving testimony to any reporter who will ask about the 'Hero of Mariupol.' "

"Offworlder healing tech is pretty darn good." Glancing down at my ankle, I flexed it experimentally. No clicking—not just as good, but better than new. "Of course, the Tetrad have their own equipment?"

"Word is, she's already halfway to filing a lawsuit against the APD and wants to march on the Capitol tonight."

I winced. Those cussed aliens. I had to catch up with Gonzalez, and fast. The department was going to be a complete wreck over this.

I looked around the food park and noticed, as if for the first time, that it was eerily empty. No foot traffic, and despite it being nine a.m. on a weekday, only the tired-looking woman manning the taco truck and I were present. All the other trucks were closed and locked.

"They've got the city spooked, huh?" I asked. "Most of these food trucks are closed."

"After a UFO sighting at the Capitol, are you surprised?"

"No."

"Tonight'll be packed," Annabelle said. "The biggest protest yet. People will want to see the UFO."

"Tanamir hasn't been making a habit of showing up in the same place twice. That would make him predictable."

"I'm getting tips every minute from my readers about protests being planned in other cities, but Austin is the biggest one."

I heaved a sigh. "I need to get Gonzalez and Simmons up to speed."

"OK. I'll check in after a while." She paused. "Roads are empty in this direction, so I'm making good time."

My heart skipped a beat. "Where are you going?"

"Don't take that tone with me, mister," she said. "I'm not the one who broke his ankle and nearly drowned last night."

"Point taken. But please, promise me you'll be careful."

"Always."

"Where are you headed, anyway?"

"Isn't it obvious? I'm on my way to interview the survivor about her miraculous healing."

CHAPTER ELEVEN

POLICE HEADQUARTERS in downtown Austin was an imposing stone building. Two flagpoles flanked its front entrance. One flew the Star Spangled Banner, the other the solitary star of the Lone Star State.

Today, the place buzzed with activity.

A hundred protesters had gathered to march in a circle on the sidewalk where Eighth Street met the frontage road. Officers positioned themselves at measured distances, monitoring the gathering. Patrol cars circled the building. Occasionally, one stopped to let officers out, either to escort perps inside or to run for the glass doors on some errand or another.

News crews loitered in the parking lot across the street, representing most major news stations and several I hadn't heard of. Cameras rolled on the protest. Reporters smoked or scuffed their shoes on the pavement as they waited for the action to begin.

As for myself, I sat on the hood of my truck further back in the lot, in a chill, shady spot beneath the overpass. It was gloomy enough that the curved fluorescent light poles illuminated the area. Rainwater fell in a curtain a few feet ahead of my truck's front bumper. A small group of homeless people stirred from under a worn tarp to my left, no doubt waking slowly after a long, cold night.

I'd only been surveying the scene for ten minutes when Detectives Gonzalez and Simmons crossed the street and came to meet me.

"Chaos in there," Sheila muttered as she leaned onto the hood beside me.

"I can imagine," I said, watching them. Simmons cast a distrustful eye at the press gang.

Simmons wore a loose grey suit. Gonzalez had on jeans and a sport coat. While the uniformed officers running to and fro seemed harried and half-frantic, Gonzalez and Simmons looked weary.

"What have you got for us, Gunn?" Sheila asked.

I filled them both in on the events that had transpired since we'd last connected. Gonzalez was frustrated about the intel I'd been withholding, but I had to give her credit, she rolled with the punches. I only had to endure a few of her snarky comments. Simmons, for his part, managed not to roll his eyes while I described my attacker and the tech she'd stolen. But his face grew darker and darker while I relayed the story. At the end, his expression was practically funereal.

"What crawled up your butt and died?" I asked.

"Our facial recognition system found something on the hotel security footage."

"Really?"

"A woman exiting from the hotel room the day before we got there."

"What's so special about that?"

"I checked the reservation system. The room was empty the night before."

Chills went up my spine. "Of course! She must have reversed time so she could leave when no witnesses were there to see her. That's brilliant."

Simmons looked like he'd eaten something sour. He shook his head in an instinctual rejection. "That's not possible."

"It is," I said, "Suspend your disbelief."

He pulled out his phone and showed me the footage. "Do you recognize her?"

I watched the video carefully. A fit brunette woman in joggers and sneakers stepped out of the hotel room and made her way down the hall, brazenly unconcerned. She held the motorcycle helmet in one hand.

"It's got to be her. The Sevrit."

"Are you sure?"

"She was wearing that same outfit when I saw her on the Shoal Creek Trail. She's got the helmet. It's her."

He sighed, stuffing his phone back into the inside breast pocket of his suit jacket. "I don't believe it. Time travel!"

"Not time travel. Temporal manipulation."

"Call it whatever," he muttered.

"I'd have thought checking your assumptions was something you detectives were good at."

He glared at me. "*Offworlders.*" He tore at the word as it slid past his teeth. "I hate this nonsense."

A smile spread across my face. "The first step to healing is acceptance, Simmons. I'm proud of you."

"Here's the problem," Sheila said as Simmons fell into a grumpy silence. "With the incident last night and the protests continuing into today, the force has recalled every warm body they can muster. They stole the rest of my guys for riot duty at the Capitol."

"Aw, no more Officer Daniels? I'll have to send him a ball of yarn as a consolation prize for his new assignment."

Simmons snorted. "Don't bother. It's a good chance for the big guy to hit something. Hard. He'll love it."

"Good point." I chuckled, but it came out as a dark sound because I knew the people he'd be hitting would be innocent civilians trying to stand up for what's right. "How long will that last?"

"No idea."

"We're on our own, then."

"There's more," Sheila said. "With no body and only a twelve-hour-old image of our suspect, they downgraded the case from murder to assault. They also won't recognize our suspect, given the timetable."

I grimaced. "Technically, the Torlik did get murdered."

"Not if there ain't no body, he didn't," Simmons said.

"They let us keep the case," Sheila added, "but they've already asked us to take another, in light of the circumstances. We'll have to work both to make it look like we're not chasing vapor or wasting department funds. And Gunn... I can't bill any more consulting hours right now, either."

"That's just rude," I said.

"Out of my control," she said. "They need all the extra budget they can squeeze to pay officers overtime for working the protests. And that includes us—we've gotta be back by tonight to work the protests ourselves."

I nodded and chewed over my dilemma. The cash Lulamina had given me would cover my expenses, and this was more than a case now. Since the Sevrit had attacked me, it had become personal.

A police car pulled up, lights spinning. The oversized pair of Officers Daniels and Gelder stepped out, leaving the car running. They perp-walked a cuffed hippie into the station right through the middle of the jeering crowd of protesters. The man's gray hair was pulled back into a messy tail, and he wore a tie-dye t-shirt with one of the protest slogans on it.

WE'RE NOT ALONE, it read.

And on the other side: *KEEP AUSTIN WEIRD*.

It certainly was that.

Regardless, the protester and his convictions were enough to firm my resolve.

What was the point of being debt-free and independent if I couldn't take the cases I wanted, regardless of money?

"Consulting fee or no consulting fee, I'm in," I said. "What's our next move?"

"We hunt down your Sevrit and nail her to a wall," Sheila said.

"I was hoping you'd say that!" I hopped off the tailgate and clapped my hands together. The crack echoed off the underside of the interstate and caused a nearby newsman to fumble with his camera. "Time to skin this cat. When do we start?"

"No time like the present." Gonzalez checked her watch.

I felt my cheeks tighten as a grin spread across my face.

"Why are you smiling like that?" Simmons asked me. "I don't like it."

I turned my grin on the skeptical cop. "You're gonna shit yourself when you see this."

CHAPTER TWELVE

THE RED-RIMMED EYES of Detective Simmons shone as we entered the expansive heart of Lulamina and Zavis's Opsilax mansion.

He stared, slack-jawed, at the ornate wood-beamed ceiling, the broad tiled corridors, and the rainbow-colored doorways lining the main hall. Each shimmering surface sectioned off a completely encapsulated environment: a desert landscape, a forest grove, an indoor pool, and many more.

The laboratory where Zavis conducted his quantum experiments lay behind a more discreet door at the far end of the hall. You'd miss it if you didn't know what you were looking for.

I'd spent enough time here to know that many things in this house were not as they seemed. Although the home was an average size for its location in the hills west of Austin, the inside was vast—far bigger than its outside frame could accommodate.

It was an engineering marvel beyond the reach of any human architect.

"How is this possible?" the detective whispered, wiping sweat into his thinning hair.

"It's bigger on the inside," I whispered cheekily.

Simmons glared at me.

"Opsilax architecture is popular on the oldest Federation planets, but it was pioneered on the Pinker homeworld," Lulamina explained. "My husband is among its foremost practitioners."

"Hmph," grunted Simmons.

I knew exactly how the detective was feeling. His perception of reality was expanding in painful and awkward ways. The man's narrow mind was struggling to keep up.

I'd stared around in disbelief much like he had the first time I'd come here. Although I liked to think I adjusted much more easily, I'd also had more time to come to grips with offworlders. Detective Simmons' skin was clammy, like he was coming down with the flu.

While he gawked and tested putting his arm through a blue energy barrier, I walked ahead and stepped through the green threshold that led to the library. A familiar tingle crawled along my neck as I passed through. I nodded to the hologram projection of Gina, the house's AI personality, as she appeared next to me, smiling.

Felix the Torlik sat in a reading chair by a tall window at the far end of the library, poring over his spiral notebook. When he saw me, he stood and said, "Tell me you've found it."

"Not yet," I answered.

His shoulders slumped, and he dragged his feet as he walked over to meet me.

"But I did have a nasty run-in with your killer. What do you know about the Sevrit?"

The pupil of his large eyeball widened in fear. "Nasty creatures. Warlike. They duel over minor infractions and have some bloody coming-of-age rituals, which are only tolerated because they are religious in nature." He glanced around at the shelves of books in various languages. "Perhaps there is a volume in here on them."

"Gina," I called to the hologram. "Can you help us find anything on the Sevrit that might help our case?"

She led me and Felix up the platforms to the highest shelf on the side with the green barrier. The emerald glow of the energy shield illuminated the spines of the books.

"Here you are," Gina said. "These books contain Sevrit customs, this one anatomy, and this one their history with the Federation."

We took the books back to the ground floor, where Gonzalez, Lulamina and a now flushed-looking Detective Simmons rejoined us.

"Have you seen the garden?" he asked, his thick eyebrows in disarray, with hairs sticking up at wild angles, maybe from how much he'd been rubbing his sweaty forehead. "It's incredible! I've never seen anything like it."

"You're... into gardening?"

"You got a problem with that?" He glared, as if challenging me to object or poke fun at him.

I didn't take the bait. Who says I haven't matured?

"You know what, nevermind," I said. "Doesn't matter. What's the book say, Felix? I can't read it and I don't know where that translation glass went."

Felix's single large pupil whipped back and forth over

the pages. “Says here their religious ceremonies began as mating rituals.”

I shuddered to think about what they could do with the claws I saw on our killer. She’d been strong, even without the timepiece. How was I going to beat her in a fight if I encountered her again?

“Buh buh buh…” Felix muttered as he skipped ahead. “Ah. It seems that most of the more violent ceremonies have been abandoned over the six millennia they’ve been under Federation rule. They have a dozen representatives in the voting body, but for such a small population they have a lot of influence, perhaps due to their strong representation in the military. In particular, the bombardiers and… hmm. How would you translate this word here?”

Lulamina leaned forward. “Assassins.”

I gulped. “Is that an official Army unit? Assassins?”

“Not exactly,” she said. She’d been watching our search with interest and seemed to be humming with the thrill of it. “The term ‘Black Ops’ would be more fitting.”

“No wonder the Peacekeepers wanted to keep tabs on her…”

“Peacekeepers!” Felix exclaimed as he jumped to his feet. He paced back and forth, becoming agitated. “Oh, dear. Oh, my. Wait, you didn’t tell them about the…” He glanced at Gonzalez and Simmons. “What we talked about, did you? We had an agreement!”

I held up both hands. “I didn’t tell them anything they didn’t figure out on their own. Relax. But remember, I told you I’d have to share info about the timepiece with my detective friends?”

He frowned but nodded.

"Do the Peacekeepers know about me?"

"I don't think so. However, you didn't tell me they could detect temporal manipulation. They say it's illegal to do such a thing."

He scoffed. "Only if they're not the ones doing it." He cursed in his own language, which reminded me of a more guttural Russian.

"He's calling them hypocrites," Lulamina translated. "Among other things."

"So, back to this Sevrit," I said. "Did you see one on the transport shuttle while you were traveling to Earth?"

He closed his ponderous eye. "The shuttles have pods for sleeping, as it's somewhat of a long trip, so I didn't interact with everyone on the ship. Besides, I don't always know the race of a stranger, and it's somewhat rude to inquire."

"What do you mean?"

"Offworlders often modify or disguise their physical traits, as you know."

"But surely there was a lounge or common room?"

"Yes, I did spend some time there."

"Did you talk to anyone?"

"I spent some time conversing with a Lodian I met."

"What did you two talk about?" I asked.

"Nothing," he hedged. "A mere entertainment to pass the time."

I smiled. "Humor me."

His eye seemed to dart around, seeming to want to rest on anything else but me. "We were, ah, discussing the latest Gevereaux creation." He coughed into a hand. "It was released a few cycles before the incident on Pango."

I glanced at Gonzalez and Lulamina, who were watching me and Felix. "What kind of creation?"

Felix and Lulamina conversed for a second in the Torlik tongue.

"You might call it a movie," Lulamina supplied. "Although that's not completely accurate. It's a kind of interactive storytelling vehicle that aims to engage the mind, body and spiritual senses of the Pangozil. They're very spiritual people, you know."

I frowned. How come I had never talked to Vinny about that? I knew he liked to gamble and might even have called it a problem, but I didn't even know if he believed in God or anything like it.

Gina edged closer to Lulamina. "Mistress, there is someone at the front door." Lulamina looked at the hologram, which made it seem almost as if she was studying herself in a moving mirror—the hologram was a Pinker, diminutive in stature, if less curvy and more modestly dressed than Lulamina.

The Pinker hostess frowned, said, "Excuse me," and departed from the room. Gina faded from view until she vanished.

I glanced at Gonzalez, who covertly unbuttoned the safety strap around the Glock on her hip. I rested my hand on my own weapon, concealed at my lower back, shifting my position to see the green energy shield. I wanted to make sure I had enough time to react if anyone unwelcome or dangerous came through it.

"I don't see how the latest Gevereaux masterpiece is relevant to this conversation," Felix said, exasperated. "I'm starting to lose faith in your ability to track down this timepiece, bounty hunter."

"I know more than the last time we met," I pointed out. "Let's finish our conversation. What makes you think running into a Lodian who shares your interest is such a coincidence?"

"Are you accusing me?"

"No."

"What I—But—" His face darkened, and he covered his eye with all four hands. "Oh, dear."

A winged creature came soaring through the energy shield, causing both me and Gonzalez to draw our weapons and point them up.

"Hold!" I said after a moment, averting the barrel. "Hold your fire."

Samael flapped down and landed on the table atop the books. He was a small creature, and his rough skin showed its many scars in the bright light of day. One of his little hands clutched a small, transparent cube.

"Bounty hunter," his voice grated. "The Gatekeeper sends his greetings."

Lulamina came back into the room a moment later, trailed by Gina's floating hologram.

"Is that right?"

"He said you might have use of this." He handed me the cube, which felt like heavy glass in my hand.

"Ohhhh," Lulamina said, retrieving a flat object from a nearby reading table. "Place that on here."

I did so and was rewarded with a projection of a table of information—in English. After a moment's study, I saw it was a passenger manifest. It listed the names, species, and origination point of each passenger. It also listed their checked cargo for the trip.

Most of the names were crossed off. I found Felix's name among those.

Only one was highlighted.

Species: Sevrit. Location of origin: Lodi. Cargo: None.

Name: Jaiyana Puala.

"Is he sure?" I asked Samael, picturing the remorseful Torlik who'd been separated from his soul. "Not all information acquired under coercion is reliable."

Samael hopped birdlike around the table, peering down at the information in the books we were studying. "Is it reliable if both our investigations arrive at the same species independently of each other?"

I pushed my tongue into my cheek. "That would be quite the coincidence."

"Or perhaps it's merely correct. Sevrit are not common on Earth. In fact, I don't know of any others."

"Still doesn't do us much good," Simmons pointed out. "It's not like I can look her up in our criminal database or ask Interpol or anything like that."

He annoyed me, but the man had a point. "What else did the Gatekeeper find out?" I asked.

Samael lifted his wings in a little gargoyle shrug. "This is what he sent me with."

"Well, can he look her up and get us some more info?"

"I will pass along the request. Good day."

Samael flapped up and departed from the room.

"Good-for-nothing Daacro," I muttered under my breath, "Always dropping bombs on us and flying off to do God knows what."

As Samael left, another person entered the library—a Pinker, this one male, with a shock of gray hair like an ancient troll. His face was buried in the screen of some kind of offworlder tablet. He walked right past us, hopped up onto the floating platforms, and went to the top shelf. We all stopped to watch him as he selected a volume without looking, then walked down.

"Hey, Zavis," I said when we were walking by. "What's cracking?"

Zavis flinched and looked up. His eyes widened. "Where'd you all come from?"

"We've been here a while."

"I see," he said, and made as if to leave.

"Zavis, quick question. Do you still have backdoor access to some Federation information systems?"

"I never—" Zavis glanced at Felix. "No. Absolutely not." On a Pinker, the guilty flush to his skin showed up as a deepening shade of violet. It suddenly hit me where the English translation of their name came from.

"I guess you're in as much hot water with them as I am," Zavis muttered. "Regardless, no—my connection was closed around the time Tanamir came to Earth. I did save a partial backup."

My ears perked up. "What kind of information do you have?"

"Oh, nothing was off-limits to the quantum engineers," Zavis smirked and pushed his thick glasses up his nose. "What's the English idiom? Necessity is the mother of invention."

Felix scribbled that one down in his notebook, intently focused. Capturing those phrases seemed to give his mind something to do.

"I have always found that criminals have all sorts of interesting needs..." Zavis suggested.

Felix grinned, his anxiety momentarily forgotten. "You didn't."

"I did."

Sheila's eyes lit up. She gave me a hungry look. "Zavis, are you saying you have access to a Federation criminal database?"

"Yes," Zavis said, hopping up and down. "An outdated one, to be sure. They never gave us access to live records, only copies. But we never suffered for reading material. Perhaps, this Sevrit, Jaiyana, has an incident report or criminal record. Even if it's not her real name, searching the database would still turn up records of an alias if it's one she's used before."

We used one of the strange, plastic books with transparent pages to access the database. "I chose to disguise them as books," Zavis explained after he had retrieved it from a middle shelf on the right side of the room. "It could be condensed to a cube like the one the Gatekeeper delivered here, but I found that more surface area was better for maximizing storage capacity, as well as being able to organize and access it modularly."

We spent the rest of the morning and well into the afternoon searching through a series of volumes for things like Sevrit, Jaiyana, Puala, and other relevant keywords. It took some time because Felix had to translate the words and look up synonyms using the language in which they were written, which was an ornate version of Lodian with shortcuts and encryptions designed specifically for record-keeping. The translation glass would let me extricate and read passages, but I wasn't as fond of the lookup mechanism as Zavis seemed to be.

It went slowly. Zavis eventually grew bored and wandered back to attend to his own experiments.

Gina took lunch orders, which were delivered on

autonomous delivery dumbwaiters that reminded me of miniature Zambonis.

I was eating a ham sandwich when I finally stumbled on something that made me pause mid-bite. "I've got something."

Gonzalez and Simmons came to peer over my shoulder, each rubbing their sore necks. "What is it?"

I pointed to the initials, "J.P."

Simmons scoffed. "That's all?"

"How do you know that's her?" asked Detective Gonzalez.

"It's a classified intelligence report. Half of it's redacted, but I started to wonder if Tanamir was referenced in any old records related to military conflicts. If he's the wily old Federation general people think he is, certainly there would be files on him somewhere."

"I don't see Tanamir's name anywhere," Simmons said.

"Me neither, but look here. It mentions a general sending a Black Ops team on a mission against some Lodian rebels hiding out on Pango."

"Which is important because..."

"Pango was the battleground for the early stage of the Tetrad's first rebellion," Felix offered. "So that tracks."

"Says here," I went on, "a Sevrit commando sent this message after going dark for days in the field: 'Seven casualties. Mission failed—I take full responsibility. Returning to base. –J.P.'

Simmons rolled his eyes.

"It's not much to go on," Gonzalez said.

"What's interesting is this—up till now, this unit had never failed a mission. The analyst who wrote the report blamed the officer in charge, saying they were negligent in their duty. In their conclusion, it says *she* left the service at her earliest opportunity, then fell off the grid. The author thinks she was ashamed of her failure in the field. But... what if she threw the mission? What if that's when she turned into a rebel?"

"How do you know the Sevrit you fought was a Tetrad rebel?"

"I didn't get the sense that she reported to Tanamir. She knows him well enough to know he might be interested in the timepiece, though."

Felix's face blanched. He blinked and wiped his eye with two hands. "She'll find him," he said. "If she has the time-piece, she has all the time in the world to look."

"Which makes me guilty for wasting so much time here... But this is the most we've found on the Sevrit yet."

Gonzalez stepped away and put her cell phone to her ear. She nodded once, putting on her serious work face.

That wasn't a good sign.

"I want you to look for more records with the initials J.P. and these unit numbers," I told Felix. I showed him using the translation glass where in the file I'd found them. "And see if you can confirm the name of the general—whether it's Tanamir or not."

He gave me a trepidatious look.

"Trust me," I said, "it's better than sitting here playing with English idioms and worrying. You'll be doing some good. I'd have had you start on it sooner if I had known Zavis had access to these records."

"Right," he said. "Of course."

"Bad news," Sheila announced as she pocketed her cell phone. "We have to go. They're calling all available units to the Capitol."

“Oh, my,” Lulamina breathed in a husky voice. “That sounds dangerous.”

She didn’t have any popcorn on the table. That didn’t keep me from imagining her later, glued to a news channel with a buttery bag in both little hands.

CHAPTER THIRTEEN

"COOL SIRENS!" I shouted over the keening noise. "You guys should let me ride along more often."

"Oh, yeah?" Simmons muttered, grabbing the oh-shit handle as Gonzalez drifted around the next corner. "Maybe I should treat you to the authentic experience."

"What's that mean, Mr. Officer, sir?" I asked in the most vapid voice I could summon. Gonzalez rolled her eyes in the rearview mirror.

"It means I throw you back there in cuffs and do doughnuts in the parking lot until you pass out."

"Simmons!" I scolded. "That's naughty."

"Smart aleck." He opened his mouth to say something else, then closed it again. The man actually looked *thoughtful* for a change. "These jobs you're working for Lula, are they legal?"

"They're not *il*legal. Besides, I'm not working for her, she just refers clients to me."

"What kind of clients?"

"Aren't you suspicious now?"

"Yeah, I want to know what else you've been keeping from me."

I grinned. "You've got the bug."

"The what?"

"The bug! For offworlder stuff." I met Gonzalez's eyes in the mirror. "Do you believe us now?"

Detective Simmons heaved a sigh. "Yeah, I guess I've seen enough oddball stuff."

"Tip of the iceberg. Anyway, I was thinking, we should ask Marsha to search military records about UFOs... might be useful if Tanamir is cribbing from our notes."

"Fah, that stuff's baloney," Simmons insisted. But he glanced sheepishly at Gonzalez and me as he said it.

"I'm just saying," he said pointlessly.

"Open your mind, Simmons! The truth is out there. Anyway, as I was saying, Tanamir definitely mined Earth's UFO conspiracy theories for ideas. I'm sure Marsha already thought about this, but finding Federation military records on 'J.P.' made me think that if Tanamir is ex-military, it stands to reason that one of the first things he'd do when he came to Earth was study our own military intelligence."

"We should have stayed closer to town," griped Gonzalez as she swerved between cars. "This is taking too long."

"If we did, we wouldn't have learned all that new information about the Sevrit," I pointed out.

"Are we any closer to finding her, or the timepiece?"

"Not yet," I admitted. "But we do know where she's going."

"Tanamir," Gonzalez said.

"How'd that gargoyle creature know you were at Lula's

house, anyway?" Simmons asked. "He's the only reason we found anything in the first place."

"Samael? He likes to spy on me," I said. "It's super annoying. Even if he can be useful." Now it was my turn to sigh in frustration. "The Gatekeeper's up to something, I just don't see it yet."

Gonzalez yanked the wheel around another turn, sending my butt sliding across the greased leather in the backseat.

Thankful I wasn't actually cuffed, I used a seatbelt to secure myself in place. Conversation in the car fell to silence, so I texted Annabelle to find out where she was.

"Just arrived at the protest," she wrote back.

"How is it?"

"Packed. We had to leave our cars miles away."

"Wow. What's the mood like?"

"Celebratory. Tense. Jubilant. Angry. They're calling themselves Believers."

"Isn't that a name your fans have used?"

"... yep." Then, a minute later, "Some of their theories are way off, but not the basic premise. Check my social."

I looked at her main profile. The photos showed crowds of people filling the street for blocks. Congress Avenue had been completely roped off from vehicle traffic. Police cars were posted at every intersection.

It was worse than the days of South by Southwest when the big-name bands were playing downtown.

In one of Anna's photos, the domed cupola of the Capitol building was visible in the distance.

"I'll come find you. Who are you with?"

"My witness," she tapped back.

"What for?" I wrote back.

"Documenting her journey," she said.

"What if the APD gets involved?"

"They're involved. Don't pretend like your job doesn't have hazards."

She was right, but it still bothered me. Was I being overprotective? I decided to back off a little.

"True," I admitted. "I'll work on an exit plan and let you know when we get there."

"Might want to distance yourself from G&S."

By which she meant my detective friends, Gonzalez and Simmons.

"Copy that," I wrote back.

We hit traffic as we were getting off the highway, slowing to a crawl as we neared the University of Texas campus north of the Capitol. I tapped my feet impatiently.

After a few more blocks, I could hear it. Noises, chanting, whistles, drums.

"I'm getting out," I said, popping the door handle before the vehicle had stopped moving. At first, the door didn't open. I experienced a moment of panic that Simmons had actually locked me in the back seat like I was some kind of suspect. I bent the handle in my cyborg fingertips as I stared through the cage.

Simmons gave me an amused side-eye. "What? It's unlocked."

I pushed harder, and the door came open. Along with the biting winter air came the noise of a chanting crowd.

"*Adiós*!" I shouted, and slammed the door before Simmons could complain about the handle I'd ruined.

"Not alone!" A man was shouting into a crackling megaphone to a quad full of students. "Not. A. Lone!"

The crowd chanted along with him, each syllable

distinct. It made me feel queasy hearing the volume of their conviction.

The demonstration was spread out along a lawn between a strip mall and the entrance to the university campus.

It would take me some time to get downtown, so I set off at a jog. I stopped when I felt a hand on my arm.

"Gunn!" Sheila said, yanking me back. "I said, stop!"

"Oh, sorry, couldn't hear you. What about your cruiser?"

"Made Simmons park it." She glanced around. "I was getting tired of his cynicism anyway."

"Kind of fun to poke him though."

She ignored that comment. "It's crowded! This is worse than South by Southwest."

I grinned at her. "Reminds me of our concert-going days. Noisy. Near campus. Lots of sweaty, stinky people pressing up against each other."

"Disgusting," she said, but she gave me a little smile. "At least it's not summer."

"It's going to take too long to get downtown if we walk," I said. "Have you been keeping up with your cardio?"

"I could stretch my legs a bit."

I grimaced. "Sorry, but you need to lose the jacket. You look like a cop."

"And you don't?"

"I'm not a cop." I frowned, looking down at myself. "I'm wearing jeans."

"It's your face."

"Speak for yourself."

"Fine," Gonzalez said as she folded her sport coat and tucked it under a bush nearby. "If this gets stolen, you owe me $200."

"You really paid $200 for that man-jacket?"

"Shut it." She untucked her blouse and mussed up her hair. "Better?"

I nodded at the weapon holster on her hip.

"What?" she asked. "Are you going to ditch *your* gun?"

"Mine is a bit less conspicuous..."

"Only if you don't know what to look for."

She had a point. The weapon bulging from my belt at the small of my back was pretty obvious to a trained observer.

I weighed my options. Annabelle had made a good point about separating myself from Sheila, but last night I'd been ambushed when I was alone. Since the Sevrit was probably in the area *and* she had the timepiece, I liked the idea of having someone to watch my back.

Especially since Gonzalez was not only armed but also had a duty to use her firearm in service of public safety.

So I nodded and set off at a light jog. It wasn't exactly comfortable in jeans, but I'd been running enough that the movement felt familiar. After a couple of minutes, we found our pace, with me in the lead. I could hear Gonzalez's measured breathing off my left shoulder.

Despite the chill in the air, we were both sweating by the time we reached Congress Avenue. The sun was starting to set. Streetlights were turning on, and the skyscrapers cast the gathered crowd in long shadows. The sky was painted with brushstrokes of deep amber and pink between a foreground of fluffy clouds.

The crowds were so thick here that Gonzalez and I were forced to slow to a walk. We pressed through dense thickets of people.

As we moved forward, I pointed at a pocket of police officers gathered at the next intersection. "Are those guys

APD?" I angled closer so I could read their badges. One of them said, "Round Rock," another, "Buda."

"Reinforcements from the suburbs," she said. "I didn't know they called them in, but I'm not surprised."

As I was staring at the badge of a brunette woman in blue, the metal shimmered and I made out an unusual shape on her shoulders, where her walkie talkie was clipped.

My breath caught in my throat. I quickly scanned the crowd of officers, and noticed the shimmering of cloaking shields for several of them.

"Sheila, some of those cops are offworlders!"

She frowned. "Are you sure?"

"Without a doubt."

She reached back and unclipped the safety strap around her pistol. She smiled and waved at the cops, who eyed her handgun and the flash of her badge from her pocket, then nodded stiffly before turning back to study the crowd.

She shrugged. "You said offworlders have been here a long time. So what if some of them are cops? Those are real uniforms. They're legit."

The idea of offworlder cops on the police force still made me uncomfortable for some reason. Was it xenophobia? I didn't want aliens defending human interests. Yet was I any better, a human hunting down missing offworlders? Who was I to get involved in their problems? I justified it by reminding myself that *they* hired *me*. It was a voluntary exchange.

We kept walking. I pointed at a sign that said, "Keep the faith" with a painting of a UFO sucking a tank into its tractor beam.

"They're all standing around hoping to see one of

Tanamir's ships," I whispered into Sheila's ear. "Like fans of the Beatles lurking outside their studio." Even though I was right next to her, the chattering crowd drowned out my voice.

A radio squawked on Gonzalez's hip. The crowd around us glanced nervously in her direction and gave us a bit more space.

"I didn't realize you'd brought that with you," I muttered. "So much for looking casual."

"I couldn't leave it behind," she said, pulling it from her back pocket. "What if they need to reach me?"

The wind picked up, cooling the sweat on my forehead and causing goosebumps to scurry up my arm.

While she spoke into her radio, communicating with her colleagues about where they wanted her to be, I pulled my phone out and checked Annabelle's social media feeds. The photo she posted five minutes ago placed her here on Congress Avenue, somewhere between Sixth and Ninth Street. The Capitol building now loomed much larger in the photos.

I made my way south in that direction. Gonzalez trailed me.

As we walked, I studied the crowd. I was now on high alert for disguised offworlders and the Sevrit.

Letting my mind drift, I saw several shimmering faces in the crowd. More offworlders in disguise.

One took the guise of an enterprising *paleta* vendor. The Torlik's visible appearance featured hunched shoulders and deeply tanned skin. His bottom hands were tucked down around his middle, beneath a stained white apron.

Another offworlder whose species I didn't recognize was mingling with protesters, taking slugs from a bottle of malt liquor in a paper sack. A rolled joint was tucked into his left ear. Beneath his disguise, he looked like a bearded monkey.

All these different types of offworlders reminded me of a trip to the Gatekeeper's ruined nightclub, Harbor.

I nodded at the offworlder. He glanced at my hand, blanched and moved in the opposite direction.

"What did you say to him?" Sheila asked, chuckling.

"Nothing," I said.

We were making our way south down Congress, between Eighth and Ninth, when a protester in a black mask ran up, chucked a brick at the bank building and shattered a window.

Screams and cries rose up from the crowd. Police officers shouted, "Stop!" and swarmed toward him.

He moved fast, jumping up and kicking off a stone column ten feet high, to tuck and roll on the other side.

The officers swore and raced after him.

"Offworlder?" Sheila asked.

"Yeah, but I didn't get a good look at his face. Maybe Lodian?"

Gonzalez's radio buzzed and clicked. I watched as a beefy Officer Daniels and his large partner chased the agitator down Congress, and then east on Tenth. He sprinted fast, easily outpacing the bigger men. I kept an eye on him, seeing his cloaking shield shimmer as he passed through a knot of other people in black clothing. They closed ranks as he moved through them, hindering the pursuit.

"More offworlders," I told Sheila in a low voice. "Mixed in among the crowd. Wearing black hoodies and jeans. I see a few Lodian faces now."

"They're all wearing hoodies or dark clothes."

"Yeah." The crowd jostled and shoved us into the street. A line of police officers tried to make more room on the sidewalk.

I turned and flowed away with the crowd, my eyes whipping around. Annabelle had to be here somewhere...

There.

A petite woman with a messy bun of blonde hair pointed a compact camera at the police officers. It seemed like she was standing on some kind of bench. I followed her shot to see Officer Daniels and several cops grappling with the agitators, ten Lodian males mixed in with dozens of college-age kids.

Offworlders among both sides wrestled.

Damn, but it was going to be hard to tell who was who.

Gonzalez must have seen me staring. "Peacekeepers?" she asked. "Or Tetrad thugs?"

"Both?" I said. "I'm not sure. It's not like they're wearing uniforms!"

"Black hoodies, black jeans, black boots. Looks like a uniform to me."

She wasn't wrong. The sight reminded me of video footage of the 1992 Los Angeles riots.

She snarled. "This is so frustrating! I can't tell who's an offworlder and who's not."

I could tell, but it was difficult. I was glad now that Dyna couldn't reverse what she'd done to me to allow me to see through the cloaking shields.

A shimmering disguise flashed in the corner of my eye. As I tried to focus on it, the crowd shifted and it vanished. Offworlders were becoming more common in Austin, but they didn't dominate any crowd. This one was packed with students and young adult human beings, primarily.

"Remind me to ask next time we see Zavis if he can make some kind of device to target and disable a person's shield," I muttered.

"What did you say?" Gonzalez shouted.

"Nevermind. This way!"

I crossed the street in Annabelle's direction. Overhead, I made out Samael and several other Daacros flitting through the sky. They were following the action.

Which meant the Gatekeeper was hiding around here somewhere.

Annabelle was lost in her photography. I walked right up to her and tugged on her pant leg.

She glanced down from her perch on the bench.

"Hey, sweetie!" She blushed. "Oh, um, hi, Sheila."

"Annabelle." Sheila nodded, politely looking away while she fixed her hair, which had come undone in our run here.

Officer Daniels and the other cops, both APD and the offworlders from out of town, had managed to quell the disturbance we'd seen. The thugs in hoodies drained away into a side street—no doubt planning their next incursion on the peace.

Apart from that little tiff, so far this was a mostly peaceful protest.

A hush fell over the crowd. Annabelle's attention was fixed fifty yards ahead, on a stunning Latina woman who appeared to be in her mid 30s. She had on a vintage jean jacket, worn at the elbows and wrists, and covered in faded peace patches and other badges. One of them was a simple UFO with a tractor beam angling down and to one side.

"I believe because I was healed!" she said.

Someone handed her a megaphone. Annabelle's camera shutter snapped repeatedly.

"I believe because I was healed!" she repeated into the megaphone, which squealed loudly, causing the crowd to groan.

"Last night, the police officers so aggressively defending this so-called 'Capitol' building shot me in cold blood."

The crowd, which had already focused on her, hushed.

She held up her fingers, which gripped a small caliber bullet. "I've got the proof. It's got my blood on it, and they shot me with it—one in the shoulder and one in the stomach."

"That's right!" shouted one protester.

"I was there!" said another.

"They shot me, too," said a large Black man. He stepped up next to her.

"They shot him too!" she insisted.

Murmurs filled the crowd. No one moved. She had them hooked.

Now, I recognized her jacket from the night before. The tall man next to her gave it away. He was the other demonstrator who fell under the horse's hooves in the video Annabelle had shared.

The man who'd been carrying the first weapon that fell out and discharged by accident.

Were they plants? Was this staged, or did she really get healed, like Dyna had just healed me?

The tall Black man nodded at the crowd, holding up one hand in a fist that looked... awkward. Off, somehow. It was only a matter of a few degrees, but he held his arm too far back.

It struck me as wrong. Fake.

When I relaxed my vision, the tall man's mask shimmered, revealing a scarred Lodian beneath.

I recognized him. One of Tanamir's people, who I'd seen with the Lodian leader at Lulamina's house.

"Annabelle," I hissed. "He's Tetrad."

Her eyes widened. "Are you sure? I knew something was off. He was acting weird during my interview with Yasmin."

She must mean her witness, the woman in the jean jacket.

"There are Lodians among the agitators, and among the cops. I can't tell who's who."

"I've got to warn Simmons," Sheila said. She'd been following the conversation closely. She stepped off a few feet and spoke into her radio.

Annabelle gave me a stern look. "This is why I told you to ditch her!" she hissed. "She's going to make things worse."

"Worth the risk," I said. "I needed someone to watch my back with the Sevrit on the loose. We haven't seen her yet, but that doesn't mean anything..." I glanced around nervously.

Annabelle seemed to consider that, then put her hand on mine. "What a mess. What do we do if it turns violent?"

"I'll lead you out. Stay close to me."

She nodded. "We go east, and if that's blocked, then south. My van's parked off Navasota."

I nodded, my heart thundering. "They could barricade the bridges. Or seal up the highway."

"It's a risk we have to take."

"Okay," I agreed. "Good enough for now."

I glanced around again. It was a good plan if we could get out of the middle of a panicking crowd. Even though we were outdoors, it felt entirely too claustrophobic. I studied the positions of each group of police at the intersection, looking for a weak point.

"What is it?" Annabelle asked.

"I didn't realize until today how many offworlders were on the police force. We know that tall protester is Tetrad, but that doesn't mean all the cops are on our side. They could be Federation plants, Tetrad thugs, or just unaffiliated offworlders living their life in peace on Earth."

"Now I know for sure that Tanamir will be here," Annabelle said, her camera tilting toward the heavens. The sky, now filled with more than a few vultures, grackles and, somewhere among them, Daacros.

During our conversation, I'd lost track of Yasmin's speech. The tall woman had gotten down from her bully pulpit. Now, with a raised fist and a blaring megaphone, she was leading the crowd down Congress Avenue toward the Capitol.

I felt the shift as the entire crowd began to walk forward.

Yasmin's Tetrad companion walked beside her. Trailing them, a knot of enthusiastic protesters about fifty strong pumped their fists and chanted.

"Here we go." Annabelle hopped down from her bench and began to walk.

I followed.

At that moment, my phone buzzed. My heart pounded when I saw Vinny's name on the screen.

"Vinny!" I answered happily. "I'm at a protest in Austin, what's up?"

"Gunn!" he shouted. The line crackled painfully in my ear. "You'll never... *krrktch* ...found... *krrrkkll...* bad shape." A long pause. "—wish you could see it... *krrktch*—"

"What? I can't understand you, the connection is awful! Vinny? Vinny!"

Given the number of people downtown, I was surprised my phone rang at all. This thought turned out to be a self-fulfilling prophecy. Our call dropped and when I tried to call him back, the new call failed to connect.

"Crap," I said as anxiety filled my stomach. I hoped he wasn't trying to tell me something important.

We'd walked half a block in that time, and I realized that the crowd had filled in behind me, making it impossible to move backward. We'd also lost track of Sheila, but Annabelle and I couldn't stop without difficulty—and I wasn't fool enough to try separating Annabelle from her hungry focus on her subject.

We were swept along in the current of people toward the Capitol building.

Frustrated, I shoved my phone back in my pocket.

"You okay?" Annabelle asked.

"That was Vinny," I said, "Sounded like he was trying to tell me something, but I couldn't hear him. Do you think it's important?"

"Maybe he just misses you," she said.

"Lucky rat," I muttered. "Wish I was on holiday with him right now."

Regardless, I hardly needed to be warned to be on my guard. I reached behind me and rested my hand on the hilt of my hidden Glock.

When we reached the intersection of Congress and Eleventh, the crowd stopped.

"I believe!" the healed survivor cried into her megaphone as she reached the gates of the state building. She turned her back on two rows of police officers who allowed her to stand before them unmolested and spoke to the gathered crowd.

"I was healed." She cast her arms wide and leaned her head back to gaze at the heavens. "I was given a second chance! Don't we all deserve a second chance at life?"

I recognized Officer Daniels by his height and bulk. He was standing near the center of the police line, and he shifted impatiently in place as she spoke.

"This could get ugly," I whispered to Annabelle.

She was too busy snapping photographs of the woman's dramatic posture to answer me. Yasmin was slowly walking backward toward the cops—more specifically, toward the riot shields they gripped tensely.

At that moment, a glass bottle came spinning overhead. It smashed into the pavement behind Yasmin, who ducked, and shards of glass splashed at the feet of Officer Daniels.

All commendations to Officer Daniels, who held his ground.

It was an officer to his right who reached out and *shoved* Yasmin with his shield.

She stumbled forward but didn't fall.

She straightened and glared back over her shoulder with a look that would make the body of Martin Luther King roll in his grave.

Annabelle dutifully snapped her camera's shutter.

Half a dozen more bottles soared overhead.

Some of these were on fire.

I poised behind Annabelle, ready to yank her back out of danger.

Molotov cocktails fell in a fiery rain, one bouncing off the helmet of Officer Daniels and crashing to the pavement. Another smashed near the wrought iron gate, and a couple even went onto state property, setting the grass on fire and casting eerie shadows on the cops.

Someone shouted my name. Glancing west down Eleventh Street, I caught sight of Sheila with a panting and disheveled Officer Simmons, who must have come at a dead run after parking the car, for his face was haggard and exhausted, and he was panting heavily.

"Gunn!" Sheila shouted, cupping her hands to her mouth. "Look out behind you!"

From the east, the direction from which the Molotov cocktails had been thrown, a cadre of men in black hoodies and jeans leaped over cop cars and wooden barricades. Officers ran toward them, leaving a vacuum at their posts, which was immediately swarmed by opportunistic protesters who climbed on the cruisers' hoods and kicked over the wooden barricades.

They came like a crashing wave, overwhelming the APD.

About half of the protesters had shimmering cloaking shields active on their faces. More Tetrad, I guessed, but I couldn't know for sure.

"No!" Sheila shouted. "Over there!"

Approaching from the south was a smaller unit that looked military. They came as if to support the main line in front of the Capitol, but I knew better.

I couldn't mistake the massive albino form of Kilos, nor Dyna's red topknots at the head of their group.

They were wearing SWAT uniforms. Others marched beside them wearing armor, head to toe, their faces inside the helmets glimmering to reveal cloaking shields on their faces. But the armor was no illusion.

Were those extra Peacekeepers the Federation had sent, or...? No. One of them looked familiar to me. The shape of his body and how his head shimmered. When the cloaking shield illusion fell momentarily, I caught sight of a second helmet mounted next to the first.

Connections began to click into place.

I glanced back at Yasmin. Her Lodian friend and his buddies were having a shoving match with the cops. The Molotov cocktails had drastically elevated the physicality of the situation, and while the fires had mostly sputtered out, protesters, the black-clad agitators, and riot police were tangled up in a knot that resembled an unruly mosh pit.

The chaos hadn't reached me and Annabelle yet, but it would soon.

The tall Lodian demonstrator who had marched with Yasmin shouted at his posse and pointed at the Peacekeeper's "SWAT" unit.

I couldn't make out what he shouted, but I could tell how he felt about this group. *Attack them!* He must have been saying.

His fifty men looked between the riot cops at the Capitol gates, the black-clad rioters coming from the east, and the SWAT team closing in on them like a hammer to an anvil.

They ran south, toward the Peacekeeper unit.

Innocent bystanders were shoved down or trampled.

Truncheons and shields were gainfully employed, sounding hollowly off of bodies as they struck.

Women screamed. Men shouted in pain.

The Peacekeepers picked up their pace. A creepy, crawling sensation passed over me, like a passing siren made of goosebumps, as Dyna used her telekinetic powers to clear a cone-shaped path through the crowd.

CHAPTER FOURTEEN

KILOS and the others with him held their own shields edge to edge and pressed forward like a walking fortress.

They danced in unison, carving a path faster than anyone without genetic enhancements could possibly manage. It was frightening to see military precision like that after the chaos of the protesters and riot cops.

Protesters and opportunists melted away from them, leaving only the Tetrad group. The two units clashed not twenty feet from where we were standing.

I hauled Annabelle bodily backward as she clung to her camera.

A blue spirit-creature winged out of the Peacekeeper group. It rose into the sky to join several other Daacro circling there, cementing my understanding of how the offworld alliances had shaken out.

"*That's* how the Peacekeepers have been keeping up with Tanamir," I said, leaning close to Annabelle's ear. "They combined forces with the Gatekeeper!"

Which means Dyna and Kilos knew everything I knew.

Gunn, said a voice directly into my mind. *There has been a temporal disturbance in the area.*

Dyna's voice sounded less whistle-chimey in my head, but it was still unmistakably hers.

Where? I asked internally.

Close, she said.

"We should go," I said to Annabelle.

"Not yet! Let me get on your shoulders again."

She vaulted up before I could object, wrapping her legs around my neck. Her camera shutter snapped many times as she swung back and forth between different focal points among the crowd—from the battle, to Yasmin, to the riot cops.

I bit the inside of my cheek as I studied the crowd, eyes wide open and searching for danger.

The multi-headed henchdogs grappled hand to hand with Tetrad dissidents and human protesters, all mixed up together. The Gatekeeper's furry muscle tossed each human protester who tried to stand their ground a dozen feet into the crowd. One crashed into a group of demonstrators near us, bowling them over and tangling up my feet. I almost tipped over myself, but Annabelle braced her arms on the pole of a street sign and we managed to stay upright.

The alien strength of these highly physical, genetically augmented beings appeared to be no match for your average human. However, when a henchdog engaged a wiry-looking Lodian, the Tetrad agent raised a fist crackling with electricity and drove his knuckles into one of the henchdog's ugly snouts. A pulse of force slammed it flat onto its back.

The Tetrad specialist advanced, sliding through two more blows from the Peacekeeper allies. He took two bounds, gathering speed, and sent a spinning kick at a pair of Lodians protecting the Peacekeeper's flank.

The Lodian specialist sliced through and sank his super-powered fist into the exposed ribs of Kilos while the feline hybrid was turned away. A shockwave sent the Peacekeeper flying, the blow reverberating through my body like a concert speaker. Kilos twisted in the air and somehow managed to land on his feet, plowing a furrow through the crowd.

His leonine form rippled with muscle beneath a thin layer of white fur as he bounded back into the melee.

People around us began to panic then, and several tried to flee. Protesters ran into each other, over each other, treading innocent bystanders underfoot.

I lost track of the Peacekeeper showdown fight as I wobbled away with Annabelle still clinging to my neck, trying to lead her out of danger. I ran into a mother and a young boy who got caught in the fray and tried to usher them away. She whacked me in the gut with her purse.

"Ow! Really? I was just—"

She hit me again. So I gave up and left them to their own devices.

Annabelle's camera never stopped clicking and clacking. She remained focused, intense, her thighs tight on my traps.

I gritted my teeth and waded toward the shelter of a building at the corner. We were jostled from every side. I used my cyborg hand to turn a grunting hardcore kid's nose into a fountain, then shoved a path around the blood.

We finally reached the sidewalk. I turned back to check on the conflict.

Despite the Peacekeepers' supernatural ability to maneuver, they were outnumbered ten to one. They were clearly trying to throw the protesters out of their way so they could fully engage the Tetrad fighters, who were armed with concealed melee weapons, but it was causing the people to turn against them.

Of course, I reasoned, *none of the human protesters know that.* Where I saw weaponized Tetrad insurgents antagonizing a force of Peacekeepers, all anyone else saw—and all the cameras would see—were what appeared to be soldiers or cops trading body blows with the black-clad "protesters."

At least until Annabelle released her story and set the record straight.

How many other riots had started with such misunderstandings?

Slowly, although they held valiantly, the Peacekeeper force became surrounded and overwhelmed by the superior numbers of the Tetrad insurgents, plus the rowdy protesters —or opportunists—who had jumped into the fray.

Dyna called a retreat. She moved her group south down Congress Avenue.

The APD, meanwhile, had been running down and arresting any rioters caught throwing Molotov cocktails. Young men and women were being stuffed randomly into nearby cruisers, dozens of which had been parked to make street barricades.

The APD had managed to hold the Capitol gates and was now attempting to corral the crowd west down Eleventh Street.

The crowd didn't want to go.

They rallied and pushed back against a line of shields, pushing the police officers—and us—back toward the T-shaped intersection.

I had a moment to admire the restraint of the police officers. Their chief must have had them on a tight leash after the videos of police violence from last night.

"Time to go," I said.

"Not yet!" Annabelle insisted.

I was about to take action on our exit plan—even if I had to run with Annabelle on my shoulders, which had begun to ache—when Yasmin shouted into her megaphone, drawing the crowd's attention.

"LOOK!!" she said, pointing at the sky.

I glanced up to see a tiny blue form and several Daacro buzzing around the side of a shimmering, curved shape that blended into the dark sky above.

Slowly, the cloaking shield disguising Tanamir's ship faded, revealing the battered, dull silver hull of a flying saucer underneath.

The crowd hushed, stilled.

Shock sent a wave of silence out faster than a pandemic.

Then, as if with one voice, it erupted into a confused roar.

Have you ever seen one of those flash mob videos?

What happened next was exactly like that. One moment, it was a confused melee of thousands of panicking people running every which way.

The very next moment, a hundred or more black-clad Tetrad agents surged to a single point, then spread outward, forming a rapidly enlarging circle in the center of Congress Avenue at Eleventh.

They stood shoulder to shoulder, facing outward in less than a minute.

Left to their own devices by the choreographed Tetrad unit, Dyna and Kilos shouted, and the Peacekeeper force began to move up Congress Avenue again.

On the north side, the riot cops, watching from the Capitol gate, glared down through their helmet visors. They tightened their hands on their shields and truncheons.

Tanamir's ship descended into the circular opening, blowing air down like a helicopter, but without the blades and only a fraction of the noise.

"What do we do?" I asked Annabelle.

"Stay still!" she shouted.

The crowd craned their heads upward in unison. Some clutched their friends while others stared slack-jawed at the remarkable sight.

Annabelle's camera shutter snicked. I adjusted her weight on my shoulders, trying to muscle through the pain. She wasn't that big, but my legs were shaking like noodles.

As it descended, it became clear just how much damage the ship's hull had taken. It was dirty, scratched and dented. Carbon marks had collected on one side, presumably from the gunfire and explosives the ship had shrugged off in the videos I'd seen.

Yet Zavis had engineered these ships solidly, back when he'd been under Tanamir's thumb. It held together.

Thunder rumbled from the sky above. When it was twenty feet off the ground, a bolt of lightning crackled down and struck the UFO. The crowd shouted in fright and backed up further from the cordon of Lodians, but the lightning fizzled harmlessly out.

"Show off," I muttered.

Rain began to fall from the sky in a soft trickle.

"Sorry, hun," I said, "but I need a break." I bent my knees and set Annabelle down on the sidewalk, reaching back to grip the handle of the Glock beneath my shirt tail.

Annabelle put her hand on top of mine. "Easy."

"What if—"

"Don't do anything stupid," Annabelle said. "We're outnumbered."

She nodded at the three parties—the wary APD force, the black-clad Tetrad force of more than a hundred, and the squad of a dozen Peacekeepers and their allies.

"Be ready to run," I said.

She nodded and pushed buttons on her camera, adjusting settings.

The flying saucer descended into the glow of the streetlights. It set down on the pavement with barely a sound. The crowd had calmed somewhat as it came down. They pressed against the Lodians like the Rolling Stones were about to come on stage.

Though the top of the ship sat about fifteen feet above ground level, and was easily visible over the heads of the crowd, there were so many people pushing in to get a better view that we couldn't get too close.

The same was not true for Yasmin. The crowd parted, and Yasmin walked up to the ship like a rug had been rolled out for her.

A set of hovering platforms descended from the ship like a staircase at the precise moment that Yasmin arrived.

I blinked, and another woman in long-sleeved, form-fitting activewear in grey and red was suddenly standing next to Yasmin.

"That's the Sevrit in her disguise!" I said. "Where did she come from?"

Annabelle climbed back up on my shoulders and aimed with her camera. A moment later, she drew it down to study the screen. "She's got the timepiece."

My stomach fell. Annabelle had been right. It was

foolish to think I'd find some opportunity to grab it from Jaiyana. Even if I could press through the crowd, as long as it was in her possession, I would never be able to just walk up and take it.

Annabelle's camera snapped rapidly.

"Jaiyana's holding that motorcycle helmet by the jaw," Annabelle said, studying the camera's preview screen. "There's a mechanism in the helmet's forehead that seems to have been pried open."

"Let me see."

Annabelle climbed back down and handed the camera to me. I swiped through the photos. A tangle of wires was clearly visible, stuffed into where the helmet's inner padding ought to be.

What had she done to the timepiece? It was obviously still working, as she'd just used it to appear here.

But she was up to something.

Yasmin used the platform steps to get on top of the ship, frowning as Jaiyana followed her but not stopping. It was almost like the saucer doubled as a stage, the kind you'd see in the center of a stadium concert, and I knew with conviction that Tanamir had been planning this from the beginning.

All those appearances had been foreplay.

This was the main event.

Yasmin gazed over the crowd from the saucer's roof as if in a daze. Then a hatch hissed open on the top of the flying ship, and she turned toward it.

I tried to push my way into the crowd to get closer, but it was impossible to get far without hurting someone or causing a ruckus. The crowd was incredibly thick, and no one made way for me like they had for Yasmin.

So Annabelle and I watched from a distance as a dapper Lodian gentleman wearing a tailored suit of black and scarlet rose from the hatch.

Tanamir wore no cloaking shield. No attempt was made to conceal his appearance.

He was just an offworlder baring his Lodian face and form for all of Earth to see.

I wasn't sure of his age, but to me he'd always appeared to be in his declining years, with gently wrinkled skin and deep smile lines at his eyes. That didn't mean he was weak—he was built lean but solid, and moved gracefully, like an athlete...

Or a soldier.

Tanamir bowed to Yasmin, then smiled and waved to the crowd as he walked around the saucer. A dark cape fluttered at his back, hanging by round medallions from his shoulder ridges, which swelled with his breathing—and perhaps also his excitement.

The suit was open at the shoulders, showing his skin where slits, like gills, fluttered open in the area where a human being's clavicles would be.

The last thing that made him stand out—and it was also visible—was the burn scar on his neck.

A whispered susurration spread over the crowd at the sight of him. Phones lifted and snapped photos or recorded videos. Dozens of cell phones, lifted by dozens of protesters, live-streamed Tanamir's image to the world.

The Tetrad leader stopped when he reached Jaiyana, who had stopped at the edge. He gave her a half-cocked smile, as if surprised to see her, then finished his round.

Now, all of Earth knew what a Lodian looked like, even if they didn't know what these offworlders were called.

Dyna, I knew, wouldn't stand for it.

The Peacekeeper force, to the south, finally made a run at Tanamir's saucer. Dyna used her abilities to shove open a space in the crowd. People cried out as they were tossed aside.

But it seemed that even she was hampered by the density of people gathered here. She wasn't able to move far. The crowd grew agitated and booed as it turned against her.

"Stop fighting!" Yasmin cried into her megaphone. "This is a peaceful protest!"

Kilos called a halt. He turned to his leader.

Dyna nodded, pacing back and forth like a caged animal.

She kept looking up at the sky, as if nervous there were more saucers coming. I looked up too, but didn't see anything.

Tanamir bowed generously to Yasmin, and then took her hand and kissed it. She stared at him with awe and more than a little trepidation before throwing her arms out and engulfing him in a big hug.

The old Lodian general laughed and hugged her back.

She held him out at arm's length, like he was a long-lost cousin.

"Welcome," Yasmin said. Although I couldn't hear her words, I was able to understand some of what she said by reading her lips. "Please, tell me, who *are* you?"

Tanamir took the megaphone from her and spoke into it.

"My name is Tanamir Voss and I come to bring you news of other worlds... You are not alone!"

Astonished whispers swept through the crowd. Cheers rose from a few sections, but it was, admittedly, not the majority.

One inebriated man's cry rose up near us. "I knew it, man!" he shouted. "No way!"

Dyna jumped from her small group, leaping through the crowd in bounds of twenty or thirty yards.

Kilos followed.

That looks like a useful skill, I thought—then squashed the idea. I didn't want to be like them. I'd had my Peacekeeper mods locked down for a reason.

Still, I couldn't help but be envious. How was I supposed to get up there to grab that timepiece before Tanamir got it? I had to rely on Dyna and Kilos for that.

Jaiyana remained standing off to one side, her disguise still active. Everyone ignored her for the moment.

"These enforcers don't want you to know the truth!" Tanamir said, pointing at Dyna's leaping form. "They want to erase your cameras, wipe your memories, and scrub my image from the public consciousness."

Indeed, as he said it, Dyna paused to flash-fry the memories from a group of people, leaving confusion in her wake as they blinked around at their friends, asking what was going on.

If there were no camera evidence, and I were an investigative reporter, I'm sure I would have a hell of a time piecing these events together from eyewitness accounts.

But Dyna was just one Peacekeeper. She couldn't do it all.

That's why she'd been trying, all this time, to recruit me.

Too little, too late.

"Their job is to maintain the status quo—to uphold your ignorance! Is that what you want?"

Shouts of "No!" came in return.

"Is that respecting your freedom?" Tanamir asked, "Or restricting it?"

This question needed no answer. It was as if he had heard the conversation that Annabelle and I had the other day. We exchanged a look, then turned back to watch.

"We are here to be your allies," Tanamir said. "Your friends. Look!"

The Lodians holding the cordon around his saucer flickered as they all dropped their cloaking shields at once, revealing the gray faces of Lodians, interspersed with a few orange Torlik, brown-furred Pangozil, and other beings I didn't recognize. Only a few hadn't dropped their disguises—they might have been riding in robots like Lulamina, but I thought I saw one or two human mercenaries among them.

The sight chilled me. He had already recruited other humans to his cause.

Dyna came leaping up again. In two more bounds, she floated onto the saucer's roof, landing lightly. She stood facing Tanamir, and her cybernetic nodes began to flash.

"Look away!" I said to Annabelle, turning her face and my own to the side. I knew that if we got hit with Dyna's light show, she would wipe this memory from our minds with surgical precision.

Annabelle needed no warning. She squeezed her eyes shut, dropped her camera, and clamped her hands over her ears.

Already, people closer to her in the crowd had begun to shout in surprise, as if wondering how they got here.

Astonished gasps followed.

I reopened my eyes to see that Jaiyana had seemed to teleport across the saucer. One minute she was by the staircase, the next she slammed the motorcycle helmet into

Dyna's skull. The impact crushed one of the Peacekeeper's cybernetic nodes, extinguishing its light and the light of several adjacent bulbs.

Dyna staggered back, then thrust out her hand, sending a wall of force at the Sevrit. Jaiyana's form *blinked.* The telekinetic attack passed harmlessly through her and washed over Tanamir, whose cape fluttered as he braced against it.

The impact swept over Yasmin, too, who wasn't ready for such violence. It sent her flying off the edge of the ship and into the crowd.

Tanamir leaped down after her, leaving the Sevrit and Dyna to engage in hand-to-hand combat across the otherwise empty saucer. The two moved faster than most eyes could follow, throwing elbows, knees, and palm strikes at each other.

Kilos joined her, and the Peacekeepers battled the Sevrit.

Jaiyana held them. *Easily.* She moved with fractured grace and speed. Even without the timepiece, she was a formidable fighter. With it, she was unstoppable. She maneuvered Kilos and Dyna close to each other, then used the timepiece to blink out of the path of Kilos's fist. He struck Dyna in the jaw. Meanwhile, the Sevrit drove her knee into his lower back, then kicked him off the saucer.

Two more blows sent a reeling Dyna flying. She hit the pavement with a heavy smack. The crowd dog-piled on top of her, throwing kicks and punches.

Kilos had fallen more gracefully, but he had to fight off dozens of pairs of hands from himself, and then pull Dyna loose. He gathered her up and jumped away with one of his great bounding leaps. When he landed, he and Dyna both disappeared beneath a cloaking shield.

I swallowed. If they couldn't beat her, I didn't have a chance against Jaiyana.

"Our freedom!" Yasmin shouted into her megaphone as she came back up onto the saucer with Tanamir. "Our choice!"

The crowd surged to see her. They picked up her chant. "Our freedom! Our choice!"

The noise grew rapidly in volume, echoing off the skyscrapers and filling the air with a reverberating sound that rumbled in my chest.

"Our freedom! Our choice!"

One by one, more offworlders standing in the crowd dropped their disguises.

Even a few of the cops. Which caused even *more* confusion.

Detective Simmons and Detective Gonzalez appeared at the corner of Tenth Street at the head of a group of riot cops. Gonzalez pointed, shouting orders, and waded into the crowd toward the saucer.

"Sheila, no!" I said. But she couldn't hear me. "Dammit. Didn't they see that fight? What does Gonzalez think she's going to do?"

A sudden nausea gripped my stomach as I shoved my way into the crowd.

"Get out of my way!" I snarled.

Annabelle held onto my belt with one hand. I pulled her along while she snapped one-handed photographs of the crowd around us.

Sheila and her riot cops were bogged down at the line of Tetrad insurgents ringing Tanamir's ship. When I arrived at the barricade, she was shouting into the face of a large

Lodian who had a flat nose and a chin that looked like it could take a few punches.

Atop the saucer, Jaiyana had stopped before Tanamir and turned her own cloaking shield off, revealing her true form.

I finally got a good look at her. The Sevrit had a long face like a kangaroo. It was covered with a light green fur that was more velvety than Vinny's, almost like a panther or a teal jaguar.

Jaiyana saluted Tanamir with a fist to her chest, then bowed deeply.

When she rose, she ripped the tangle of wires from the motorcycle helmet and in a few movements—fractured by the timepiece so that I couldn't see exactly what her hands were doing—she pulled the wires into a braided cord with a thick, intricately carved medallion connecting the ends of the braid.

She hung the cord around Tanamir's neck.

His lips formed the words, "What an unexpected surprise."

Tanamir turned to look right at me. He lifted the megaphone to his mouth.

"Remember, I came to greet you as a friend. I—and my people—walked among you. In the future, your enemies will come from the sky. You will know them because they will refuse to come down. They will greet you only with threats. They will steal your freedom in the name of compliance. Remember your rights—and beware the Federation of Lodi."

Air began to blow around the base of the ship. The saucer rose into the air, reactivating its cloaking shield.

Along with him, the disguises of dozens of offworlders went back up.

I thought I saw another ship chasing the saucer into the night, but that could have been a trick of the light. I could see through the personal cloaking shields, but the ships were more difficult.

Besides, it was full dark, and the streetlights made it hard to see far. Helicopter blades thrummed overhead as the line of Tetrad insurgents guarding the saucer dissolved and melted into the crowd, their illusory disguises and black garments blending into the night.

They vanished as fast as they'd appeared.

Along with any hope of keeping the timepiece out of Tanamir's hands.

CHAPTER FIFTEEN

NEWS OF TANAMIR'S appearance in Austin, his public pronouncements of extraterrestrial life, and his predictions of threats descending from the sky reverberated across the globe.

Yasmin returned the next morning, starry-eyed from her tour with Tanamir. She blabbed on any news channel that would have her about this benevolent alien leader and his vision for peaceful coexistence.

Barf.

Her words rang tinny and hollow to me. Liberal and conservative news channels, on the other hand, were having a field day with it.

I kept tabs on the news as I traveled around town, checking in on my offworld and local contacts. Yasmin transformed into a celebrity, dragging Marsha Marshall with her into the spotlight. This notoriety made Annabelle deeply uncomfortable, even as the media invitations piled up in her inbox.

The UFO demonstrations weren't as big or rowdy on the

second night, but protests against police brutality continued to rage in Austin. Like a virus, public demonstrations spread to other major cities across the country.

Offworlders made themselves even scarcer than usual. As more people flocked to Austin to see Tanamir and our offworlder residents, traffic grew congested. I borrowed an old motorcycle Alek kept in his shed so I could move around town faster while spending less on fuel.

Hotels that had already booked up during the protests turned people away. Even the crummy motel where the Sevrit had murdered Felix was full. Tent cities poured out from under the freeways and overflowed into sidewalks and green spaces. The cops were too busy to do anything about them.

I was careful with my money. But after paying rent and filling up the motorcycle a couple of times, I found myself counting the weeks until my checking account bottomed out. Not only had gas prices doubled overnight, but ammunition prices skyrocketed, too.

Even the best gun stores in town were running out of everything but the most common rounds.

I came to the reluctant realization that maybe the Gatekeeper had been right about my needing the extra cash.

I brought my anxieties to a check-in meeting with Felix, Annabelle and Lulamina in The Poached Pig.

"Oh, what have I done?" the Torlik moaned, gripping his head with four hands in the booth across from me. He kept his cloaking shield active, but each time he used his bottom set of hands, the disguise flickered in my vision. Watching him gave me a headache, like watching one of those anime shows with the flashing lights.

"This is the worst thing that could have happened. And

the worst part is that I know better! I'm such an idiot. What was I thinking, bringing it here?"

"I'm sorry," I told Felix. "I've tried everything I can think of. I talked to Rashiki's people, but they hadn't heard of any Sevrit and wouldn't let me below the barn level."

His head jerked up, and he examined me like a faulty engine. "Why not?"

"... because of what happened with the Jel'ka last time."

Felix looked sideways at Lulamina.

"Story for another time, dear," she said, giving his shoulder a soft pat.

My face heated. I hurried on. "I went out to the junkyard to talk to Gwurk, but he would only talk to me through the door."

"That's not unusual," Lulamina said.

"Yeah, I know, he's always been paranoid. I've talked to a few of my other contacts as well. Tanamir's still lurking about, and my best guess is the Sevrit—and your timepiece—are in hiding with him." It twisted my gut to say the next part, but I had my professional pride to uphold. "I'll give your deposit back as soon as I have a chance to get to the bank and withdraw the cash."

"What? Don't tell me you're giving up. This is your world! Surely, you can locate Tanamir and devise a way to recover the timepiece. The damage he could do if we don't is... frightening to consider."

"Like what? Alter the timeline?"

"No, no, nothing like that," Felix said. He looked up. "More like... imagine if you had a redo button for everything that went wrong with your life. Don't like how a conversation went? Redo! Took a punch in the face? Redo!"

"He can really travel back and get unpunched?"

"Sort of. He still feels the hit and the pain. But, if he rewinds time, the bruise will vanish. He'll then be able to dodge the attack since he knows it's coming."

"Yeah. The Sevrit pulled that one on me a few times before I caught on."

Remembering made me bitter. What person, leaving a trail of mistakes like footprints in the sand, wouldn't want to have control of such a device?

But how was I supposed to outsmart a guy like him, with a device like *that*?

I glanced at Annabelle, who leaned her shoulder against me as she scrolled through her news feeds. I hooked an arm around her shoulder and squeezed. She patted my leg without looking up.

"So, what then? I ask nicely and expect Tanamir to hand over the timepiece? He's not exactly the kind of guy who can be charmed or coerced into complying with that kind of request."

Felix's face darkened. "We have to find a way! This may be just another job for you, but for the Pangozil, it's existential."

I pulled back. This was the first time Felix had shown me that he had a spine.

The Torlik must have seen something in my face he didn't like, for he fell back into despair, gripping his head in all four hands. "Oh, what am I saying? Of course you can't do anything about it. It's too late. We're doomed."

What would Vinny want me to do? I thought of my friend—who I hadn't been able to reach, despite several attempts—and nodded slowly as my conviction hardened.

I didn't know *how* I was going to retrieve the timepiece. But I couldn't give up yet. Not if it would help Vinny's people save their world—or if it was my only chance to get Tanamir *off* of mine.

Besides, wasn't helping people why I had expanded beyond bounty hunting to other types of cases? Sure, it felt good to haul a scumbag off the street. But my favorite jobs were the ones where I got the privilege of helping someone find something they'd lost, like a treasured family heirloom or a long lost relative.

Vinny was doing a similar thing. He went looking for his people to reconnect with them, to support them. I thought I knew what he'd want me to do in this situation. The same thing he'd done when it came down to it—he'd want me to step in and help.

"Pull yourself together," I told Felix. "We're not giving up so easily. There's got to be a way to get the timepiece back. Does the device have any loopholes or weaknesses we can exploit?"

"Every piece of technology has constraints." He rubbed water out of his oversized eye, a very gooey process. "Technically, this is a limited-use device," Felix said. "It allows the user to fast-forward or reverse time within a local radius."

"How?"

"The user can shape and direct the dilation to selectively affect objects or people in the vicinity."

I remembered how Jaiyana had held me underwater while standing on solid ground beneath me. "And what's its range?"

"It has a temporal radius of about twenty meters."

"You engineers and your standard units," I muttered. I closed my eyes, doing the mental math—twenty meters was about... sixty-five feet. "We could set a trap for him. We'll need to do our fighting at a distance, long range. Maybe use nets?"

"That wascally wabbit," Annabelle snarked. "You're going to need a bigger net, Elmer Fudd."

"Hush, you." I smirked at her. "That still means we have to track him down first. He's not a normal skip. I can't just interview his neighbors or track his credit card purchases."

"What about the Peacekeepers?" Lulamina asked. "They were able to track the location of temporal disturbances before, weren't they?"

"Yes," I said, "but I haven't been able to get ahold of Dyna since the protests."

The whole table fell into silent thought.

"What do you think Tanamir still needs?" asked Annabelle. "What's he missing?"

"He's obviously trying to win Earth's loyalty with this honorable hero routine. Although who knows," I said. "Maybe he actually believes it."

"Scary. The most dangerous villains are misunderstood heroes," Annabelle said. "Do *you* believe him?"

"I don't believe he gives a rip about peace on Earth, but I don't doubt that what he's really trying to do is win us over to his side. He wants us to be against the Federation." I thought about that scar on his neck and wondered how he got it.

"That tells me about his intentions, but not his strategy," said Annabelle.

"How does debating it help us catch him, though?" I asked.

"You're both missing my point," Lulamina said. "What if we don't hunt him down? What if, instead, we draw him out?"

I opened my mouth, then shut it. The pipsqueak had a point. “How?”

“Hmm. I’m not sure yet.” Lulamina—still riding in her robot with rainbow hair—glanced behind her at the TV behind Barry’s bar.

There didn’t used to be a screen in the Pig. Barry had installed one after the light phenomenon at Lake Travis because customers kept asking him to turn on the news. I didn’t love what the television did to the ambience, even as I acknowledged its usefulness.

On the screen, CNN was currently covering a stabbing in Washington, DC. The anchor warned about the graphic nature of the clip and then cut to a pudgy Lodian hurling a Coke bottle at two men in hats and white tank tops. They rushed him with switchblades at the far end of a subway platform. A short scuffle ensued. The Lodian was left bleeding on the floor as the two thugs hurried up the stairs.

Most of the witnesses looked on in horror, and then ran. Only one brave young man went to help the Lodian.

Random acts of violence against offworlders were being reported across the country, the anchor said as the footage ended. “Unfortunately, many victims of these crimes aren’t even aliens, but human beings. They are the victims of two tragedies: random violence and mistaken identity.”

Another minute of heavy silence passed as we all watched the news. The anchor shifted to another pattern journalists had identified. Landlords were evicting offworlders from their rental homes all over Texas. Their offense? Being offworlders and daring to show their true faces.

One disturbing story came from Denton, where a home-owners association had forced a family out of their home.

Angry neighbors had camped in their yard, shining spotlights into their bedroom windows until the offworlders chose to leave rather than be harrassed.

It made me sick. Sick, and deeply furious.

"Ugh, it's so shameful," Annabelle said, turning her phone's screen up on the table. It showed an anonymous editorial that was an elaborate argument for why offworlders didn't have the same fundamental rights as human beings.

Some folk had already made up their minds on the issue. Tanamir wasn't the "hero of Mariupol" to everyone. Despite his publicity stunts, he had detractors.

Yasmin, the vocal protester, may have been ready for peaceful coexistence. But not everyone was as optimistic as her. Humanity would be slow to accept this new reality.

"Tanamir's playing us like puppets," I said. "If enough people see him as a hero, he can direct that anger wherever he wants."

"What about your police friends?" asked Felix. "They still have my case open with the Sevrit as their chief suspect, don't they?"

I blew out my cheeks. "Since they downgraded the case from murder, it hasn't been their top priority. I tried reaching out, but they're giving me the cold shoulder right now. That's why I've been driving around doing my own investigations."

I glanced at Annabelle for her thoughts. She was buried in her email again. She responded without looking up.

"The police force is struggling to hold themselves together," she said. "They haven't said so publicly, but I have a source on the inside who tells me that between all the overtime they've been pulling on protest security, and an internal investigation to discover who among them is an offworlder in disguise... they're not operating in peak condition."

I stared at her. "You didn't tell me you had a source in the APD."

"Oh, sweetheart." Her smile was gentle yet full of mirth. "There's a lot I don't tell you."

"We're doomed." Felix closed his oversized eye and put his forehead on the wooden table. He added a few extra phrases in his own language that made Lulamina wince and pat his back in sympathy. "I'm going to be sick."

"Look," Lulamina said, pointing at the television. "They're playing your clip again."

A blush rose in Annabelle's cheeks.

Barry had the volume muted, but I read the captions. "They're people like you and me," Annabelle said. "I've known about offworlders for over a year. I've spoken to them, shared meals with them, visited their homes. The vast majority simply wish to live their lives in peace."

"Why didn't you report anything before now?" the anchor asked her.

"I did. No one believed me."

"You could have used your source's names."

"If my sources wish to remain anonymous, I respect that."

That was only half the truth. I could feel Annabelle squirming in her seat through the vinyl of the booth bench we shared.

We watched in thoughtful silence for a couple more minutes. The next segment that came on said that the APD investigation into the riot was still underway. They showed a couple clips of Dyna and Kilos tossing protesters into the crowd. Then, they showed one of Tanamir's caped form atop the saucer as he caught Yasmin, saving her from injury.

My phone buzzed in my pocket. When I saw the caller ID, my heart pounded. "It's Vinny!" I said, sliding out of the booth and walking a few feet away. As I did, a couple of young punks pushed through the front door. They bellied up to the bar, perhaps to get a jump on the night's festivities.

I answered the call. "Hey man! What's going on?"

Garbled static responded.

"Vinny, can you hear me?"

"Gunn! There you are." His voice was coming through clearly now, if a little distant. "Finally. I had to come all the way into town to get service!"

"Where are you?"

"Tiny little mountain town," Vinny said, his voice full of energy. "I found them, Gunn. I found my people! It's way worse than I thought, though. Pango is in a bad state. The only consolation is that we all saw this comin' and they managed to get a lot of our people out in time."

He sounded happier than I'd heard him in a long while, despite the bad news. "What do you mean?"

"The Federation and the Tetrad been fightin' over my homeworld since before my parents were born. I don't really take stock in prophecies, per se, but there are more than a few infamous Pangozil who been sayin' this was foretold. It's a conflict older than time."

"Freedom versus slavery? Federation versus the Tetrad?"

"More like... do we migrate to another world before ours blows its atmosphere into the vacuum? Or do we stay put and go down with the ship?"

"That sounds pretty negative whichever way you look at it."

"Hullo! Earth to Gunn! It's a prophecy. When are prophecies not negative?"

I laughed. "It's good to hear your voice, man! It's been bad here, too. Have you seen the news?"

"Not much. Don't really have service in the place I'm stayin'. It's a cave system that reminds me of the warrens I grew up in. I wish you could see it! They even brought ever-burners to keep the place warm. Cold on the surface of Pango is one thing I do *not* miss, but the warrens were always cozy. Crowded, but certainly cozy." He paused. "Come to think of it, you'd probably hate it."

"The news is ugly, man. Offworlders are out of the closet. Hate crimes are way up. I'm glad to hear you're safe."

"I've heard a few of the stories. We may like hiding out in caves, but when Pangozil are together, they talk. A few of the people here are cousins of local residents."

"Lot of cousins among your people?"

"We have big families."

"I don't think I've ever asked. How many cousins do you actually have?"

"Seventeen hundred and change, by my last count. We were a small clan. Anyway, I know what you mean. The Elders are in council tryin'a decide what to do next."

"What do you mean, the Elders?"

"It's what we call our government leaders. They relocated a small community to Earth to establish roots. But as you can imagine, seeing the Tetrad here has got 'em spooked. They don't want to endure a repeat performance of what happened on Pango, or bring the rest of their people from exile unless it's sustainable to stay long-term. And some of these Elders... they remember Tanamir."

"It sounds like they see the writing on the wall," I said.

Vinny's voice fell to a somber whisper. "If they go, I have to go with them, Gunn. Amberen keeps saying that we have to stick together. That Pangozil are best in community, and I gotta say, I haven't felt so connected in years."

I felt a sudden heartburn. It reminded me of when I was a kid and my best friend moved to another state. We'd promised to stay in touch, but life got in the way.

"I understand if that's what you decide," I said, surprised at how my voice shook when those words came out. I cleared my throat. "Wait... did you say Amberen? As in Amberen Gevereaux?"

"... how do *you* know that name?"

"Hold that thought."

I turned around to find the punks harassing my friends.

"Come on, let me see it!" said one guy with greasy black hair. He shoved Lulamina's shoulder. "I'll bet you're cute beneath the costume."

The other had leaned down so he was nose to nose with Felix. The Torlik had his lower fists balled up.

"These holograms are really incredible. But I saw you messing with it. Come on, let me see!"

"Mind your own business!" Annabelle said, standing. She placed herself between my clients and the black-clad punks with their spiky, studded jewelry.

"Easy, friend," I said. "We don't want any trouble."

I put my cyborg hand on a shoulder and squeezed.

"Ow!" he said, his knees buckling beneath him. "Okay! Geez! Take it easy, asshole."

"Hey," the other punk said, reaching into a cargo pocket and gripping a weapon he had hidden in there. "You don't own this place."

They took a few steps back toward the door. I pushed my

shirt up, resting my left hand on my Glock. I'd moved it from my lower back to a more accessible, obvious holster since the protests.

"Whoa, whoa! No disrespect, man. We were just excited to see some aliens!"

"Find somewhere else to drink."

"Is this your bar or mine?" Barry said as he stepped out of the kitchen holding a baseball bat against his shoulder.

"Sorry, Barry."

He nodded at me. "Find somewhere else to drink. I have the right to refuse service to any gutterpunks who forget their manners."

They looked between me, Barry, and the other customers at the bar. Everyone was nursing their beers and watching nervously. Several of them had come to their feet. They weren't small guys.

"Man, forget this," the one with his hand in his pocket said.

The two hurried back outside.

"Take it easy, Gunn," Barry said to me after they had departed.

I raised my hands. "My bad."

I sat back down and put my phone on the table so my shaking hands didn't drop or accidentally demolish it. Weird how a cyborg hand could still tremble when my system flooded with adrenaline.

I waited until everyone had gone back to their drinks before switching the phone to speaker mode.

"Vinny, are you still with us?"

"Yeah. What was that all about?"

"Some punk kids trying to start trouble," Annabelle said.

"Andy puffed up his chest and scared 'em off. How are you, Vinny?"

"Annabelle, doll! What a treat it is to hear your voice."

She smiled. A genuine grin, not the embarrassed blush this time. "Yours, too."

"Vinny," I said, "I want you to meet Felix. He's the Torlik engineer Lula introduced me to."

"Hiya," Vinny said.

"Can I tell him what you just told me?"

"Long as you don't go blabbing around town about it, I guess. Why?"

"Vinny said he knows Amberen."

"Oh, nooooo," Felix cried. He slammed his head on the table, smothering a wail with his bottom hands.

The remaining customers glanced worriedly at us, then filed out of the bar, leaving us alone. Barry came back out and glared at me. I gritted my teeth and grimaced, mouthing, "Sorry."

I resolved to leave him a big tip, even though I couldn't afford it.

I had bigger problems at the moment. "I thought you'd be excited to hear about Amberen! Weren't you trying to find him, Felix?"

"Yes, when we had the timepiece! I'll bet he's halfway off this planet now that the Tetrad are loose."

"Heh, you're more right than you realize, Felix," Vinny said as he caught the thread. "But what do you want to meet Amberen for, anyway? Apart from the obvious."

"Because," Felix said, "I have—or I *had*—an idea for how to make the world of the Pangozil whole again."

A stunned silence was all we received from Vinny's end of the line.

"Vinny, did we lose you?" I asked.

"I'm still here," said Vinny. "Are you bein' serious? Actually *reverse* the singularity? I'm not losing my hearing, am I?"

"Well, it's only a theory," said Felix, "but I—" He glanced around the bar. Even though no one else was there, he was still acting cagey. "Ahem. I can't talk any more about it here, but the science works. I'd like to speak to Gevereaux about the details. From what I understand, he saw the singularity form."

"That's what I heard, too," Vinny said, somewhat surprised that Felix knew that.

"So can you arrange a meeting?" I asked.

"Well, I wouldn't normally interrupt a session of the senior council... but this qualifies as urgent. Yeah, I'll give it a try."

"There's no point in meeting unless we have a chance of recovering the timepiece," Felix said. "I don't want to give you false hope."

"It's not false hope," I said. "I don't know how, but we'll get it back."

Felix studied my face for a long minute. He must have seen something in there that he trusted because he finally nodded. My resolve strengthened.

I didn't know *how* I was going to do it, but I'd get that timepiece back. For Vinny.

I clung to that idea like a raft in rough seas.

"All right, then," I said, "It's settled. Vinny, by the way, have you talked to Rashiki? I went out to his place, but he won't let me in. I feel like he's up to something."

"Hmm... I'll give him a call. I'm not surprised to hear about increased security, though. If news about offworlders is out, Rashiki will lock that place up tighter than the warrens in winter."

"Text me with a place and time. I'll bring—"

The Pig's front door slammed open against the bar.

"What now!?" Barry said, exasperated as he came back out of the kitchen.

An imposing, dark-haired woman stood in the doorway, backlit by the setting sun.

My throat constricted in panic as I fumbled to draw my weapon. *Was this the Sevrit?*

I relaxed as my eyes adjusted. It wasn't the Sevrit but it was a woman: Detective Sheila Gonzalez. She carried fury like a thundercloud. I took in her posture, and my fear of the Sevrit melted into a puddle.

Detective Gonzalez was beyond angry—she was livid with rage. She marched across the room and slapped a piece of paper down on the table in front of me.

"Our new case." She spoke the words as if she were accusing me.

On the paper were two pictures and a few lines of text. One photo was a still frame of the news video. It showed Dyna using her telekinetic powers to toss protesters into the crowd.

The other showed Dyna pointing a gun at what appeared to be a human.

I knew it wasn't a human, but a Tetrad dissident with his cloaking shield active. But without that context, from the outside? It looked pretty damned bad.

"Well, look at that!" I spoke lightly, hoping to defuse the situation. "They still print warrants on paper, huh? I'd have thought it would be easier to send an email blast."

Annabelle bit her lower lip so she didn't smile and averted her face.

"Where are they?" Simmons demanded. He stood a few feet behind Gonzalez, near the open front door. "You're the last person they spoke to, as far as we can tell."

My heart thundered and my thoughts raced as I considered my response.

As far as I was concerned, the Peacekeepers were responsible for their own actions. Especially because the pair had ditched me after the protest. I'd agreed to work with them to find the Sevrit, yet after the initial warning Dyna had sent, they'd gone radio silent.

But I wasn't a snitch. The way Simmons spoke to me pissed me off.

"I'm not their keeper," I said.

"These warrants are posted in every station," Sheila said. "In Austin and surrounding metros. Even the Rangers have them."

"That means they're to be arrested on sight," Simmons said. "Including *your* sight."

"I haven't seen them. But why'd the APD give the case to you? Aren't you busy with other cases?"

I wanted to distance myself from the situation. At the same time, I felt like chasing the Peacekeepers was a waste of time. Whatever issues I had with Kilos and Dyna, they'd done good for the people of Earth by cleaning up offworlder scum.

Gonzalez glared at me, her lips pressed into a thin line.

"Ah, I see. It's because you hired me. They gave you this case to punish you."

I turned to Simmons, who was scuffing his boots against the doorframe and avoiding my eyes.

Sheila's eyes widened as she read the same thing I'd read in his body language.

"You didn't," she said.

He shrugged. "So what if I did?"

"Simmons," I said, "you're *officially* the worst."

Sheila's face flushed red. She turned to stare at her partner. "You promised me you wouldn't say anything."

"Well, who are they to run around like some kind of vigilantes?" Simmons demanded. "They aren't officers of the law—not *my* law. They have no authority here."

"They're not working *against* us," Sheila said. "They're working against the Tetrad!"

"Tetrad, shmetrad," Simmons spat. "They're outsiders. They don't have any right to be roaming around policing *our streets*. And don't think I'm okay with alien police officers either! I'm not! I'm not doing it! As far as I'm concerned, they can piss off back to their own planets. This one's taken!"

Simmons was wide-eyed and panting by the end of his tirade. He stormed out, leaving the door hanging open.

Annabelle had gone pale. She was staring at the television. "Gunn."

"Hang on," I said. "Sheila, what about your other cases? We could still use your help tracking down the Sevrit."

If I didn't come up with something clever to lure Tanamir out, that was the only backup plan I had.

"This is the only case that matters now," she said in a quiet, defeated voice. "I have a job to do. I'm sorry, Gunn."

"*Andy,*" Annabelle said.

Something about her tone seemed urgent, but my mind was still fixated on Gonzalez. "Well, can you at least do *something* to keep Simmons off our back? I can't believe I took him out to Lula's house. He better not go around harassing her because he's out of the closet as a racist."

She snorted. "Speciesist, maybe."

"Same difference."

I noticed everyone else in the bar was staring at the television. I turned toward the screen and, for a moment, my mind struggled to take in what I was seeing.

I recognized Austin's skyline. But what was that in the sky, filling the screen like a dark cloud made of circuit boards?

The headline at the bottom of the screen read, "Massive spaceship appears over Austin, TX."

My heart hammered. I walked out of the bar as if moving on stilts. Felix, Lulamina and Annabelle followed me.

We all stood on the sidewalk and looked up.

Above the level of the clouds, a giant ship filled the sky as far as the eye could see. It was as vast as the ocean. Its underside was an intricate pattern of armored plating, thrusters, portholes and what appeared to be weapon systems.

Chills ran down my back and arms. Annabelle put one hand around my waist and gripped my forearm with the other.

My eyes traced the ship's length to where its nose pierced the horizon.

It was so big I couldn't see the end of it. It must have been fifty miles long.

"How is it even flying?" I asked aloud.

"I have no idea," said Annabelle.

"Someone tell me that's not what I think it is." Felix shaded his eyes with his top set of hands and wrung the bottom set near his belly. He finally bent over and braced himself on his knees, as if nauseous.

"Federation battlecruiser." Lulamina took a deep breath, shaking out her rainbow hair and sighing. "It was only a matter of time."

A red laser swept over us, like we were being checked out at the grocery store. I and the other humans—but not the offworlders—flinched.

"And now they know I'm here," Felix said, wiping his mouth. "I'm definitely going to prison for this."

"No, you're not," said Lulamina. "I'll Arbitrate for you."

The Federation had arrived at last. That scan was them taking stock of their belongings.

Up and down the street, several bystanders burst onto the sidewalk and screamed. Conversations were fearful and hushed. Parents shuffled their children into the nearest building to hide.

My cybernetic hand continued to tingle long after the rest of my body did, almost as if in recognition.

I felt an urge to fly up and board the ship.

Had that idea come from my hand? I wondered.

I resisted it with an effort of will, making a fist, and turning south in the direction the ship seemed to be moving. After a moment, the urge faded to a distant craving.

Gonzalez cussed as her phone vibrated in her hand. A walkie-talkie barked and fuzzed from inside Simmons' jacket.

"All units, report for duty!" the operator said. "Repeat, all available units, report for duty."

CHAPTER SIXTEEN

WITH THE BATTLECRUISER drifting ponderously toward the Gulf Coast, the Peacekeepers were my best hope of anticipating the Federation's next move.

In addition to trying to get the timepiece back from Tanamir, now I also had more motivation to find Dyna and Kilos, wherever they were hiding—preferably before Detective Gonzalez and Simmons arrested them.

I figured the Peacekeepers were probably hunkering down in their invisible ship, waiting to receive their next orders. Since I had no way to contact them, and Dyna wasn't responding to my attempts to broadcast my thoughts to her, I had to gamble on my fallback.

I drove out to Hub with Annabelle in the hopes that the Gatekeeper could put us in touch with Dyna again.

"The idea of going to the Gatekeeper for help leaves a bad taste in my mouth."

"Do you have a better idea?" Annabelle asked.

"At least I know he's not on the Tetrad's side," I said.

"He's made it clear that he only cares about his bottom line."

When we finally arrived at Hub, we were shocked to find the private runway deserted inside the shield barrier. The chain-link gate had been hanging wide open, unlocked.

I drove along the empty runway. "Well, shit. Now what?"

Annabelle, who sat beside me, tapped away on her phone.

"I swear, I'm not yanking your chain. I met the Gatekeeper here just the other day."

She glanced up, across the vacant tarmac, then back down at her phone. "Looks like they evacuated when the big ship arrived."

It would have been a staggering amount of equipment to disappear so quickly—spaceships, cars, hangars full of supplies. Where had they stored everything?

Had the Gatekeeper's people already left the planet?

"I knew the soulsucker didn't want to stick around after the Federation arrived, but I'll be honest, I didn't expect him to disappear quite so quickly."

"That ship's got everyone spooked. The White House is in a furor. The Army mobilized the National Guard of Texas. The Navy deployed almost its entire fleet to the Gulf Coast. The Army Corps of Engineers is already in Corpus Christi building up the harbor's coastal defenses."

"Any new sightings of Tanamir's UFOs?" I asked, trying to ignore the feeling of dread that had settled into my gut.

"Mostly in this area, but none of them have been confirmed. I'm also starting to see reports of smaller ships in New York, Paris, Las Vegas, Sydney, Australia, and several other places."

I drove around the grounds trying to find a cloaking shield or some other hidden entrance. It never happened. We made three laps before I gave up.

"We have a greeting party," Annabelle said, pointing up at the sky.

I glanced up at a flock of vultures that were circling overhead.

One bird had detached itself and was descending in lazy circles until it finally settled on the runway in front of us. Samael shook himself as he dropped his disguise.

I parked my truck, and we got out.

"Hey, Sammy Sosa, my favorite outfielder!" I said. "Fancy seeing you here. Why do we keep meeting like this?"

The Daacro cleared its throat to express his amusement, a sound like a rock polisher. "You have an odd sense of humor. Samael will do."

"No one likes my nicknames. I guess if you're here, that means the Gatekeeper hasn't left town yet."

"My employer has relocated to a more... discrete location. He is well along in making preparations to depart. However, he believes that there's a small chance the situation can still be salvaged."

"Maybe he just told *you* that because he's planning to ditch you at the first opportunity."

The Daacro bristled and gave another rumbling growl, this one with a distinctively more aggressive tone. "My loyalty is not in question."

"What I'm wondering," Annabelle said, touching one finger to her lips as she assessed the Daacro, "is what, exactly, the big boys want your boss to do, now that they've arrived." She pointed up, where the Federation cruiser still took most of the southern horizon.

"The Federation has halted all traffic into and out of your star system."

"Like a blockade?" I asked.

"Effectively. Of course, we had to relinquish our supply routes. Several of our vessels were acquired for patrols. Only the Gatekeeper's detailed preparations kept the rest of his fleet from being commandeered."

"They don't want his help?" I asked. "I thought he worked for them."

"His agreement with officials in the Federation was... you Americans would call it a handshake deal. Not a contract they can overtly acknowledge under the guidelines for the governance of silent planets. And not enforceable by the Federation machine. They saw ships they wanted, so they took them for their own use."

"Bummer." I put my human hand over my eyes and squeezed my temples. "Hey, Samael, I've got a favor to ask. We need your help to get ahold of Dyna and Kilos. I know the Gatekeeper was working with them at the protests. How do I reach them?"

He just stared at me.

"Throw me a bone here, would ya?"

"Our interests are somewhat aligned, but it's not something my employer wants to be made public knowledge. If that happens, both your Peacekeeper friends and our organization will be in danger from retaliation by the Federation."

"I need to talk to the Peacekeepers."

"To warn them about the warrant out for their arrest?"

"Among other things, yes." I turned to Annabelle. "The Gatekeeper's annoyingly up to date. He always seems to know things we haven't told him yet."

"He is well-connected," Samael said.

"If anyone knows what the Federation is planning to do now that they're *here*, it's Kilos and Dyna. Help me reach them."

"This is misguided reasoning. You seem to think that the Federation will behave like sentient beings."

"Won't they?"

"First of all, the Federation is beyond reason, impersonal and faceless," Samael said. "Secondly, you're being followed."

I looked around at the empty runway. "Don't change the subject."

"This is what I came down to share." Samael pointed at the entrance. "Beyond the gate, about a half mile down the road, an unmarked police vehicle is parked on a wide shoulder. They followed you here."

"Is it Detective Simmons?" I asked.

"And his partner."

I glowered. Sheila and I hadn't parted on good terms, but I didn't think she'd continue working so closely with Simmons after he'd gone behind her back.

Yet here she was, tailing us with him.

"I'll get rid of them," I said.

"Then I will ask my employer if he is willing to help you get in touch with the Peacekeepers. That is, of course, assuming they want to be found."

"Of course," I gave him a thin smile.

Samael flapped his wings once but didn't lift off.

"What?" I asked.

"There is a condition."

I groaned. "There's always a condition. I don't want to borrow any money from the Gatekeeper."

"That offer is no longer on the table," Samael said. "Your funds have been absorbed into our organization's exit plan."

"So what do you need me to do?"

"Not you," he said. "His request is for her."

He was looking at Annabelle.

My hackles rose like an angry dog facing down a home invader. "I don't think so," I said.

"Easy, Andy," said Annabelle. "What would he have me do?"

"You'll soon receive an invitation to speak with a high-ranking official in your government. We want you to take the meeting."

"You want me to take a meeting? That's it?"

He inclined his narrow head. "In person."

"You know I can't do that. My identity is still a secret."

"You must. If we are to salvage this situation, we need Earth's political leaders to hear the truth from one of their own. And to believe them. Ms. Marshall, you have a reputation as the top journalist for breaking stories on offworld activity. You are the ideal fit for this task."

"I don't work for the Gatekeeper."

"All we're asking you to do is take the meeting. No further commitment required."

She took a deep breath and gave me a look. If I didn't know better, there was real fear lurking beneath her appearance of tall confidence.

Annabelle knew better than almost anyone what it meant to hide behind a mask.

If her true identity were revealed, she'd be in as much danger as any offworlder currently being targeted for hate crimes.

"If I accept, Gunn comes with me," she said. "I need protection."

Samael gave a slight bow of his head, baring the pebbly skin on top of his head. "As you wish."

"Okay," Annabelle said. "Who does your boss want me to meet?"

"The invitation should arrive momentarily."

Annabelle looked down at her phone, then gazed back up at me with wide eyes as a new email appeared in her inbox.

CHAPTER SEVENTEEN

SECURITY at the Texas State Capitol building had ramped up since I'd last been for a tour.

"Please remove your shoes and any metal items, such as coins, belt buckles, and jewelry," recited a bored Officer Daniels, who loomed over me and Annabelle. I stood over six feet tall, yet the man's height made me feel like Mario to his Luigi.

A broad, buff Luigi.

There were maybe a dozen cops in the entrance hall. A crowd of reporters was gathered on the steps outside. The noise of their conversation was harder to keep out, and while the cops hadn't let them follow us in, they made no effort to close the door and block their cameras.

Red dots and lenses pursued us inside, indicating live recordings or at least video footage taken by professional camera equipment. I could tell Annabelle was nervous being on the receiving end of such attention. She, perhaps, was all too conscious of broadcasting power dynamics.

Reporters shouted questions at us from outside.

Questions like, "Who are you?" and "How did you get a meeting with the governor?"

We ignored them as best we could. The invitation hadn't been publicized, but plenty of journalists were chomping at the bit for a new story. They'd been lurking when we arrived.

It was better not to respond to them. They'd figure it out in time, and keeping a low profile was to our advantage.

Annabelle pulled down her hat and pressed her sunglasses against her rosy cheeks. The shades covered most of her face. She chewed on a fingernail, showing the adorable gap between her front teeth.

"Be cool," she whispered.

I chuckled.

She put her hand down, worked her mouth, and turned her back to the reporters, donning a regal, stoic expression that looked beautiful in a "half-veiled supermodel" sort of way.

I'd lost track of what Officer Daniels had been saying to us, so I turned back to him now.

"—the scanner," he said, "Backpacks and large purses are prohibited. So is that camera bag, miss."

"It's just lenses and SD cards," Annabelle said, handing it over. "You can inspect them if you want."

"No bags allowed." He turned his gaze on me. "Also prohibited are firearms, blades and incendiary devices."

"Daniels! I would never." I withdrew my Glock, popped out the magazine, ejected the bullet from the chamber, caught it, and slapped the gun and the bullets into his large hand.

He muttered and threw the weapon down on a nearby

table, like the metal was hot to the touch. “Are you serious right now?”

“Hold that thought.”

I pulled a small pistol out of my jacket pocket, a double-edged knife out of my boot, and a set of lockpicks from my back pocket.

He refused to take them from my hands this time, so I set them down on the table beside Annabelle’s camera bag.

“I suggest you return to your vehicle and lock these inside,” said Officer Daniels.

I thumbed back at the crowd of reporters. “After they’ve seen them all? That’s not wise.”

His face was impassive stone.

“Besides, you wouldn’t make a lady wade back through the gauntlet, would you?”

“She can wait here.”

“Wherever he goes, I go,” Annabelle said.

Officer Daniels hesitated.

“Before you make up your mind,” I said, “two more things. Here’s my license to carry.” I handed him the card. “And this is for you.”

I held out the package.

When he didn’t take it, I shook it gently.

He took the manila envelope and squeezed it open. When he saw what was inside, his nostrils flared, and he fought back a smile. He closed the envelope with precision and set it on the tabletop next to the rest of our things.

Officer Daniels maintained a practiced, professional expression that made Annabelle’s blank face seem positively forced. I supposed, as a cop who often worked with the public, he had a bit more practice than a reclusive writer who rarely showed her face in public and didn't use her real name.

Annabelle gave me a silent, questioning look.

I waited for Officer Daniels to respond.

Legally, I was on shaky ground, seeing as I was standing on state property with loaded firearms. But we'd both been invited here and I *did* have a license to carry. Technically, I could take my weapons right up to the door.

And I had. Partly because I liked giving Daniels a hard time... but I wasn't about to go unarmed if my job was to protect Annabelle.

Not with Tanamir and the Tetrad still on the loose.

After learning our destination, I had ditched Gonzalez and Simmons with some erratic driving on the back roads. I then called Alek and had him use his connections to find out who was on duty. When he told me it was Officer Daniels, and why he'd been given security detail at the Capitol, I felt bad for the guy.

"Sorry to hear about Officer Gelder," I said, quietly, so none of the other officers on duty or reporters outside would hear it. "Wasn't right what they did."

The gift was to soften him up, my words to indicate my understanding. I thought I knew where his allegiances lay, but I wanted to make sure.

His square brow scrunched together. "How do you know about that?"

"People talk."

"Gelder's one of the best officers I know. I'd trust him with my life—hell, I already have, many times over."

"Seems like overt prejudice if you ask me."

"He stood strong at the riots. Right at my shoulder the whole time."

"I know. I saw you two there."

"We've worked together for years." He cut himself off when he realized his voice was rising. He dropped it back to a whisper. "*Years, Gunn.*"

"Did they warn you before it happened?"

His lips clamped together. He shook his head.

"Found out afterward, huh? You're on your own, just like that. I bet you feel betrayed."

"What do you know about it?" Daniels spat. "Butt out."

I held up my hands. "Look, I get it. I went through the same thing with one of my friends last year. Finding out the truth was a shock to the system."

"Last year?" he asked, suddenly intensely interested. "How long have *you* known?" *Known about offworlders*, he meant.

"Most of a year." I glanced at Annabelle. "She's had her own encounters. That's why we're here."

Daniels licked his lips. "They're putting my partner through a formal review."

I winced. "Sounds like department speak for 'shit-canned'."

"They won't find anything. Mo's squeaky clean."

"Is that his first name? I didn't expect that. He doesn't look like a Mo to me."

"Mooney Gelder. We call him Mo for short."

"Tell him to look me up. My business partner knows a bunch of attorneys. He might be able to help."

He nodded slowly. "I will. Thanks."

"Sure. Be careful not to stab anyone with those, eh?" I pointed to the manila envelope.

A blush crept out of Officer Daniels' collar. "Go ahead."

"By the way, I hope you don't mind... would you keep our things locked up while we talk to the old dove hunter?"

Officer Daniels hedged for just a second more before relenting. "Fine. We've got a locker over there we use for this sort of stuff. You'd be amazed how many senators try to attend sessions with loaded weapons. It's like they're trying to make some kind of point."

"I'm sure they are."

Daniels busied himself stowing our gear. He let us keep our phones but Annabelle wasn't allowed to bring the big camera, and the only weapon I could bring was my cybernetic fist. Fortunately, it was attached, but it *did* set off the metal detector.

Daniels had to pat me down.

"I know I brought you a gift," I muttered as his hands moved up my thighs, "but don't think you owe me any favors."

"You're a troublemaker." He snorted. "Get lost, you two."

At last, we entered the statehouse.

"You boys were awfully buddy-buddy by the end of that conversation," Annabelle whispered. "What was in the envelope?"

"New knitting needles." I held up my hands. "Big ones to fit the big man's hands."

With tourist visits on a temporary hiatus, we were the only ones inside. Except for a secretary, who was waiting for us in the rotunda. She led us through the soaring marble columns, past portraits of the governors of Texas dating back to 1845, up a flight of stairs to the second floor, and into the office of the current Governor of Texas.

In keeping with his public image, Hector Enrique Erazo III had mounted a dove-hunting shotgun across from the stained mahogany desk. A taxidermy display of three doves stood in one corner. Several other stuffed game animals had been placed around the room: a full cougar, a mounted buck's head and—to my delight—a jackalope.

Governor Erazo himself stood at the window looking south in the direction of the ship. The curtains were open wide to show the backside of the Federation battlecruiser where it squatted on the horizon. According to news reports, its nose was sticking out into the Gulf of Mexico now.

Several squadrons of elite fighter jets patrolled the spaceship as it moved out to sea. There was also a rumor that bombers circled high overhead in case we needed to retaliate quickly.

Despite the company, the Federation ship had continued its slow, unhurried way. It flew on the same heading it had shown since its first appearance over Austin.

"Welcome in," Governor Erazo said, pumping my hand and kissing Annabelle on the cheek. "Thank you both for coming."

He had a booming speaking voice with just a hint of a Spanish accent. He was bilingual, and, as the first governor of Texas with Mexican heritage, he was something of a local folk hero. His background, fiery speeches, and far-right views had set him up to unseat the incumbent last year.

The state was still reeling from it, and I could tell Annabelle was not unaffected by his charm.

Made me a bit jealous, to be honest.

"Please, have a seat," the governor said, gesturing to two deep leather armchairs.

We did, and I sank into the cushions deep enough to feel small in front of his oversized desk. He settled into his own chair, adjusting several times as if he couldn't sit still. He tapped his fingers. The man's eyes were puffy and red. Faded coffee stains marred his otherwise clear white button-down, like he'd attacked them with Tide pens.

"Now, I don't mean to be rude, so please don't take it that way, but I have a spaceship parked in my sky and the only reason I'm taking this meeting is because I am waiting on responses and was told you had relevant information. Miss..." He checked some printed notes. The man was a bit old-school in his habits. "Miss Marshall."

"What we have to say will be well worth your time," said Annabelle. "I promise you that."

"And you... Mr. Anderson Gunn," he tapped the desk with two fingers in an alternating beat. "I can see why the journalist is here, but what is a bounty hunter doing here?"

"I double as a bodyguard," I said.

"I see."

"He's aiding me in my investigations," Annabelle said. "Security, surveillance and intel."

The secretary blew in with more papers and dropped them on the Governor's desk. Without saying a word, she spun and walked out, her heels tapping on the wooden floor.

Erazo glanced at them, picking up the papers. "It says here you own a business called Gunn Bounties LLC and are partnered with the city's most popular bail bondsman, Alek Ludwig."

I shrugged. "We don't advertise it, but that's all public record."

"So what's this," he snapped, slapping the papers onto his desktop. "Got to do with *that?*"

He gestured angrily out of the window at the ship.

I took a deep breath. The man was under a lot of pressure, yet he'd been convinced to take this meeting without knowing many details. I was dying to know how the Gatekeeper pulled it off, but I decided it was probably best to just get to the point.

"I've met a lot of offworlders," I said, "and I know several of them very well."

"Well enough to get them to buzz off and leave us alone?"

"It's complicated. The Federation doesn't take orders from its people any more than you do."

Governor Erazo grunted.

"We have other information you'll be interested in, too," Annabelle said.

"More than what you published on your website, Ms. Marshall?" he asked, looking at Annabelle. "By the way, I know that's not your real name."

She smiled. "It's not. And yes, more than what I've published. I can't make a lot of what I've seen public for various reasons. Gunn, you better start, and then I'll fill the Governor in on the details."

So I told my story. I gave the governor the high-level overview of how I'd first been hired to chase down an offworld fugitive, and went all the way up to my first run-in with Tanamir in Rashiki's.

I left out specifics about my clients and only made vague references to my friends. But when it came to my understanding of the Federation, what they were doing on Earth, and how Tanamir was opposing them to undo Earth's status as a silent planet—and align Earth's interests with the Tetrad's—I held nothing back.

Governor Erazo asked a few clarifying questions while I was detailing the main points, but he withheld his personal opinions about my story until the end. When I finished, he simply looked at me and shook his head.

"Why should I believe any of what you say? Where is your proof?"

"Well, I've got their prosthetic in me," I offered, holding up my right hand so he could see the metallic joints mounted in my wrist. "It set off your metal detector. Apart from that, you've got Annabelle's testimony to corroborate, and several photographs."

Annabelle had put together a dossier on Tanamir for him. She handed it over now—the only thing she'd been allowed to take through security. It was a few pieces of printed paper laying out her theory of how Tanamir was using seemingly altruistic and highly visible publicity stunts to garner support among humanity. And how, at the same time, he'd used his own people at the protests to agitate the crowd, drawing the Peacekeepers and police against them, and provoking violence.

She provided photos from the protest as evidence.

"Why bring this to me instead of the police?"

I gripped the arm of my chair, but let Annabelle answer —I knew she'd be more polite.

"Pardon my frankness, sir," she said, "But they just put all their offworlder officers on immediate suspension. Even if they had the resources, do you really think they'd be objective?"

"Do you think we should have let the offworlder officers continue to serve when they've been lying about their identity, some of them for *years*?"

"If they have a history of complaints and problems? Definitely not. But from what my sources say, most of them have exemplary records."

The governor chewed the inside of his cheek as he studied us, like he was weighing whether he could trust us or not.

He then asked permission to forward this information to his team. Annabelle agreed, and Governor Erazo called his secretary in to take the papers and printed photographs, plus an SD card containing more evidence.

"I'll be honest with you two," Governor Erazo said as he stood up from his seat and paced behind the desk. "Part of me thinks this is bullshit. I don't want to believe you. But... some of what you're saying matches up too closely with the events of the past 24 hours for me to ignore it."

Annabelle and I exchanged a glance.

"What did we miss?" she asked.

"We've kept it under wraps and away from the press, so if I tell you any more, you've got to swear that you won't leak it or write about it. Not even under a pseudonym."

We both agreed.

He pulled out two thick stacks of paper from a drawer in his desk. "Sign these NDAs."

"What happens if we don't?"

"Then I tell you nothing."

"What if we sign the papers and have to divulge the information?"

"You'll be tried for treason under Texas law." He turned the page and tapped on the text. Sure enough, there it was.

"Even under duress?"

"Even so."

I swallowed and exchanged a worried glance with Annabelle. That was a frightening prospect. But what other choice did we have?

One wrong turn from that battlecruiser floating on the

horizon, and my world could explode. What was a little signature on a piece of paper in the face of that alien starship?

I scribbled some nonsense that could be mistaken for someone else's name and signature. Annabelle took a cursory look through the papers and signed her pen name.

"We're all ears," she said.

"Since its arrival, the Federation ship has been broadcasting the same message on repeat using an encrypted channel. My tech guys only cracked it this morning."

"You can understand it?"

"It's broadcasting in English and a dozen other languages—languages from our world."

"They've known about us a lot longer than we've known about them," I said.

Annabelle opened her phone screen on her lap and pushed record without looking at the screen. "What did it say?"

"It said, *'By the authority of the Federation of Lodi, in accordance with Directive 4113, Earth is no longer classified as a silent planet. All sentient beings are now under Federation jurisdiction. Any attempts to resist will be met with deadly force.'* "

I blew out my breath. "I'm surprised they're letting our jets fly so close to them."

"Well, they're not attacking us, and having the planes there makes the President feel better."

"I'll bet. What are you most afraid will happen?"

"Isn't it obvious? Retaliation leading to all-out war. Or worse, colonization. Last thing anyone wants is for these bastards to stick around."

Annabelle opened her mouth to object, but she decided against it.

"Pretty sure Tanamir and the Tetrad would agree with you," I said. "Which is part of the problem. We can't take their side."

"What if they'd make good allies?" asked Governor Erazo.

I drew in a hissing breath. "I don't think you really want that."

"The enemy of my enemy…" he said, quoting Churchill or some such nonsense.

"Have you responded to their message?" Annabelle asked.

"It's not a dialogue by any stretch. They broadcast the same message on a loop, every quarter of an hour on the dot. Don't know if you can tell, but the nose of their ship is pointed at Cuba."

"Is that going to be a problem?"

"Yes," Erazo scowled. "We're lucky they haven't leveled the island yet. Those idiots launched missiles at the battle-cruiser at three o'clock this morning."

So *that* was why he had coffee stains on his shirt. Erazo probably hadn't slept in two days.

"How did the battlecruiser respond?" Annabelle asked.

"They dismantled the attack with some kind of laser defense system and kept cruising south at the same speed."

"No retaliation?"

"Not yet," Erazo said as he glanced out the window over his shoulder.

I blew out a breath. Annabelle sighed heavily.

"That's good news," I said. "They're not afraid of us."

"Good news? It's goddamn terrifying," Erazo said. "Means they don't consider us a threat."

"We've got to arrange a talk. A parley of some kind."

"I'm not sure that's possible, or even desirable at this point. We sent a message reassuring them that we were not responsible for the attack, but again we've received no response."

I took a deep breath and tried to think about this from Tanamir's point of view. What would his next move be in the face of this massive ship? How could we possibly anticipate him? Or keep him from making things worse?

"Look," I said, "From my point of view, whatever you do, we have to show them that we're peaceful. That we're *not* on the same side as the Tetrad. Because if we align ourselves with the Tetrad, I guarantee they will crush us. The Federation takes a scorched earth approach to insurgency. And in this case, Earth is the supply depot they need to wipe out."

"Sounds like even if we do nothing, they've already decided they're taking charge. And let me tell you, that doesn't sit well with the President, his cabinet, or the American people."

"So what are you going to do about it?"

"Hang tight until I hear from the President, and in the meantime, try not to get us all killed."

"Can I offer one idea that might help?" I asked.

"If you have a suggestion, spit it out," Erazo said. "I don't have any more time to waste. In fact, I'm late for another meeting."

"Don't take sides. No matter what you choose, you'll anger one group of offworlders or the other."

Governor Erazo heaved a sigh that aged him by ten years. "One thing I've learned about politics, Mr. Gunn. If you don't pick a side, someone else will pick it for you. Here's a phone number you can use to reach my team. Call if you learn anything else that might be of use to us. Call right away."

He handed a card to Annabelle and walked out of the room without another word.

"I guess we're dismissed," I said.

"Why don't I feel any better than when we got here?" Annabelle asked.

"Better?" I asked. "Since when was talking to a politician supposed to make a person feel better?"

CHAPTER EIGHTEEN

IN THE BIG RED BARN, I kicked aside a layer of hay and stomped on the hatch. "Hey, Rashiki! It's Gunn, let me in."

Nothing happened. The hatch stayed shut.

I was determined not to be rebuffed a second time. After all, this time I'd received an invitation. Vinny was bringing Amberen down, and he told me to meet him here.

"Vinny's expecting me," I said. "Come on, open up!"

I looked into a corner of the ceiling, where I knew hidden cameras were mounted in the rafters. Rashiki had made some improvements to the barn to conceal his place of business, and his security staff were on high alert.

Annabelle strode in behind me and gave the cameras a cheeky wave.

There was a hiss as the pressure released, and then the square hatch popped open. The rich smell of alien bodies and cooking food wafted out.

"I know she's cuter than me," I said, "but you don't have to be rude."

We dropped down the hatch, which drew closed and sealed behind us. A sloping path led us down into the rich miasma of Rashiki's underground racetrack.

Truth be told, this place offered quite a bit more than a racetrack. The Jel'ka track was located at the very bottom of the hive-shaped structure, which was enormous—easily fifty times the width of the barn at its widest and twenty stories deep. The top levels were accessible by a spiral wooden walkway that descended on a gradual slope. Arcades on each floor were packed with shops. They sold offworlder food, drinks, entertainment, and other... desirables.

My pal Vinny loved coming to Rashiki's, and I understood why. It had the same appeal as a casino, and offworlders could indulge in a broad selection of vices. It was full of lights, good smells, and a hard-to-pin sense of warmth and welcome.

As we descended, I noticed some things had changed since the last time I'd been here. The upper levels were the same, but the middle levels had been converted into a series of enclosed pods or dwelling units. These apartments consumed much of the space, forcing other shops down and crowding the lower levels near the racetrack. On the levels of the apartments, the walkway thinned and wound between buildings.

"These look pretty permanent," Annabelle said, moving aside to let a trio of Torlik youths pass by. They averted their eyes and rushed away when they saw us. "I wonder how much Rashiki's making on rent now."

A thick plume of smoke puffed up from the floor below us as a humming, buzzing sound announced the arrival of Rashiki on his hover chair. The massive Torlik looked like a pile of orange pudding scooped into a copper bowl. He had one massive, drooping eyelid, a red-shot eyeball which peered through a haze of smoke, and four arms entangled in a hookah hose.

"Anderson Gunn," he boomed in his Russian accent. I don't know why he talked like that; the eccentric Torlik owner of this establishment was quite the character. "And *beautiful* Annabelle. How are you, darling? Long time no see."

"Rashiki, ever the flatterer. Nice to see you, too."

Rashiki was flanked by two Torlik security guards—both much fitter than their boss—who approached on foot at a nod from Rashiki. The guards ran handheld scanners up and down our bodies as they circled us, searching for hidden weapons. I'd removed my firearms, as I knew guns weren't allowed inside, but the scanner beeped noisily when it reached my cybernetic hand.

"Weaponized mods are strictly prohibited," stated the guard.

"Sorry, but this one's attached." I rotated my hand. "Got it here, as a matter of fact."

"I am familiar with your augment," Rashiki said. "As long as you don't use it to cause trouble, is okay today. I came to warn you, however. Rashiki's is more than casino now. Is also home to many offworlders. See?"

He pointed at the apartments on the levels immediately below us. A lean creature with transparent skin tottered out of a narrow door. It belched lime-green water into a bucket, which was there for that purpose. Acidic-looking steam rose from the waste.

Even Rashiki wrinkled his nose. He shrugged apologetically. "It is work in progress."

The ghostly offworlder turned, nonplussed, and began to stroll down the walkway. It carried a bin of what looked like rags.

"Is it headed to the laundromat?" I joked.

"What, you think offworlders don't wash their clothes?"

"Not what I meant." I said. "Why the pivot? Gambling and Jel'ka races don't pay enough?"

"I give back. Charity work," Rashiki said, pulling on his hookah hose so hard his cheeks caved in. "Besides, real estate is good, steady business now. Many offworlders feel living on surface carries too much risk. What with Tanamir on news and"—he gestured vaguely at everything around him—"Federation parked in sky. Plus, easier to get front row seats at Jel'ka races when you live nearby."

"How'd you do the construction so fast?"

"That's nothing. Many hands in need of work right now."

"You'd think you'd feel more safe, not less safe, with the Federation battlecruiser here."

Rashiki snorted. "These folk come here because the Federation has taken over their worlds. They are not fools."

"So why not leave?"

"For many, too expensive to get home. For others, no home."

"And the Tetrad? Are their agents giving you any trouble?"

Rashiki gave me a dark look. "Tanamir's revolutionaries are not my... how you say... not my cup of tea. Bounty hunter, you know this."

"Have they come knocking, though?"

"We turned away a few," Rashiki admitted. He'd been outraged to discover that Tanamir had used his prize Jel'ka to smuggle drugs to Earth, so I didn't think he'd get into bed with them. But I had to ask, in case there was any risk of us being followed or spied on while we were here.

"Fah," Rashiki said, "Tetrad want war. I want good living. Very different, us."

"You sound like the Gatekeeper."

"Gatekeeper and I are both business people."

"Yet he's pulled his crew out of Austin, while you dug in to stick around."

Rashiki gave me another dark look. "Where I go, then? You have ship can transport Rashiki's?"

I grunted in acknowledgment. Rashiki had confirmed it: The Gatekeeper possessed the resources to leave. Rashiki, despite his success running this establishment, did not. He made the best of his situation, expanding the business laterally to meet an evolving need.

My estimation of the Torlik climbed up a notch. It wasn't a charity case like he claimed, but he wasn't turning tail and running for the hills, either. He was here to stay.

"I respect that," I said. "Can you point us in Vinny's direction? As I understand it, his friends are trying to keep a low profile."

"So I heard." Rashiki leaned in and lowered his voice. "Is this secretive Pangozil new client of yours?"

"You don't know who it is?" I asked, surprised.

"I do." Rashiki gave me a knowing smile. "Do you?"

Felix and Lulamina descended the walkway and came to join us. Lulamina was no longer riding in her vessel, so her undersized hand gave my leg a reassuring pat in greeting as she passed. Her head only came up to my mid-thigh.

She introduced Felix to Rashiki. He turned from our conversation to study the other Torlik with interest. He lowered his chair to Felix's height, and the two shook hands, each crossing his body to grip the other's opposite hand—an eight-handed handshake.

The hookah hose fell from Rashiki's mouth and hung, forgotten, over the side of the hoverchair. He grinned broadly with brown teeth. Then he offered the hose to Felix, who took it between his lips and inhaled deeply as he released Rashiki's hands. His large eyelid closed in satisfaction as he exhaled a thick plume of smoke.

"Oh, that's good. I didn't know you could get Midian Farnum here! And I haven't seen a hoverchair of this model in ages. I see you've made some adjustments."

The two of them moved off together, switching from English to their own language and talking amiably, like old friends. Felix hadn't encountered another Torlik since he'd been on Earth, and Rashiki was always in a talkative mood when he encountered new customers and the potential of their wallets.

We trailed along behind the two Torliks as they got to know each other, trusting Rashiki would eventually lead us to our destination.

"How much do you think he's charging for rent?" I whispered to Annabelle. "And do offworlders get tired of living in a neon cave like this? It would drive me crazy if I didn't get any sunlight or fresh air."

She shrugged and chewed off a sliver of her pinky nail. "Probably better than the alternative." She offered nothing more. Annabelle had been lost in thought since we left the governor's office, so I didn't press her.

"Rashiki!" Annabelle suddenly called ahead, her voice impatient. "Are you going to take us to see Vinny, or just waste our time with chit-chat?"

"Twelfth level, north side," he told her.

"Come on," Annabelle said, all business. She brushed past the pair of Torliks so quickly that I had to pick up my pace to keep up.

Lulamina followed, and Felix came loping after us.

Felix's eyelid was drooping when he caught up to me. He appeared flushed and wasn't wringing his hands nervously —first time since I'd met him.

"What's in that hookah?" I asked. "Ora?"

"Oh, stars, no" Felix said. "That junk is lethal. Midian Farnum is like your tobacco, but stronger. It mixes a stimulant with a mild sedative."

"No wonder Rashiki is always in such a good mood. How long does it last?"

He shrugged. "Few hours."

"Sounds like cannabis."

"What's that?"

"Remind me when this is all over, and I'd be happy to show you."

Felix took a deep breath. "I'm still nervous to meet Gevereaux."

"Why? "

"He's the mind behind many dramatic masterpieces played across Federation space," Felix said, suddenly chatty. "Not to mention peaceful social movements against heavy-handed Federation oversight. It was he who got the Federation to hand governance of Pango back over to the Pangozil leaders. That was before the Tetrad created a singularity that threatened to destroy the planet. Many of my people look up to him. I did a little snooping around on your Internet to give you a better sense of things. He's kind of like the Ronald Reagan of the Pangozil."

"Not sure if that's a compliment," I said. "Where did you get your information?"

Annabelle shot me a sly smile.

"What I'm trying to say is that he's an accomplished artist *and* an elected leader. What's not to admire?"

I shrugged. "I don't know the guy."

"Regardless, it is common for a Pangozil to excel in one field, but rarely in two."

"Vinny's a chef. He makes the best pizza I've ever had, and he's a good friend. That's two things."

Felix waved his hand. "They are social creatures, and your friend chose a career that is very much in line with a Pangozil temperament. They love devoting themselves to a craft and will spend a lifetime dedicated to doing one thing. A well-prepared meal is a masterpiece in its own right, isn't it?"

My stomach grumbled in agreement. "Which fields do the Torlik excel in?"

"Trade. I'm somewhat of an anomaly." Felix gave a high-pitched chuckle. "My father always wanted me to go into logistics with him, but I never had a brain for details. I'm more of a big idea type. In fact, quantum engines used to fascinate me so much that when he was in interstellar medical supply sales, I used to sit in the engine room and watch..."

Felix's voice trailed off. His now-droopy eyelid widened as a pack of stoop-shouldered Pangozil emerged from the building, about twenty yards down the curved walkway in front of us.

Their bodies and faces were covered in loose fabric. Only their snouts, eyes, hands, and fur-covered feet showed. They wore no shoes.

What little I could see of their fur surprised me. Some had thin, velvety coats like Vinny's, but others had longer, wiry hair. Of the half dozen fur coats I could see, each was a different shade of dark blue, red or purple.

The Pangozil bowed to us in greeting. The one with wiry blue fur had toes ending in wickedly sharp claws. He stepped forward, tapping long fingernails—also sharpened—together with soft clicks. His beady black eyes searched us from beneath the folds of black fabric.

Unfortunately, his raspy voice was completely unintelligible to me.

"Greetings from the Pangozil nation," Lulamina translated.

"Hi," I said, giving him a little wave.

Felix gave me a sharp look. "It is not polite to show open hands to a Pangozil soldier," he whispered. "Unless you're looking for a fight."

I choked. "Warn me next time, would you?"

The black-clad Pango drew up to his full height, which was a head taller than me. He was much bigger than Vinny, bigger even than Vinny's late cousin. Other than those two, this was three times as many Pangozil as I'd ever met in my life.

Maybe Vinny's tales of childhood hardships had affected him and his cousins more than I realized. This fella in front of me was enormous. Even under the loose wrappings covering his body, I could tell he was jacked and would easily best me in a wrestling match.

I sized him up. The chat between Lulamina and the black-clad, blue-furred Pango continued. Abruptly, he turned and gestured toward the apartment. Two of the

Pangozil went in ahead of us. We were beckoned in after them, and the rest of them brought up the rear.

"That was easier than I expected," I said. My heart still raced from the anticipation of a fight.

"I told him we had something that could help Gevereaux restore their planet."

"Straight to the point. That's why I like you, Lula."

I saw we were stepping into darkness, so I squeezed my eyes shut as I walked inside. I opened them on the other side of the threshold. Even so, it was all fuzzy shadows. I used my hands to find the sides of the corridor.

I braced myself for some kind of betrayal—a sucker-punch, a gun in my face, a tackle from the side.

The only thing that assaulted me, however, were smells of roasted meat, baking bread, and sautéed garlic and onions.

I expected the wet rat smell of a rodent den. Yet I was rewarded with the powerful smell of Vinny's cooking. I'd recognize that smell anywhere.

I had to force myself not to run forward. The two Pangos ahead of us turned through a few narrow corridors until the drywall gave way to stone walls.

As we came around the final corner, the corridor opened into a large cave. Dozens of Pangozil were gathered in groups. At the far end, Vinny was removing a round pastry from a brick oven. The smokestack wound up into the ceiling and back the way we'd come.

"Vinny, is that you?"

"Hey, pal!" I waited until he set the food down on a large boulder with a flat top. The flour-dusted stone was being used as a cooking surface. "Good to see ya, Gunn."

He brushed his hands on his apron and I chucked him on

the shoulder. I wanted to hug him, but he glanced around, saw that all his kin were staring at us, and went back to his work. He removed three more pastries from the oven, then cut them all into slices with quick gliding motions of a half-moon blade.

The food was distributed among the Pangozil waiting in the cave. They made it disappear as fast as it came out. Vinny danced through the kitchen, spinning even more dough into the hot stone oven.

I realized they had been staring not necessarily because of our friendship, but because they were hungry.

Or both. It definitely could have been both.

"Sorry," Vinny said, "Long day of travel. My people have an appetite."

One Pangozil didn't eat—a tall, lean male with maroon fur. A wispy grey beard hung from his long snout, and tall ears swiveled expressively.

The ears pointed at us as he separated from a group and approached. His eyes were blurry like a blind man's, but he moved like a karate master, almost sweeping his feet as he walked forward. He moved through the crowded cave as if he was aware of everything happening around him. Despite the lack of vision in those misty eyes, I noted a deep intelligence. In the manner and attitude of the Pangozil he passed, I sensed a deep reverence. They moved out of his way and bowed their heads to him ever so slightly.

When his face turned in my direction, it felt as if he were... Not looking into my soul, exactly, but sounding me out with those ears, as if by divination.

The blind elder stopped before us and dipped his head.

Vinny cleared his throat and stepped away from the

stone ovens. "Gunn, Annabelle, friends. Allow me to introduce you. This is Elder Amberen."

"Pleasure to meet you, sir." He took my hand and squeezed—tight enough to give even my cybernetic hand some pressure.

"Hi there!" Annabelle said brightly. "If you don't mind my saying so, we've heard quite a lot about you."

The Elder inclined his head, then muttered a few words in his own language. When he spoke, his mouth hardly moved at all.

"That's a traditional Pangozil greeting that means 'peace to your clan'." Vinny looked away, as if embarrassed. "He says he's also heard a lot about you two."

"Where would he have heard that?" I asked.

"I may have put in a good word," said Vinny. "No big deal." His ears twitched a few times, a Pangozil expression of shyness, or maybe embarrassment.

It warmed my heart.

"Thanks, Vinny. But it's not me who asked for the meeting. I'm just the go-between. Sir, this is my client, Felix, and our mutual acquaintance, Lula."

The Torlik avoided Amberen's eyes. "It is truly my honor to meet you, sir. I'm a big fan." He worked his mouth, blinked, then muttered a clicking, whispering phrase. It made Amberen smile warmly and chuckle.

The two exchanged a few more phrases that sounded like they were quoting from a movie.

"Guess he's seen the Elder's dramas," Vinny said, smiling.

I was getting frustrated at not being able to follow the conversation. Amberen must have detected the change. He clapped a hand on my shoulder and pointed at his throat with a clawed finger.

"Don't worry, I can speak your tongue also," he said in a tinny voice with a perfect midwestern American accent. He pointed at a small bug-like machine, no bigger than a quarter, which lay half hidden in the fur of his neck. Its six tiny prongs embedded themselves into his skin. "No more inside jokes, I promise. Let's find somewhere warm to sit, shall we?"

So that's how they do it, I thought, studying the translator. *Well, that's one mystery solved. Not everyone who speaks English has to learn our language.*

I was sure the Peacekeepers downloaded languages into their brains using that nanobot tech. Others, like Rashiki and Vinny, had lived here long enough to learn the tongue. It seemed that some offworlders who were new to Earth had tech to help them communicate.

Vinny stayed at the oven, cooking in a kind of trance-like state. Amberen led everyone else to a round heating element on a stand six inches off the floor. It looked like a little camp stove, but without the smoke.

His Pangozil form lent itself to sitting on his haunches more effectively than human anatomy, and he squatted with his back against the cave wall. Following his example, I sat cross-legged on his right, while Annabelle folded her knees under her on his other side. Felix and Lulamina sat opposite us, completing the circle.

"Now," Amberen said, "time is short, so I'll cut right to it. I am only here because you told Vinkalathis you could restore our homeworld. My kinsman seems to trust you."

Those attentive ears swiveled to focus on Felix.

"I am skeptical, and I do not have much time," he

continued. "The council of elders has voted for our small colony to leave Earth the day after tomorrow."

I blew out my breath. I had half expected him to say that, but it was still a disappointment to hear it. If they went, Vinny would go with them.

Felix took it worse. He looked like someone had abandoned him on the side of a country road near nowhere and nothing. His face crumpled, and a tear leaked out of his eye.

Amberen held up a hand. "I aim to hear you out. It is not every day that such a claim is made. If what you say is valid, there is time for the council to reconsider. Convince me."

Vinny, who had remained standing at his makeshift food counter kneading dough, swiveled his ears in our direction.

Others in the cave—Amberen's entourage, his friends and advisors—pretended not to pay attention to the conversation. They were being polite.

Felix swallowed and began to wring his bottom set of hands like he was squeezing out invisible water. He glanced at me.

I gave him a thumbs up, encouraging him to proceed.

"It is, uh, possible to restore the Pangozil world," he said. "As I understand it, the singularity has been arrested. Is that correct?"

He nodded sadly. "Yes, they coldsealed it in resin from the mines of Panaseah."

Felix drew in a sharp breath. "That is... yes, that might hold. For a while, anyway. Who's monitoring it right now?"

"The Federation evacuated the continent and set up an orbital blockade. Still, half of our population remains there. If the coldseal fails, the singularity will tear a chunk out of the planet. It will vent our atmosphere into space and render our homeworld unlivable."

Felix said, "It'll be worse than that, I'll bet. It'll tear the planet in two."

"We pray our kin survive," Amberen said. "But even if they do, where will they go? We need a permanent solution."

"Reverse the singularity," Felix said. "Or rather, prevent it from coming into being in the first place."

"But how?"

"My invention—the timepiece. You can use it to reach into the past and dismantle the singularity as it forms," Felix said. "Effectively prevent it from coming into being in the first place."

"Even if such a thing were possible," Amberen said, "temporal manipulation is against Federation mandates. They'd destroy it if we tried to use it."

"Or... they'd confiscate it and its inventor, forcing them to study the device in their secret weapons research facility. They might even reverse-engineer it, making it possible for the Peacekeepers to detect and hunt down such a weapon."

Amberen's ever-moving ears paused in what I interpreted as surprise. "Or they might do that," Amberen allowed. "Are you saying what I think you're saying?"

"It's already happened." The Torlik bobbed his cyclopean head. "I invented the device, and they confiscated it. In order to continue my experiments, I worked for the Federation for half my life before I stole it. If they find me, they'll take me into custody, and it won't be voluntary this time. The device was in high security lockdown until I took it and came here to find you."

"I suppose even a fragment of a clan's exodus is a difficult secret to keep quiet." Amberen leaned forward, cloudy eyes piercing Felix's center. "Can I see this device?"

Felix grimaced and clenched his hands together. He stared down as his great eye watered.

When it was clear he'd lost his voice, I spoke for him. "The timepiece was stolen. Felix here was attacked, but he survived."

"Correction," Felix said. "I was murdered, and only my forethought in installing a backup personal rewinder saved my life."

"A Sevrit took the device. She gave it to Tanamir."

"A Sevrit?" Amberen asked. "Working with the Tetrad? They tend to be extremely loyal, even under duress."

Annabelle said, "We believe it was a crime of opportunity. She came to find Tanamir, and when she saw the device, she stole it and delivered it to him to gain his favor. They have a history, the two of them."

It was Amberen's turn to scowl. He stared at Felix as if he would eat the chubby orange offworlder. But he did not lash out or move a muscle. "And now Tanamir has it."

"He hasn't used it yet," I offered. "He seems to have gone into hiding after the Federation ship appeared."

"And how do you know? With the timepiece in his possession, if he doesn't want you to see him, you won't."

Annabelle nodded. "I'm with you on that one."

"The Peacekeepers can detect temporal anomalies—Felix just explained that. The Federation developed detection tools as a countermeasure. Tanamir hasn't used it yet, or I would have heard about it from Dyna or Kilos. My guess is he's waiting for the right time."

Amberen took several slow breaths while he reflected on this information. "What is your plan to recover it?" he finally asked.

All eyes turned to me. Now it was my turn to feel the heat of the spotlight. "Working on that. Any ideas?"

Amberen searched the room. Pangozil bodies turned on their haunches to regard us, their ears swiveling and reaching to hear.

"Well, the council has made their decision," Amberen said. "I am but one member of the body. Changing their minds is not up to me alone."

Felix deflated.

"But..."

The dejected Torlik perked up. As did every Pangozil head in the room.

"The fate of our homeworld is at stake," Amberen said. "And we are presented with an opportunity."

Over fifty Pangozil rose to their feet and turned to face us. Even Vinny, whose hands had been busy during this whole conversation, stepped away from his oven, brushing floury paws on his apron. He seized a pastry as he stepped forward, one that had been cooling on the stone, and tossed it to a tall, lean soldier wearing those loose wrappings. This Pangozil stood nearly seven feet tall, towering over the others in the room.

He snapped the snack hungrily out of the air and chewed it with relish.

Others around the room began to chant something in the Pangozil native language. I didn't understand the words, but they filled the room with an excited tension.

"We will abide by the decision of the council," said Amberen over the noise. "Until then... We have thirty-six hours to draw the enemy out. There is much work to be done. Let us begin."

CHAPTER NINETEEN

AMBEREN WAS RIGHT.

We'd never be able to outwit Tanamir if he saw us coming.

Our best chance to get the timepiece back was to draw him out and take him by surprise.

After some brainstorming, we settled on one of two options: a devastating smash and grab... or a stealthy pickpocket.

I argued for the former.

The major vulnerability of the timepiece was that it had to be worn by the operator—initially as a helmet, but the last time I'd seen it, as a necklace.

Which meant Tanamir would most likely be wearing it.

Jaiyana had told me that I couldn't move faster than she could think. Felix said the device's touch created a neural link with the wearer. It read their intentions and let them control it with their thoughts.

"Then a smash and grab won't work," Annabelle argued.

"It will if he doesn't see us coming."

"You only have one try to get it right. What if you can't find it?"

"It's a necklace. He'll be wearing it. I'll just yank it off."

"What if it's under his shirt?"

"Fabric won't stop me." I flexed my dangerous hand. "I'll knock him out so I can have more time to search."

"Like he won't have bodyguards."

I gestured around to the twenty Pangozil who had spread out around the cave to do calisthenics. "That's where they come in."

"No," Felix said, slashing all four hands across his body. "Way too dangerous. We can't afford to damage or destroy the timepiece."

"If it gets damaged, can't you fix it?"

"Not easily! Argh. Idiot human—"

"Watch it," I said. It seemed that Felix got mean when he was frustrated. And I guess my temper was getting shorter, too.

The Torlik blanched. "I have neither the time nor the tools here on Earth to repair serious damage to the timepiece. No. Stealth and coercion are the only viable options."

"Let's say it does get damaged, but you still take it from Earth. Can't you fix it before you need it on Pango?"

"Probably. If I have the right tools. If the Federation doesn't catch me and lock me back up first."

I sighed. "Even if we try to be sneaky—and I'm not sure that's best—there's a real chance things could go wrong. Let's say Jaiyana or Tanamir do manage to activate the timepiece. How do we fight them if they can predict our every move?"

Felix shared more about how the timepiece functioned. It wasn't time travel. Not exactly. You couldn't travel back years and stay there like Marty McFly, working to alter the flow of time over a span of weeks or months. You had to work locally, one event at a time.

It could only keep you in the past for about an hour before you snapped back to the present. You also couldn't activate it, say, and then run across the city. It would need to be amplified to work across a wider area, much like it would need a substantial power source to reverse the singularity on Pango. Felix mumbled some technobabble about its density and that it would detonate if it focused too much power on a single point. I didn't follow the nuances there. Math was never my strong suit.

What I honed in on was what Felix called the device's *depth*. The device could take you back decades or even centuries, to a specific moment in time.

But it could only transport you a few weeks into the future.

"Traveling into the past is easy," Felix said, "It's going forward that's hard. The future is too... fungible, especially if you don't stay there, but it does allow you to jump forward."

"How so?"

"It's like looking into a foggy mirror. I've tried going too far into the future. It can be... disassociating." He shuddered. "Anyway, when I came back on the street the night Jaiyana killed me, my personal rewinder brought me back at the edge of the device's range."

"You're lucky the Sevrit didn't kill you again on the way out."

Felix's orange skin blanched, turning a pale, yellowish tint. "Don't remind me."

"Whether we 'smash and grab' or use stealth to divest the old general of the device," Amberen said, "they're really two different ways to describe the same scenario. One is simply a bit more heavy-handed." He glanced at me.

I guffawed, then smiled broadly. "Heavy handed! I like him. He's funny."

With Amberen mediating, we aligned on what mattered. Namely, that our best chance to get the timepiece back was to lure Tanamir out with bait. Then, we had to hit him from his blind side—hard and fast. He couldn't see us coming or he'd use the timepiece to escape.

Felix started to have another anxiety attack. Since he wasn't going to be on the team that executed this plan, Lulamina took him by the hand and they departed.

We continued the discussions. As it turned out, the Pangozil were face-to-face fighters, not stealthy ninjas, but that didn't mean they weren't good at disguising themselves. Some of the big marsupials amazed me with their cloaking tricks. They didn't just disguise someone as a human; they could also blend into the shadows of corners.

"This might really work," I said to Vinny while we were taking a break. "Your guys seem like capable operatives."

"They are. Hard not to be when you're raised in conflict."

The other Pangos had gone for a walk to stretch their legs. Annabelle and Amberen were the only ones left in the cave with us. They chatted quietly while Annabelle held her palms out toward the heat of a warmer. Amberen made a joke, and Annabelle laughed with a warm smile. It was good to see her without anxiety creasing her brow or her eyes perma-glued to her cell phone screen, even if only for a little while.

They must have seen me watching. Annabelle glanced at me, then came over to join us.

"How are you feeling, Andy?"

"We're still missing a few pieces, but I'm encouraged. We have allies now. Numbers are on our side, and the Pangozil soldiers seem capable."

"It still doesn't seem like a sure thing," Annabelle said.

"It's the best chance we've got."

"Better a small chance to recover the world of the Pangozil than no chance at all," Amberen said, nodding at me.

"This sort of stuff is your specialty, Anderson, not mine," Annabelle said. "I'm better with research and story." She shook her phone, as if to indicate her superpower. "What if Tanamir's got a bunch of flunkies around him? He likes to use crowds to insulate him from the authorities. Or what if he stays on his ship?"

"We've got to lure him off it," I said.

"As I also concluded," Amberen said.

I nodded my agreement

"So," Amberen said, "the only question that remains is... who will be our bait?"

"Who?" I asked dumbly.

Annabelle's jaw set. "I'll do it."

All eyes turned to her.

"Wait, no!" I said. "That wasn't part of the plan."

"It's simple, Andy. Tanamir wants to gain cachet among humanity," she said. "All we have to do is offer him a stage. That'll get him off his ship *and* away from his people."

"What kind of stage?" I asked.

"I have a couple of ideas," Annabelle said, glancing at her cell phone, and then up at Amberen again. "If your people can stomach the risk, then so can I."

"The continued existence of my entire species is at risk, Ms. Summers. There is little I won't be able to tolerate."

Amberen studied her curiously. “How strong is your stomach?”

Whether due to frayed nerves or one too many meat pies, Annabelle dashed to the side of the cave and dry heaved into a trash can.

I came over to meet her, rubbing her back with one hand.

“Some journalist I am,” Annabelle muttered. “I’m more scared of showing my face on camera than a Federation battlecruiser. I wonder if I was this scared when Elekatch snatched me off the street.”

I frowned at her. We’d never know, since Annabelle had lost those memories.

“Different kind of danger,” I said. “In your defense, the mystery meat upset my stomach a bit, too.”

“Hey, don’t spread rumors about the chef, ” Vinny said, “It was seasoned beef. Nothing you haven’t had before.”

She gave me a weak smile, then wiped her mouth with the back of one hand. “I’ll do it.”

“I wish I could contact the Peacekeepers. I want to tell them our plan. They could detect the anomaly and warn us when it was activated.”

“I’ll bet they’re up on that flying fortress,” Annabelle said.

I remembered the way I’d wanted to fly up there when the ship first arrived. If I had a plane of my own or a practical way to get there, I might have done it. “That’s probably why they dipped out,” I said, “The commander summoned them to the mothership.”

Amberen and Vinny disagreed with this assessment.

“You’re talking like the Federation is run by reasoning people, or your own officers of the law,” Vinny said.

"Isn't it?" I asked.

"Ehhhh," Vinny said. He had packed all his ingredients into lidded plastic bins. Now, he was washing his tools in a shallow sink set into the cave wall. "No. It's more impersonal than that. The worker bees flying that ship aren't trained to think for themselves. It's more like the Borg in *Star Trek*."

"Resistance is futile," I said in a robotic voice.

Annabelle rewarded me with a sparkling laugh. "Dork."

"Sort of," Vinny said. "There are definitely Lodian officers on that ship. Maybe officer is the wrong word... More like, a combination between 'politician' and 'bureaucrat.' Button-pushers, we sometimes call 'em."

"And they're here to enforce the law."

"They're here to push buttons. The Federation enforces the law."

"I don't understand the difference," I admitted.

Amberen waved one wiry-haired paw. "It's not important right now. Let's focus on the plan."

"Is that why you fought them on Pango?" asked Annabelle.

Amberen seemed as concerned as I was about Annabelle's role in it. But he seemed inclined to humor her. He considered her question before answering. "Among other reasons, yes. For the Pangozil, the Tetrad's cause is compelling: an independent, autonomous future where we control and enforce our own laws, independent of the Federation. We are a community-oriented people, and the way the Lodians have augmented themselves and outsourced control of their society to the Federation machine is distasteful to us. They take things to the extreme."

I squeezed my metal fingers into a fist again, taking a second to marvel at the strength I felt there. It was truly amazing what their technology could do. It felt like real skin and bones—I didn't necessarily have all the touch sensation I used to, but I had no trouble visualizing the hand in my mind's eye *as if it were my natural hand.* It lent me incredible strength, and could also withstand great suffering in ways other parts of my body could not.

The Peacekeepers had locked down the rest of the augments that lay dormant within me. I wondered what else I was capable of.

And what did that imply about what the Federation ship overhead could do? If Lodian tech could weaponize my hand, how would they equip their battlecruisers tasked with maintaining intergalactic security?

"Which of these two evils is worse?" Annabelle asked. "How do we know we're making the right decision?"

Again, Amberen took a deep breath. "The Federation has caused plenty of harm, but if you ask me, the Tetrad are worse. They work by causing chaos and discontent, at least in the short term. If they gain the upper hand here, Earth will be much worse off than under Federation rule."

"We'll just have to hope the Peacekeepers are still on our side," I said, "If Dyna's still watching, she'll do her best to give us advance warning. But if Tanamir's smart—and I think he is—he'll know they're watching and won't use it until and unless he's forced to."

"So we have to force his hand," Annabelle said. "Like I said, I'm the best chance we've got."

Over the next few hours, Annabelle laid out an ingenious trap for Tanamir. It was, apparently, an idea she'd gone directly to Amberen with. It hurt to know she bypassed me like that, but it made sense at the same time because hearing it out loud made me sick with worry for her.

And yet, once she'd finished explaining, I had to admit that it was brilliant in its simplicity, for it appealed directly to Tanamir's primary weakness—the vanity of his reputation and his desire to be in the spotlight at all times.

I hated the idea of using Annabelle as bait... she'd been put in horrible danger because of me on more than one occasion.

And yet she remained firm in her resolve.

"If we do this right, the world will be watching," Annabelle said.

"If he hurts you..."

"He's invested a lot into building a certain reputation as a speaker of truth and a helper of humankind," Annabelle said. "I don't think he'll resort to violence against me. At least not on camera."

"I think you're right," I admitted. "Which scares me. Because if he doesn't resort to violence, he probably has something worse in mind."

CHAPTER TWENTY

ANNABELLE MADE several long phone calls and called in a few favors. She teased the announcement to her fans through a network of private email relays.

The next morning, KXAN announced that Marsha Marshall would do an exclusive interview with the pilot of the flying saucer, the Lodian known as Tanamir Voss, *live* on television this coming Thursday night.

The news spread like wildfire.

It was the first time anyone had named the Lodian species publicly, drawing the interest of national outlets that had been using "extraterrestrial" and "alien" in their terminology.

Simultaneously, Annabelle published a dossier on Lodians that included everything she knew about them: summaries of their biology, history, culture, some photographs, even a brief passage about mating rituals (somehow she had discovered that they were monogamous, which she claimed made them more relatable). All this lent credibility to her position, as well as some criticism that she'd been holding out on folks.

No use hiding it, Annabelle tweeted. *I waited until the time was right.*

Some of this, Annabelle told me, came from Lulamina's library. But she had put together most of it from observation and first-hand accounts.

I knew she took extensive notes and always tried to sneak photographs of offworlders for her private collection. But this was the first time I'd realized the full extent of her obsession.

Later that night, she landed a national syndication deal with CNN.

They invited her out to Atlanta to do the interview at their station. She insisted on keeping it at home here in Texas.

Annabelle threw another piece of bait into the bloody media waters. A juicy one for long-time fans and curious onlookers alike.

Marsha Marshall—the woman who first broke the news of offworlders on Earth—promised to show her face for the first time.

The only kicker? Tanamir had yet to RSVP.

"Think he'll show up?" Annabelle asked me.

"He'd be crazy not to," I said. "You're 'Internet Famous' now."

"I think I'm gonna be sick," she said, rolling down the window of her minivan and dry heaving into the wind. A stream of cold air whipped into the vehicle, chilling the back of my neck. I leaned into it, bracing, and felt my nerves settle. My pistol was heavy again in its shoulder holster beneath my left arm, hidden by my jean jacket but within easy reach. Comforting.

I glanced up at the sky, a new habit I couldn't quite break. The bright blue sky was clear, both of clouds and of the Federation battlecruiser, which had finally parked over the sea several miles off the coast of Corpus Christi. It hadn't moved in about twelve hours. The US Air Force still circled, waiting for the order, but held its fire. The media suppressed the story about Cuba's missiles—we'd seen rumor threads on various social networks and online forums, but nothing that could be confirmed.

Annabelle leaned back in the van and wiped her mouth on her sleeve. "If he doesn't show, I'm ruined."

"Give yourself a break, eh? If he no-shows—and I don't think he will—your fans will forgive you."

"It's a big risk. Can you imagine? My first interview with a national syndication deal, and my subject doesn't show up."

"You can always spin it as a refusal to cooperate. Cast doubt on his motives. That sort of thing."

"CNN expects an interview, Andy. If he doesn't show, and it turns out we lied to CNN… it's CNN, Andy!"

"You're right. I hear you," I said, trying to avoid riling her up even worse. She was anxious about the interview. "But we talked about this. It's too good an opportunity for Tanamir to pass up—he'll be there."

"How do you *know*? Journalistic integrity is everything. If he doesn't show, it hurts my reputation. I'll be ruined."

"Even the most beautiful girls get stood up once in a while."

"Is that supposed to be comforting? I don't like that metaphor. I don't like it at all."

We reached the station a few minutes later. Even though we were two hours early, there was a crowd waiting for us by the front door, a mixture of Marsha's fans, reporters and other rubberneckers. I drove around and parked a block away at the rear. We had called ahead, and when we arrived, we were ushered in through the side door. The crowd, noticing, ran to greet us, waving signs and shouting for Ms. Marshall to answer "just one question," but we slipped into the door and avoided any interaction.

Annabelle got set up while I checked the exits and secured the building.

Slowly, our friends began to arrive, and when they did, I let them in through the side door—a dozen or so Pangozil, all wearing cloaking shields to disguise themselves as nondescript men in jeans, polo shirts and baseball caps. I snuck the first few Pangos in unnoticed. When Vinny arrived with the third group, the cameramen and showrunners started giving me nervous looks, but I shrugged and told them they were security staff for Ms. Marshall.

"Not even the governor had this much security," said one camera operator.

"Yeah," a skinny blonde producer added. "We interviewed him last summer during his campaign."

I shrugged again. "I don't give the orders. Just follow 'em."

Someone went and got the station manager. "No more people inside," he said, "We're at capacity for the fire code."

"Are we?"

He lowered his voice. "I'm worried about the crowd out front. We don't... This doesn't usually happen."

"Of course," I said. I tried to be accommodating. "Should we call the police?"

"No," he said. "No, of course not."

Alek texted me when he arrived. I went to the side door to let him in, and one of the producers stepped between me and the door. I dodged left, and when he stepped into my way, he went down hard, hitting the tile floor and hurting his shoulder as he twisted.

"Enough!" cried the producer. "Stop it. We said no more people inside."

"But he's my boss," I said.

"Boys." Annabelle came running. "Boys!"

After a tense standoff, she convinced them to let Alek inside.

Given his height with that cowboy hat, the snakeskin boots, the accent, and the way I introduced him as my "boss", the staff immediately deferred to him. He just had that air about him that made him seem important. And, by this point, they were happy to deal with someone other than me.

"Here's what we're gonna do," Alek said, and went on to negotiate the right for himself and "Ms. Marshall's personal security team" to stay inside. Vinny—who'd been one of the security staff I sneaked in—took the lead. I trusted him to keep Annabelle as safe as possible, and we didn't want Tanamir or any of his people to recognize me.

The enormous Pangozil with the snapping jaws, the jovial leader with the big appetite who told us to call him Feriss, left with me and four other Pangos.

As we departed, I caught Annabelle's eyes one last time. She nodded, then slipped back into her dressing room.

"Good luck," I mouthed. Then I ducked out of the building along with several of the Pango soldiers.

And none too soon, either. As we stepped into the

sunlight, shouts and the noisy volume of intense conversation rang out from the front of the building.

Tanamir's escort had arrived. The razor edge of a saucer shimmered into sight. Waves of heated air rippled underneath, making the view of the street behind him blurry as the craft landed. They set down smack dab in the middle of the parking lot, gridlocking the whole situation.

"Go, go, go!" I said, shooing Feriss and four of his Pangozil comrades toward the rear of the building.

CHAPTER TWENTY-ONE

WE RAN flat out to our vehicle.

Tanamir's people didn't give any sign they'd noticed us, which was good. But if they had, and then turned back time, would we even know about it?

It hurt my head to think about, so I stopped trying and focused on action. I used the key remote to unlock our rental car when we got near. A dark blue Ford Expedition flashed its lights at me. Feriss moved to the driver's seat, while I climbed into the front passenger side, and the others piled into the back.

I'd had to scour the Austin suburbs to find the right car, but I finally did. It was the same make, model and color as the newer police cruisers, only without the twirling lights on top and APD markings on its side.

Fortunately, it didn't need to have the lights or decals for the disguise to work—it needed to be close enough to trick the eye.

As the others got comfortable, I slapped the cloaking

shield Zavis had made for me onto the roof of the vehicle. It was held in place by two adhesive strips.

When I hit the button to activate the device, the Ford Expedition sprouted light bars and APD logos. The lights spun brightly, blue and red, illuminating nearby objects just as well as the real thing.

I grinned. "Perfect."

I hit the button on my second device—the one in my pocket. This one went on me, turning me into a generic-looking dark-haired cop with light brown skin.

I looked into the mirror and admired cheekbones that were higher than mine and a thick brush mustache. I still felt like myself with a six-day stubble, but the mustache in my rearview mirror was thick and black.

"Hah!" I said. "Look at that."

My eyes moved over my shoulder to the four junior police officers, now squished in the back seat behind an illusionary metal grate separating the front and back compartments. "You four look like the Super Troopers got arrested for drinking and driving."

They gave me a funny look.

"Yippee ki-yay!" I hooted.

They stared back at me blankly.

"What are you talking about?" asked Feriss.

"Forget it. Let's go. I'm sure news about that saucer is spreading fast."

While Feriss drove us around front, I took out my phone and found the interview's live feed, making sure I had a good connection to hear Annabelle when it started up. I put in one headphone so I could hear even if I wasn't looking at the screen. The feed showed a countdown for two minutes.

Tanamir had cut his arrival close. They were probably miking him up right now.

We circled back toward the station and waited in a parking lot on North Lamar, across from a parking garage covered in green vines.

I'm sure reports about the saucer were making havoc on the police department's radio channels. We waited at the intersection until the first cruiser came screaming down North Lamar. As it skidded onto MLK Blvd, I recognized Officer Daniels. Two other cars followed close behind him, sirens blaring. Feriss stepped on it, joining the rear of the caravan.

We tailed them to the front of the KXAN building. Blood pounded in my ears. Feriss parked, and I jumped out of the SUV. Officer Daniels headed toward the crowd to secure the alien ship.

At our arrival, cars and people dispersed. They vanished down the sidewalk and through the alley like underage teens at a fraternity kegger.

Although most didn't keep running. Once they were out of range of the cops, they stopped and turned to watch from behind corners and hedges, and on the lawns of houses. That was fine by me. We didn't need them to leave, just get out of range so they didn't become collateral damage.

"Clear the area!" Officer Daniels was saying to a crowd of stubborn reporters and Marsha Marshall fans who insisted on staying closer by. "I don't want anyone within a hundred feet of the entrance. I don't care if you're with the press. It's not curtailing your freedoms to make you watch from over there."

"Daniels," I said, "we're headed around to secure the side and rear entrances."

Daniels nodded, not taking his eyes off the two groups of onlookers. If he thought it weird that I knew his name, he gave no sign.

With my gut doing somersaults, I loped around the side of the building. While our plan to arrive early and plant people in disguise inside and outside the building had worked so far, the real test was what happened next.

We didn't know how long the interview would last, or which exit Tanamir would choose. So we had to secure them all and then wait for Vinny to tell us which one he was trying to leave by. Their job on the inside was to encourage him to leave by the side exit.

"Do you have eyes on our target?" I asked into the comms we'd established. The audio for that didn't come from my headphone, but one of those ear-bugs the offworlders preferred.

"I've got eyes on him," Vinny whispered, his voice seemed to resonate in my skull. "He's in makeup. If he's wearing the device, he's hiding it well. I don't see it on him."

Shit. My heart hammered in my chest. "Then where is it?"

"Don't know. Do you see the Sevrit out there?"

"No. The saucer is still parked out front, but there are no offworlders near it."

I peeked around the building to see it standing stationary and closed. A police officer—one of the Pangozil—had climbed atop it. He squatted down and picked at a seam with his fingers. He stood again, frowning. He looked in my direction and shook his head.

"Must be sealed up," I reported to Vinny. "None of his people are out here that I can see. Who came in with him?"

"Two Lodians, not armed. He walked right into the

makeup room like he owned the place. Okay, he's coming out now."

As Vinny went radio silent again, I looked around me, searching for any of his other people lurking in the bushes or around a corner. I tensed, terrified that the Sevrit would jump out and kick me in the balls.

I forced myself to breathe through my nose. I didn't believe she could see through the cloaking shields—that modification was reserved for Peacekeepers and those who took their drugs. To her, I would look like just another uniform searching the exterior of the building on behalf of the APD.

At least, that's what I told myself in order to stay calm.

"You two," I pointed at the group of four Pangozil who'd followed me. "Post up."

They nodded and took up positions on the side and rear doors like we'd rehearsed. They already knew that if Tanamir came out of one of these exits, they were to grab the timepiece and scram with it.

We only had one chance to get it before he manipulated the situation at the speed of thought.

I circled the building on my own. When I came back around front, I saw a new police vehicle—this one unmarked—had arrived. I groaned.

Detective Simmons climbed out of his car, eyes scanning the parking lot and building.

My heart skipped a beat when his gaze rested on me. Would he see something wrong with my disguise, and get suspicious? Simmons frowned, the ever-present creases of annoyance on his brow deepening. It must have been indigestion or something because he turned and moved on.

Simmons picked out Officer Daniels and approached the man. "What's the situation?" he asked.

"Vehicle is illegally parked." Daniels thumbed at the UFO.

"Is that freak inside?" He meant Tanamir, but Officer Daniels was too professional to take the bait.

"You mean the alien leader with the cloak? We think so. First priority was to secure the area."

"We've got trouble," I whispered to Vinny through the earpiece. "Simmons and Gonzalez are here."

Detective Gonzalez had gotten out and moved toward the street. Passing cars were parking along Martin Luther King Jr. Blvd and getting out to photograph the saucer with their phones.

It was starting to jam up traffic. She was trying to get them to drive on.

"I'll get eyes on the offworlders," Simmons said, walking toward the front door. "You do something about the traffic."

I stepped in front of Simmons and stopped him with a hand on his chest. Feriss, flanking the front door with one other Pangozil, would have stopped him before he went inside. But why let *them* have all the fun?

"Sorry, Detective," I said. "No one goes in or out."

A quizzical look came over Detective Simmon's face. Had he recognized my voice?

"Why not?" he asked.

"Fire code," I said. "Plus, they lock it down before they air live broadcasts so that no one can interrupt it."

I made that part up, but what did this fool know?

His curiosity about me crumbled under the heat of his sudden anger. "They can't possibly be at capacity already. How many people are in there?"

More than anyone knows. "Lots of production crew," I said. "Not sure exactly. Just what they said."

The frown lines in the detective's forehead formed writhing crevasses. "I'm a detective on official business." Flecks of foamy spit flew from his dry mouth. "Move out of the way."

"It's your funeral,“ I said, forcing a smile into my voice. "But I'll warn you, the station manager doesn't take any crap. Apparently, the fire department is strict about their codes, and even if they weren't, it didn't seem like she wanted to be interrupted. We agreed to stay outside."

"I'm going in."

He shoved past Feriss and tried the door.

It was locked. I figured Vinny must have heard our conversation and gotten it.

"Fine," he said, "I'm not here for that alien freak anyway."

Chewing on his cheek and wandering back toward his car, Simmons glanced around him, as if expecting bad weather. I knew he was looking for Dyna and Kilos, and the only reason he was here was that the last place we'd seen the Peacekeepers had been in front of Tanamir's ship at the capitol riot downtown.

They probably figured the Peacekeepers would show up.

All I knew was that if Gonzalez figured out I was here or Simmons interfered with the legitimate officers because he felt affronted, it would throw the whole plan into disarray.

"Thanks for locking the door, Vinny," I whispered into my mic, taking up my post beside Feriss.

"Uh, that wasn't me."

My blood froze. "Was it one of your guys?"

Segment opening music played on the audio feed.

"We're live in 10... 9... 8..." I heard someone say in the background of Vinny's mic.

"Vinny, what's going on in there?"

"Don't think it was one of us, Gunn." Vinny said. "They're starting. Tanamir is on stage with Annabelle."

"Everyone in position?"

"So far, so good." He drew in a sharp breath.

"What is it?"

Nothing.

"Vinny? Vinny, can you hear me?"

Vinny was panting heavily when his voice returned. "Gunn, that Sevrit is in here with us."

"What happened?" I asked.

"Found one of your soldiers in the stairwell," Vinny said. "His throat's cut clean through."

CHAPTER TWENTY-TWO

FERISS GROWLED deep in his chest. The large Pango shook his head and his lips quivered as they peeled back from his teeth in a feral snarl.

I seized the front door handle and shook it. It was locked. What's more, the space between the doors was now filling with some kind of sealant foam. It oozed out through the cracks and hardened before my eyes. I chipped off a piece with my fingertips and it was replaced by more oozing foam, growing so fast it soon covered half the glass.

"Break down the door," I said.

The oversized Pango snapped out of his revenge daydream and drove his shoulder into the glass. It cracked, but the foam held it in place. He grunted like he'd hit a brick wall, recovered and pulled back to strike again.

Shards of glass tinkled down to the pavement as he struck a second time. His shirt ripped, but he didn't get through. He clawed at the glass with his hands, snarling with rage. The foam bubbled and oozed, glomming onto his fingers where it hardened within seconds. He had to crack it off like dried clay, striking his fists against the building's exterior walls to dislodge it.

"Side entrance," I said, "Go!"

I turned to see if anyone else had noticed what was happening. Officer Daniels narrowed his eyes and reached back for his pistol. Detective Gonzalez had turned from her conversation with a reporter. She looked cross yet perplexed.

"You two!" Simmons shouted, starting toward us with wide eyes. "Why are you leaving your posts? Hey! I want to see your badge number and identification, the both of you. Stop!"

"Walk," I whispered.

"They already know!" Feriss snarled back.

"Just walk until we're out of sight."

"I said stop!" Simmons shouted.

As soon as we turned the corner, we broke into a dead run. One of the Pangozil soldiers posted at the side entrance hauled the door open when he spotted us. I reached him in a few breaths, almost tripping as I slowed. My body fetched up against the door's frame, but it was already filled with expanding foam that had hardened at the edges.

Only the Pangozil's quick reaction of pulling the door open to reveal the blockage had given me any chance of getting through. I had three or four seconds—maybe—before it hardened into a solid wall like the front door had.

I took a deep breath, pulled back my cyborg hand, and slammed my fist through the softest part of the foam in the center of the doorway. The foam bent and cracked under the power of my alien hardware. I pulled back and struck again, this time twisting from the hips and putting my whole body into the punch.

My arm sank up to the elbow. Fissures in the material spread out from the puncture I'd made. Feriss kicked a booted foot into the stuff below my arm, and we broke through into a dark and empty hallway.

"We're in," I panted, crumbling the hardening plaster off my jacket. It was heavy like cement with the flaky consistency of freeze-dried ice cream. Weird.

I drew my sidearm and flicked off the safety. "Where are you?" I whispered to myself.

The hall was dim and quiet. I found a switch and turned on the light. Fluorescent bulbs flickered to life in the ceiling.

"Southern stairwell," Vinny replied through my earpiece.

"I was wondering about the Sevrit, not you," I said. "She tried to seal the exits. Front door is blocked but we got in through the side door."

"Stay put. I'm coming to you."

A minute later, Vinny stumbled through the doorway, eyes wide. His hands and jeans were stained dark with blood.

He glanced down when he saw me staring and cursed. A smart clicking sounded, and his cloaking shield re-cast itself, the blood stains disappearing beneath a fresh coat of optical illusion.

I still saw them, like red spots in my vision, provided I looked away and relaxed my eyes. I tried not to.

"What happened?" Feriss asked. "Did he say anything before you lost him?"

"No," Vinny said. "He was dead when I got there."

Feriss spoke into his earpiece for a minute. He spoke in his own language, but I figured he was checking in on the others we'd planted in hiding.

"We're missing two others."

"Annabelle?" I asked.

"She's safe," he said. "Ritga and Polem have eyes on her."

"Jaiyana knows we're here," I said.

We took that in for a moment. The Sevrit commando could be anywhere. If she had the timepiece, we'd never see her coming.

"So, she's killing us off one by one," Feriss growled. "Catching us when we're alone. We stick together now."

"She could be anyone, too," I pointed out. "You sure you can't see through it like I can?" I asked. I nodded at Vinny's pants. I could see the bloodstains if I relaxed my gaze, but only for a second. "The cloaks don't flicker for you?"

"No," Vinny said. "Told you. Peacekeepers only gave *you* the performance-enhancing drugs. Put it to good use and spot this Sevrit before she jumps us next time."

There was shouting behind us. The "cops" standing guard outside had closed the door to stop Detective Simmons from getting in, but they needn't have worried. The expanding foam had finished filling the hole we'd made and dried. Simmons and the other cops were stuck outside.

The three of us put our backs together. I studied shadowed corners and ceiling panels. If she was hiding behind a cloaking shield of her own, only I'd be able to see her coming, and only then if I was looking when it happened.

"Oh, damn," I said, pulling my phone out. "We missed the start of Annabelle's interview." In the run here, the app had closed and I'd lost the feed. I hadn't even noticed. "Screw it, if the Sevrit's lurking around I want eyes on her. Let's go."

The three of us made our way through the building. We passed several bewildered-looking staff who ogled our weapons. I stiffened my spine and nodded at them. A cop was the only person in a building who could stalk through, bearing a weapon, and cause people to calm instead of panic. The reporters still weren't used to seeing firearms in the workplace.

None of them gave the telltale flickering sign of a cloaking shield, however, and I felt we were safe to proceed. My neck itched and I kept glancing over my shoulder.

As we entered the waiting room adjacent to the studio, two producers objected to our approach in strained whispers. A secretary, startled by the sight of us, dropped a water glass.

It hit the floor with a crash and a splash.

So much for calming people.

"There," Vinny said, pointing at a set of double doors while people hurried to clean up the mess. "The studio's through that door."

"Pardon us." I let my gun drop to my side and gave what I hoped was a reassuring smile to the news crew. "Anyone seen the other offworlders?"

They all pointed toward the studio.

Putting my pistol behind my back with one hand, I opened the door and slipped inside.

When I laid eyes on Annabelle, sitting poised and serious-looking with a notebook open in her lap, I sighed in genuine relief.

She was so focused she never glanced our way. To my right were several expensive-looking cameras and camera operators laden down with headphones, stabilizing frames and handheld equipment.

In the armchair facing Annabelle sat Tanamir. He was

turned away from the door with his cloak draped over the armchair behind him, his legs crossed casually.

Standing between us, behind the camera operators, was the production team: the director, several producers and several more assistants, about a dozen in total.

Two Lodians stood among them, undisguised—Tanamir's people. They looked more like businessmen than soldiers.

The Sevrit was nowhere to be seen.

Several of the news crew frowned in our direction. I sheathed my gun and put up my empty hands. They left us alone to watch.

The two Lodians in the crowd frowned and conversed quietly, but didn't move to intercept us. One of them took notes, the other had an armful of jackets and bags.

I eyed them as I settled into a shadowy corner. They weren't making any attempt to hide their true forms. I glanced around, searching for our hidden allies, and found them in the odd shape of a shadow in the far corner, and the way the light bent on the near side of the stage.

"You see her?" Vinny asked.

I shook my head.

We put our backs to the wall and, finally, I allowed myself to focus on the interview.

"Enough background," Annabelle said. "Let's get to the real question: You say you want to be our ally. Our friend. Why should we believe you?"

"If you don't believe my words, measure me by my actions," Tanamir said. "I've done some good here on Earth."

"You mean like saving that girl's life at the Grand Canyon?"

"That is one example."

"It seems an unusual coincidence that you were there at the right moment to intervene. The Grand Canyon National Park staff hadn't had any accidents in over six months. What were you doing there that day?"

"Sightseeing." Tanamir smiled affably, then shrugged. "I noticed the girl coming close to the edge several times, so I had my pilot keep an eye on her. I can't stand idly by and watch others come to harm. It's my biggest character flaw."

"What about in Mariupol? Were you sightseeing in the middle of a war zone?"

He smiled. "What can I say? I'm a mission-driven person."

"Is that another character flaw?"

"I try to be helpful wherever I go."

"It's not like your interference changed the outcome, you know. I spoke to a reporter on the ground. The Russian army came back a few days later and took over the part of the city you repelled them from."

The screens cut to a close-up of a photograph. The street where I'd seen Tanamir's saucer absorb the tank fire was completely demolished.

"That is unfortunate. But the damage caused by your own territorial conflicts will pale in comparison to what that Federation battlecruiser will do if you don't address the problem."

"You think they'd attack us?"

"If they're provoked? Absolutely."

"You told me earlier that you had a long career as a military general for the Federation of Lodi. Did you leave by choice or were you forced to leave?"

"The separation was mutual. I didn't agree with how they treated the peoples they annexed from new worlds."

"Is it true that you were responsible for starting a civil war on a planet called..." She checked her notes. "Abacon."

"That's not true. Abacon's first rebellion was already firmly underway before I arrived."

"My sources tell me that, under your leadership, Federation armed forces have 'scorched' or 'glassed'"—Annabelle used air quotes—"at least five different worlds using planet-busting weapons. One world in particular, home to a species known as the Pangozil, is on the verge of destruction due to your actions."

Tanamir frowned. "Not my actions."

"The Tetrad's—the organization you work for."

"All I know is that the Pangozil held the singularity like a knife to the Federation's throat. The Federation called their bluff, and the imminent destruction of their world is the result."

"What was your involvement?"

"Personally? None." He looked down, then gestured with two open hands. "I wasn't there."

She looked frustrated. I'd be willing to bet that Annabelle wanted to push back on this, but lacked sufficient evidence to make a convincing argument. So she switched tactics. "It appears that the Federation don't take resistance lightly."

"It's different with a core world like Pangozil than it would be with a place like Earth."

"And why is that?"

His smile this time was tight-lipped. His cloak flared up like a serpent who'd been cornered. "Silent planets don't have status yet. Your world is more of a blank slate, and certain ancient regulations govern how they're treated. To the Federation, your world is still primitive. Somewhat of a 'backwater,' to use one of your terms."

"It doesn't seem like you think much of Earth."

"Oh, but I do. I've been touring your world. It's a beautiful place you call home."

Annabelle frowned. "You visited the Grand Canyon, Mariupol, Cairo... What brought you to Austin and to the protests earlier this week?"

"Injustice."

"And what's your opinion on how we should handle the situation in our city?" Annabelle asked, pushing her glasses up on her nose.

"I am here to remind you of the *interplanetary* implications, not to meddle in local politics, except to make you aware that fighting amongst yourselves will prove counterproductive. Your world, especially Austin, has become a destination for offworlders who wish to escape Federation rule. As you have pointed out, Lodians and other species have been here for many years precisely for that reason. I would prefer to keep it that way."

"But this isn't *your* world. You don't get to decide that."

"Don't you think that it's in our mutual interest to send the Federation battlecruiser away?"

"You brought them here, Tanamir. That very large, very intimidating spaceship is here because of you and your public proclamations."

"All I did was speed up the timeline, Ms. Marshall. It was going to happen eventually. The Federation of Lodi is, if nothing else, predictably intractable." Tanamir's smile didn't reach his eyes.

"So you admit it—you brought the Federation's battlecruiser here on purpose."

"I merely removed obstacles to its arrival. The Federation follows a specific playbook when a civilization like yours finally wakes up to the existence of alien life. Once a planet wakes up to the existence of offworlders, it kicks off a series of events and procedures that no one, least of all me, can stop."

"Which brings me back to my point. How do we know we can trust you, since you brought this danger to our shores?"

"As with anything, you have a choice in the matter. You get to decide who to work with, and who to show to the door. But I ask you—would you rather believe the one here today, speaking with you face to face? Or whoever is commanding that Federation battlecruiser parked in your sky, broadcasting orders and ultimatums from behind the safety of their shields and weapons?"

"What orders and ultimatums would those be?" Annabelle asked.

"Don't play coy with me, Ms. Marshall. I know you spoke to the Governor. He must have told you what's been keeping him up at night."

She blinked at him.

"You don't know? Well, I have it on good authority—and they always operate in this way—that the Federation battlecruiser has been broadcasting the same message on repeat. And that the United States Air Force has standing orders to defend this country at the first sign of aggressive action."

"And when did you speak with the governor?"

He leaned forward in his seat with a sly smile. "This morning."

"That seems like something the people of Texas might want to know. What did you two talk about?"

"I won't share details of a private conversation." He smirked at her. "What matters is this broadcast. Don't you think 'We the People' have a right to know what they're up against?"

Annabelle regarded him with a lifted chin. "Of course they do."

Tanamir put his hand into his cloak. I jumped when he did so, my hand flashing to my pistol. But he didn't draw a weapon. He turned as he reached, digging into a pocket inside his cloak while his shoulder ridges flared. Tanamir didn't look at me, but the two Lodians standing with the camera crew watching the interview glanced over. I let my hand drop to my side, doing my best to look bored even though my blood rushed like lava through my veins.

Instead of a weapon, Tanamir withdrew a small handheld electronic device from his pocket. As he did so, I caught a glimpse of the timepiece—a braided silver cord was lashed to the inside of his cloak, secured around his left bicep. The timepiece's shining blue face seemed to pulse with an unnatural shimmer that warped my vision. A moment later, it was covered back up with his cape.

Damn, but that was going to be hard to grab without him noticing.

At the same time, at least the Sevrit didn't have it. It gave me hope that we'd be able to stand against her if she decided to jump us.

"I had my people record the battlecruiser's broadcast," he said. "The governor gave me his leave to share it, given the circumstances."

"Did he now?" Annabelle asked. "I'll have to confirm

that off-air. I would think he'd be more sensitive to national security. You know, under the circumstances."

Tanamir smiled and pressed play on the digital recorder, holding it by his microphone. Annabelle, though she looked unhappy, made no move to stop him.

"By the authority of the Federation of Lodi, in accordance with Directive 4113, Earth is no longer classified as a silent planet. All sentient beings are now under Federation jurisdiction. Any attempts to resist will be met with deadly force."

Marsha Marshall appeared to take this in. She glanced at me—the first time she'd given any sign that she noticed I was in the room. She couldn't see through the cloak, but I made sure she saw my disguise beforehand so she would recognize me.

"It's a variation on the same theme on every world they annex," Tanamir said, putting the digital recorder back. "They never ask your opinion. They simply declare their sovereignty and order you to follow their rules... or else."

"Can you clarify what you mean by 'annex'?" asked Annabelle.

"Earth belongs to the Federation now. You'll have a seat at the table. But one or two representatives from Earth are insignificant in the face of its huge, intergalactic bureaucracy."

"But we would have representation."

"Not in the grand scheme of things. To them, Earth is a speck of dust. A minor blip on the radar."

"How would you suggest we respond?"

"That's up to your leaders. But I pose them a question: What gives the Federation the right to take over? Who put them in charge? Earth is an independent world. Your planet's governments are a Federation of their own! So you have a choice now: Would you like it to stay that way? Or are you ready to bend the knee to your new overlords?"

"Tanamir, isn't the Federation governed by *your* people?"

"The Federation of Lodi is ancient. The government is no more made up of *my people* than the Babylonian Empire is of yours. Besides, only about sixty percent of the functionaries who work in the government are Lodian."

"But still the majority."

"Yes, granted."

"How many species are represented in the Federation?"

"Thousands, but only about a hundred are considered sentient beings and given a vote."

"Suppose the people of Earth decline to participate?"

"Good luck with that. I've seen it on dozens of worlds, Ms. Marshall. Because I have such a fondness for humanity, I came ahead to warn you. You can *say* you're independent as much as you want. But I tell you truly, unless you convince that battlecruiser to leave this planet, your world belongs to the Federation of Lodi."

"So how, exactly, do we get them to leave?" she asked.

"Declare your independence." He looked away from her into the camera lens. "Let the United States of America be the first nation to sign its name on a new document for the whole of Earth, as befits your nation's history."

"Just sign a piece of paper? If it were so easy, why haven't other worlds done so?"

"That is merely the first step. You'll have to send a representative to the button pushers on that ship to plead your case. They will be quite specific in their demands." He gave her an arrogant half-smile.

"What kind of demands?"

"For example, your world must offer political asylum to offworlders before you can submit your declaration. The Federation loves bureaucratic procedure."

"If it's just a matter of procedure, why haven't the other worlds they've annexed tried this? You've implied that what's happening here on Earth has happened before."

"It has, but not in the same way. Here's the catch, and the reason why I made myself known here on Earth to begin with. In order to submit your declaration, it must meet certain requirements. Legal protection for offworlders is one point. Another is that the declaration must be co-signed by a citizen of the Federation with expertise in interplanetary treaties."

Annabelle's face went dark. "You mean you."

"I am at your service."

"How convenient. And what would we owe you for the favor?"

"I simply want to see you keep your freedoms."

"I'm sure you're not the only one who qualifies. What else is the Tetrad after?"

"Truly, Ms. Marshall, we need nothing from you. We have a mutual interest in this. But you must understand how the Federation works. Otherwise, your bid for independence will fall on deaf ears. It's taken me... several attempts to map the depths of their procedures. With Earth, I believe it's possible to succeed. I'm here to help, and I will help, however I can."

She studied him for a long, drawn-out moment. "And if we do this, the Federation will declare Earth an independent world and just leave?"

"Well," Tanamir said, "of course, you still have to manage your own security."

"Do elaborate." Annabelle's voice had dried out like a desert plain.

"All in due time, Ms. Marshall. I didn't say it would be easy. Just that it would be worth it. You have no idea how many have died to give the people of Earth this information at the very moment it matters most. Now, it's up to your people to recognize the opportunity before you. I hope your leaders are listening. Trust me, Ms. Marshall, this moment *will* pass. If you do nothing, based on my experience, you have about a day before the Federation announces your forthcoming assimilation."

Tanamir stood, drawing the cameras away from Annabelle to himself. He stepped forward. The frame zoomed in on his head and broad, ridged shoulders as the main camera operator moved in.

"What say you, America?" Tanamir stared into the camera, lifting his chin to bare the burn scars on his neck. "Are you with me? What's your freedom worth?"

Freedom, my ass.

I pictured the Pangozil bleeding out in the stairwell. I couldn't help but see this as another of Tanamir's tricks.The problem was, he had just enough evidence to sound believable. He knew how to appeal to people's fear of being enslaved or destroyed by some alien power they couldn't comprehend. People feared for their lives, and so they were listening.

One of the production assistants hurried up to Annabelle's chair and passed her a note.

"Where did you get this information?" she whispered.

"Governor's office." He gestured at the two Lodians deep in conversation with a hungry-eyed producer, who held a phone to his ear. The man caught Annabelle's gaze and gave her a big thumbs up.

"You're sure?" she asked again. "It's confirmed?"

He nodded, waving her on.

"And you want *me* to say it?"

"Yes," he mouthed silently, pointing over to a screen showing their live viewership numbers. It was in the hundreds of millions.

Annabelle paled as she turned to face the camera. "This just in," she said. "In an unprecedented move, Governor Erazo has just issued an executive order declaring that offworlders living in Texas are now eligible to apply for Temporary Protected Status as asylum seekers under U.S. Code, Title 8, Chapter 12, Section 1158."

CHAPTER TWENTY-THREE

"AND WE'RE OUT," called the director. Crew began to mill about as they cut to a commercial break.

"And now," Tanamir said, planting his feet and turning to Annabelle, "we officially meet the Federation's qualifications. This is good. The Federation cares *deeply* about making sure all the blanks in their forms are filled in."

Annabelle crumpled the note in her fist. "There's no way this'll hold up in court."

"It satisfies the Federation's requirements."

"What did you say to get him to issue the order?"

"I simply explained the situation. Governor Erazo gave the order. Still, I applaud him for his visionary leadership. If they're wise, other leaders of your states will follow suit. Now, I'm afraid our time here is up. It was nice speaking with you, Ms. Marshall."

With a flourish of his cape, Tanamir stood and moved across the room toward the exit.

Toward *me*.

The two other Lodians in the room moved to join him.

When they got close enough for me to see the burn scar on Tanamir's neck, I held the door open for him.

Vinny and Feriss closed in on either side, making as if to block the way, like police officers protecting a charge.

A blurry form dropped from the ceiling. I shouted a warning, but too slowly. Vinny clutched at his back, where, as he turned, a stubby triangular handle jutted out.

Feriss fell on the cloaked form, grasping with his hands against the invisible foe. He couldn't see her. No one could except me, and all I saw were snatches of sharp claws and oversized kangaroo-like feet that struck blows to his midsection.

As Feriss deflected the attacks, bloody red gashes appeared on his ribs and thighs.

Vinny shoved over to help, but she drove a knee into his waist, crushing the gadget that created his cloaking shield.

It flickered and went out. People in the studio screamed as this cop was revealed as a Pangozil—one whose clothes were covered in blood. The other Pangozil ran out of hiding to help, but the Lodians protecting Tanamir took their charge and rushed toward the doorway—toward me.

I held the door open. This was my chance. "Hurry!" I said, "I'll close the door behind you."

Tanamir covered his head, acting scared, but I could see it was a ruse. He was pretending, as if the Sevrit was here to attack *him* and not *us*. The reporting played out in my mind —the reporters would say the station was raided by an assassin. Tanamir would pin the blame on the Federation. He would be painted as a hero.

I gestured them through the door. As the nearest Lodian approached, I pretended to trip and shouldered him aside, reaching into Tanamir's cloak at the same time.

My cyborg fingers wrapped around the chain and tore it free.

The timepiece tumbled through the air. I hit the top of it with my other hand.

Time slowed and stretched like taffy. I struggled against the strange sensation as I tried to control its abilities, but it was like trying to grasp hold of water. Tanamir's nostrils flared wide. His muscles flexed as he grasped for the device.

I tried to reach out to stop him, except my arm wouldn't move. It was stuck, suspended as if the air was thicker than gel.

While I rotated a mere two degrees, Tanamir grabbed hold of the timepiece. An interlocking set of metal plates puzzled together into a frame containing a bright gem suspended, as if with magnets, at its center. He revealed a second wire, which was attached to his belt, untangled the chain from my fingertips, and pocketed the timepiece back beneath his cloak.

"I didn't expect such cleverness. But I did come prepared. The device is still attached to me, you see."

My blood went cold as I realized what had happened. I'd been able to touch the timepiece's abilities while I was in contact with it, but since the second chain was still attached to Tanamir, I hadn't been able to wrest control of it from him.

Tanamir moved his hands and time slammed back into motion. Instead of barreling into him, my face slammed into the doorframe, bursting my nose and splitting my lip. I cried out. Blood streamed down my face, into my mouth. I spat it out as a strong pair of hands shoved me back. I reached out for where their belt ought to be, grabbed the device and crushed it in my super-powered fist.

Revealing a lithe, panting, sleek-furred Sevrit in our midst.

Pandemonium broke out. People trampled each other in their haste to get out of the room. More offworlders had appeared from somewhere, and now they outnumbered the producers and cops-in-disguise. The Sevrit was like ten soldiers. Vinny's Pangozil comrades and a roaring Feriss tore the enemy from me. She stabbed, slashed and hamstrung my allies with her claws.

I turned and stumbled out of the studio. Tanamir's cloak fluttered through the next doorway. My boots slipped on a slick patch as I ran after him.

"He's running," I said into my comms. "Alek, where are you?" I hadn't seen my business partner since I let him into the building an hour ago.

My question was answered when he slipped a rope around the neck of a Lodian blocking my pursuit. He yanked the Tetrad soldier to the side and I met him with my cybernetic fist, knocking him out cold.

"Go on, then!" Alek said. "We'll hold 'em off."

Another Lodian punched Alek in the jaw. He shook it off and returned the effort with a haymaker of his own. Brass knuckles on his fist glistened wetly.

I was worried about my friends—especially Annabelle and Vinny, still in the studio with the Sevrit. But they had been prepared ahead of time, and we'd placed the Pangozil around the room to protect Annabelle. They also outnumbered the Sevrit. Deadly though she was, she couldn't best them all. I knew Vinny had more battle experience than I did, Feriss fought at his side, and obviously Alek could hold his own.

My friends could take care of themselves. My mission was to recover that timepiece.

I found my footing as I ran after Tanamir, winding through the building's narrow halls.

Drawing my pistol in my left hand, I caught a flash of Tanamir's cloak as he turned the next corner into an office lined with desks. He disappeared through another door, and then another, staying just ahead of me until I reached the hall where we'd entered the building.

Two more Pangozil were on the ground, bleeding out. That foam seal held against the police outside. It was a bland reddish-brown color when it dried, like bricks.

Tanamir stood beside the door, holding an alien weapon glowing orange in one hand and the blue timepiece in the other.

I hadn't even heard the shots fire.

The timepiece's face faded to black. Tanamir rested his hand on the button.

"So we meet again, Mr. Gunn."

"Give me the timepiece. That doesn't belong to you."

"Did you really think I wouldn't plan for this?"

"Admit it, you were surprised when you saw me. I almost had it."

"I could smell the Pangozil crouching behind your lady's chair. Those creatures do have a particular stench. I knew you would try something. But I'll admit, your disguise was convincing."

I raised my gun and sighted down the barrel at him. "The timepiece, or I shoot."

He stuck out his lower lip in a very human expression of petulance. "But I've barely gotten to try it out. And I still have need of it."

I pulled the trigger. Two shots. They passed right through him and he didn't even flinch. Tanamir grinned at me, then held the timepiece up.

I lowered my weapon a few inches.

Gunn, are you in there? Dyna's voice popped into my head.

Dyna? I wondered internally. *Hell of a time for you to show back up.*

We have detected a temporal signature in your area. The device is being utilized again.

"No shit, Sherlock," I muttered under my breath.

We are on our way to you. Hold him there.

Typical of the Peacekeepers to come running when it was convenient to them, while making themselves impossible to reach in the meantime.

Tanamir didn't give me time to follow this train of thought. He knitted the brows of his gray forehead together. "Ah, it's the Peacekeepers, is it? I knew they'd come calling. That's why I waited as long as I did to use this."

I scrambled to think of a way to stall him long enough for Dyna and Kilos to arrive. "Did you modify it?"

"It's easier to use now. Plus, it's far more interesting to look at."

"You mean it has better crowd appeal."

"I'm sure I don't know what you're implying."

"What are you playing at, Tanamir?" I glanced over my shoulder as shouts sounded in the office rooms and halls we'd passed through. "I don't believe you have Earth's best interests at heart."

"I never said I did. I simply pointed out that, in this endeavor, our interests are aligned."

I fired again. This time I was sure I'd hit him, but he

moved a step to the side and remained unharmed. He frowned at me like a disappointed father.

"Give me that timepiece back and we can go our separate ways."

"I don't think so. But I do believe we'll be seeing each other again soon."

With that, he flicked his finger, activating the device. I shot again, twice, but I knew they'd miss before I even fired. A flash of blue exploded outward as my body slowed to glacial speeds. My mind continued to perceive events as if they were happening in real time, but the bullets crawled to a stop in mid-air.

He stepped out of the line of fire, studying me. He was toying with me again. A volcano of rage burbled up into my chest, my anger boiling over.

Tanamir held me pinned in the time dilation. I strained my leg muscles, trying to force them to move. Gravity held me in place, fixed like an insect in a glass case.

I released my hold on everything like Dyna had taught me when learning to control my new abilities after she'd first dosed me with their nanobots.

It didn't work. I didn't move like I wanted to. My cybernetic fingertips, however, did twitch.

Tanamir smirked at my helplessness. He stepped toward the doorway. As he approached, the foam sealant filling the door retreated steadily, like the air itself and Tanamir's very proximity could dissolve it. In actuality—if I understood correctly—it was growing backward as time reversed, revealing the jagged opening I'd torn there before, and then an empty doorway untainted by the blockage.

"You're a part of this too, you know," Tanamir said. "What the Peacekeepers did to you—it violates every one of their ethical codes. For Dyna to use their genetic modification technology on a citizen of a silent planet without their knowledge is tantamount to treason. She'll hang for it, mark my words. But thanks to her mistake, you and I will be Earth's salvation."

Chills raced over my skin as goosebumps gathered all along my neck and arms. I wanted to ask him what that meant, but I couldn't speak.

I focused my mind intently. I thought about my nanobots and the passcode Dyna had given me—and suddenly my lips and tongue lolled free.

I drooled, then asked, "What are you talking about, Earth's salvation?"

Tanamir didn't answer. He smiled and stepped through the open doorway. Outside, I spotted a crowd of police officers bearing a battering ram between them, faces frozen in a grimace. Tanamir had stopped them mid-swing. They were frozen, just like me.

Tanamir seemed to have second thoughts. He paused and turned back one more time.

"Did you really convince yourself you were playing a bit part?" he asked.

"What do you mean?"

"Annabelle stepped into the spotlight today, true. But the Federation has a very particular idea of procedure, Anderson Gunn. No, you're essential to the way this is going to play out."

He glanced behind me, in the direction the Pangozil were brawling with the Sevrit.

"I'm sorry, but you can't have the timepiece back. At least not until I'm done with it."

A terrified, throaty yowl of pain pierced the bubble of

slowed time he had trapped me in. It reverberated through the air like a rippling heat wave at the edge of the timepiece's range.

"But if Jaiyana can't control her bloodlust and kills you..." He shrugged. "No matter. I have a backup dose of the Federation's nanobots. If you die, your lady will do quite nicely in your stead."

CHAPTER TWENTY-FOUR

TANAMIR STEPPED through the doorway and out of sight.

My cybernetic hand vibrated in place as I tried to force it to move. Then my whole body was released at once as time began to run forward at the normal pace once again.

My shots cracked into the hardened foam where Tanamir's chest had been moments before.

I hurried over and clawed at it with my robot hand. The cops on the other side must have been banging on it for quite some time. The bullets weakened it further. Using my fingers, I widened the hole and gave them enough of a breach to finally bust it open.

"Move!" I shouted, shoving my body through the hole while they hauled back to strike again.

I staggered out like a drunken monkey, breathing hard. I gained my feet and made to run—only to bowl right into Detective Simmons.

He toppled onto his backside in the alley—I snorted a short laugh. A few days ago, it had been me falling on my ass in the alley. Things had really come full circle.

"Hey, asshole!" he shouted. "What gives?"

"Where'd he go?"

"Who?" Simmons climbed to his feet and brushed off his wrinkled slacks.

"Tanamir! He came out this way."

"We only saw you shoving through that wall like a baby walrus clawing its way out of its mother's womb." He reached out and picked a piece of the dried sealant from my hair. "Not quite as bloody, but still gross."

I shoved him out of the way and ran to the front of the building. I was breathing hard when I got there.

Tanamir was standing atop his UFO, eyes fixed on the distance, waving to the crowd.

Just standing there and *waving*!

I gawked. "What in the Twilight Zone is happening right now?"

My jaw dropped further when Kilos's white-furred form fell onto Tanamir from his cloaked ship above. He growled angrily. Tanamir activated the timepiece and vanished in the moment before he landed. Kilos slammed down on the closed hatch atop the saucer.

The Peacekeeper snarled. "Don't hide from me, coward! You're finished."

The saucer wobbled, throwing off the Kilgar mutant. Kilos flipped and landed in a crouch on all fours beside me.

Dyna drifted down from above, using her telekinetic abilities to lower herself lightly. She had also jumped from the ship above, a ship whose thrusters I could feel pushing heated air down on top of us. It was a balmy relief in the sharp cold of the winter air, but nothing could melt the chill

I felt knowing that Tanamir was inches from escaping with the device.

Our gambit had failed. The wily old general had been one step ahead of us the whole time.

Detective Simmons rounded the corner then. From the other side, Detective Gonzalez approached.

They both drew their firearms and leveled the guns at me and the Peacekeepers.

"Freeze!" Detective Gonzalez shouted. "Hands where I can see them."

"Yeah, freeze!" Simmons said.

I rolled my eyes. "Are you serious?"

I didn't have any more time to mock them. The saucer began to rise. Knots on Dyna's head lit up in a shimmering red-and-yellow pattern, and she strained. The saucer wobbled, struggling in midair as if tied down by invisible cables.

The sight caused the crowd of police officers and onlookers to stagger back in fright. People ran to get away from the very heavy ship that would definitely crush them if they got caught underneath its hull.

A glass bottle whizzed through the air and shattered against the back of Dyna's head. Somehow, she held on, unperturbed. More objects were thrown. Most missed their mark. The cops tried to quell the troublemakers. Turning, I saw a mob of young offworlders of mixed species retreating around the corner—at least one Pango, two Lodians, and several other oxygen-breathing species whose names I didn't know. They jeered and made lewd gestures at the Peacekeepers as they retreated.

Dyna shook her head, as if to dispel an annoying fly buzzing around her eyes, and held her ground.

"Put down your weapons!" Simmons shouted. "Right. Now."

"Make me," I said.

"Not you, idiot," Gonzalez sighed. "Her. Dyna of the Federation of Lodi, you're under arrest."

"I submit to a higher authority than you, young constable."

The UFO above us shook dangerously.

"Release the ship!" Gonzalez demanded.

I gawked at her. "You're defending *Tanamir*? After what he did to us?"

Tanamir had tortured us *together*. Gonzalez had been there beside me as he forced us to murder each other in melee combat inside a realistic simulation that felt indistinguishable from real life, except every time I passed out, I came back to relive the horror. I couldn't *believe* she'd arrest Dyna over Tanamir, orders or no orders. It was a betrayal of everything I thought she stood for.

"There's a warrant out for *their* arrest," Sheila said. "Not his."

"But he's the criminal! And if she releases the ship, he's getting away with the timepiece!"

Gonzalez sighed. "Doesn't seem like he needs a fancy device. He's been one step ahead of us this whole time."

Which is what *I'd* thought a moment ago. I sputtered.

"I have a job to do, Gunn. Move out of my way and let me arrest her."

Dyna considered the situation, looking from Gonzalez to me and back. "I cannot put them down, Detective. My nodules are mounted on my skull, but their circuitry extends into my brain."

"And I carry no weapons," Kilos growled, flexing the claws of his fingers. "If you like, I'll show you why."

The weapon in Officer Simmons' pale hands shook, rattling against his wedding ring.

Gonzalez worked her mouth and swallowed. Her hands, at least, remained steady.

"Release the ship and come with us peacefully," she said. "You heard what Tanamir said. If we make this declaration of independence, they have to honor it. Isn't that right?"

We all stared at Dyna, rapt to see what she'd say. She worked for the Federation, so it seemed like she would know.

"Technically," Dyna said, "yes."

"If that's the case, I'm guessing that your disobeying an officer of Earth law would make the Federation look pretty bad. They won't like you causing any trouble that would require their direct involvement."

Dyna considered this a moment. Then, without further argument, she released her hold on Tanamir's ship. The UFO bearing our target and the coveted timepiece launched itself into the air. It banked sharply and sped off into the distance.

"Dammit," I muttered.

"You make a good argument," Dyna said, ignoring my comment. "Very well. Arrest me, but let my partner go free."

"He was at the scene of the crime."

"Yet he did not commit one. I am familiar with your bylaws. You do not have cause to arrest my partner."

Gonzalez glanced at Simmons.

"We can still bring him in," he said.

"But not keep him. I promise he won't talk while in custody. Our conditioning is very clear on that point."

"Fine," Gonzalez said, sheathing her weapon and withdrawing her handcuffs. "If you come with me, he can go."

"Hey!" Simmons shouted, his voice shrill. "You're out of your mind! We've got to bring them both in."

Gonzalez ignored her partner.

As she came close, Sheila met my eyes. I saw regret and shame on her face, and then I knew that, although she'd pursued Dyna, bound by her sense of duty, and although she was following through and making the arrest she'd been charged with making, she was still trying to help our cause.

She'd left Kilos out so that I could still use him.

"Let's go, Fluffy."

He didn't get mad at me for calling him names this time. He seemed to understand. He exchanged a look with Dyna and then backed away.

As Detective Gonzalez put Dyna into handcuffs, Kilos and I pushed past Simmons and the other police officers who had gathered to watch the conflict. We rushed back toward the building's jammed front door.

With the enhanced power of both of us together, we made short work of the sealant in the door and hurried through the hallways between the front door and the studio.

The place looked like a slaughterhouse. We found six dead Pangozil, three dead Tetrad soldiers of the Lodian species, and one other insectoid creature with an exoskeleton who'd taken a pair of scissors to the space between its plate armor. It twitched in its death throes.

To my relief, I found Vinny in triage in the capable hands of several of his comrades. Annabelle was badly shaken, but unharmed. The Pangozil behind her chair had rushed her to the safety of the dressing rooms after the Sevrit jumped Vinny.

According to our friends, the Sevrit and the surviving Lodians who had come to her aid had disengaged and skipped out the rear exit moments before we arrived.

Alek held a bleeding cloth to a head wound, but otherwise he was unharmed. His knuckle dusters were covered in gore.

"What now?" I asked him.

"Make a hasty retreat. Take your friends with you."

I rounded up Annabelle, Vinny and the Pangos who could walk.

"Cops and press are gonna have an absolute field day with this mess," Alek said. "I'll handle it. Now go on, git outta here while the gettin's good."

Kilos called his ship from the sky. It sucked us up into its belly, and took us away.

CHAPTER TWENTY-FIVE

"THIS IS the weirdest conference call I've ever been on," I said.

Shaken and stirred, we'd come together in the crew lounge on Kilos's spaceship to regroup. He'd ferried the injured Pangozil fighters back to Rashiki's. We were now floating, cloaked, somewhere over East Austin.

On the screen, Felix moved his lips, but no sound came out of the ship's speakers. I rubbed my swollen nose and jaw. Kilos's healing tech had eased my pain, but I'd insisted he use his remaining medical supplies on the Pangozil, who'd taken by far the worst of the damage.

Annabelle glanced at me. "Felix, honey, I think you're on mute."

The nervous Torlik fumbled for the unmute button.

"These machines are so primitive. Can't they tell when I'm talking? Haven't they ever heard of a photonic neuron micromanometer?"

It wasn't just him. We were all on edge.

Chaos had erupted in the hours since Tanamir's escape and Dyna's subsequent arrest.

Despite Governor Erazo's vocal opposition, the president unilaterally ordered an attack on the Federation battlecruiser, bringing war to the Gulf Coast.

The Air Force's trigger-happy flyboys obeyed their Commander in Chief, but their attempt at intimidation backfired.

Satellite videos showed the fighter jets arrested midflight by some kind of stasis field before being flung back toward the shore. One exploded against the hull of the USS Lexington, a World War II vintage aircraft carrier turned naval museum docked in the harbor at Corpus Christi.

A few civilians were injured in the destruction, and the pilot was killed.

The starship didn't retaliate further. This casual display of force sent a clear message.

We're the power here, the Federation was saying.

The battlecruiser drifted out to sea and dropped some kind of cables into the ocean—to cool its systems or to resupply? No one could be sure—and then it just *sat* there.

Annabelle had tried to crack their broadcast encryption, but no one in her network had the skills for it. The famous Marsha Marshall was thwarted.

Similar behavior had been observed in the other, smaller ships stationed in the skies over major cities around the globe.

Now the whole world watched while the president of the United States met with global leaders to determine their next course of action.

Zavis took the laptop from the Torlik, freeing all four of Felix's hands to rub his neck and chest with anxiety. Also on the call were Lulamina, using her phone camera in her library, and Amberen Gevereaux, who joined us from near one of the low warmers in the Pango den. His camera pointed straight up, so all I saw was his whiskers waving around.

"Can you see me?" Geveraux asked.

Kilos, Annabelle, Vinny and I exchanged amused glances. They sat next to me on the couch. I was impatient to get going, so I said, "We can. Now, Felix, what were you trying to say?"

"Right. We've got the amplifier's harness ready. We can't do more without mounting the timepiece into it. And even if we had that, we're still missing a few major parts of the assembly."

"Which parts?"

"We've tested it with electricity, but to use it on Pango to reverse the singularity, we'll need something with a lot more power."

"How much more?" I asked. I was no longer worried about the situation on Pango. I was thinking we might need their tools to undo whatever Tanamir was planning to do here on Earth.

"Think on the level of a nuclear reactor. Or a starship engine's power core."

"Does this ship have a power core we can use?"

"You're not touching my ship," Kilos growled. "Even if the authorities would agree to let me relinquish it, which they won't, we might need it."

To escape with our lives, he meant.

Felix shrugged. "Your ship's core isn't powerful enough to reverse a singularity on its own. Maybe a fleet of them would be."

"How much more power do you need?" I asked.

Everyone fell silent as he thought about it. Felix muttered calculations under his breath.

"More," Zavis finally said. "A lot more."

Another person logged into the call. They were listed as "anonymous," and when the video loaded, it showed someone I'd never met before, a young lady who might have been a college dropout but had the sad eyes of a tired female escort. She was young, with smooth, beautiful skin and a low-cut dress that accentuated her features.

Geveraux turned off his camera. Felix looked like he was going to hurl.

"Excuse me, but this is a private line," Lulamina addressed the stranger. "I don't know who you are, but you need to leave. "

"I invited him," Annabelle said. "Hello, Gatekeeper."

The young woman nodded. "Ms. Marshall."

"It's nice to confirm that my favorite anonymous tipster is an offworlder in origin."

The woman's eyes flashed blue and a genuine smile spread across her face. "You tricked me with that email routing. Well played."

Annabelle tipped her head in acknowledgment.

"I feel like I missed something," I said, "What just happened?"

"My anonymous tipster—the reason I missed breakfast the other day? Same one who's been sending me leaked videos and making introductions to foreign independent news channels... it's been him all along."

I grunted. *Meddling offworlders.* "I figured your abandoning Hub was a scam."

"It was no scam, Mr. Gunn. I did, indeed, abandon that

base. We've shut down almost all my operations in the wake of the Federation's arrival, and we are waiting in orbit to depart."

I wasn't sad to see him leave. He'd been a thorn in my side ever since our first encounter. "Why haven't you left already?"

"I was on my way out when I heard something very interesting." The Gatekeeper's vessel tapped a finger to her lower lip. "It gave me pause and I wondered if you'd heard..."

He looked around—he had everyone's rapt attention.

"I am always on the lookout for new opportunities." New victims, he meant. Things he could suck the blood from like the parasite he was. "Truthfully, I am loath to abandon Earth as I've made a significant investment of both time and money here. But if the Federation annexes you, they'll move their own customs agents in and there will be no place for my modest import/export operation."

"Coward," I said. His smug tone riled my anger and the absence of his physical presence must have emboldened me. Either that, or the threat of the Federation battlecruiser made the Gatekeeper seem small by comparison. "You're like the criminal boss of one of those old west outlaw gangs. You walked into the town, named yourself sheriff, and shot anyone who crossed you. And now, with the civilizing authorities finally showing up, you're hightailing it to the next town."

"There's no operation if I'm dead. I never thought it would happen, but... it seems the Federation would like to consider Tanamir's proposal. Now, where's that pesky share button... stupid Earth computers... aha! Volume up, please."

The young woman's face lit up in a bright smile as an

audio reel played through the speakers in a somewhat robotic voice.

"Planetary annexation halted. Injunction X-9485 has been issued. Requesting the presence of approved intermediaries onboard. Please appear before the Justice of the Peace and give testimony. You have 24 hours to comply. Failure to do so will result in the lockdown of this sector."

I ground my teeth. "It's happening like Tanamir said it would."

"Who are the approved intermediaries?" asked Annabelle.

"I'm glad you asked," the Gatekeeper said. "That first one is on the public broadcast channel. But this message was sent on a private channel and, fortunately, I know how to decrypt it."

He pressed play again. That same robotic voice—it reminded me of Dyna's but colder somehow, cold and hollow. *"Would the following citizens please approach our ship: Hector Enrique Erazo III, Governor of the State of Texas; General Tanamir Voss, citizen of the Federation and of Texas; and Anderson Gunn, bounty hunter."*

They all turned to stare at me, slack-jawed.

"What the hell, Anderson?" Vinny said.

I hadn't told anyone what Tanamir had said to me before he disappeared. Not even Annabelle. There was the old protector in me coming out. Grimacing, I decided not to repeat my past mistakes. I told them all what I felt I could, given present company.

"He told me I still had a part to play in all this. I don't know what his plan is, but he's setting me up somehow. This is proof."

I refused to mention his insistence that if I didn't cooperate, Annabelle was on the chopping block next.

"Why those three names, and not, say, the president?" asked Annabelle, full of healthy suspicion.

"The President delegated Governor Erazo as his representative." Kilos spoke in a soft voice. "As for Tanamir, even though he's technically a war criminal, he's never been convicted. and he comes from a long lineage of prominent Lodian citizens. As a result, he has standing to file the injunction."

"And why ask for Gunn to be there?" Annabelle asked.

"He's had the most interaction with offworlders of any human alive. This all started when he took that first case to help us find the criminal Elekatch. But from the Federation's perspective, it's due to his augmentations. He's the *only* human who has ever received them."

Kilos gave Annabelle an apologetic look. She huffed, her mouth scrunching up in that cute way.

"I'll have you recall that I was the one who got kidnapped by that wicked squid."

"But I'm the one with the Peacekeeper nanobots in me," I said. "For better or worse, only Tanamir and I have a foot in both worlds."

"Yes," Kilos admitted. "I'm sorry, Gunn. I never wanted to get you involved in this."

"Way too late for that, big fella." I didn't have the energy to select another clever nickname on the spot.

"Don't trust Tanamir," Kilos warned. "He may say he wants peace, but what he actually wants is to see the Federation burn."

"Would that be such a bad thing for us?" I asked.

"Depends on whether or not you want your planet to go up in flames with it."

"Well, we can't let him go up there alone with Governor Erazo," Annabelle said. "You have to go, Andy. And I'm coming with you."

"No way." I felt guilty almost immediately but didn't take it back.

She glared at me. "Why not?"

"Too dangerous. Tanamir's pulling the strings. For all we know, I'll be walking into a death trap up there. That, or Tanamir will try to get himself named King of Earth and trick me into endorsing him."

My attempt at levity fell flat. The others studied me.

"You have an inflated view of your own influence," Annabelle said.

"Can't you do something about this?" I asked Kilos. "You work for the Federation."

"Different departments," Kilos said. "I don't know how Tanamir unlocked this outcome. But now that it's in motion, they'll no more listen to me than you would to a single insect."

"One thing you have to understand about the Federation of Lodi," Amberen Geveraux spoke up. "They follow their own inscrutable algorithm. It's not personal. 'Justice of the Peace' is just a translation to help you better relate to the request, to position it in a familiar mental model. In Pangozil, it would be 'Clan Elder'. In reality, there's no single person up there deciding things."

"Just button pushers and a big computer," I said.

Kilos shrugged.

"No one you can appeal to?" I asked Kilos.

"No," he said.

I rubbed the heels of my hands into my eye sockets.

"Gatekeeper, did you see this coming?" I asked.

"I knew it was theoretically possible, but no silent planet has ever entered Arbitration. There have long been rumors stirring of ancient procedures that could lead to a bloodless revolution. That's ostensibly been the Tetrad's mission on a dozen planets, including Pango, but every time they've tried it, it's resulted in all-out war or planetary destruction."

"And what makes Earth so different?"

"You're new," Vinny said. "Unaffiliated. The Pangozil were already part of the Federation, just oppressed by them."

Kilos snarled loudly, a burbling sound that came from his chest. Then he jumped toward the door to the cockpit.

He moaned as he went to his knees at the door's edge. Kilos battled with something inside himself, squeezing his eyes shut and snarling.

The young lady ferrying the Gatekeeper in her head smiled as her eyes flashed blue. "And so it begins," she said. "Oh, I'm *so* glad I didn't miss this part."

My cybernetic hand tingled.

"You disgust me, Gatekeeper," I said. "What in the heck is happening to him?"

"Better lock him up before he gets violent," the Gatekeeper said.

I shot to my feet. "Violent? Why?"

"Your fleshy human forms won't stop him if he needs to go through you."

Kilos turned. Through bloodshot eyes, I saw a semblance of sanity. "Med station," he grumbled, crawling toward it.

"I got you," I said, and lifted him over to the med station, bearing most of his weight under me as he thrashed. I earned a few scratches on my shoulders from the effort.

Kilos tried to cuff his own wrists to a metal bar, but fumbled the bulky powered cuffs.

"Gunn, help!"

Vinny got there first. I held Kilos's wrists while Vinny secured the cuffs. The beefy Kilgar jerked his head at an injection gun nearby.

"Sedative," he snarled. "In me. Now."

I did the honors, slamming the pointed nozzle into his right pectoral muscle. Kilos sighed as the drugs went in. His body relaxed, but he still twitched every now and then.

"Better," Kilos said between panting breaths. "Gunn, go to Dyna." He stared at me with wide eyes. "We don't have long. She can't speak mind to mind now, so you have to see her in person. Hurry!"

He snapped at the powered cuffs. "With the drugs, I can resist, but not for long."

CHAPTER TWENTY-SIX

I WAS tense and breathing hard by the time Gonzalez and I reached the front door of the police station.

A crowd of protesters shoved against a cordon of police officers in a half-circle around the front door. They staggered but held the line.

We looked back over the heads of the crowd, catching our breath for a moment before we went inside.

I'd seen angry mobs before, but none of them had ever jeered at *me*. It felt different to be the target of such hatred. Rather than being an invisible bystander, I was the center of attention. It felt exposed and dangerous. Chasing bail jumpers and then offworlders had always been an adrenaline rush for me. But I did not like this kind of conflict.

As the thought passed, someone spat in our direction. The loogie splashed across the toe of my boot. One of the cops, part of the cordon around us, punched the offender in the gut and shoved him back into the crowd.

"What about them?" I asked, gazing at my friends on the far side. Vinny had convinced several Pangozil to serve as an impromptu security detail for Annabelle. They gathered in a protective bubble around her.

"They'll be okay," Gonzalez said, jerking her chin. "I've got Officer Daniels over there keeping an eye on them."

He stood a head taller than every officer around him. Nearby, a line of police vehicles and gates blocked through traffic.

"Has his partner been reinstated since the governor's order?"

She shook her head. "No. The mistrust runs too deep."

"Bet that's tense." I studied Gonzalez.

"Everyone's doing the best they can," she said. "On all fronts."

"This is a mess," I pointed out.

"You're telling me. The Feds said they wanted to take over this case, but they must be as swamped as we are because they haven't shown up yet. Probably too busy managing the rash of interspecies hate crimes and the riots."

"Making files on everyone who's sympathetic to offworlders, no doubt."

She snorted. "You and Annabelle have the thickest folders, I'm sure."

The roar of jet engines split the air overhead as fighter jets zipped across the sky. I followed them with my eyes.

"And then there's the situation in the Gulf," I pointed out.

"They flung those F-15s around like toy planes." Gonzalez shuddered. "Frightening."

"But they didn't retaliate."

"You don't call that retaliation?"

"Not compared to what they could have done."

In the days since the Air Force's first attack, the alien starship had begun to drift back toward Austin. It zigzagged over populated urban areas, perhaps to discourage another attack, to be seen, or both.

I couldn't make it out yet, but I sensed it. The starship's presence loomed beyond the southern horizon, calling me from beyond the blood-red sky.

"You'll find out eventually, and I don't want you to think I shut you out when you do," I said to Sheila. "The Federation ship asked for me by name. I think that's why they're moving back toward Austin."

"What do they want?"

"They're asking me to come up and give testimony about Earth's status. Tanamir is supposed to be there, and Governor Erazo, too."

Her eyes softened as she turned to face me. Worry creased her brow. The crowd shouted, which was good cover for a private conversation.

"Sounds like a bad plan," she said. "Remind me how you got mixed up in all this again?"

"Ah, you know my luck."

"You always did know how to turn up in places you weren't expected. It's one of the things that makes you a good bounty hunter."

"My business looks different these days. I'm not chasing deadbeats and catching bail jumpers anymore."

"It's good you recognize that. This is bigger than you, Andy—*way* bigger."

Back in college, when we tried dating, we fought like cats and dogs over minor breaches of trust. We'd break up and get back together, only to do it over again the next week.

I didn't want that memory to cast a shadow over our relationship any longer. We were both too strong-willed to be compatible as romantic partners. Nonetheless, through our shared experiences with offworlders, and then with me working as a consultant for the APD on offworld-related cases, we had finally started to rebuild a sense of trust.

Despite what had happened with Dyna, I liked this new dynamic with Gonzalez. I didn't want to lose it.

"I know," I said. "I'll be careful."

She seemed to think about it. "I'll go with you."

I shook my head. "No. I already asked Kilos. They won't let in anyone else who wasn't invited."

She scowled. "Then promise me you'll be careful up there. Keep your head on straight and don't get distracted."

"Are you worried about me?" I smirked at her. I was feeling sentimental. I knew that if I did answer the Federation's call, I might not come back.

She snorted and looked away. "So what if I am? I'm your friend, Andy. I hope you know that."

"I do."

"Make sure someone's watching your back when I'm not around, would you? I don't trust these Peacekeepers."

"You don't trust anyone. It's one of the things that makes you a good detective." I glanced toward the blood-red horizon. "You've got your own duties to attend to. Just do me a favor. Look out for Annabelle and Vinny while I'm gone."

"I will." She nodded once, sharply, and pulled the doors open. "Ready?"

"Let's do it."

We stepped inside and let the door swing shut behind us, closing out the noise of the jets and the shouting crowd.

Gonzalez faced the station's interior. Officers gathered to "welcome" us, forming a hostile aisle for us to walk through. After the briefest hesitation, Gonzalez led me forward in silence. I tried to ignore the cold looks I received. Some glared, others took hushed phone calls or whispered together at their desks. Most stood with arms crossed or fists clenched. They resented me being given an audience with Dyna. They might even have resented Gonzalez helping me. She bore their ire with grace—she had ever since she took over as head of the Special Incident Team, so this wasn't all that different, I supposed.

Or they resented that offworlders had lived among them for so long without their knowledge.

That said, the officers watching us all looked haggard and exhausted. Detective Simmons stepped out of the crowd. "Remember whose side you're on," he said. He had dark circles under his eyes and the smell of whisky on his breath. "We know they've been paying you."

"So have you," I said. "I take cases, not bribes."

"You're working for them." He jabbed me in the chest with one bony finger. "Why else would they invite you up to represent humanity instead of a real cop? One wrong move, and I've got a judge standing by who will happily sign a warrant with your name on it. As a *bounty hunter*, you should know how warrants work."

"Can it, Simmons," Gonzalez said. "He hasn't broken any laws, and you know it."

"Not yet."

I had. Minor infractions, to be sure—but I wasn't about to give him the satisfaction.

We stepped around him and continued. I believed Gonzalez when she said he had no authority to arrest me.

But I also noticed how no other cops challenged him or stepped up to intervene. I felt the detective's mistrustful glare boring holes in my back until we passed through the next door.

After a short walk, we reached the area of the station containing the few prison cells they had on-site. Gonzalez walked me all the way to the back, to an isolated unit with a single cell. I found Dyna in there, sitting in a lotus position on the floor and meditating. The bulbs on her head shifted from soft pink to purple in a wave pattern.

She looked as relaxed as a person could be in a prison cell. I waited for her to notice me.

She looked up with glazed eyes, fixed upon a horizon only she could see. As she focused on me, she came back to the present, and her brow knitted together as if in pain.

"Hello, Gunn," she said in that strange musical voice I'd come to associate with the Peacekeepers.

"Dyna," I said. "Never seen that color before."

"The softer hues appear when I am suppressing my telepathic abilities."

I looked around me. Gonzalez was still within hearing distance, but she'd walked back to the door at the end of the hall. I glanced up—there were cameras. Nothing we said was going to be private. But Dyna seemed unconcerned.

"You look like you're in better shape than Kilos."

"I am more skilled in mental control. My mind understands my situation and shields me from some pain. If I weren't in this cell, things would be different. All the same, I cannot communicate mind-to-mind while I am actively suppressing the symptoms of a Federation summons, so I appreciate you making the trip on a deadline."

I grunted and asked the question that had been bothering me most. "Is that why you let yourself get arrested? It seems like an awfully inconvenient way to ditch work."

She looked at me and smiled. "Your detective friend was correct... and so was I. As Peacekeepers, we serve a higher power. However, since the arrival of the Federation's representatives, until your planet's status has been decided, it is prudent for one such as myself to adhere to your laws. That way, no matter the outcome, I cannot be seen as being at fault."

"By our laws, you're already at fault," I said, gripping the cell's bars and shaking the door. "I saw the video of you with that protester."

Dyna sighed. "It is unfortunate how it appears. But tell me this—have the police found a body?"

I glanced back at Gonzalez. She scowled and shook her head.

"He was a Tetrad agent. Not a human being."

I grimaced. Although she had betrayed my trust, I knew she took her duty seriously. Maybe *too* seriously. But I also didn't think Dyna would hurt a person if she didn't have cause to. She'd put herself in harm's way for humanity too many times.

"So it was a ruse to make you look bad."

She nodded. "Part of Tanamir's plan to paint us as the villains."

"So why did you let Tanamir get away? You had him in your grasp."

"Even if I had held his ship, it would not have prevented this outcome."

Her hair knots flared a bright, fiery red. She fought them back, subduing them to soft pink and purple hues.

"They're calling you back to the ship," I said. "But why?"

"They want my testimony to be submitted as part of their deliberations. Same as yours."

"And why don't you go do that?"

"Because once I do, I cannot help you any longer. They will lock us down or send us away on another mission. And as much as I do not agree with Tanamir's ways, he is right about one thing. The Federation is ripe for change. You, Anderson Gunn, could be that change."

"Don't tell me you're working with him."

"I am not," she said. "I would have preferred this Illumination never happened." She paced back and forth across the cell, speaking slowly and carefully. Resisting the Federation's call taxed her physically. It was the nanobots in their bloodstream, I reasoned, that allowed the Federation ship to summon her like that.

The same nanobots that were, even now, mostly dormant in my own body.

"However, now that it is happening," Dyna continued, "we must work for the best possible outcome. You can help keep Earth safe from war."

"Tanamir is using me. He thinks I'm the key to this whole thing."

"Tanamir is correct. But it is my fault, not yours. He used me as much as he used you. He knew that I was starting to question the Federation's procedures on silent planets. He knew that if he sent a criminal here, I would intervene."

"Why?"

"Because I wanted to prevent what happened on the other worlds from happening here." She took a deep breath. "That is why I put the nanobots in you. To make you... what is your phrase here? 'A shoo in'."

She smiled, the idiom seeming to amuse her. A wince of pain banished her smile.

"I never understood that one," I said. "Like, a shoe in the door?"

"Apparently the phrase's origin has to do with horse racing. If there was a predetermined winner, the other jockeys would hold their horses back to 'shoo' the winner in."

I thought about the dead Jel'ka racing raptor under the floor of Rashiki's track, its stomach bursting with drugs.

"It would give you standing with the Federation. You could plead humanity's case. From their view, I made you a party to Federation interests."

I pondered this, feeling the corners of my mouth turn down. I hated being used like a pawn in offworlder games. It turned out that what I suspected about Dyna was true, she *had* used me, and here she was admitting it.

Only, I didn't feel anger at her anymore. What she'd done may have given humanity a chance. Unfortunately, as she was pulling one way... Tanamir pulled the other.

"There is something else you need to know," Dyna went on. "About the Sevrit, Jaiyana."

"You know her name?" My blood went cold. "And you're just telling me this now?"

"I know you have been kept in the dark quite a lot, Gunn. I am telling you the truth about her, so I hope you believe me. She is a former special operations team leader for the Federation's assassin unit. She worked for Tanamir back when he was leading the invasion force. Her team was responsible for eliminating local rebel warlords."

"And now she's working for one." It was vindicating to learn that our research into Jaiyana's past had been, if not complete, at least pointing in the right direction. "Invasion force sounds ominous."

"You have no idea. It was used on any planet that rebelled against Federation oversight or ousted their representatives."

"So Tanamir was oppressing people as part of the invasion force before he became the Federation's enemy number one? And his right-hand assassin has now come to work for him?"

"Does it surprise you?"

"Not really. So what do you want me to know about Jaiyana?"

"It's my fault she turned against us. She's here because I rejected her application to join the Peacekeepers."

"Why?"

"For one, I suspected her of being a Tetrad agent. Secondly, she failed our psychographic screening. She's a natural-born killer."

"So she joined the Tetrad instead."

"They have no such quibbles. Perhaps I was... too hard on her. But know this: you will never beat her without your augments. We augment all our soldiers, and she was one of the best."

"So how do I beat her?"

She just looked at me.

"You want me to unlock my nanobots." I shook my head. "No way. Not if they give the Federation that kind of control over me."

"It is your best chance. You have only just begun to tap into their true capabilities. Activating them will give you more access to the Federation's systems because they will be forced to recognize you as one of *us*—as a Peacekeeper. These nanobots are a special strain."

That would be an advantage, I thought. But still, I hesitated.

"Remember, Gunn, I gave you the nanobots as a failsafe. To keep Earth from falling into Tetrad control in a situation like this. Remember the training I gave you. I taught you to resist the mental control of the Pharsei, to see beyond his veil of mental illusions and manipulation. You will have to use these skills—and more—if you want to keep Earth safe."

"Tanamir says he wants Earth to declare its independence. What happens if I can't stop him and he gets his way?"

"To him, independent from the Federation means allied with the Tetrad. My plan was to use you to make sure that Earth assimilated peacefully into the Federation. But Tanamir has made me realize that there may be a viable third path."

"What's that?"

"True independence," she shrugged. "There is no precedent for it. No Illumination has ever resulted in an independently governed world. The Federation uses the Peacekeepers to monitor the silent planets. When one becomes aware of offworlders, they get assimilated. There used to be more silent planets, but only a few remain. And among those that do, only Earth's civilization is advanced enough for this to be viable... It is a small chance, but it is a chance."

"I don't know anything about your Byzantine galactic regulations. It doesn't even seem like *you people* do. How am

I supposed to convince this Federation Justice of the Peace of anything?"

"Unlock your augments, and Kilos will show you how to use them to communicate with the ship. Show them Earth's goodness and your commitment to galactic security. You have to show them that humanity is young, has made some mistakes, but is still full of promise—and do not forget to frame it as an experiment. The Federation is strict on obedience to its regulations, but they are *also open to experimentation*. If you win that argument, it will buy you time to prove your case. Will you do it?"

I thought about it, growing sadder by the moment. Every argument I formulated against activating my nanobots seemed like a lame excuse.

If this was my chance to win Earth's independence, wasn't exposing myself to Federation control worth the risk?

And if I had to pay with my life—wouldn't that be worth saving the rest of humanity?

As for the nanobots... Dyna and Kilos were able to resist the summons, even if it hurt. I knew pain. And it seemed like I could always lock my nanobots up afterwards, if what happened this time was any indication.

I did what they'd shown me before, squeezing the bones of my cyborg wrist with the thumb and forefinger of my opposite hand.

A display popped up, like a window into my palm. Behind the translucent square, I made out a tangle of cables, joints and motors.

I tapped my passcode into a translucent keyboard tattooed on my skin.

Immediately, an incredible urge—like hunger combined with an intense wanderlust—roared through my body. My cyborg hand clenched into a fist. My nostrils flared as a deep inhalation saturated my system with oxygen.

"What *is that*?" I asked.

"The Federation summons."

I immediately tried to resist, and a cramping pain in my stomach pitched me over.

"Don't try to resist," she said. "Tell it you're on the way."

"Tell it how?" I asked through gritted teeth.

"Think it. Form the words in your mind."

Cool it, bub. I'm coming. I don't even have a ship to fly up there yet.

The intensity of the sensation subsided. I felt it like a light that pulsed in my peripheral vision. Distant, but lurking.

"I only have a few hours left," I said. The deadline became known to me instinctively, like a physical urge.

"Remember to breathe," she said. "Relax your mind. Exactly like when we faced the Pharsei together."

"All right," I said, inhaling and exhaling through my nose. "I wish we had more time to train."

"Kilos can explain the rest. He'll take you up there. Go to him. I'll join you when I can."

"You do that," I said, already turning to walk away, my feet carrying me out. I'd get Kilos and we'd go up to the ship together.

For Earth's sake, I'd answer the call.

CHAPTER TWENTY-SEVEN

KILOS HAULED BACK on the pilot's control stick, bringing us level with the Federation battlecruiser. He growled in annoyance. "No turning back now."

I was sitting in the cockpit with him. It was the first time he'd ever let me inside. I was strapped into the co-pilot's seat as the enormous starship grew larger in our front windshield.

"How could I?" I asked.

He grunted. He felt it too and knew exactly what I meant.

Butterflies flapped in my stomach, along with a kind of thirst I'd come to recognize as the Federation summons. It drew me onward with a relentless pull that felt almost *spiritual* in nature, going deeper than my physical needs to the very core of my being.

It lived in me, and it had an appetite. I now felt like a starving man after a three-day fast. Or, like a pack-a-day smoker craving a cigarette.

I had learned to push it down. To calm my blood, I

breathed. But it was always there, gnawing at the edge of my awareness.

As we got closer, that gnawing finally began to lessen.

"It'll go away once we're inside," said Kilos.

"I'm still afraid they'll use it to compel my decisions."

"Not how the button pushers operate. You'll see."

The battlecruiser was sleek in some parts, blocky in others. It was generally an oblong, black shape with a fin on top and silver streaks down its sides. Its surface area was greater than most major metropolitan areas. Structures of various shapes and sizes rose along its flanks and roof, like the skylines of a dozen small cities strung together.

All this vanished from my view as we drew closer until all I could see was an endless curve of matte black hull. The ship's nose yawned open, lowering like the jaw of an enormous whale. He, the Leviathan, and us, the helpless drifting kelp.

Inside the giant gaping maw was a hangar *chock-full* of starships. An entire armada's worth. As the jaw opened, sunlight reflected off thousands of metallic wings and crystalline blades and engine ports and windshields, lighting the Leviathan's interior in a dazzling array of colors.

The hived interior reminded me of Rashiki's, but on a much larger scale.

Kilos pointed his ship's nose at the bottom row of landing pads, which were empty. A signal on the ship's command screen authorized our entry and showed us where to go.

We flew toward the beast's mouth. An alarm blared from Kilos's leftmost control panel.

"What was that?" I asked.

He frowned and tapped the ship's reverse thrusters.

"Temporal manipulation readings coming from about two miles in front of us."

"Tanamir must be nearby."

As if in answer, one of the saucer-shaped ships appeared above us. It slowed to a breathtaking pause as it hovered. Then it darted into the ship's maw ahead of us.

Kilos's frown furrowed his broad forehead. "It's different from before. This reading seems larger. And it seemed to be coming from below the ship, not from that saucer."

"What are the odds the battlecruiser has its own temporal devices?"

Kilos grunted and flew forward again. "Not likely. They don't allow that sort of contraband."

As we fell into the rainbow glint of the hangar, I spotted chopper blades on a rearview monitor.

"There's the governor."

"Right on time." Kilos said.

Shortly after I had left Dyna in the APD lock-up, the Federation's tech hacked my phone. It replaced my home screen with an invitation showing the location and time I was supposed to arrive, along with a countdown timer. As the Peacekeepers had anticipated, it said I could bring one person for backup, and I chose Kilos. He was a fighter, he knew the Federation's nuances, and he was the only one who could show me how to use my nanobots if I ran into trouble.

Annabelle was pissed, but I was glad to have an excuse to keep her out of Tanamir's reach. The Pangozil had gone back into hiding at Rashiki's and were preparing to depart. Vinny was planning to go with them. Even if I didn't make it out of this alive, I didn't expect to see him again. The thought put me in a dark mood.

My heart was a real melting pot of emotions right now. It had all happened too fast. Had I made the right decision? Could I have avoided this?

I didn't think so. I'd worked my way into it, starting from the first moment I'd cornered Elekatch on that rooftop.

"Remind me what happens to Dyna when we hit the deadline?"

"She'll be neutralized."

"They have that kind of control over you?" I asked.

"Over Peacekeepers? Yes."

"But not over me?" I'd asked him this a hundred different times.

"Not until you agree to their terms."

We landed on the platform indicated, setting down in the spot highlighted for us in the pilot's display. Tanamir's saucer landed on another platform to our left, the governor's helicopter to our right. We followed prompts on the screen, connecting to their systems and locking down the Peacekeeper ship the way they wanted. Kilos put on some kind of emergency brake, disengaged weapons and disconnected power systems. I assume the other ships did the same because no one got out yet.

With a mechanical hiss, all three platforms began to slide toward the wall. I was apprehensive as we drew closer. Before we made contact, the solid wall parted like so many tiny boxes folding in on themselves, forming a ship-shaped aperture for us to slide through.

Once inside, the wall sealed itself up, leaving us in a soft green darkness.

We were now in a room the size of the landing platform. Kilos and I finally disembarked. He pointed at the wall across from us. I shrugged. He led the way toward it.

The wall opened like the aperture that had swallowed our ship. It broke into tiny pieces and moved with a fluid, almost organic grace. This was tech on a level I'd never seen. It was as if the entire structure was made up of small interlocking Lego bricks, which could arrange and rearrange themselves at will.

Was this the nanobot technology, writ large?

I leaned in to peer at the material. It was neither metallic nor organic. Not exactly silicone, but like it, both soft to the touch and hard if you applied pressure. I inhaled slowly as my nostrils widened in shock. Tiny creatures, no larger than the smallest of ants, with no legs visible, rolled across the surface. They were like small metallic beads of silver, gold and sapphire swimming across the surface of a pond.

Unless you got in close while the material was shifting, you couldn't tell it wasn't an unbroken sheet of metal. Like a pointillist painting, the whole was greater than the sum of its parts.

I stared at the shifting patterns. As I watched, one of the lines seemed to skip back and retrace a pattern it just made. Was that intentional, or an error? I stared at it, relaxing my mind and trying to peer through it, but it was no illusion. It was, however, mesmerizing, and on a level of technological advancement far beyond anything humans were capable of today.

This entire ship was beyond us. Humanity didn't stand a chance.

Except... My melancholy at leaving my friends melted in the face of a fierce determination. A fire bloomed in my gut which had nothing to do with nanobots.

Humanity had a chance. They had me.

I hurried to catch up with Kilos and picked up the pace,

following a long, serpentine hallway that opened before us as we moved. It wound back and forth several times before dumping us into a large, cube-shaped chamber. Tanamir smiled as we came through the door. The wall was sewing up behind him, so he'd just arrived.

The Sevrit stood at his right shoulder, as though she had always been there.

I looked around for his other guards, but there appeared to be none.

"Seems you found your new lieutenant," I said to get him talking. "You know, since the last one betrayed you."

Entirely unemotional, Jaiyana stared at me with soft golden eyes. They had vertical slits and eyelids that closed from the sides when she blinked. A medium-length broad blade was strapped to her right thigh, and she cradled a snub-nosed gun of some alien craftsmanship in her arms.

"Jaiyana and I have a long working relationship." He smiled at her and gripped her arm, as if she were his daughter or another female relative. "She's demonstrated leadership and initiative on countless occasions."

"But only recently come back into the fold," I said.

I was rewarded with the slightest hesitation from the feline creature. Not much, barely a moment where her breathing paused. "I saw the error of my ways," she said.

"Sure you did."

Tanamir gave me a lizard-like smile, then paced slowly around the edge of the cube. He stuck his hand into the wall—the nanobot material parted to make way for him. If he carried weapons of his own, they were concealed. His cloak swished, and although I searched for the timepiece, either it was hidden underneath the garment or he didn't have it on him.

Did Jaiyana have it? I couldn't tell.

A third doorway appeared, and a familiar, petite blonde woman strolled out. She stared around with characteristic wide-eyed wonder.

"Anna?!" I said, mortified. "What are you doing here?"

She was burdened by cameras on two shoulder straps. Wait, scratch that, a camera and an M3 rifle. And a pink Glock in a hip holster that was definitely not mine. She sniffed.

"You didn't think I'd be content to let you have all the fun without me, did you?"

I frowned at her. Having her here was going to make it harder for me to focus. She handed me the rifle and said, "This isn't mine."

I frowned at her, but I took the gun and checked the ejection port and magazine, then loaded it. I turned back to Tanamir and Jaiyana, flipping the safety off and holding it across my body.

"Fun," I said, my fear giving way to bewilderment. I couldn't help but laugh and shake my head ruefully, despite the danger. Tanamir watched us. "I always try to keep you out of harm's way, yet you keep walking back into it..."

I glanced back at Tanamir. *He* must have orchestrated this. He smiled at me, confirming my fear.

"As long as you do the right thing," Tanamir said, "no harm will come to her."

"It better not."

"That's up to you," Tanamir said.

Annabelle stared between us in confusion. "I came at the governor's request," she insisted.

I started to explain, but someone screamed and then a human body was forcibly *ejected* from the tunnel Annabelle had come through. A man in a suit tumbled between us, slamming into Jaiyana and Tanamir, bowling them over.

Governor Erazo. He struggled to rise, pushing against the two offworlders. There was cursing and cries of pain as they tried to untangle their limbs and weapons from each other.

The wall slurped closed again, ejecting a pocketful of warm air. I didn't know a wall could get irritable, but apparently, yes, it could. This ship had a personality of its own.

"*Puta madre*," said Governor Erazo. "Hey! That was extremely rude!" He pointed up at the ceiling and shook his fist.

"What happened?" I asked.

"The ship stripped me of my security staff without my consent! Not a very good start to negotiations, is it?" He tilted up and spun, addressing the ship.

"Ah, Governor Erazo, sir... I did point out that they weren't invited," Annabelle said. "Only one representative and their guest."

He heaved a deep sigh, burdened and world-weary. Poor man. I could see he was still trying to accept the existence of offworlders and struggling with this situation. There was a cold fear lurking behind the anger in his eyes and demeanor.

"Should have named one of my guards as 'Earth's media representative'," the governor muttered. "Do you even know how to use a gun?"

Oh boy, he gets angry when he doesn't get his way. This could get ugly.

"I do," Annabelle said with a soft determination. "And someone's got to tell this story. Why not me?"

The governor gathered himself with an effort, dusting off his jacket and straightening his lapels. He studied the rifle I now held, as well as the other weapons holstered and concealed on my person, and seemed to re-gather his dignity. With an air of command, he immediately took charge of the situation.

"I'm the best negotiator in the Republican Party, and the leader of the great state of Texas." Governor Erazo marched toward the wall with a confidence he had no right to possess. "I'm not about to let some uppity alien ship tell me how to serve my country. Let's go."

To my astonishment, the wall parted the moment before he made contact with it.

This seemed to give the man—who was beginning to bald at the peak of his pate, I could see from this angle behind him—even more confidence. He strode ahead, followed by Tanamir and Jaiyana, while Annabelle, Kilos and I took up the rear.

I walked deeper into the heart of the starship among my friends and enemies.

CHAPTER TWENTY-EIGHT

WE HADN'T MADE it twenty paces when a pale, worm-like creature slid from the wall. Its skin was semi-translucent, and it was about the height of a large child. Nanobots glittered in its wake like a slug's slime trail.

"*Díos mio.*" The governor stepped back, startled. "What is this?"

The worm spoke in an alien language. Tanamir glared at it with hatred clear in his eyes. Jaiyana drew the blade from her thigh, which caused Kilos to flex his claws.

"Whoa, whoa, whoa," I said.

"Hold," Tanamir ordered, soothing Jaiyana with a glance. "We need him."

A brown cloth hung loosely over the segmented, fleshy body of the worm-like creature. Hundreds, maybe thousands, of nanobots the size of small beads crawled all over its body. They gathered in the folds between its segments and glittered among the short bristles of hair on its head. Two forearms extruded through the cloth, each ending in three long, multi-jointed fingers.

It bobbed forward in a rhythmic dance, waving like a pudgy serpent. When it got near to us, it reached one arm out to the wall, drawing forward a stream of nanobots. As it did so, I *heard* them, like a water faucet being turned on. There was no audible noise, but I could feel it in my mind.

It made me shiver all over.

“You feel that?” Kilos whispered.

I nodded. He’d explained how these secondary senses had been available to me ever since I’d received my own nanobots. Earth lacked the tech to trigger them, however. It was like the old idiom about a tree falling in the woods. I hadn’t been able to hear it before.

But I was *definitely* in the woods now.

“Take us to your leader,” Governor Erazo demanded impatiently.

The stream of nanobots joined the worm, crawling up its arm and gathering around its throat to form a box on its neck.

“Welcome to Federation Vessel X-4695, *The Axiom’s Edge*,” it said in a slithering voice. “I am Administrator 317. I will be your guide.” As it spoke, I searched for the creature’s eyes and found none. It was disturbing. I looked at its long, anteater mouth and the metallic box that had solidified out of the nanobots. It hung around its neck like a speaker used by some throat-surgery patients. I suppose it was exactly like that. A kind of translator and speaker combo, one suitable for this species’ vocal cords.

“This way,” it said.

“Button pusher?” I whispered to Kilos.

He grunted his assent.

The worm turned and my feet began to move, as if called along. It wasn’t that I was compelled, necessarily, but I did feel drawn forward, like water running downhill. It felt rude to refuse, and every time I thought about stopping, my neck itched.

Kilos kept his eyes on Tanamir and the Sevrit and made sure they walked in front of us. He was more close-lipped around them than he had been with me. I respected that. I, too, was suspicious.

Annabelle's curiosity had fewer such qualms, and she took the opportunity to continue her interview with Tanamir.

"Tell me more about this Justice of the Peace," Annabelle said.

"A misconception," the Tanamir said. "The Federation is a faceless machine that runs itself."

"Is that why you oppose it?"

"I don't oppose it. That would be like opposing gravity or holding back the ocean tides. I'm simply trying to set a new precedent."

The worm twitched, twisting around.

"Lodians are founding members of the Federation," Jaiyana said, joining the conversation. "One of the most ancient and populous species. But no *one* race rules. The Neth"—she pointed to the worm-like creature—"isn't in charge."

"He's in charge of executing the Federation's procedures," Kilos pointed out.

The Neth didn't dispute it. We walked on.

"Where are you taking us?" Annabelle asked the creature.

"To the Processing Center," Administrator 317 said. "Where you will present your case for Arbitration."

He glided forward. Hundreds of small tentacles below

his worm-like bottom half, like a centipede's hundred tiny feet, wiggled constantly, carrying him forward.

"You know, you're kind of cute," Annabelle said

"Egh," I said.

It wiggled its head side to side.

"Hey, I'm just kidding."

"We don't mean to offend you," Annabelle said. "Excuse my friend."

It slithered forward, ignoring us for now.

Administrator 317 took a right turn, then a left, then another right. As he moved toward some unseen center, the shifting structure opened before him in ways we could never navigate alone. The governor was uncharacteristically quiet on the journey. The wind must have been taken out of his sails by the administrator's arrival. Erazo pretended to be aloof and unbothered, but sweat stained the starched collar of his shirt.

We moved into a large hallway with walls so high they seemed to vanish overhead. At the next intersection, several metallic robots the size of small gerbils scurried over every surface. One was adding nanobots to a door frame. Another was nose-deep in an electrical panel of some sort, soldering something—an action that seemed strangely human to me. Sparks shot out from around its body, lighting the tangle of equipment within, machinery of a similar make as the intricate design of my cybernetic hand.

We passed a large maintenance drone, a machine made of several orbiting, spinning pieces suspended as if by artificial gravity around a small blue orb. It was straightening banks of monitors and what might have been computer towers.

We continued to walk, passing through different

sections of the ship. The hallways sometimes resembled an Earth building. At times, they curved oddly or opened into hive-like rooms. In some areas, they dropped off sheer edges that gleamed like mercury. When Annabelle asked, Administrator 317 told her those shafts were designed to be traversed by methane-based life forms.

The bones of the ship were always made of that nanobot-like material that resembled steel or carbon fiber. Bright spots of color gathered as we passed, forming strips of light to illuminate our path, and then separating and fading behind us. The ship only ever used as much light as we needed, never more, so it was usually dim and hard to make out many details unless you were close up.

As we proceeded, the structure became more deliberately formed, with straighter walls and smaller halls. These seemed made to fit bipedal creatures. We crossed into another section of the ship, and the ceiling lowered. I breathed a sigh of relief, feeling less overwhelmed by the openness of my surroundings.

"How are we going to get back out if we get lost?" I asked Kilos.

"Ask the ship." He tapped his ear knowingly. "It'll show you the way."

"But not how to get in?"

"No. For security, finding your way in is a labyrinth that only the Neth can navigate."

I sighed, focusing inward while clearing my mind to become more aware of the ship itself. I felt silly. The most I could sense was a light fuzzing, like an untuned TV channel. But even that could have been my imagination.

A window up ahead glowed with sunlight. Annabelle and Governor Erazo both hurried over to it, peering out at

Austin's skyline in the distance. Annabelle took some photos while I frowned. My sense of direction was completely disoriented by this point. By the location of the city, it put us on the port side of the long ship. Or had the starship turned? I couldn't be sure.

The Administrator's every move took us deeper into a maze of halls and shifting walls, a labyrinth of ever-changing nanobot technology.

"Sometimes it helps to touch it," Kilos whispered, jerking a chin at the nearest wall. I glanced at the Administrator. Though he said he would lead us, he'd given no other instructions. He simply stopped at occasional corners, checked panels, and adjusted maintenance drones, moving them from one location to another before moving on.

Sometimes the Administrator would change the direction of the next hallway—rather than curving right, it would slide left. As we reached the next corner, I watched him do this again. He reached his arms out and sank his long fingers a few inches into the wall, seemed to consider for a moment, staring up blankly as if he were calculating.

As he did so, I leaned my left hand toward the wall and felt a tingling pressure—fuzzy and indistinct. Annabelle did the same, then shrugged and shook her head as if she didn't sense anything.

I reached out with my right hand, my cybernetic appendage, and like the button pusher, pressed my fingertips against the wall. I paused, then slowly pushed *into* the material.

The sensation was sudden and overwhelming—like a jolt of adrenaline to my system. A coldness spread through my hand and up my forearm. Suddenly, the corridors ahead bloomed in my mind like the petals of an elaborate flower. I could see what the Administrator was doing, moving those corridors to lead us inward, around a large glowing power source—the engine room, perhaps.

We were close to the edge of the ship right now, about halfway down its length. Next, he was taking us toward the middle.

The Administrator swiveled and fixed his eyeless attention upon me—both physically and with his own senses deep in the ship's slipstream system.

It shoved my fingers out of the pliable wall, severing my connection.

"Sorry," I said. "Did I do something wrong?"

He glared at me with a face that had no eyes, his attention firmly rooted on me. "Do not attempt to tamper with the ship's systems."

I glanced at Tanamir and the Sevrit, who were watching the exchange. Did they have the ability to sense the ship? It would make sense if so—they were former Federation military and would have received augments of their own. I couldn't be sure how much access they had, or what the differences were between the Peacekeeper's serum and what they gave their military officers and assassins.

We moved onward. Next, we passed a maintenance drone buried in an electrical box, as if it were chewing wires. Sparks shot out around its body. I blinked, a feeling of *déjà vu* overtook me.

"Didn't we see that drone a minute ago?" I whispered to Annabelle and Kilos.

Kilos glanced back. "There are many maintenance drones."

"I didn't see anything," said Annabelle. She was taking photos of our surroundings. Seeming annoyed at our interference, Administrator 317 rearranged the route and sped up. We were obliged to walk quickly to keep up with him.

After a few turns, we passed another window. We weren't near the edge of the ship anymore, and seeing sunlight unnerved me, but maybe this was a video screen instead of a window. I paused to look. It sure looked like a window. Several helicopters and not a few fighter jet trails were visible in the distance. This time, Austin's skyline was further away and to the left. Daylight was fading.

"Have we really been in here that long?" I asked. "What time is it?"

"Quarter past three," she said, checking her watch. "Come on, we have to keep up."

I put my arm out to slow her down. Kilos stayed with us while the others moved on ahead. "Awfully dim for mid-afternoon, isn't it?"

She glanced at the sky, which was speckled with bats out hunting for their dinner. "Now that you mention it, yeah..."

I reached out a hand to the wall and sank my fingers into it. This time the fuzzing seemed to crackle—static on a TV turned up way too loud. What was going on?

My blood went cold as I realized what could be causing the temporal weirdness.

"The timepiece," I whispered. "Could they be using it somehow?"

Kilos scratched a furry cheek. "Possible."

"How?" Annabelle asked. "I looked inside his cloak when we were talking. I don't think he has the timepiece on him."

Administrator 317, Tanamir and Jaiyana rounded the next corner, leaving us in darkness. We hurried to catch up with the group and met them in an archway at the edge of a vast silo. I felt dizzy, overcome with a sense of vertigo as Annabelle and I studied the enormous open space.

The curved wall was speckled with thousands of stars, or that's how it seemed. Each star was an archway like the one through which we'd entered. Our platform was fifty feet deep and ringed by a floating railing at waist height, but with no other safety precautions.

The railings led from this platform to the next, and occasionally from there it would shoot out toward the center of the open chamber, where a sphere floated, suspended as if by artificial gravity.

"Let me guess," I said. "The Processing Center."

For the first time, I spotted other Administrators, all of them soaring around the vast silo. They weren't flying, but gliding. What I took to be guardrails were actually some kind of travel system for them to slide along, using their tiny appendages to cling to it. There weren't many of the creatures, maybe a dozen in total that we could see. But they were also far away, so I couldn't make out individual characteristics. Each administrator was clothed in a uniform brown cloth. Some carried devices made of nanobots, like 317. A few shepherded large groups of maintenance bots off to do some errand or another, ducking into the archways far above us.

I flinched as an explosion detonated to my right.

Instinctively, I swung my rifle to my shoulder and turned to place my body in front of Annabelle, scanning for danger. Kilos bristled, bared his claws and fangs and stood beside me.

Administrator 317 rushed over to the wall. An electrical panel poured smoke into the air. Several of those small metallic gerbils had been turned into shrapnel.

Erazo coughed, waving the smoke out of his face, while Tanamir patted him on the back.

Jaiyana sprinted away from us.

"Where's she going?" I asked.

Annabelle swung her camera up. Its shutter snapped rapidly. She caught Jaiyana mid-leap for the briefest moment before she fell.

I ran to the railing, where the floor dropped off at a sheer edge.

I looked down, staring open-mouthed.

Jaiyana saluted me as she plunged into the depths of the starship.

CHAPTER TWENTY-NINE

"REGULATION 4566-B PROHIBITS freefall in the Processing Center!" Administrator 317 screeched as he ran to the burning electrical panel—apparently, ship safety took precedence over stopping Jaiyana. He made a few motions, and nanobots jumped to smother the panel, choking off the fire. Other automatons swarmed the area and immediately set to repairing it.

Jaiyana had produced some kind of parachute to slow her fall. She glided toward the sheer chamber's edge and slammed her blade into the wall near a lower level. It was an incredible feat of strength that impressed and terrified me, stuck, as I was, up here. I saw bright flashes, as if from a discharged weapon or a torch, and then watched as glittering sparks were flung aside.

"She must be going after the timepiece!" I said.

"I'll go after her," Kilos growled. "You have to stop Tanamir from hijacking the Arbitration."

"Got it."

Kilos jumped over the edge without a moment's delay,

although he didn't jump out as far as the Sevrit had. I felt him interface with the nanobots, and a rope of them separated from the wall. They looped around his ankles as he fell in a graceful dive.

"Gunn!" Annabelle said. "Look."

Tanamir was striding across a narrow bridge, moving toward the sphere at the silo's center.

"I don't think he can start the arbitration without us, but if the timepiece is in play, expect him to have the first-mover's advantage."

Annabelle was snapping photos down into the silo. "Go! I'll catch up."

I ran along the walkway. It flared inward, narrowing to a rail on the left and a thin path on the right. I tried to step with care without slowing—I'd come too far now to let impatience take me out of the race inches from the finish line.

I didn't have a parachute like the Sevrit, and it was a *long* way down to the bottom.

My heart hammered. I swallowed with a dry mouth. There hadn't been any water on this trip, and I was feeling lightheaded.

When I slowed, Governor Erazo stumbled into my back. "Out of my way!"

He snarled, grabbing at my shoulder to stabilize himself and pulling me off balance. Bending my knees to lower my center of gravity, I reached out and gripped the rail to keep us both from falling to our deaths. The rail squealed when my thumb pressed into the material, indenting it.

Again, I felt a sudden and intimate contact with the starship. It had a weight like a law of nature. Its heavy presence hung all around me. It was not human, but its weight could be felt. Like gravity. If you wanted something to fall, you could *rely* on the law of gravity. But try to work against it, and everything would become difficult.

With a thought and another squeal, my thumbprint in the metal rail popped back out.

The starship's presence pulsed its thanks.

"I don't trust you, bounty hunter," said Governor Erazo.

"We're on the same side," I said, detaching his fingers from my forearm. He was holding me with an iron grip, like he was afraid of heights.

"Are we?" he demanded, studying my eyes.

"*Yes.*"

"They haven't turned you?

"Turned me into what?"

"One of them!" He released me in disgust. "Whatever it is you're doing with this ship, it's not normal."

I studied the man. "You don't want to be here, do you?"

"No! It wasn't my idea! Sending me up here like some kind of tribute. Stripped of my guards! Sent to some kangaroo court to plead for humanity."

"Calm down."

Tanamir watched us from the doorway of the sphere.

He spoke in a strained whisper. "If we can't convince this ship to leave the planet, the President is going to nuke it and burn half of Texas along with it!"

A cold shiver passed over my body. I spoke in a strained whisper. "Listen, bub. Now is not the time to be questioning my loyalty. I don't like this any more than you do, but we're here now and we need each other. So let's get in there before this alien rabble-rouser throws humanity to the jackals."

This seemed to awaken some halfhearted sense of courage in the man. He nodded and we turned our attention to moving with a measured pace across the rest of the distressingly narrow bridge.

Tanamir didn't try to stop us or seal off the entrance like I expected. He simply smiled, waited until we started moving toward him again, then entered the sphere.

As we neared the sphere, Administrator 317 came squealing down the slide rail past us, grasping it with his little appendages. "What are you doing?" he demanded, shouting at Tanamir's back. "Cease and desist!"

"Whatever do you mean, Administrator?" Tanamir asked playfully, his voice coming from inside.

"Your second has breached the hull of *The Axiom's Edge*! She's attempting to violate the operating system." As he spoke, his form seemed to glitch, jerking in unnatural and sudden motions. "Your second has—" he glitched again. "—are you *doing*? Cease and desist!"

We entered the room and my knees went weak as I struggled to comprehend an alien fountain, or moving sculpture, taking up the back half of the concave space.

"All parties are present," Tanamir said, "please open the Arbitration and leave us to it."

"You don't have the authority to order me—" The Neth glitched again. "You don't have the—you don't—"

Administrator 317 disappeared and reappeared in another place across the room, glitching back and forth. He moved around the room in a dizzying series of flashes before spreading his serpentine body over a console at the room's center. He shoved his long fingers into a large stream of flowing nanobot-like material.

I got that sense of vertigo again as my mind struggled to grasp what I was actually seeing. It was alien, beyond human ken.

Governor Erazo averted his gaze and gagged. "What *is* that?" He dry-heaved with his head between his knees.

Annabelle staggered into the room behind us, breathing heavily. When she saw it, she immediately averted her eyes. She was too smart to avert her camera, however. The camera shutter snapped, taking dozens of photos and letting her see something—a rendering of the monstrosity—through the camera's preview screen.

Tanamir seemed to be unaffected. I realized belatedly that he and Administrator 317 were already *connected* to the ship's systems and that I was missing things.

I bent to the floor and placed my cybernetic hand on it. With an inhalation that was both physical—air moving through my nostrils—and cognitive—opening to the ship's weighty presence—I drew a stream of the ship's nanobots into myself.

Immediately, my normal perception expanded, and the ship's contours appeared in my mind's eye once again. This time, Administrator 317 didn't try to shut me out.

The alien horror we bore witness to was a flowing river of nanobots. Each nanobot was an engineered creature, a perfectly balanced organic-machine hybrid.

The reason we felt nauseous seemed to be that, gathered together in such a dense mass, they emitted a psychic energy that even those without the augments were affected by. Deep within the flowing stream, a dense mass of nanobots pulsed. It seemed to be some kind of brain or—or Processing Center, I realized.

The alien matter flowed up from the floor and passed over, around and through the dense mass, a kind of brain. The liquid oozed from holes in the floor, which were vents that connected to every area of the ship. As they passed through the mass, they were replenished like blood cells, dying and being made anew, continuously re-energized, and then transferred out to flood the rest of the starship's body and bones.

And, describing it as a brain didn't do the thing justice. What I was seeing was the starship's beating heart. The nanobots were this ship's blood and bones, the atomic unit of its being. It was *alive* and *powerful.* Way beyond the mental forces of the Pharsei I'd first faced on Earth; way larger than the machinations of two mortal alien beings fighting over our world's allegiance; nearly infinite in its capacity. I could sense, as if through a fog, that the ship's brain was connected to a vast network of other such concentrations of mass, neurons in other star systems far from here.

It wasn't anything *I* was doing. My connection with the shipheart through my alien augments, which I knew now came from it, like its children, allowed me to—if not see—at least become aware of the greater whole.

The Federation.

The Federation of Lodi was not any *one* person. It was, itself, this network, a collection of neurons, each one made up of a concentration of nanobots from the same source, spread using starships across the galaxy. I sensed some of the nodes on starships like this one, in distant star systems. Others were on planetary bodies. One such body was a dying planet. The network had put this world into isolation and walled it off to protect the Federation. In the ship's senses (or my interpretation of them), that planet appeared cracked down the middle. *That's Pango*, I thought. I tried to reach out to the world, but a giant awareness shoved me back.

This all happened in a flash. Before I could react, I was walled off from the greater network, isolated to this starship, *The Axiom's Edge*, once again.

This time, my connection held, and no one booted me out.

"Begin Arbitration," Administrator 317 finally said, drawing my focus out of the ship's alien systems and back to our group inside the Processing Center. "For case 998-XF-415, regarding Earth's status as a silent planet. All parties are present and accounted for. Testimony collection may begin."

I watched the Neth's eyeless face. He seemed to find nothing amiss about his own behavior. He ignored me and shuffled out of the sphere as the flowing nanobot waterfall formed three distinct platforms. Tanamir stepped onto one and gestured for Governor Erazo to stand in the middle. This seemed to please the man's ego, and he complied.

I held my ground, refusing to stand on the third. "How'd you get the timepiece on board?" I asked.

The wrinkles deepened around Tanamir Voss's ancient eyes. He regarded me for a minute, then shrugged as if revealing his plans would cause no harm. It probably wouldn't, if he could just hit undo on the conversation.

He deftly manipulated the *Edge's* systems through his connection with it. I didn't know what *deft* even looked like until he did it. The starheart put up a bit of a fight, but not too much. Its flowing form glitched before giving way.

I saw Kilos and Jaiyana fighting. I watched as the Peacekeeper deflected blows from her blade with the palms of his hands. He swung out—faster than I could follow—and sent the timepiece tumbling from her hands.

Jaiyana dove for it, rolled, and when she came up, she

tossed it into the air. The flat of her whirling blade caught the timepiece and batted it toward a blazing ball of fire at the bottom of the room—the starship's power core, I assumed. It landed in a funnel that fed directly into the core's heart.

"Now it's embedded in the ship's systems. I have secure access to its capabilities."

The visuals he'd summoned melted back into the flowing stream of nanobots, demonstrating his mastery of the starship's systems.

I reached out with my mental senses and felt the temporal disturbance there, but I couldn't grasp it. I shoved with my mind, and Tanamir pulled it away, like an adult holding a toy high up out of a child's reach. It felt like what Administrator 317 had done before when he'd booted me out of my connection, but more slippery, as if I'd grasped it and he wriggled away by reversing time and anticipating the move I'd already made.

I recalled what Felix had said about needing a power core—something with far more capacity to amplify the timepiece's capabilities. It seemed he hadn't been the only one to come up with that idea. This starship provided the perfect power source. Not only that, but its unique interface allowed Tanamir to operate it from a distance.

`VIOLATION DETECTED`, the Federation announced, speaking directly into our minds. `INITIATE EMERGENCY SHUTDOWN PROTOC—`

The enormous presence dissolved as Tanamir reversed the flow of time. He grunted, obviously frustrated and putting in an effort, but the stream of nanobots reversed.

"I'm ready to give my testimony," Tanamir said.

`YOU ARE A WAR CRIMINAL`, the ship's systems spoke.

"I've never been tried or convicted, so my testimony is valid under Federation law."

TRUE.

Nanobots grew into the arched open doorway we'd entered through, forming a lattice and closing us into the sphere.

YOU ARE UNDER ARREST. YOU MAY PROCEED.

Tanamir fiddled with the timepiece's functions, reversing the growth of the bars and rolling back time again.

YOU ARE A WAR CRIMINAL, the ship's systems spoke once more, repeating the phrase it had used a moment ago.

"We are not here to plead my case."

ACCURATE, BUT INCOMPLETE.

"Arbiter, hear me. My life and experience make my testimony even more relevant, given my expertise in silent planets, annexations and worldwide revolts. Is there a single living individual in all the Federation systems who knows more about the Federation's most pernicious of problems than I?"

YOU ARE A WAR CRIMINAL.

"Allow this trial to proceed without delay, and I will agree to submit myself to a separate judgment."

No bars grew down over the doorway this time.

AGREED. PLEAD YOUR CASE.

CHAPTER THIRTY

"REGARDING EARTH'S STATUS," Tanamir said, "it is my assessment, as a Lodian citizen, as a credentialed expert in interplanetary treaties, and as the former head of the Committee to End Separation, that from this point forward, Earth should be considered a self-governing and autonomous world."

`THAT IS A HIGHLY UNUSUAL CONTRAVENTION OF PROCEDURE FOR SILENT PLANETS`, the ship's brain said.

"The facts are clear. Even you must recognize that this case has no historical precedent."

`WHAT QUALIFIES EARTH AS AUTONOMOUS?`

"Humans, as self-aware, intelligent beings, created a society that reached space on their own. Interplanetary treaties state clearly that spacefaring technology is a requirement for planetary self-governance."

`FEDERATION CITIZ—`

The flow of nanobots glitched as my senses lit up. Was Tanamir messing with time again? He was getting more subtle at controlling it. I reached out through the systems, but I couldn't see how he was doing it. I only felt a sense of decay somewhere far below us, as if a piece of meat had started to rot.

The Federation node pulsed as it processed.

"Yes," Tanamir said. "Criminals and refugees came here in secret to hide. They violated the laws of this world to do so—another reason to recognize Earth's autonomy. As you know, silent planets have no say in their status. And since they lack the technology to track the transit of modern starships, Federation bodies exploit them to rid their systems of unwanted criminal elements."

WE ARE NOT HERE TO ARBITRATE THE TREATMENT OF FEDERATION CRIMINALS.

Tanamir held up his hands. "My apologies."

PLEASE CLARIFY. HUMANITY REACHED SPACE ONLY AFTER SPACEFARING SPECIES WERE PRESENT.

"Has any evidence been filed showing that an offworlder gave illegal Federation secrets to human engineers in order to develop spacecraft?"

NEGATIVE.

"As an example, Federation starship drives don't use combustible fuel. It's terribly wasteful."

TECHNICALLY CORRECT.

I wanted to object to his argument, but so far I couldn't find any fault with his logic or a place to intervene. Annabelle followed the conversation with her lips pressed into a hard line.

"Yet, that is how humanity reached space. On their own, using a technology the Federation considers too dangerous and inefficient for its own use." He glanced at the Governor.

"I also have it on good authority that they're on the verge of developing faster-than-light technology."

Annabelle's jaw dropped. "Is that true?"

Tanamir leaned forward, letting time roll forward at its own pace.

THIS… ALTERS OUTCOMES.

"It is true," Governor Erazo said. "A breakthrough was made at an engineering lab at Baylor about two years ago."

"How did you keep *that* under wraps?" I asked.

"It is a matter of national security," Governor Erazo said. "My familiarity with the project was one of the reasons I was asked to be here."

"As you can see, their understanding of quantum physics is far superior to that of any other silent planet that has ever been annexed by the Federation," Tanamir said. "So, as I said, this particular case has no precedent."

AGREED, the ship said. IT IS A UNIQUE SITUATION.

Tanamir spread his hands and grinned as the stream of nanobots flowed upward through the mass.

WHO WILL GUARANTEE EARTH'S SECURITY?

"We'll guarantee our own security," Governor Erazo said.

HOW? The Federation ship demanded. YOU DO NOT POSSESS A SPACE NAVY.

"Give them a ship," Tanamir said. "To establish a precedent. Consider it the first gesture of goodwill to a new neighbor."

HIGHLY UNUSUAL…

Nanobots flowed upward slowly as the shipheart seemed to consider this. Power flowed from the mass through invisible connections to other nodes throughout the ship in engineering, weapons, navigation, life support...

At last, the ship seemed to accept Tanamir's testimony. It turned its attention to Governor Erazo next.

WHAT SAY THE LEADERS OF EARTH? the ship asked Governor Erazo.

"I have it on good authority that the President supports this request, and he has the cooperation of the UN. I can't speak for the rest of the leaders of Earth's nations."

WE DO NOT REQUIRE UNIFORM CONSENSUS, ONLY A MAJORITY. DO YOU SPEAK FOR THE MAJORITY?

"As much as we don't always see eye to eye with China or Russia... Yes, I can say with confidence that Earth's leaders will not bend the knee to an intergalactic overlord they don't know. We wish to make our own decisions, govern our own people, and administer our own justice."

I found myself nodding along.

AND WHAT OF THE FEDERATION CITIZENS WHO LIVE ON YOUR WORLD?

"I've already granted refugee status to offworlders in Texas," Erazo said, glancing at Tanamir. "I have assurances from the president that Congress will follow suit. From there, our position as a world power will encourage other countries to do the same. I'm told you like calculations. Run the odds, if you'd like."

The ship reached out and seemed to shuffle through Governor Erazo's mind like a deck of cards. Once finished, the ship released him. Erazo huffed out a disgruntled breath. "Warn me before you do that again, would you?"

ARE YOU WILLING TO OFFER SAFE HARBOR TO

OFFWORLDERS, SHOULD OTHER NATIONS DECLINE TO RECOGNIZE THEM?

“We can establish a sanctuary here in Texas,” Governor Erazo said, “if that’s what it takes to safeguard our independence.”

I glanced at Tanamir and my heart sank. *Harbor: the Gatekeeper’s name for his former nightclub.* Had Tanamir already pre-negotiated this with the alien parasite? It would make sense if the Gatekeeper had encouraged me because he had a stake in the outcome. If Earth governed itself, he could profit from manning the customs desk between the two authorities.

Tanamir refused to look my way, but I knew I was right. The promise of profit is the only thing that would make the Gatekeeper stick around.

VERY WELL. The intelligence turned its attention to me. I felt very exposed all of a sudden. AND YOU, PEACE-KEEPER OF EARTH?

“Oh, no,” I said, shocked to my core. “No, no. You must be mistaken. I’m no Peacekeeper. I’m just a bounty hunter.”

YOUR PEACEKEEPER AUGMENTS ARE ACTIVE. YOU HELPED TRACK DOWN AN OFFWORLD CRIMINAL NAMED ELEKATCH AND EXTRADITED HIM FOR TRIAL. THIS IS THE ROLE OF A PEACEKEEPER.

All that was true. And yet, the idea that I was some kind of Peacekeeper for Earth terrified me.

“Managing local Peacekeeper forces—or at least liaising with Federation Peacekeepers when they come knocking—is a requirement of independence,” Tanamir said. “To be recognized as a separate jurisdiction, Earth has to uphold all the functions that the Federation expects of its neighbors.”

I had a strong urge to distance myself from the concept.

"How am I supposed to represent all of Earth's law enforcement authorities? I'm just one man, and I'm not even a cop."

My words hung in the air, and I felt embarrassed. My voice didn't sound brave or bold—though I'd come here thinking I was being courageous. I knew deep down that this was the same voice that set me up with a career as a bounty hunter instead of becoming a cop or another kind of lawman. I preferred to chase my skips and wash my hands of them when I was done. I didn't have to build a case against them. My personal conduct wasn't going to be closely scrutinized by a review board. I was rarely asked to testify in court. I did my job and went home, and I liked it that way.

I liked it because I didn't have to worry about living up to the high standards of the law itself.

"You're a representative," Tanamir said. "The Federation only needs one. It can run its models from there."

"Don't screw this up, Mr. Gunn," Governor Erazo warned.

No pressure. Just the future of humanity on the line.

Even though Annabelle nodded encouragingly, the sense of responsibility sent me into a panic.

Tanamir called out to that rottenness that was the timepiece. He looked meaningfully between me and Annabelle, drawing an injector gun—with a large needle—out of his cloak and showing it to me behind her back.

His meaning was clear. If I didn't accept this responsibility, he'd inject Annabelle with a strain, and *she* would say the words I couldn't. After Tanamir went back in time to remove me from the situation, she'd be too scared to say no.

I couldn't let that happen.

"It's true, I've helped stop offworlder criminals," I said,

gathering my courage like shards of broken glass, "a few of them, anyway. I've helped keep the peace on Earth. I didn't do so as a Peacekeeper, and they injected me with the nanobots against my will. But one experience has taught me how much of your mess the Peacekeepers have to clean up. The Federation is far from perfect. You have criminals and opposing factions within your citizens that don't abide by Federation law, much like we do."

WHAT IS YOUR POINT? the ship asked.

"All this procedure and regulation is fundamentally flawed. You still have plenty of crime and wars. Innocent people still die—just look at Pango! So, who are you to decide what should happen to Earth? Who are you to force us to join your Federation? For better or worse, Earth deserves the right to determine its own future." I met Tanamir's eyes. "And correct our own mistakes."

WILL YOU ASSUME RESPONSIBILITY FOR INTERPLANETARY MIGRATION AND SAFE CONDUCT?

"What's that, like a customs checkpoint for Federation traffic?"

AND THE EXTRADITION OF OFFWORLD CRIMINALS.

"Well, that makes sense. I don't want to run it, but assuming we had some sort of independent bureau, then I think it would work."

REQUEST DENIED.

The judgment struck me like an off-key piano note. I'd barely winced before Tanamir reached out and *wrenched* time backward.

We experienced three more denials before I figured out what was happening. Tanamir kept rolling back to different points in the conversation, trying to find a way through the failure.

Every time, we got to the part about safe conduct and ran up against a `REQUEST DENIED` response. The Federation was not satisfied.

We did it a dozen more times. Whether it was because I testified last, or simply because it didn't like my answers, each time ended in that sharp and sudden denial.

Apparently, the Federation didn't trust us to police our own borders. They had a point. Earth didn't have the knowledge or the technology. We needed help.

In the end, the ship seemed eager to deny our requests and appeared to dislike the idea of Earth as an independent world.

I got temporal whiplash as the ship's systems reversed and repeated once again, Tanamir pulling us back through time.

Before the next `REQUEST DENIED`, Tanamir forced his way past the verbal interface and spoke directly to the ship's brain with a series of images—his memories as a Federation general.

Scenes of war on dozens of worlds passed between the Federation's network and Tanamir's mind. Governments fell. Species were enslaved. Worlds were glassed, gassed, cracked. A sentient but primitive race of ocean-dwellers was sterilized and forced into manual labor. A colony moon was later plunged into the ocean of a different world, sundering its atmosphere and destroying it to prevent a rebellion.

Every world that fought the Federation for control was eventually brought to heel.

On most of those worlds, peace won the day, but always at the cost of many lives.

The exchange ended with a world called Charr. Tanamir had been sent there with a Federation invasion force, carrying orders to crush the latest rebellion. When his forces arrived, the rebels on Charr were ready with floating bombs. Tanamir lost half his fleet in the first confrontation. After a siege lasting three hundred of the planet's local days, the famed general went down to the surface to negotiate with a trio of rebel leaders.

It was during this parley that he defected from the Federation. Tanamir joined the three rebels, forming an alliance of four. They called themselves the Tetrad.

Charr got blown to smithereens, anyway, but not before the Tetrad's leaders had escaped.

He stopped the replay and returned to his closing argument.

"Granting Earth's independence will prevent a conflict like this from destroying the world, and humanity along with it. Allowing humanity to govern itself will do more to uphold the peace than if the Federation usurped control," Tanamir said. "And isn't that why the Federation was created? To keep the peace between worlds. Yet, your Peacekeepers are nothing more than interstellar janitorial staff, cleaning up the mess that your imperfect order has made. I'll acknowledge that what the Tetrad has been trying to do was not a bloodless path forward. But you must acknowledge that this third way is viable. It's the best possible way to maintain the transparency the Federation requires without violating Earth's autonomy."

It turned to Governor Erazo. `YOU AGREE TO OFFER SAFE HARBOR TO OFFWORLDERS?`

Erazo agreed, same as he had before.

`AND YOU, PEACEKEEPER OF EARTH,` it said,

focusing on me, WILL YOU ASSUME RESPONSIBILITY FOR INTERPLANETARY SAFE CONDUCT?

This time, instead of offering unsatisfactory answers about the huge responsibilities the Federation wanted me to take on, I remembered Dyna's advice and caught myself.

"Yes, I will... but I propose we run it as an experiment."

Tanamir looked over, shoulder ridges billowing as a glare pierced through me.

EXPLAIN.

"I'm not sure what makes the most sense. Let's run it as an experiment first."

LIKE A TRIAL? the ship asked.

"Exactly. That'll give us time to make any adjustments and iron out the kinks," I said. "This is our first time upholding interplanetary treaties—I'm sure there's a lot to learn."

INDEED.

Annabelle's eyes lit up. "Can I help?"

"Sure." I shrugged. "Why not?"

"No," Tanamir said. He looked furious but exhausted, having just negotiated with the feckless, faceless machine for hours on end. "It has to be decided today."

"Says who?" I retorted, my natural stubbornness coming out to play. "We don't have to decide anything today."

THIS ARBITRATION WOULD REMAIN OPEN UNTIL THE EXPERIMENT HAS CONCLUDED.

Annabelle was hastily typing these notes into her phone. She'd been recording the whole exchange, I knew, but much of the communication passed mind-to-mind between us and the Federation's network, and much more had been lost to Tanamir's temporal manipulations.

The ship turned to Tanamir. NOW, AS FOR YOUR CRIMES. OPENING CASE XF-97—

"I don't think so," Tanamir said, his voice trailing off, glitching into a series of garbled messages.

YOU CAN'T DO THAT, the ship said. NO, STOP IT.

The nanobot flow reached out like a big hand and tried to snatch Tanamir. He used the timepiece to avoid being snared, moving out of reach before the nanobots could seize him.

"It's time for you to leave."

REQUEST DENIED. YOU MUST PRESENT YOUR DEFENSE.

"I don't think so," Tanamir said. "You may consider what I've done a crime, but I will not stop until every sentient world is liberated from your tyranny! Long live the Tetrad."

Nanobots sealed the sphere's arched doorways with a slurp. My ears popped in the sudden change of atmospheric pressure.

Tanamir reached out through the ship's systems. I felt something turn, opening like a valve.

"I planted a device that can create a temporal rift in your power core," Tanamir told the ship. "Once activated, it will pull the past into the present, creating a temporal anomaly that will destroy the core powering your main thrusters, causing your ship to fall and crack on the ground."

TENS OF THOUSANDS WILL DIE, the ship said. WE'RE FLOATING OVER OF A DENSELY POPULATED URBAN AREA.

"Yes," Tanamir said, "the people of Earth will be very angry that you killed so many of their citizens. It won't predispose them to think kindly of the Federation. How sad."

I reached out again into the ship's systems, searching for a way to grab ahold of the timepiece.

How had he done it? Could I undo the damage or otherwise disrupt their plan somehow?

Jaiyana. I felt her presence near the engine room. Kilos was nearby, alive, but his presence was thready and faint in the ship's senses.

I reached out, feeling for the source of the rot, seeking through the systems like searching for a needle in a pile of sand.

A quiet presence appeared near where I felt Kilos. Administrator 317. The Neth sensed me. I jerked back, but it reached out and gently guided me to where Jaiyana had planted the timepiece in the engine room—specifically, in the control panel monitoring the power core's vitals.

The Neth guided me to a seam where a section of the software had been cut out and patched. There, I found the timepiece's influence. It had been wired in, activating the timepiece to give the ship access to its abilities, and then rigged with a trigger on the anomaly.

Its clock read north of ten minutes. It counted down, which meant that if Tanamir didn't activate it manually, it was set to destabilize on its own.

As I watched, a powerful presence reached out, poising its finger over the trigger.

I lashed out, batting Tanamir back. Guided by Administrator 317, I formed a mental barrier around the device, blocking Tanamir from detonating it.

This gave me access to the timepiece. I kicked it, and the countdown timer froze.

With a shout of rage, Tanamir grabbed my right forearm —not in the ship's systems, but in the physical world. I realized that my cybernetic hand had sunk into the flowing waterfall of nanobots while we wrestled in the cyberspace of the ship's systems. He stepped on my rifle, which had fallen, to keep the barrel pointed away from him.

"Let go of the timepiece," he said.

"Make me," I snarled, tightening my mental hold on the timepiece while shifting my legs beneath me in the real world.

Behind Tanamir, Annabelle drew her sidearm and pointed it at the back of his head. "Let him go," she said, wide-eyed and panting.

"Boom," I said.

Annabelle squeezed the trigger.

CHAPTER THIRTY-ONE

TANAMIR'S face twisted in a snarl as the .38-caliber bullet crashed into his temple.

It exploded from the opposite side of his skull...

...and froze as time crawled to a halt.

With a desperate shove, he wrested control of the timepiece back from me and rewound the moment.

I saw it happen in slow motion. Not using my physical senses—which were far too slow to comprehend what was happening in each moment—but with my connection to the starship through my alien augments. It was extrasensory perception at a level of detail I'd never imagined. I tumbled through the psychic obstacle course.

"Boom." The words spilled from my lips a second time as the moment replayed. I yanked control of the timepiece back, stopping his reversal well before he intended.

From the wall, Tanamir called a needle-thin cord of nanobots to deflect the bullet, sending it off at a slight angle. That kind of accuracy was unprecedented and would have been incredible to me if I weren't so irritated about not anticipating the move. But it wasn't enough. Tanamir threw his head back. The bullet missed his temple and pierced the ridge of flesh connecting his shoulder and neck on the opposite side.

When it ruptured, the flesh collapsed in on itself, deflating.

He tried to reverse time again. I felt him pulling it back and threw all my willpower against him, wrestling for control of the slipstream. I couldn't figure out how to take the timepiece's functionality back, but I blocked his efforts to rewind the moment through psychic brute force and sheer stubbornness.

Tanamir screamed, staggering backwards as he disengaged. He kept his momentum going, running for the sphere's exit despite his injury.

Governor Erazo, the coward, fled after him.

I pointed my rifle at his back, but couldn't get a clear shot thanks to the Governor. I snarled, lowering the weapon.

"Are you okay?" I asked, reaching down and helping Annabelle up.

"Come on, he's getting away!"

Annabelle ran for the door, and I followed, out of the sphere and back onto the bridge. I joined her at the rail. Annabelle's face went pale as she stared down the curve of the opening. It was like gazing down the face of the Hoover Dam. My stomach quivered.

Tanamir's cloak billowed as he fell.

I couldn't see Administrator 317, Tanamir, or Jaiyana down there, but I could sense them.

And Kilos, with his fading pulse, somewhere in the vicinity.

I hoped the tough Kilgar made it out of this one, and that we could get him back to his healing chambers in time.

The thought hadn't crossed my mind for more than an instant when I remembered his healing tech was fresh out of medical supplies.

"We have to jump," I told Annabelle as I refocused on what we had to do next. I could see Tanamir down there, falling through the open space that seemed to taper, like an upside-down teardrop, to a point. A translucent veil of nanobots was strung from straps beneath his armpits.

"What's that noise?" Annabelle asked.

A whirring hum I hadn't noticed before came from below, like a giant microwave was running somewhere in its center.

"Weird image," I muttered.

He must have noticed us watching. Tanamir pulled the chute in and increased his speed. I drew my rifle on him and fired a few testing shots.

They either went wide or deflected off the nanobot chute.

"Is that where the power core is?" Annabelle asked. "It must be like a nuclear reactor or something."

I gripped the rail and reached out through the ship's systems to sense the area. "All thick walls and a nested trio of containment chambers," I said. "Control room's on the far side. I think that's where the timepiece is."

"That's where he's going, then."

I slung the rifle back behind me and picked Annabelle up with my good arm.

"What are you doing?" she asked.

"Do you trust me?"

"What?!"

"I said, do you trust me?"

"Oh hell, Gunn, this isn't some Disney movie, I—"

I'd stepped over the rail before she could finish.

Annabelle screamed as I plunged my cybernetic fist into the slanted wall of the silo, using my fingers like a brake to slow our descent.

I formed the mental image of a board beneath my boots and one appeared, securing my feet. I leaned forward onto my toes, and we carved our way around the silo like a reckless snowboarder tilting down the slopes at a breakneck speed.

I grinned into the wind, thrilling in the adrenaline rush.

"Do you even know how to break?" she asked.

Annabelle had wrapped her legs around me and squirmed onto my back. Tanamir's chute rippled as he hit the shadowed floor. We fell into the darkness.

"Break what?" I asked, enjoying the ride.

"BRAKE!!"

Stop me, I pleaded with the ship. *And try not to shatter our squishy human bodies in the process, would you?*

Whatever mind was aware inside this networked system of reconfigurable nanobots—the Federation, Administrator 317, or the faceless machine—it responded to my commands, nanobots flowing out from where my hand sank into the wall. The snowboard's nose broadened into a plow and slowed us down enough to jump off.

Busted doors, dented walls, and scorch marks lined the entryway. I followed the trail of destruction into a control room made of that nauseating, shifting material. The entire far wall was a window cracked diagonally across its face.

Beyond the window shone a blue plasma orb, blinding in its brightness.

Annabelle shaded her eyes and snapped her camera's shutter. "The power core."

Its light was pulsing, strobing the room in violet flashes which leaked, like liquid, through the cracked window to illuminate more collateral damage. Two administrators lay dead, eviscerated by Jaiyana's blade, in horrible messy piles near splashes of nanobots that flowed out of scars in the wall.

Nanobots were rapidly filling the room, multiplying with every flash.

It strobed like a heartbeat. *Ba-dum. Ba-dum.*

Kilos lay nearby, his large body caught in the hatch doorway of some kind of airlock. His head and shoulders stuck into the room we'd just entered and his normally pale fur was matted around his mouth and chest, soaked in a brown liquid which I took to be alien blood. And maybe some of his own blood from many slashes mixed in. He turned his head toward us.

"Look out," he said, reaching with one hand.

I turned in time to block an upward-arcing elbow to my chin with my cybernetic hand. My cybernetic wrist pinged off Jaiyana's elbow with a metallic twinge that shot up my arm and shoulder.

She attacked me like Bruce Lee, a whirl of fists, knees and broad-bladed feet. I used my rifle, forearms, and even my own feet to block her attacks, but her speed overwhelmed me. Three blows landed on my neck and torso. She kicked me with a foot so powerful I flew by Annabelle and landed near Kilos.

I rolled and came up with the rifle to my shoulder. I fired at her midsection, a double burst. One of my shots took her in the flank. She snarled, and that half second allowed me to glance down and see that the starship's nanobots had caught me.

EMERGENCY PROTOCOLS, came the clarion call from the ship. PEACEKEEPER: ELIMINATE THE THREAT.

Its voice thundered out of the nanobots holding me three feet off the ground.

That hungry compulsion returned with a vengeance.

I'd say I tried to resist... but after taking a beating from Jaiyana and chasing her and Tanamir around the city for days, I didn't *want* to resist anymore.

The nanobots gathered around my cybernetic fist like a glove, reshaping it into a gauntlet. They climbed in spindly lines up my arms, lacing around my biceps and shoulders to reinforce my limbs and straighten my spine.

The lines encircled my waist and legs, I felt *strong* in its embrace, stronger and more capable than I'd felt in years. I thrilled with the power. It was intoxicating.

The M3 rifle was pulled from my hands. I didn't need it, so I let the ship take it. Around my other arm, the nanobots formed a cast that sculpted into a long barrel extending a foot out from my hand.

For the first time, Jaiyana actually looked scared.

Scared... and a little bit surprised.

This gave me confidence. It was my turn to attack. Laced with alien armor and armed with an offworld plasma weapon, I advanced. I squeezed my trigger finger and bolts of light shot out like lasers, making Jaiyana dance to avoid getting burned. I backed her into a corner with the weapon, but she jumped up and gave a double-footed kick to that arm. I swung with my reinforced fist, and her arm came up to block me.

A slashing kick struck at my knees, then she drew a

handheld firearm of her own, some alien model I didn't recognize. I knocked the barrel away and a laser burned a line across the wall. We wrestled for the weapon, and I managed to get my fingers around the barrel and squeeze a shot off. It scorched the ceiling.

I shoved her back and she stumbled away. She rebounded quickly, coming in with acrobatic roundhouse kicks. I moved quicker and hit harder than I ever had. My movements seemed to be choreographed, programmed in advance. Still, she matched my every move.

She was a hell of an opponent.

In shock, I realized something. She wasn't *just* a skilled opponent. She was also stalling for time.

"Gunn, hurry!" Annabelle's voice cut through the fog of combat. "Tanamir's inside the engine room. I think he's... he's doing something with the timepiece! Gunn! Andy!"

With a cold fear, I reached out with my mind and felt a presence approaching the timepiece virus.

Inspiration struck me. With a speed I'd not yet matched, I sprinted toward Jaiyana and drove her toward the pile of nanobots that now covered the Neth bodies. I called to the ship, and as I approached, the material glommed onto her back and sucked her inside of it.

The Sevrit thrashed and screamed, but her elbows and kicks weren't effective against the intelligent particles as they hardened.

In response to my thoughts, they formed a personal prison around Jaiyana, making a shell with only a hole for the tip of her snout.

It quivered in anger.

I didn't waste time gloating. I turned and ran toward Kilos and Annabelle. Annabelle gestured for me to move forward, then backed away from the Peacekeeper, who was now unconscious.

"Kilos said the radiation would melt the skin from my bones without the ship to protect me. So, you have to do it. When you go in, I'll pull him out." She nodded at the unconscious Kilos.

Hairs raised themselves all along my arms but I wouldn't dream of putting her in harm's way if I could do the dirty work. "He's heavy. You got it?"

"I'll manage."

I glanced through to the next door in the airlock, another hatch-like entrance made of super-dense nanobot material.

"How does Tanamir survive something like that?"

"Same way you will."

She gestured to my person. The nanobot material would protect me, she meant.

I reached for the timepiece, feeling it with my mental senses inside the engine room. It was active, but the device wasn't rewinding time. Instead, Tanamir seemed to be taking a single point in space and shoving it forward into the future. The device could only go so far. It reached its limit, and the fabric of reality tore—the tiniest rupture, no bigger than the width of a single atom.

The future poured into the past in a disorienting loop.

`CONTAIN THE ANOMALY`, the ship demanded. Again, its words stirred my blood, and I felt that compulsion to do as the voice commanded.

I fought for control of the timepiece, but my psychic grip slipped off like it had been greased. Tanamir increased the flow rate, shoving the point even further into the future.

Like an engine redlining, the air shook as Tanamir pushed the device beyond its normal limit.

I gave up the mental wrestling match and returned my attention to my physical body. If I couldn't control it, I could still punch Tanamir in the jaw.

I pulled more nanobots from the piles of it writhing around the room, thickening my armor until it was a full-body suit.

I hadn't made it three steps into the airlock when an explosion inside the chamber rocked the ship, forcing me to my knees.

The timepiece had detonated.

INITIATE EMERGENCY LANDING PROCEDURES, I heard the ship say.

Having bent down to pull Kilos out of the threshold, Annabelle bashed her head against the frame. When I looked back at her, blood oozed out through the fingers of the hand she held to her head.

There was another horrible rending sound, then a shudder.

My feet lifted from the floor as the Federation battle-cruiser dropped from the sky.

CHAPTER THIRTY-TWO

CARRYING KILOS'S UNCONSCIOUS, three hundred some-odd pound body between us, Annabelle and I staggered out of the engine room and into the bowl-like basin into which we'd descended.

The curved floor was pulling apart, tearing in jagged, unpredictable seams. The nanobots struggled to re-adhere, and the floor deepened as it separated, sloping downward in sinkholes. The exoskeleton of nanobots I had formed around myself was starting to slough off in sections, too.

Without power from the ship, its nanobot systems were dying.

The breakdown was slow enough for us to move away from the sinkholes. I was able to use some of the exoskeleton's strength to support Kilos. Each step forward was like doing a set of squats, though. I was fading fast, huffing and puffing and feeling more like my weak human self by the moment.

The compulsions in me had gone when the ship turned its attention to damage control.

I didn't know how I was going to get us out of here. Unlike Tanamir, I couldn't make a parachute.

Or could I?

The floor several yards in front of us finally yawned open, revealing clouds and a blue sky below, which frightened me out of pulling another harebrained stunt.

As I took in this terrifying sight with my wide eyes, Tanamir staggered out of the door of the engine room.

His heavy cloak was in tatters. His flayed and cracked skin glowed with a radioactive light. He only had one boot on. Something had punctured his shoulder ridges in several places, so he struggled to breathe. He clenched the damaged timepiece in one fist.

As he went, he gathered up loose nanobots from the floor, pulling them around himself, smoothing layers over his damaged skin like bandages.

We watched in horror as he tried to patch himself. The nanobots sloughed off in sheets, making him look like a B-movie horror monster with loose skin.

Tanamir finally seemed to notice us watching. He grinned, his face like a glowing Halloween skull.

We stared at the mutilated offworlder. How was he even standing? It didn't make sense, and my mind struggled to process what I was seeing.

All I could imagine was that he'd gotten more augments than I had if he could survive that kind of radiation.

"Should I put him out of his misery?" I said.

Annabelle shuddered. "Ugh."

The damaged timepiece Tanamir held fell to the floor with a soft thunk.

"Mission accomplished," Tanamir rasped. "The Tetrad will be in touch."

He saluted us with a raised fist, then stepped into the nearest sinkhole to plunge through the ship's porous floor and the storm clouds hundreds of feet below.

Annabelle took one step forward, then halted and stared back at me in wide-eyed shock.

I sighed, relieved not to have to kill him, even as I made a mental note to locate and ID his body... assuming we got out of here alive.

Gunn, it's Dyna—are you there?

"Dyna?" I asked aloud so Annabelle knew she had made contact. "We're here. I thought Kilos said you'd be neutralized."

The Federation's dampening effect wore off when the power core ruptured, she said.

Is that him? That was Vinny, somehow communicating through the Peacekeeper. *Jesus, Gunn, where you been?*

"Long story."

Do you have Kilos? Dyna asked

"He's unconscious and badly hurt, but alive."

Good. Good. Can you find an exit?

"Define exit..." I explained about the holes in the ship's floor.

His tone became immediately professional and urgent. *We're approaching your location. I'll have the ship positioned below you in thirty seconds.*

They did as promised. We had to put Kilos down and drag his body back several steps to stay on solid ground. The hole continued to widen, and material now dripped down out of the ship like it was bleeding streams of nanobots.

Dyna's ship turned off its cloaking shield and appeared—fifty yards below us.

I could make out individual houses on the ground

beyond now. We were positioned over a suburban neighborhood.

Incoming! Vinny said.

Three harnesses arced into the hole in the battlecruiser's belly. They had glowing green lights on them, which allowed us to locate them with ease, although gathering them up was a dangerous game.

Put those on, Vinny said, *Dyna's gonna use 'em to airlift you down to us.*

Annabelle and I shrugged into the vests. They were made of nylon straps and buckles, like something you'd see lift an actor across a stage. We hauled Kilos into his, somehow. I pulled a neck muscle in the process.

"What about that?" Annabelle said, pointing at the timepiece where Tanamir had dropped it.

I rubbed my neck and frowned. Was it radioactive? Would it burn me? I decided to take the risk. Careful to use my cybernetic hand, I first gathered a sheet of the remaining nanobots, the ones near my waist that still had some adherence, and used it like paper to wrap up the timepiece in a little ball. The nanobot material seemed to insulate the heat emanating from the device.

Quickly, if you please, said Dyna.

"We're ready," I said.

Jump.

"Twice in one day?" Annabelle asked. "I really don't like this part of the gig."

"All in a day's work, m'lady. Hold onto me if you'd like."

We held each other tightly and, with two booted feet, kicked Kilos's enormous body into the sky.

"Ten, nine, eight," Annabelle said, "Seven—WHY, ANDY? WHY!?"

Wind roared around our ears. My vision blurred with tears, and cold air rushed at me.

We slowed. Despite the fluttering panic in my stomach, Dyna caught us with her abilities and brought us safely down onto the roof of her ship.

Annabelle stopped screaming. She smacked me in the shoulder several times in vengeance before settling into my arms, soft and trembling. It was reassuring to hold her.

We'd made it out alive.

Dyna's ship moved away from the falling battlecruiser. From out here, the streams of nanobots seemed to pour from many holes in the ship like waterfalls that dissipated before they hit the ground. The ship bent inward, no longer straight, but bowed up so that its center—where we'd exited—would hit the ground first.

It fell slowly as its engines and thrusters lost power. But even if it didn't hit at full velocity, its sheer size would crush and destroy anything it landed on.

Dyna finally stopped her ship. The wind calmed as the battlecruiser fell past us.

We stayed up there, in the cold air, as the starship made impact. A shockwave rolled out across the city, leveling buildings and flooding the river's banks.

Dyna came up through an elevator topside. After checking on us, she levitated Kilos's body and took him back inside.

Annabelle went next, and I followed, holding the broken timepiece in my alien hand.

CHAPTER THIRTY-THREE

DYNA SAT across from me at the round table in the common area of the Peacekeeper's ship.

"So how'd you get out of jail?" I asked.

"When the power core ruptured, the Federation released me," Dyna said. "At that point, I was free to go from their perspective. However, I waited for the detective to open the cell."

"And how'd you get clearance to release her?" I asked, turning to Gonzalez, who sat next to Dyna like they were old friends and she hadn't arrested her the other day.

Detective Gonzalez shrugged. "We had no body, and Officer Daniels' partner, Mo, discovered that someone had doctored several of the videos we'd filed as evidence of her crimes. With people congregating in Austin, our jails were also overflowing. We couldn't afford to hold onto them anymore. After that, it wasn't a stretch to get her released on her own recognizance along with several other protesters from that night. The Texas DAs will still try to charge Dyna with aggravated assault."

"Surely, you won't stick around for that, will you?" I asked, looking back at the Peacekeeper.

"If I do not, who is going to help you run your trial?"

I cocked my head at her. "The Federation would let you do that? Don't you and Kilos have other responsibilities?"

The Kilgar was in Rashiki's, recovering in the medical facilities I had used after an alien beast crushed my hand. The medical technology there wasn't as good as that on the Peacekeeper ship, but since they'd run out of supplies, it was his best option—Dyna sped him there the moment we'd boarded.

By all indications, Kilos was going to survive, but Dyna didn't know if he'd make a full recovery this time. Too much damage to his spinal cord. She said they could make some augments to suit him, but he'd never be the same.

"I will send my resignation to Lodi. If the Federation wants me back, they will simply have to send another Arbiter to compel me."

"The smaller ships they left in orbit can't do that?"

"Their nodes don't have enough mass to compel me."

As the massive battlecruiser had crashed to the ground, the Federation ships stationed in its hangar lifted off and flew to safety. They parked in geostationary orbit over Austin, where they broadcast an encrypted signal back to Federation space. To my surprise, they didn't communicate with Earth or do anything to retrieve or secure the wreckage of their starship, which the FBI, NSA, DHS, and every other alphabet-soup agency were now combing through on the ground.

Any average Joe could see the ships up there on a clear night, like a dozen space stations clustered close together. The media were calling them 'sentinel ships' or 'the alien overwatch'. Yasmin's fanatics and Annabelle's fans preferred terms like 'guardian angels' or 'the offworld protectorate'. Whatever they were called, our country's leaders did not like seeing the enemy overhead, and the U.S. Space Force had the starships under constant surveillance.

According to Dyna, the smaller ships stayed to observe and report our movements back to the Federation, but would no longer interfere. Another Arbiter would be sent to finalize the judgment we'd begun, once our experiment concluded, but neither of us knew when that would be. The battlecruiser had been destroyed before we could discuss the timeline. Dyna said it would take years. The Federation took a long-range view of these kinds of experiments.

Annabelle and I had received invitations to the governor's office to discuss "the situation." He'd been found unconscious in an escape pod a mile from the crash site's outer edge. Dyna thought he'd been launched to safety by the battlecruiser in the moments before impact, as part of its emergency landing procedures.

I felt Governor Erazo's trepidation through the terse note. It was co-signed by the White House and the director of Extraterrestrial Affairs—whatever that was.

Other pods had been found near the governor's, presumably for the Neth and other lifeforms we'd encountered aboard the ship. Jaiyana may have been among those the battlecruiser ejected. I couldn't be sure.

Unfortunately, Tanamir's body had not been found either.

"We'll do our best to get those charges dropped," Annabelle said, patting Dyna's hand. "I have some photographs of you protecting protesters when Tanamir landed his UFO on Congress Avenue and released those thugs to stoke the riots. That'll show that you were on the right side of the riots and actually protected people instead of harming them."

"Gratitude, Annabelle." Dyna dipped her head. "What will you do with that?"

The busted timepiece sat in a radiation containment pouch on the table between us.

"As useful as it might be," I said. "The Pangozil need it more than we do."

"HERE YOU GO," I said, handing the busted timepiece to Felix.

The Torlik took the containment pouch into his four trembling hands, glancing up and down the boardwalk like he was scared someone might snatch it. We stood outside the Pangozil residence in Rashiki's. "I don't know if I can fix this," Felix said.

"All you can do is try."

He glanced up at me, flabbergasted, only to realize a moment later that I was being earnest rather than my usual sarcastic self.

"It was never meant to be used the way Tanamir used it," I pointed out. "It's not your fault it broke."

"I know."

"You can make it right. Fix it and use it for a higher purpose."

A group of Pangozil exited the residence carrying large trunks between them. Amberen Gevereaux emerged, followed by his retinue. Felix watched them file out, swallowed hard and ginned up his courage.

He slowly approached the group, holding the device out to Amberen, who admired it with a skeptical curiosity. The elderly Pangozil made a comment I couldn't hear, but it must have been positive, for Felix stood a little straighter and responded in authoritative tones as he spoke about his device. The Pangozil leaned in, ears attuned to his every word. The longer Felix spoke, the more animated he became, gesturing with his three free hands. His audience ate up every word. Of course they did. He was feeding the Pangozil refugees a rare delicacy—*hope.*

A light pat on my leg drew my attention down to Lulamina's pint-sized person.

"Good work, Mr. Gunn," she said. "A job well done."

"Thousands of people died." I swallowed, thinking about the damage the battlecruiser's wreckage had done when it came crashing down on the city of Austin and its suburbs.

"And billions more still live."

I nodded at Felix and the group of Pangozil. "You think it'll make a difference?"

"Zavis thinks the device can be rebuilt, with the right tools and a skilled engineer."

"Does Felix have what it takes?"

"Zavis thinks so," she said. "He wants to go with them."

I glanced up the boardwalk to see Zavis coming down the way, dragging a suitcase behind him. "He packed light."

"Half of his workshop is in that suitcase."

"Ahh, I see, more of your opsilax containers. What about you, Lulamina? Will you go, too?"

All around us, offworlders packed to leave. Rumor had it that the Gatekeeper's shuttles were resuming operation and many were eager to leave Earth behind, given the hostile attitude of some humans toward offworlders. Not as many as I expected, though. Most, it seemed, were going to take their chances here on Earth.

"I'm not going anywhere," Lulamina said. "Someone has to keep an eye on the house. Plus, word on the street is that you got yourself into a pickle. I figure you might need an advisor, or at least a listening ear, before too long." She smiled and handed a white envelope to me. "The rest of your payment for this case."

I took it gladly. "Thank you."

"You know where to find me." She departed, moving down the spiral boardwalk to speak with Annabelle.

Vinny separated himself from the group and hurried over. He stopped in front of me, giving me a shy smile and a half-shrug. "How can I ever repay ya?"

"You don't owe me anything, pal. I'm happy to be of service."

"Thank you, Gunn. I wish it weren't goodbye again, but..."

"You've got to be with your people," I said, glancing over at Annabelle. "I get it."

Amberen saw us talking, handed the timepiece back to Felix, and joined us.

"You've given hope back to our people," he said. "We won't soon forget it."

"Like I was telling Vinny, I'm glad I could help, even if I only played a small part."

"Yet you made an effort—and at no small risk to your own life."

I shrugged. Annabelle joined us at that moment, entwining her arm in mine and resting her head on my shoulder. "His heart's in the right place."

"You have a monumental task ahead of you, Gunn. Just know that should you ever need assistance, you may call on me."

He handed me a square piece of plastic with a computer chip in the middle. "My personal calling card."

I pocketed it. "I'll keep that in mind."

Amberen nodded and walked back to join the Pangozil. They took Felix and Zavis into their room with them, where they were packing to depart.

"I'll miss ya, pal," Vinny said.

"Pfah, don't get all mushy on me." I wiped away some wetness from the corners of my eyes. "Stay in touch?"

"Of course. Can't call you on the phone from Pango but I'll send a message when I arrive to let you know we made it safely."

"Good," I said. I couldn't manage any more words. I embraced Vinny, squeezing him tightly. "Gonna miss you, pal."

"I'll be seeing you," he said gruffly, and went his own way.

I turned to see a long-legged woman in a short skirt sauntering down the boardwalk in absurdly high heels. Her eyes flashed blue. She paused by Dyna, who stood about twenty yards away, leaning against a doorframe while we said our piece. The Peacekeeper didn't look surprised to see the Gatekeeper.

Annabelle and I went to join the Gatekeeper and Dyna.

"Guess you decided to stick around," I said when I got close.

Samael flapped down and landed on the doorframe above us to listen in on the conversation.

"I heard about your little experiment," the Gatekeeper said. "Bold strategy!"

I wrinkled my nose. "Thanks for the heads-up," I said. "I know you were only looking out for your own interests, but you didn't have to tell me what you'd heard, so I appreciate it."

"Certainly." The leggy blonde grinned at me like I was a snack. I squirmed as I imagined the Gatekeeper diving into my mouth and sucking out my soul.

I sighed. "I can't believe I'm going to say this but... We talked, and the only way this trial is going to work is if we cooperate. We'd like you to take up your old mantle again. Earth needs the Gatekeeper."

"Well, if the local Peacekeeper captain wants me to do that, I suppose I shall have to endure."

"Don't act like it's an inconvenience. You keep all your profits from enforcing customs at the border and regulating imports and exports. The only difference now is that you'll have to abide by Earth law, too. That means no more torture or murder, even of offworlders."

"Or what?"

"You'll have to deal with us." I gestured to encompass me and Dyna.

"And what recourse do I have if someone tries to steal from me, or smuggle something to Earth on my shuttles?"

"Give me a call. I'll investigate."

The leggy woman with the glowing blue eyes pouted for a minute, then sighed. "Very well. As you wish. And if the U.S. government sends agents sniffing around? They'll definitely want to get involved."

"Last time I checked, they don't have any spaceships."

"Not yet, they don't."

"One day at a time. Do we have a deal?"

"We do, Mr. Gunn."

The Gatekeeper turned and sauntered off, swinging his host's shapely hips. The Daacro flew up toward the exit, leaving me, Annabelle and Dyna alone on the boardwalk.

"I hope that was the right choice."

"We couldn't very well prevent him from setting up his business again," Annabelle said.

"Removing him would have left a power vacuum," Dyna said. "We agreed on that. At least this way we know who we're dealing with."

"We did. And as they say—better the enemy you know, et cetera. He, at least, is predictably profit motivated."

My stomach growled. I glanced around and sniffed. "If Vinny's not cooking, I don't want to eat here. How do you two feel about cheeseburgers?"

"I do not believe I have tried one of those yet," Dyna said.

I stared at her, mortified. "Are you serious?"

"Quite. We have rations aboard the ship."

"Oh no, that won't stand. If you're sticking around, you'll have to get used to the local cuisine."

We left Rashikis, drove to The Poached Pig, and enjoyed the best meal I'd had in days.

I didn't know what would happen with our experiment, but we ate Barry's burgers knowing that, at least for now, Earth would live to see another sunrise.

DRIVING HOME AFTER DINNER, I flicked on the radio.

"Flash flood warnings are in effect across Travis and Bastrop Counties tonight," the DJ on Sun Radio was saying, "as heavy rains from the Gulf move north and west across the state. Stay safe out there, folks. Turn around, don't drown."

My chest tightened as a hunch came over me.

Confirming my instincts were correct was going to be a wet affair. I'd have to wait to get that good night's sleep I'd been craving.

Later that evening, I stood on the shore of Shoal Creek as a gushing flood of stormwater rushed through the creek.

I didn't mind the wet or the cold. For once, I'd come prepared in a heavy-duty rain slicker and waterproof waders. I carried a swift-water self-rescue kit: rope, carabiners, multi-tool, and a large belt knife.

I waited patiently, checking my diver's watch and listening for just the right moment.

My patience was rewarded. As the waters of the creek rose to historic levels, I heard a voice shouting for help.

My voice.

I followed it into the water and waded to the spot where I'd dropped my Kimber in the fight with Jaiyana. I'd looked for the gun here after Dyna had pulled me to safety, but I hadn't found it.

I noted the spot, waded into the water, and plunged my arm in, feeling around.

Wet mud squelched between my fingers. Grass or weeds, maybe a bush, the hard edge of the pavement—

There. My fingers wrapped around the rough grip of my Kimber handgun. I felt the trigger guard where its curved edge met the barrel. I pulled, but it was caught on something.

ment in ankle-deep floodwaters. I felt like I might be the happiest man in the world at that moment.

I'd disassemble the Kimber inside and let it dry overnight. For now, I was just glad to have it back.

Grateful to be alive. Overjoyed to be free of debts, at least of the monetary type... I'd rarely known such freedom. I'd made a big promise to the Federation, but there was time to sort that out. For now, I could enjoy the moment. Everything else could wait until tomorrow.

HERRON'S HEROES

Join thousands of like-minded sci-fi fans in M.G. Herron's reader group.

Sign up at **mgherron.com/bookclub**

You'll get behind-the-scenes updates from the author, exclusive short stories, and be the first to know about new books by M.G. Herron!

ALSO BY M.G. HERRON

THE GUNN FILES

A sci-fi mystery about alien encounters in Austin, TX

Book 1: **Culture Shock**

Book 2: **Overdose**

Book 3: **Quantum Flare**

Book 4: **Nick of Time**

RELICS OF THE ANCIENTS

An action-packed and spellbinding space opera series

Book 1: **Starfighter Down**

Book 2: **Hidden Relics**

Book 3: **Rogue Swarm**

STARFIGHTER ORIGINS

The origin stories of characters from *Relics of the Ancients*

Book 1: **Spare Parts**

Book 2: **Raptor**

Book 3: **Operation Heartstrike**

TRANSLOCATOR TRILOGY

A portal science fiction adventure trilogy

Book 1: **The Auriga Project**

Book 2: **The Alien Element**

Book 3: **The Ares Initiative**

STANDALONE

A sci-fi thriller novel

Riot

A sci-fi short story collection

Boys & Their Monsters